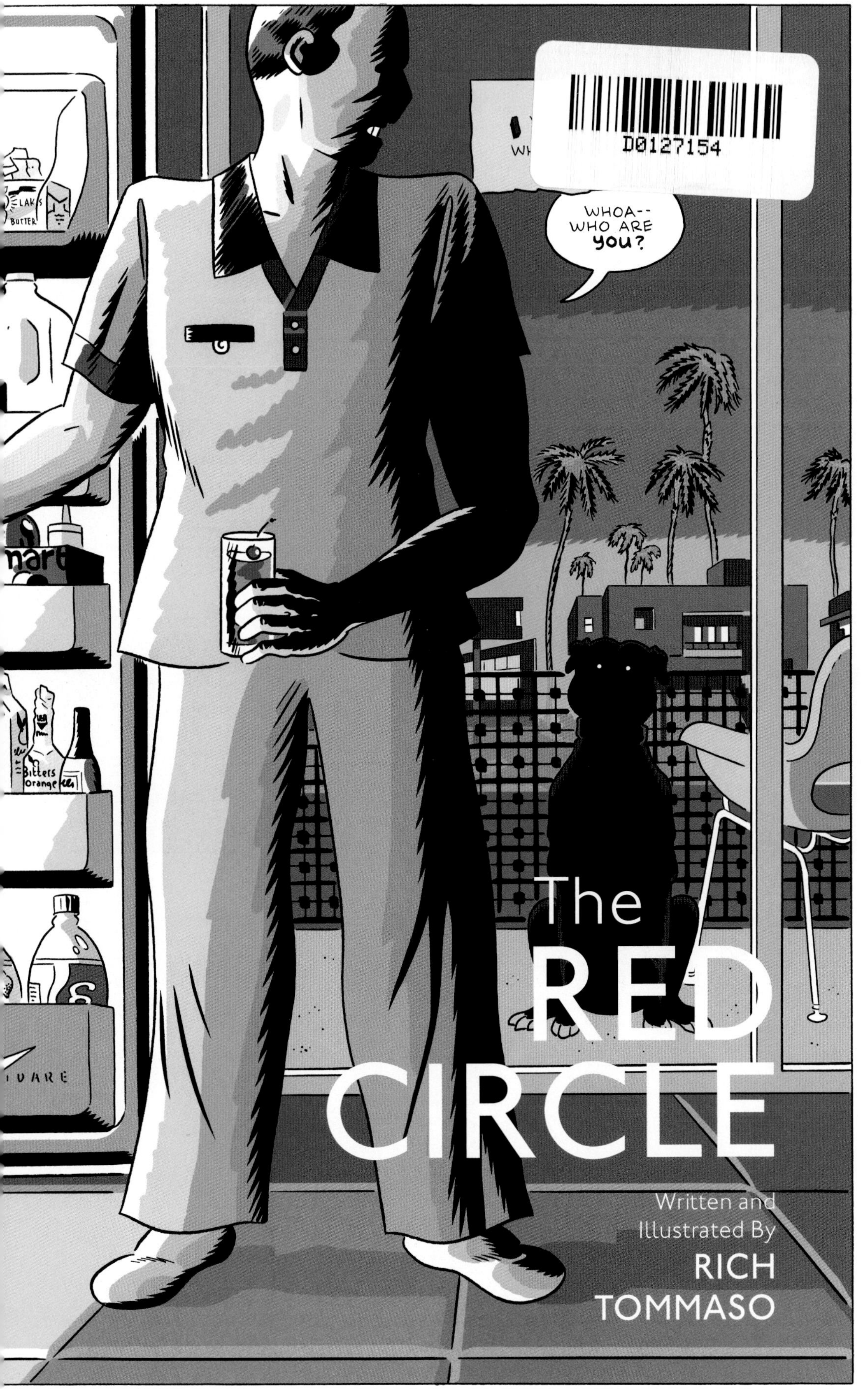
WHOA--
WHO ARE
YOU?
BUTTER
Bitters
Orange

The RED CIRCLE

Written and Illustrated By
RICH TOMMASO

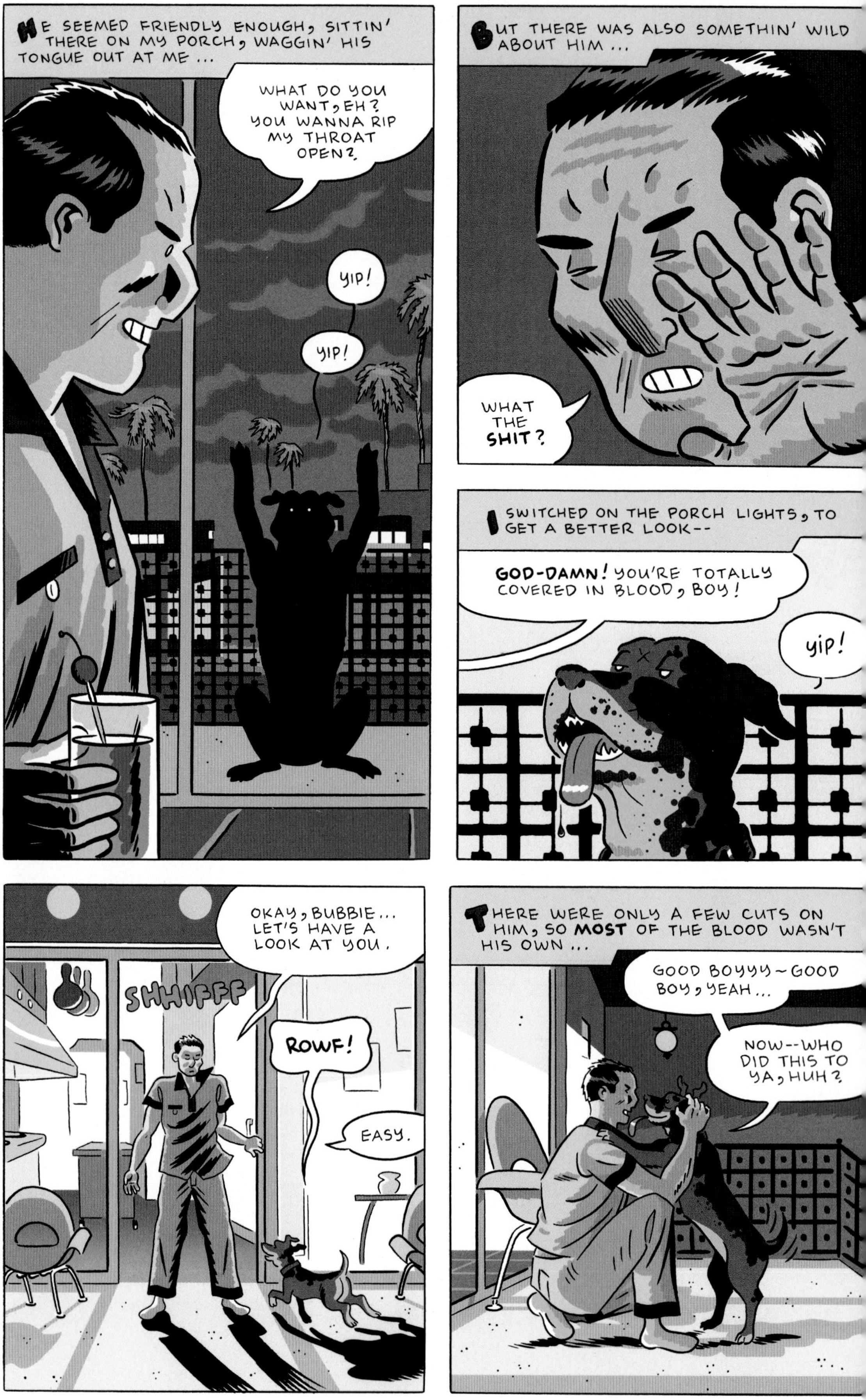

HE SEEMED FRIENDLY ENOUGH, SITTIN' THERE ON MY PORCH, WAGGIN' HIS TONGUE OUT AT ME ...
WHAT DO YOU WANT, EH? YOU WANNA RIP MY THROAT OPEN?
YIP!
YIP!
BUT THERE WAS ALSO SOMETHIN' WILD ABOUT HIM ...
WHAT THE SHIT?
I SWITCHED ON THE PORCH LIGHTS, TO GET A BETTER LOOK--
GOD-DAMN! YOU'RE TOTALLY COVERED IN BLOOD, BOY!
YIP!
OKAY, BUBBIE... LET'S HAVE A LOOK AT YOU.
SHHIFFF
ROWF!
EASY.
THERE WERE ONLY A FEW CUTS ON HIM, SO MOST OF THE BLOOD WASN'T HIS OWN ...
GOOD BOYYY~GOOD BOY, YEAH...
NOW--WHO DID THIS TO YA, HUH?

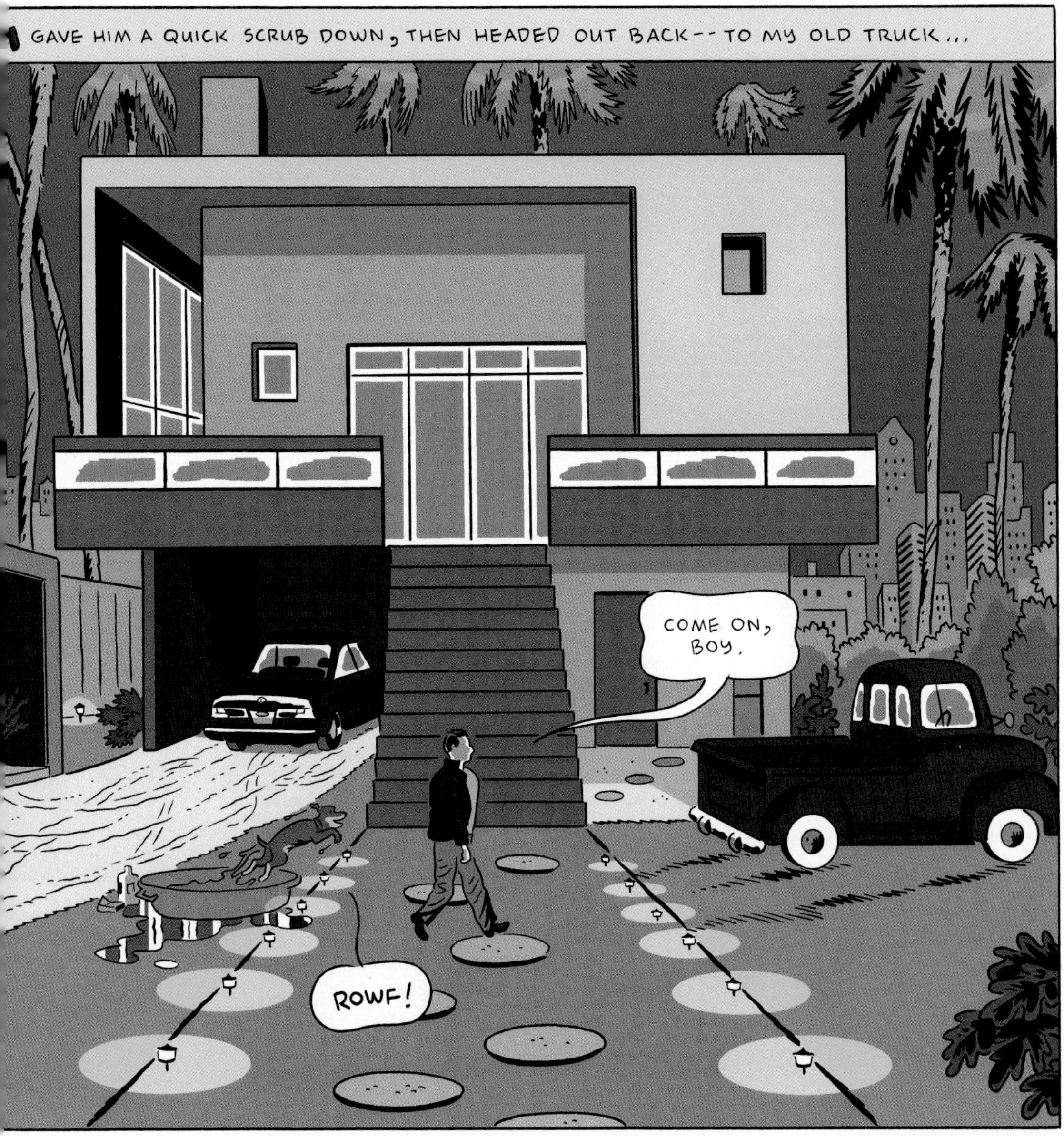
I GAVE HIM A QUICK SCRUB DOWN, THEN HEADED OUT BACK-- TO MY OLD TRUCK...
COME ON, BOY.
ROWF!

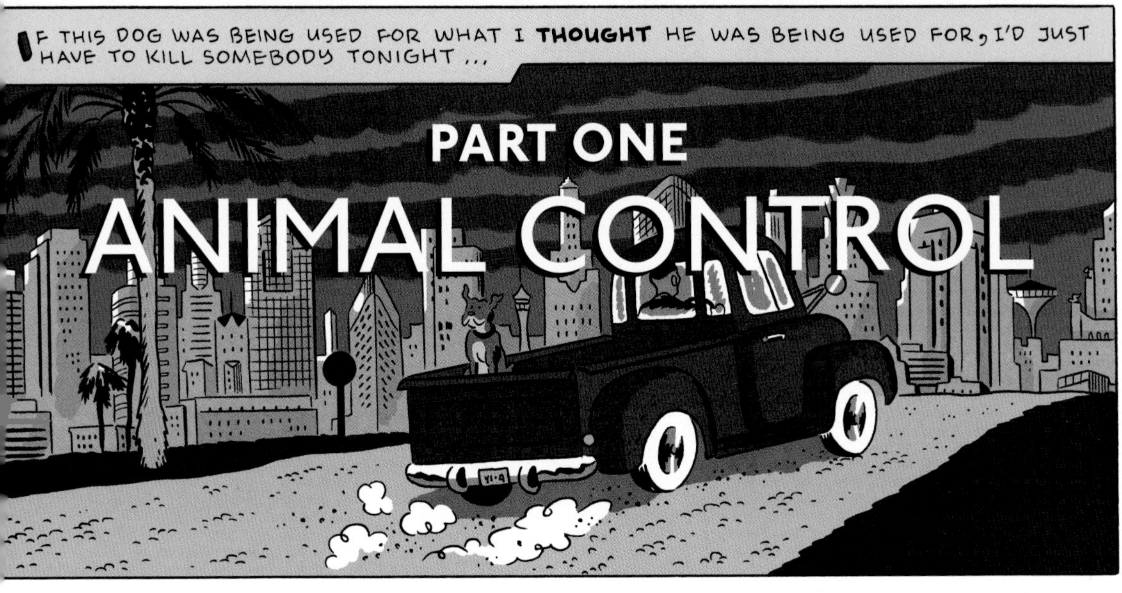
IF THIS DOG WAS BEING USED FOR WHAT I **THOUGHT** HE WAS BEING USED FOR, I'D JUST HAVE TO KILL SOMEBODY TONIGHT...
PART ONE
ANIMAL CONTROL

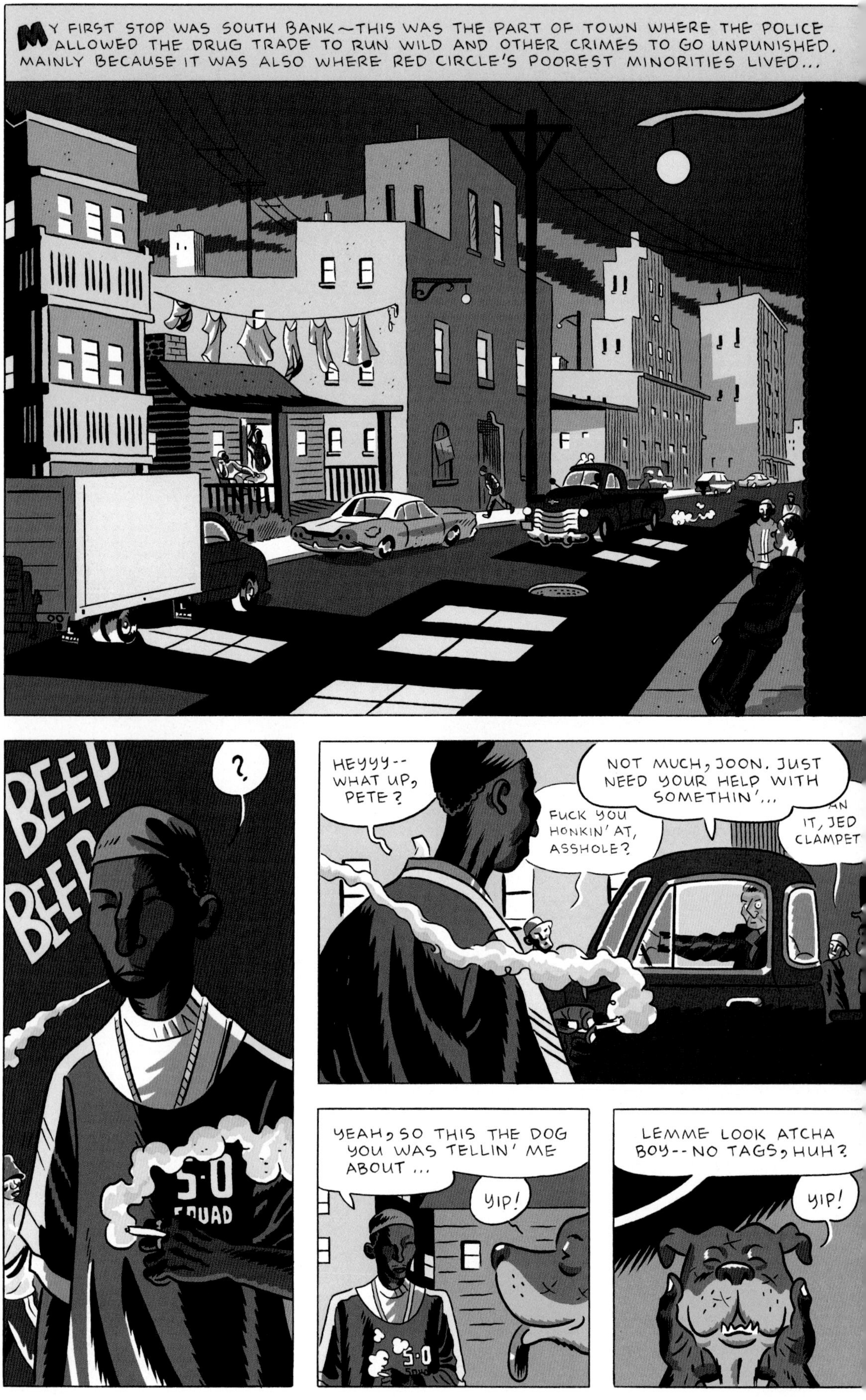
MY FIRST STOP WAS SOUTH BANK~THIS WAS THE PART OF TOWN WHERE THE POLICE ALLOWED THE DRUG TRADE TO RUN WILD AND OTHER CRIMES TO GO UNPUNISHED, MAINLY BECAUSE IT WAS ALSO WHERE RED CIRCLE'S POOREST MINORITIES LIVED...
BEEP BEEP
?
S-O SQUAD
HEYYY-- WHAT UP, PETE?
NOT MUCH, JOON. JUST NEED YOUR HELP WITH SOMETHIN'...
FUCK YOU HONKIN' AT, ASSHOLE?
AN IT, JED CLAMPET
YEAH, SO THIS THE DOG YOU WAS TELLIN' ME ABOUT...
YIP!
LEMME LOOK ATCHA BOY-- NO TAGS, HUH?
YIP!

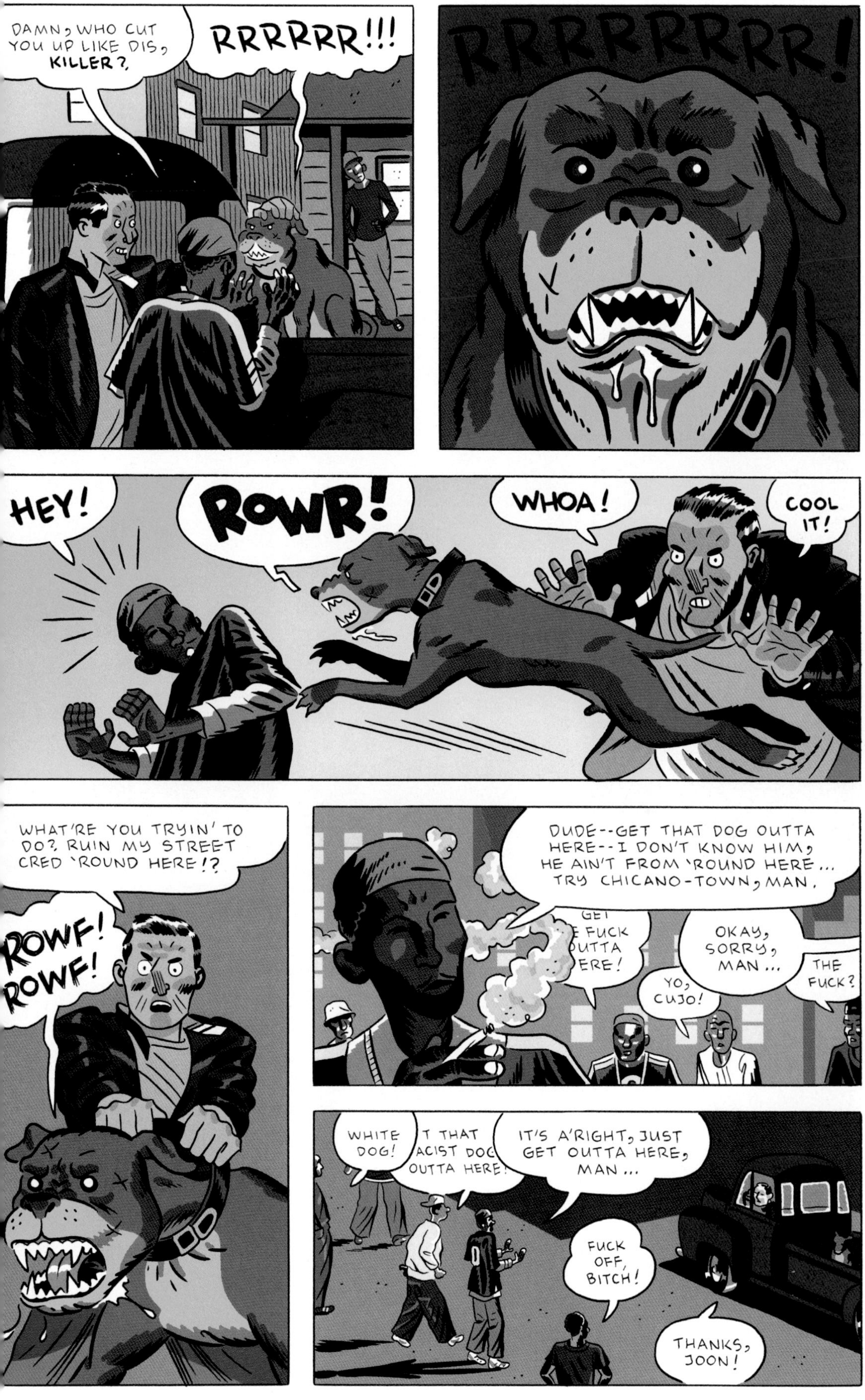
DAMN, WHO CUT YOU UP LIKE DIS, KILLER?
RRRRRR!!!
RRRRRRRRR!
HEY!
ROWR!
WHOA!
COOL IT!
WHAT'RE YOU TRYIN' TO DO? RUIN MY STREET CRED 'ROUND HERE!?
ROWF! ROWF!
DUDE--GET THAT DOG OUTTA HERE--I DON'T KNOW HIM, HE AIN'T FROM 'ROUND HERE... TRY CHICANO-TOWN, MAN.
GET
E FUCK
UTTA
ERE!
OKAY, SORRY, MAN...
THE FUCK?
YO, CUJO!
WHITE DOG!
T THAT
ACIST DOG
OUTTA HERE!
IT'S A'RIGHT, JUST GET OUTTA HERE, MAN...
FUCK OFF, BITCH!
THANKS, JOON!

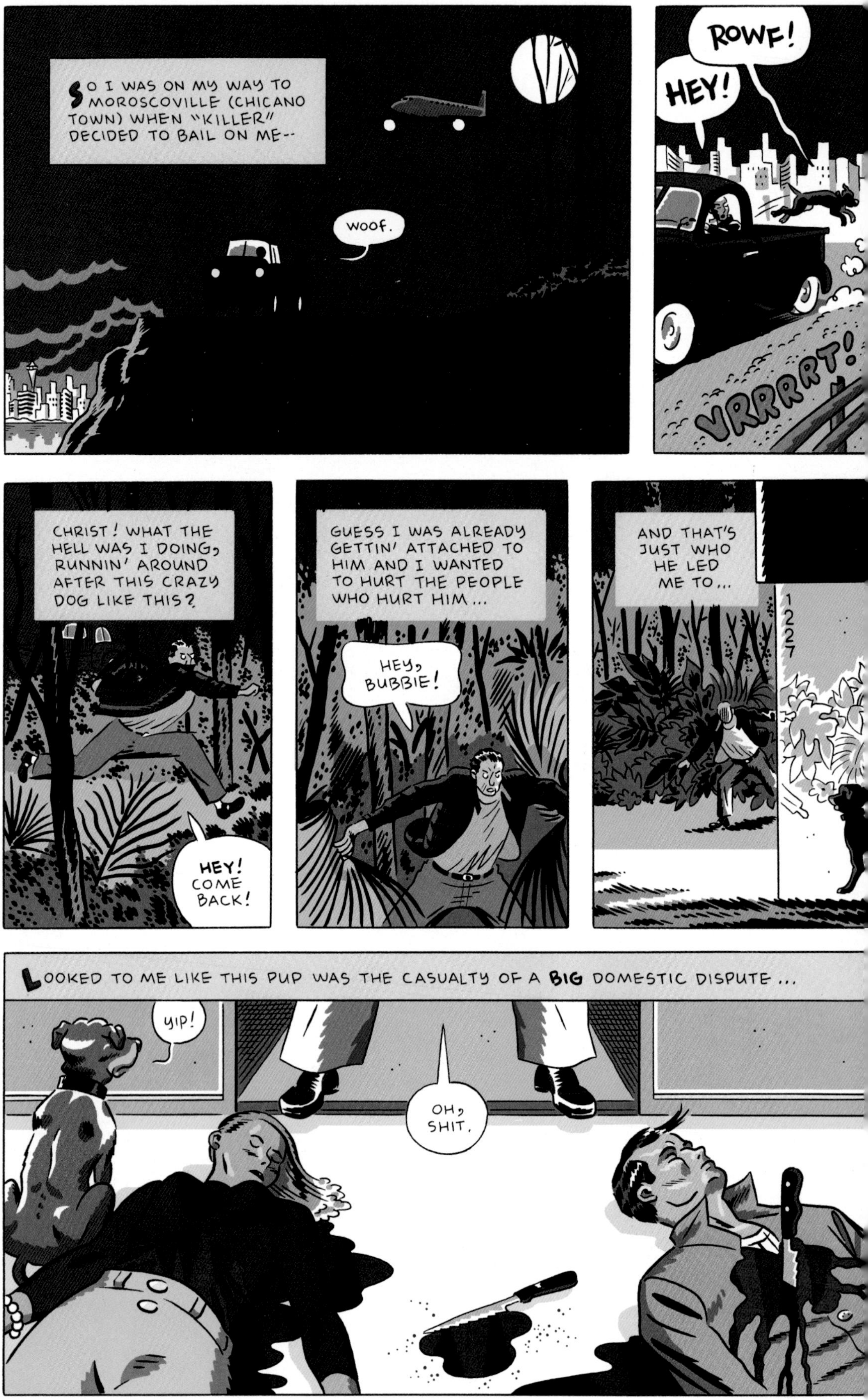
SO I WAS ON MY WAY TO MOROSCOVILLE (CHICANO TOWN) WHEN "KILLER" DECIDED TO BAIL ON ME--
WOOF.
HEY!
ROWF!
VRRRRT!
CHRIST! WHAT THE HELL WAS I DOING, RUNNIN' AROUND AFTER THIS CRAZY DOG LIKE THIS?
HEY! COME BACK!
GUESS I WAS ALREADY GETTIN' ATTACHED TO HIM AND I WANTED TO HURT THE PEOPLE WHO HURT HIM...
HEY, BUBBIE!
AND THAT'S JUST WHO HE LED ME TO...
1227
LOOKED TO ME LIKE THIS PUP WAS THE CASUALTY OF A BIG DOMESTIC DISPUTE...
YIP!
OH, SHIT.

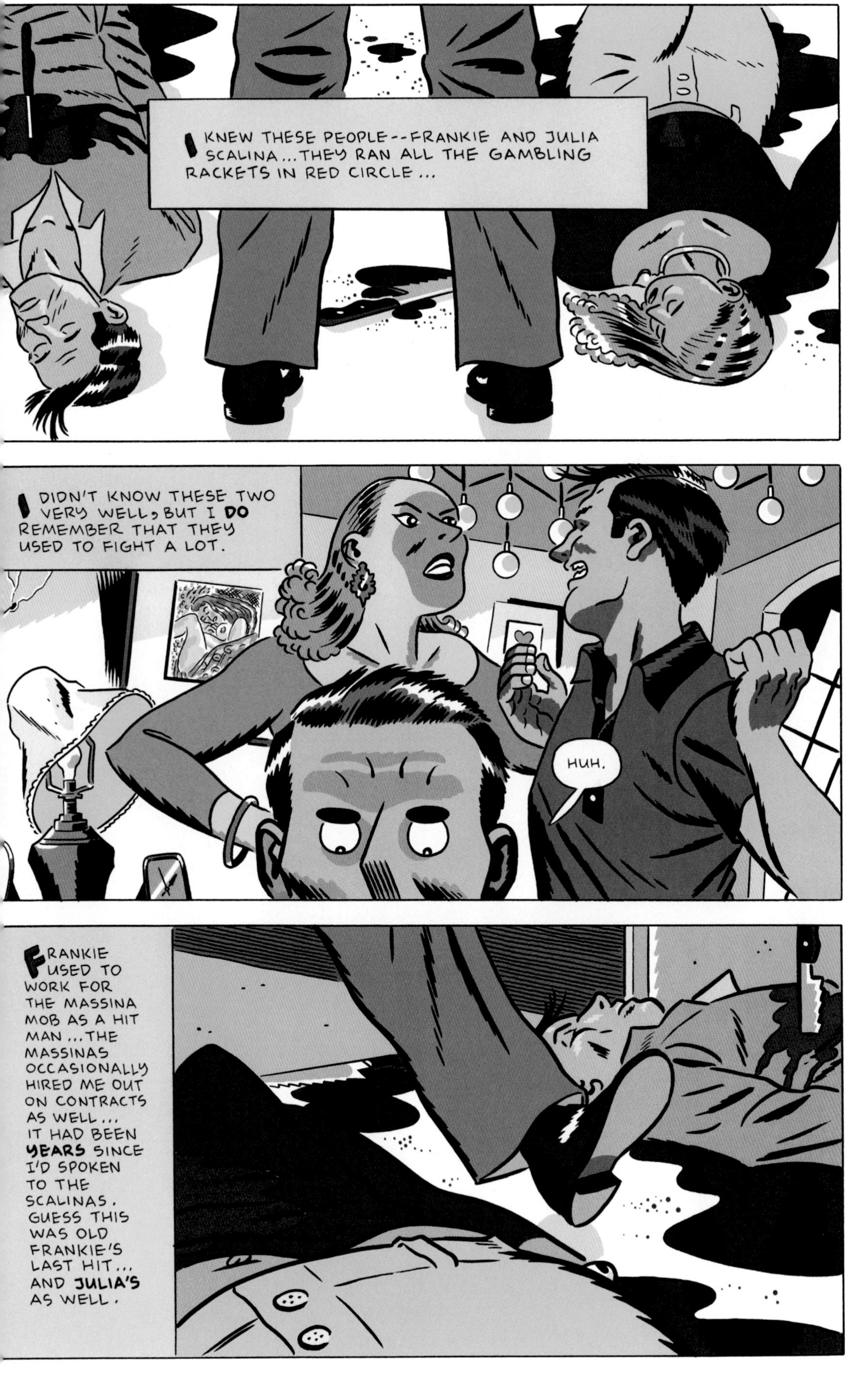
I KNEW THESE PEOPLE--FRANKIE AND JULIA SCALINA...THEY RAN ALL THE GAMBLING RACKETS IN RED CIRCLE...
I DIDN'T KNOW THESE TWO VERY WELL, BUT I DO REMEMBER THAT THEY USED TO FIGHT A LOT.
HUH.
FRANKIE USED TO WORK FOR THE MASSINA MOB AS A HIT MAN...THE MASSINAS OCCASIONALLY HIRED ME OUT ON CONTRACTS AS WELL... IT HAD BEEN YEARS SINCE I'D SPOKEN TO THE SCALINAS. GUESS THIS WAS OLD FRANKIE'S LAST HIT... AND JULIA'S AS WELL.

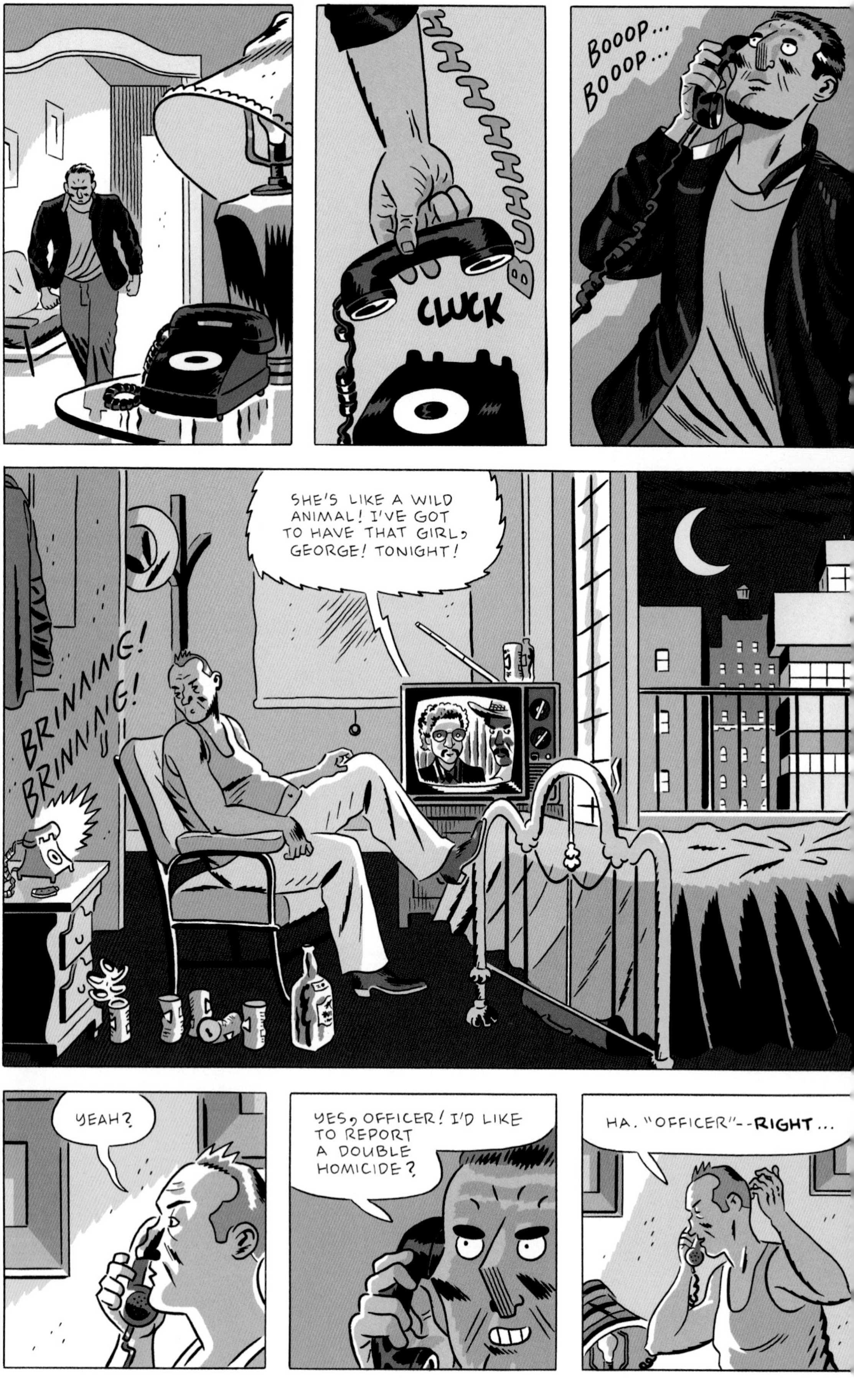

BUHHHHHH
CLUCK
Booop... Booop...
SHE'S LIKE A WILD ANIMAL! I'VE GOT TO HAVE THAT GIRL, GEORGE! TONIGHT!
BRINNNNG! BRINNNNG!
YEAH?
YES, OFFICER! I'D LIKE TO REPORT A DOUBLE HOMICIDE?
HA. "OFFICER"--**RIGHT**...

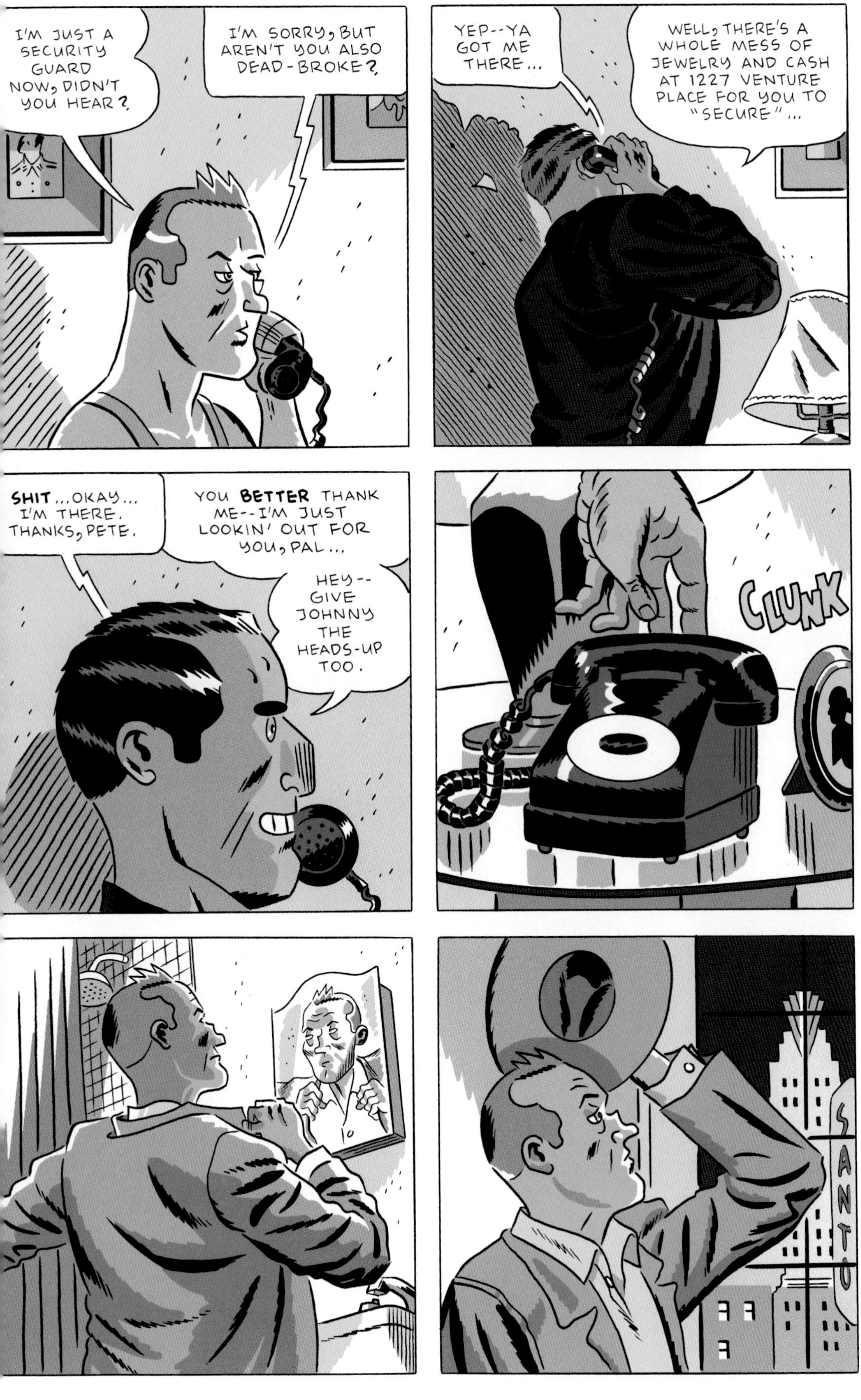
I'M JUST A SECURITY GUARD NOW, DIDN'T YOU HEAR?
I'M SORRY, BUT AREN'T YOU ALSO DEAD-BROKE?
YEP--YA GOT ME THERE...
WELL, THERE'S A WHOLE MESS OF JEWELRY AND CASH AT 1227 VENTURE PLACE FOR YOU TO "SECURE"...
SHIT...OKAY... I'M THERE. THANKS, PETE.
YOU **BETTER** THANK ME--I'M JUST LOOKIN' OUT FOR YOU, PAL...
HEY--GIVE JOHNNY THE HEADS-UP TOO.
CLUNK
SANTU

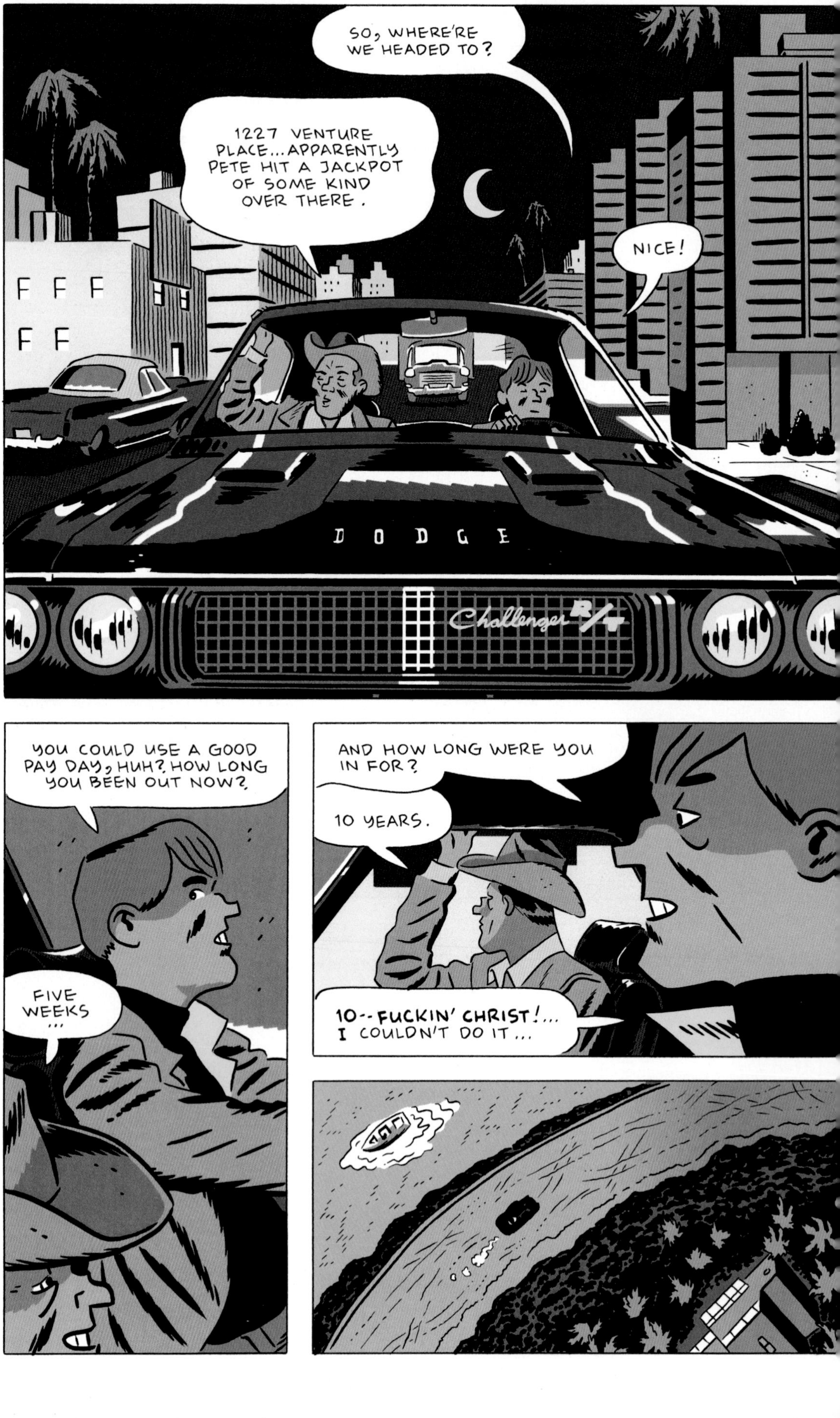
SO, WHERE'RE WE HEADED TO?
1227 VENTURE PLACE... APPARENTLY PETE HIT A JACKPOT OF SOME KIND OVER THERE.
NICE!
DODGE
Challenger R/T
YOU COULD USE A GOOD PAY DAY, HUH? HOW LONG YOU BEEN OUT NOW?
FIVE WEEKS...
AND HOW LONG WERE YOU IN FOR?
10 YEARS.
10-- **FUCKIN' CHRIST**!... I COULDN'T DO IT...

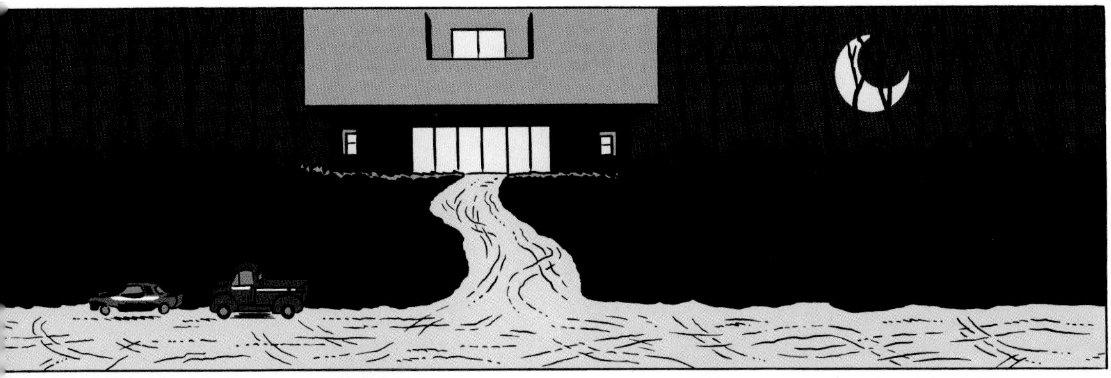

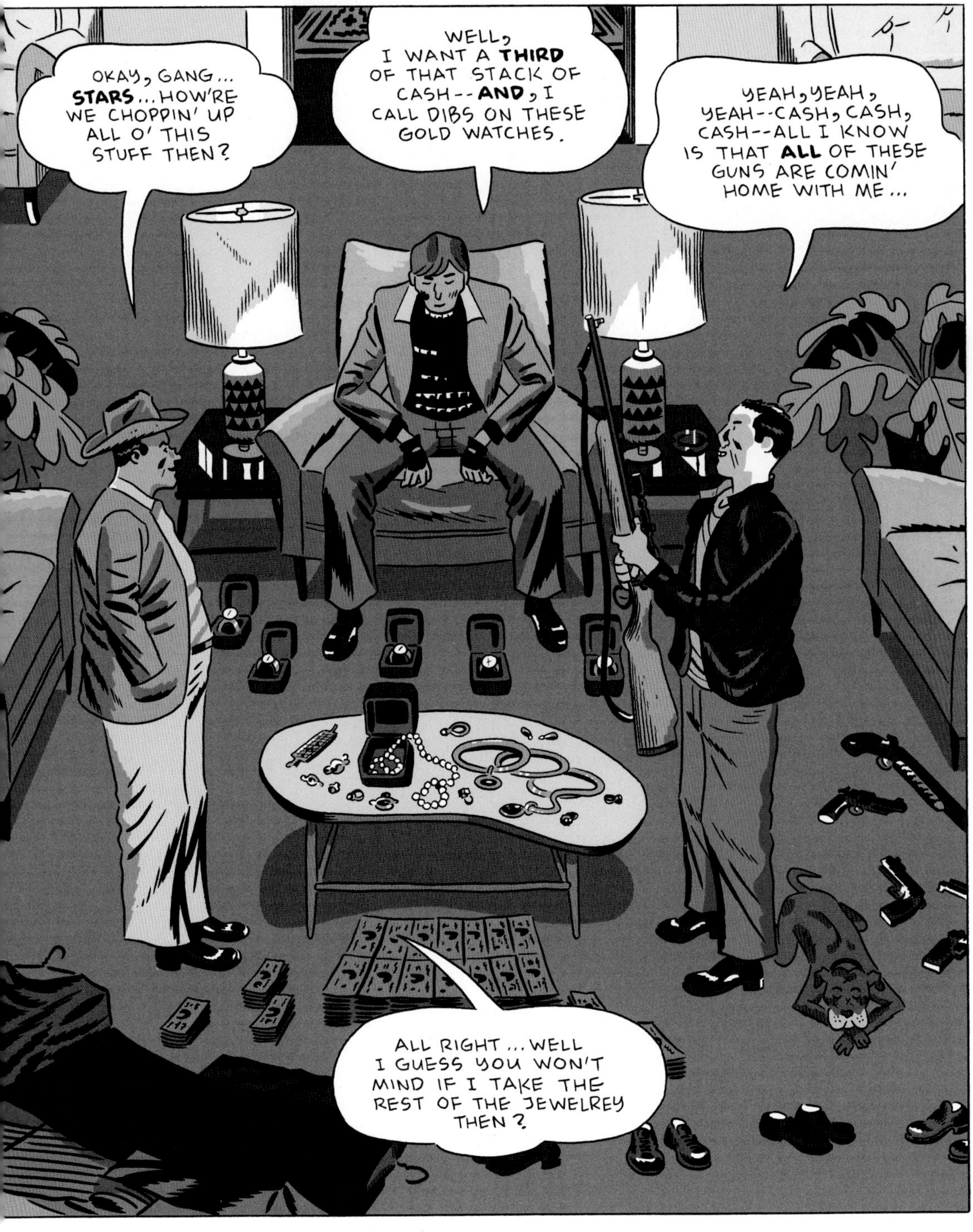
OKAY, GANG... **STARS**... HOW'RE WE CHOPPIN' UP ALL O' THIS STUFF THEN?
WELL, I WANT A **THIRD** OF THAT STACK OF CASH--**AND**, I CALL DIBS ON THESE GOLD WATCHES.
YEAH, YEAH, YEAH--CASH, CASH, CASH--ALL I KNOW IS THAT **ALL** OF THESE GUNS ARE COMIN' HOME WITH ME...
ALL RIGHT... WELL I GUESS YOU WON'T MIND IF I TAKE THE REST OF THE JEWELREY THEN?

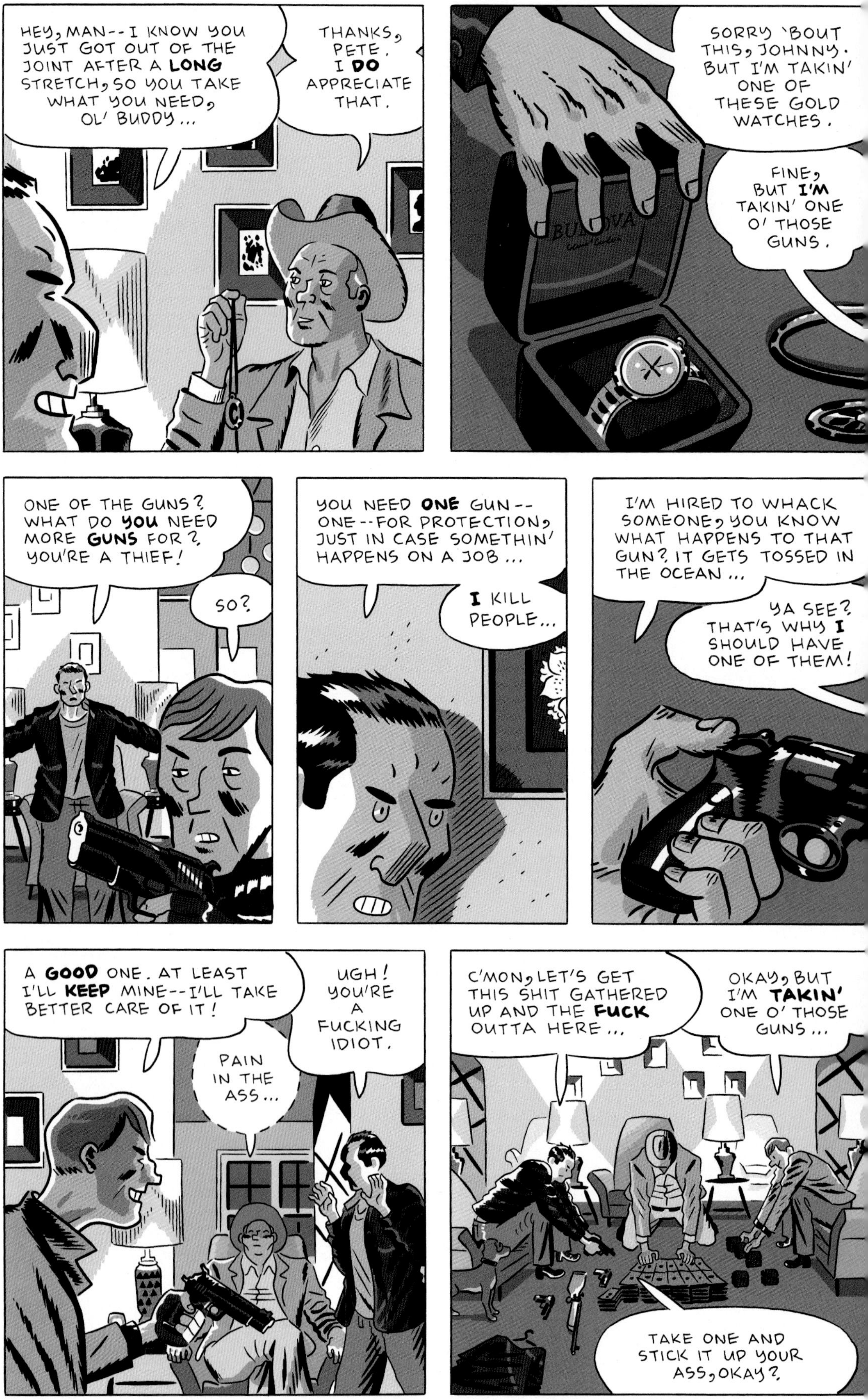
HEY, MAN--I KNOW YOU JUST GOT OUT OF THE JOINT AFTER A **LONG** STRETCH, SO YOU TAKE WHAT YOU NEED, OL' BUDDY...
THANKS, PETE. I **DO** APPRECIATE THAT.
SORRY 'BOUT THIS, JOHNNY. BUT I'M TAKIN' ONE OF THESE GOLD WATCHES.
BULOVA
FINE, BUT **I'M** TAKIN' ONE O' THOSE GUNS.
ONE OF THE GUNS? WHAT DO **YOU** NEED MORE **GUNS** FOR? YOU'RE A THIEF!
SO?
YOU NEED **ONE** GUN-- ONE--FOR PROTECTION, JUST IN CASE SOMETHIN' HAPPENS ON A JOB...
I KILL PEOPLE...
I'M HIRED TO WHACK SOMEONE, YOU KNOW WHAT HAPPENS TO THAT GUN? IT GETS TOSSED IN THE OCEAN...
YA SEE? THAT'S WHY **I** SHOULD HAVE ONE OF THEM!
A **GOOD** ONE. AT LEAST I'LL **KEEP** MINE--I'LL TAKE BETTER CARE OF IT!
UGH! YOU'RE A FUCKING IDIOT.
PAIN IN THE ASS...
C'MON, LET'S GET THIS SHIT GATHERED UP AND THE **FUCK** OUTTA HERE...
OKAY, BUT I'M **TAKIN'** ONE O' THOSE GUNS...
TAKE ONE AND STICK IT UP YOUR ASS, OKAY?

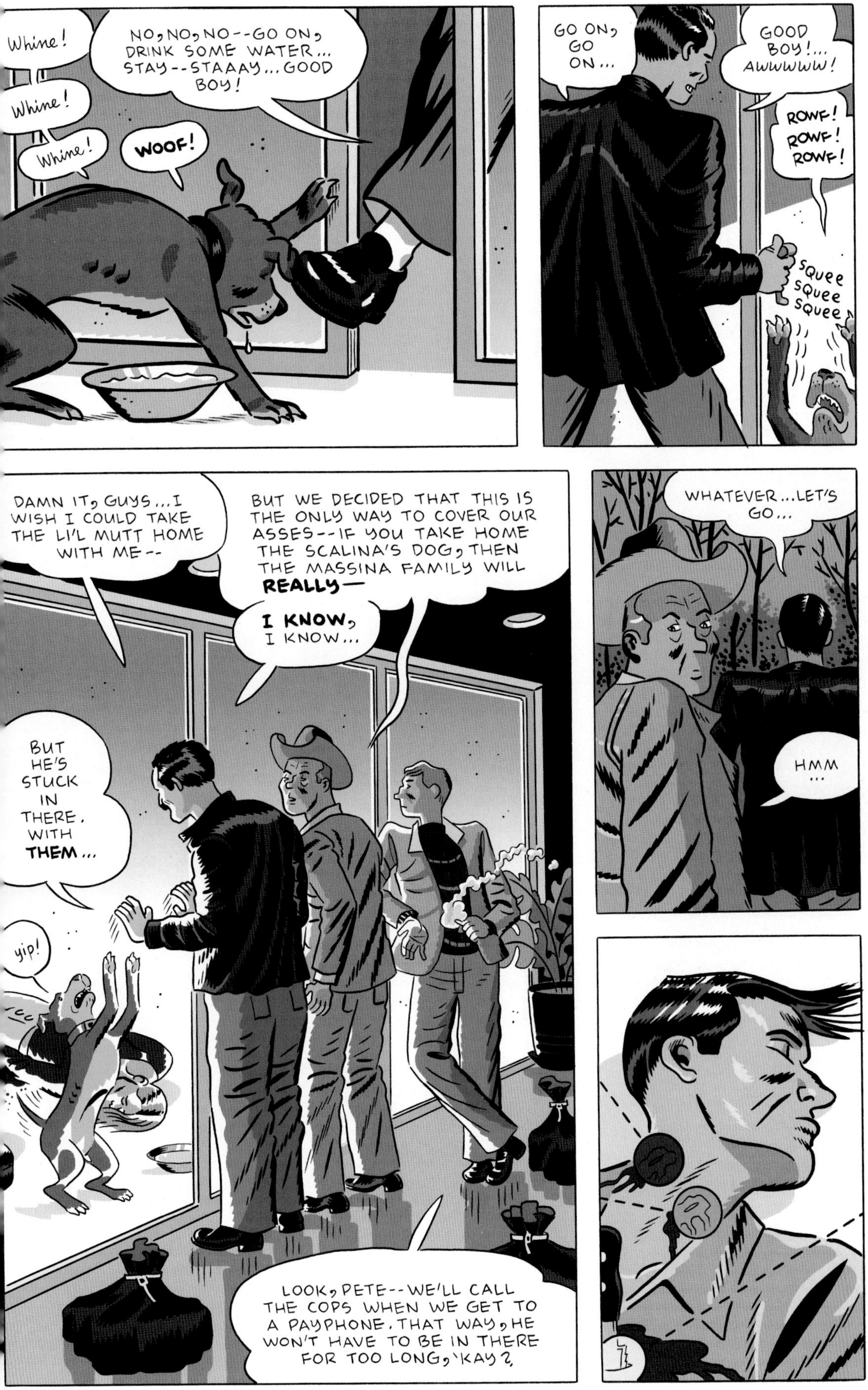
Whine!
NO, NO, NO--GO ON, DRINK SOME WATER... STAY--STAAAY... GOOD BOY!
Whine!
Whine!
WOOF!
GO ON, GO ON...
GOOD BOY!... AWWWWW!
ROWF! ROWF! ROWF!
SQUEE SQUEE SQUEE
DAMN IT, GUYS... I WISH I COULD TAKE THE LI'L MUTT HOME WITH ME--
BUT WE DECIDED THAT THIS IS THE ONLY WAY TO COVER OUR ASSES--IF YOU TAKE HOME THE SCALINA'S DOG, THEN THE MASSINA FAMILY WILL REALLY—
I KNOW, I KNOW...
BUT HE'S STUCK IN THERE, WITH THEM...
yip!
LOOK, PETE--WE'LL CALL THE COPS WHEN WE GET TO A PAYPHONE. THAT WAY, HE WON'T HAVE TO BE IN THERE FOR TOO LONG, 'KAY?
WHATEVER... LET'S GO...
HMM...

INTERESTING.

WHAT?

NUTHIN'... LET'S GET A DRINK.

HELL YEAH, LET'S...

SOUNDS GOOD.

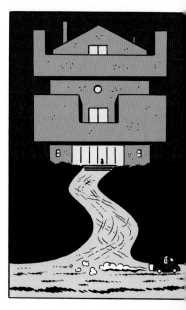

ROWF!

YIP! YIP! YIP! YIP! YIP!

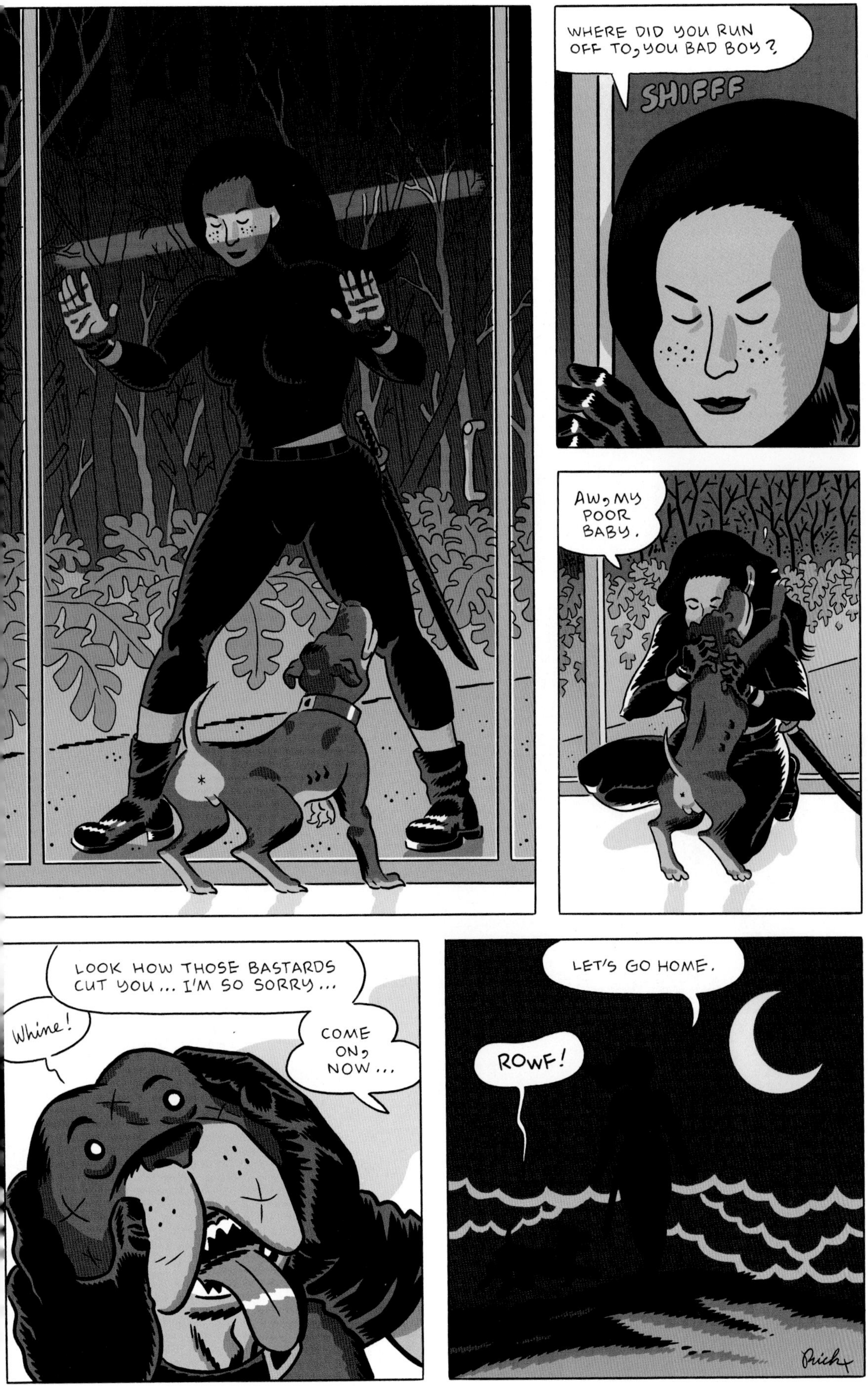

WHERE DID YOU RUN OFF TO, YOU BAD BOY?
SHIFFF
AW, MY POOR BABY.
LOOK HOW THOSE BASTARDS CUT YOU... I'M SO SORRY...
Whine!
COME ON, NOW...
LET'S GO HOME.
ROWF!
Rich

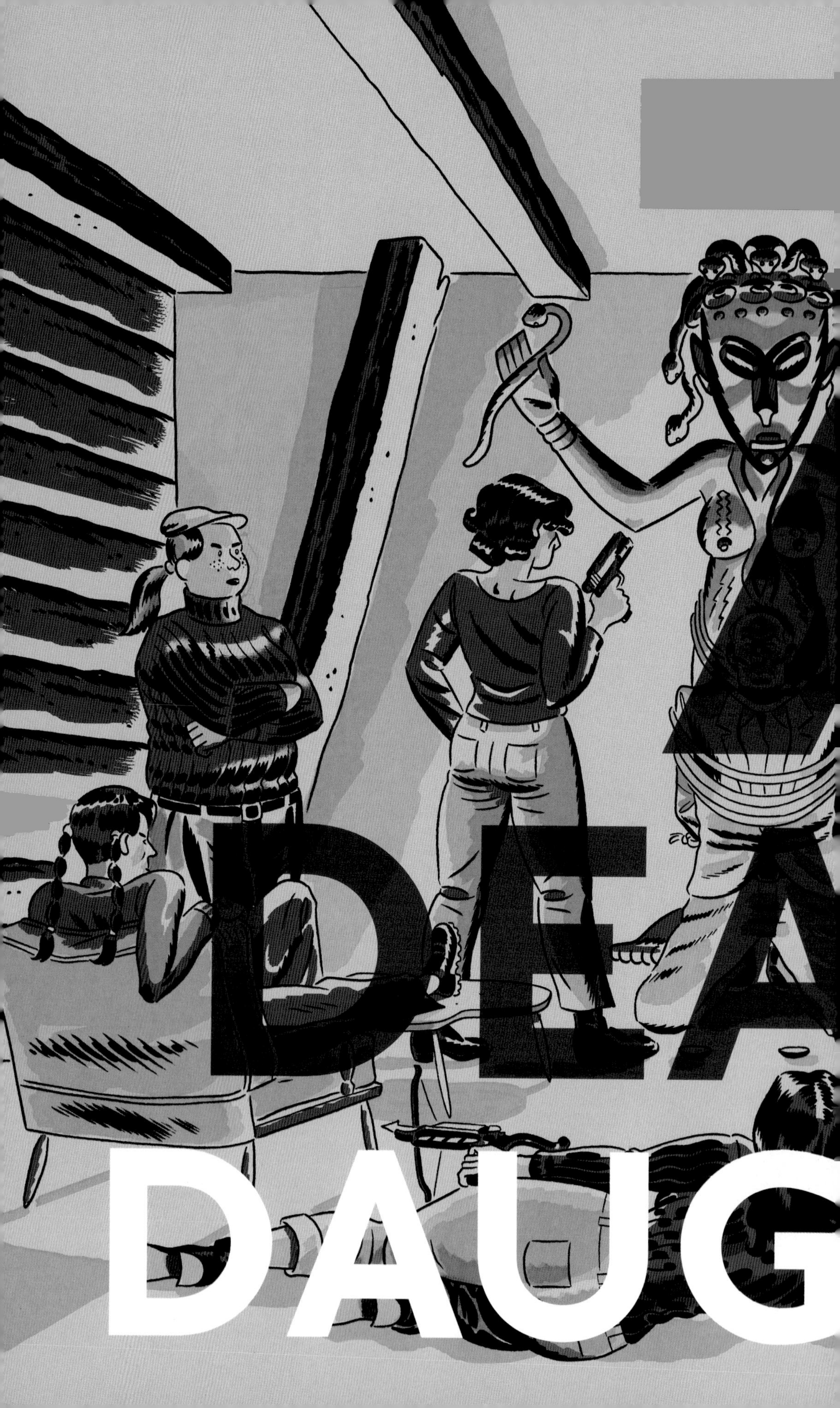
DEA
DAUG

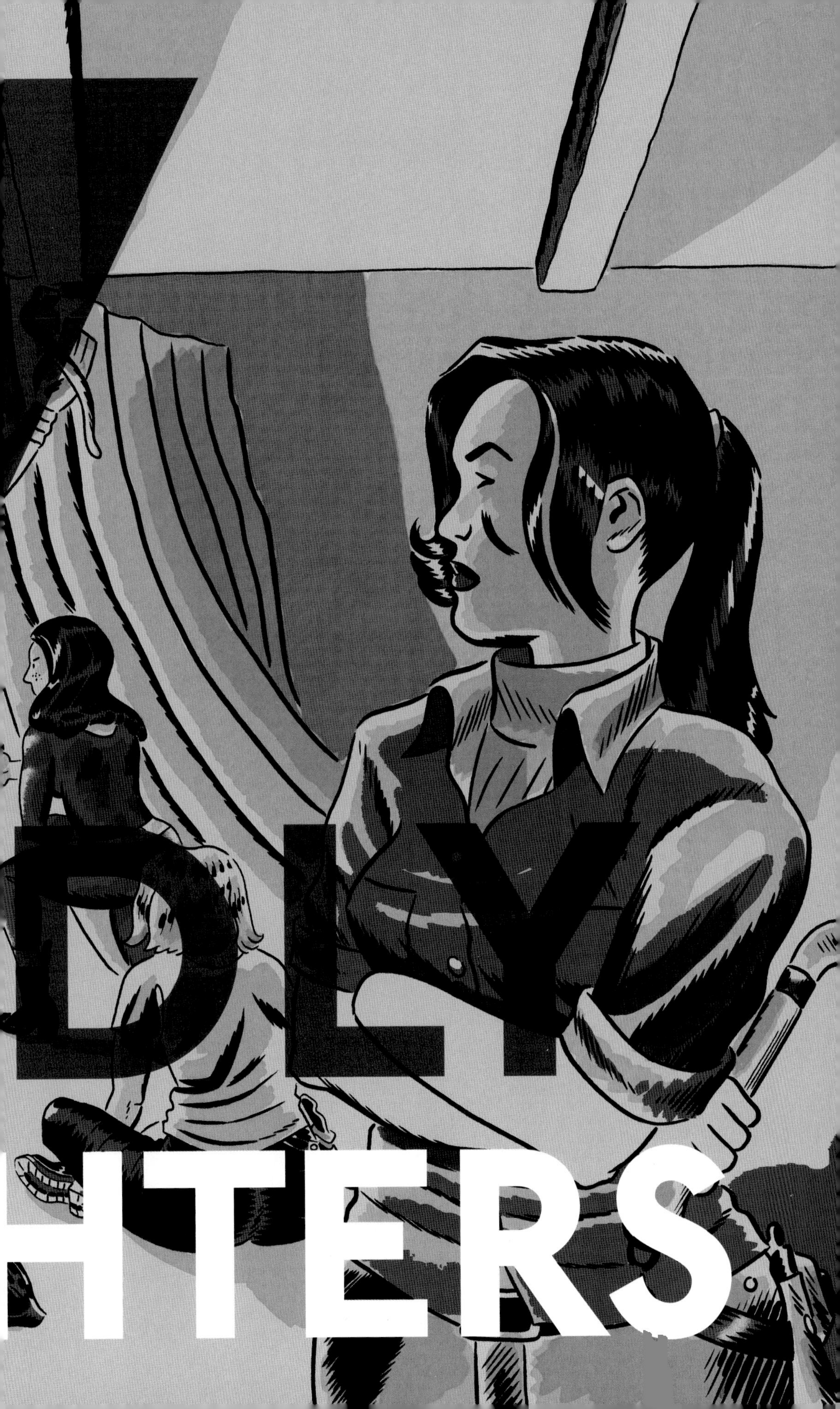

DLY
HTERS

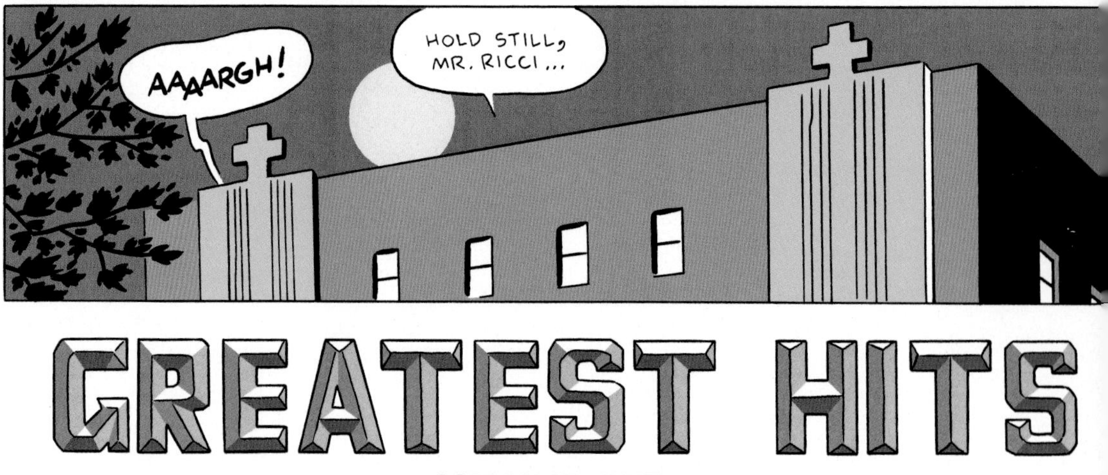
AAAARGH!
HOLD STILL, MR. RICCI...

GREATEST HITS

VOLUME ONE: MARIE CASTELLA

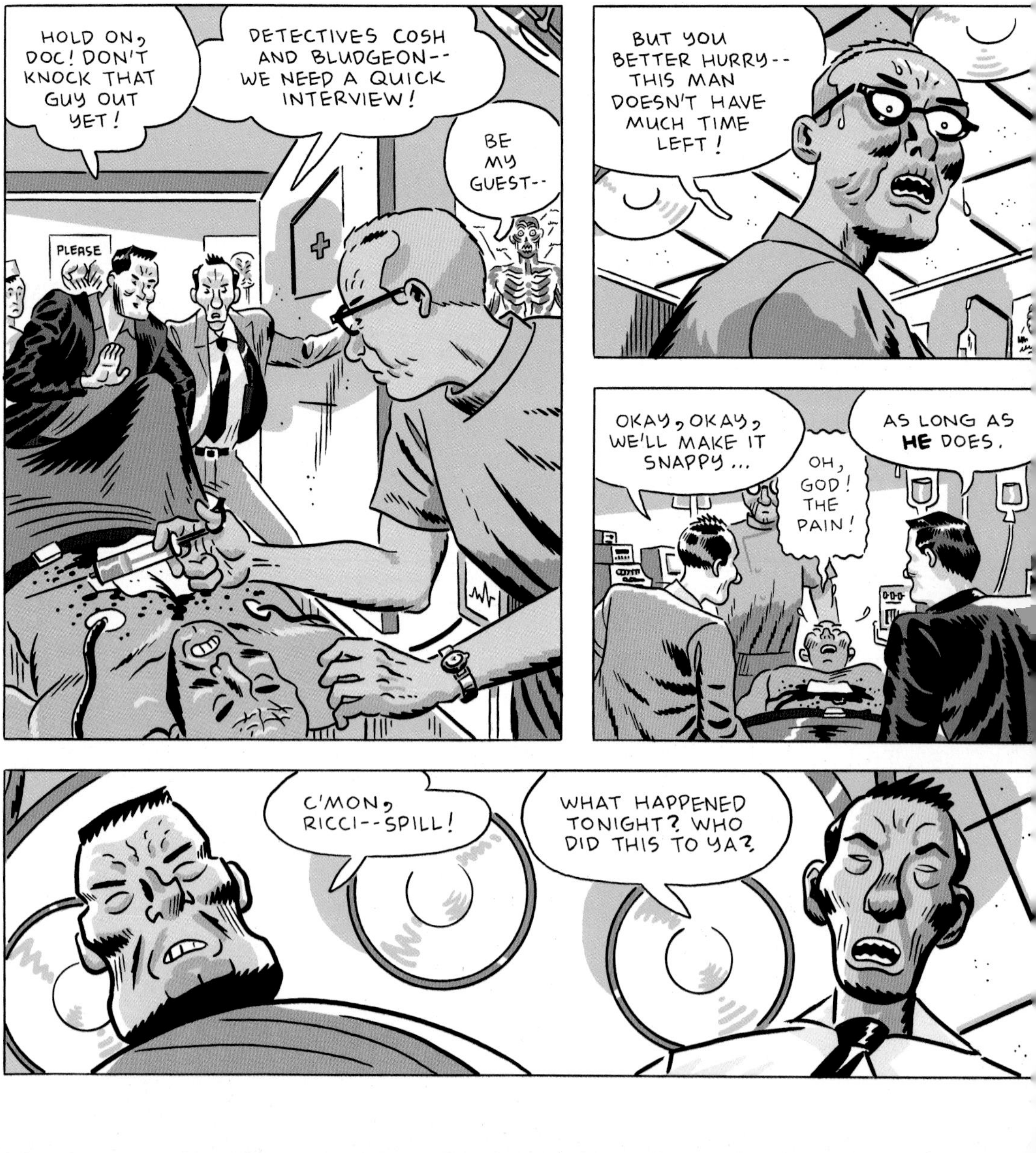
HOLD ON, DOC! DON'T KNOCK THAT GUY OUT YET!
DETECTIVES COSH AND BLUDGEON-- WE NEED A QUICK INTERVIEW!
BE MY GUEST--
PLEASE
BUT YOU BETTER HURRY-- THIS MAN DOESN'T HAVE MUCH TIME LEFT!
OKAY, OKAY, WE'LL MAKE IT SNAPPY...
OH, GOD! THE PAIN!
AS LONG AS HE DOES.
C'MON, RICCI--SPILL!
WHAT HAPPENED TONIGHT? WHO DID THIS TO YA?

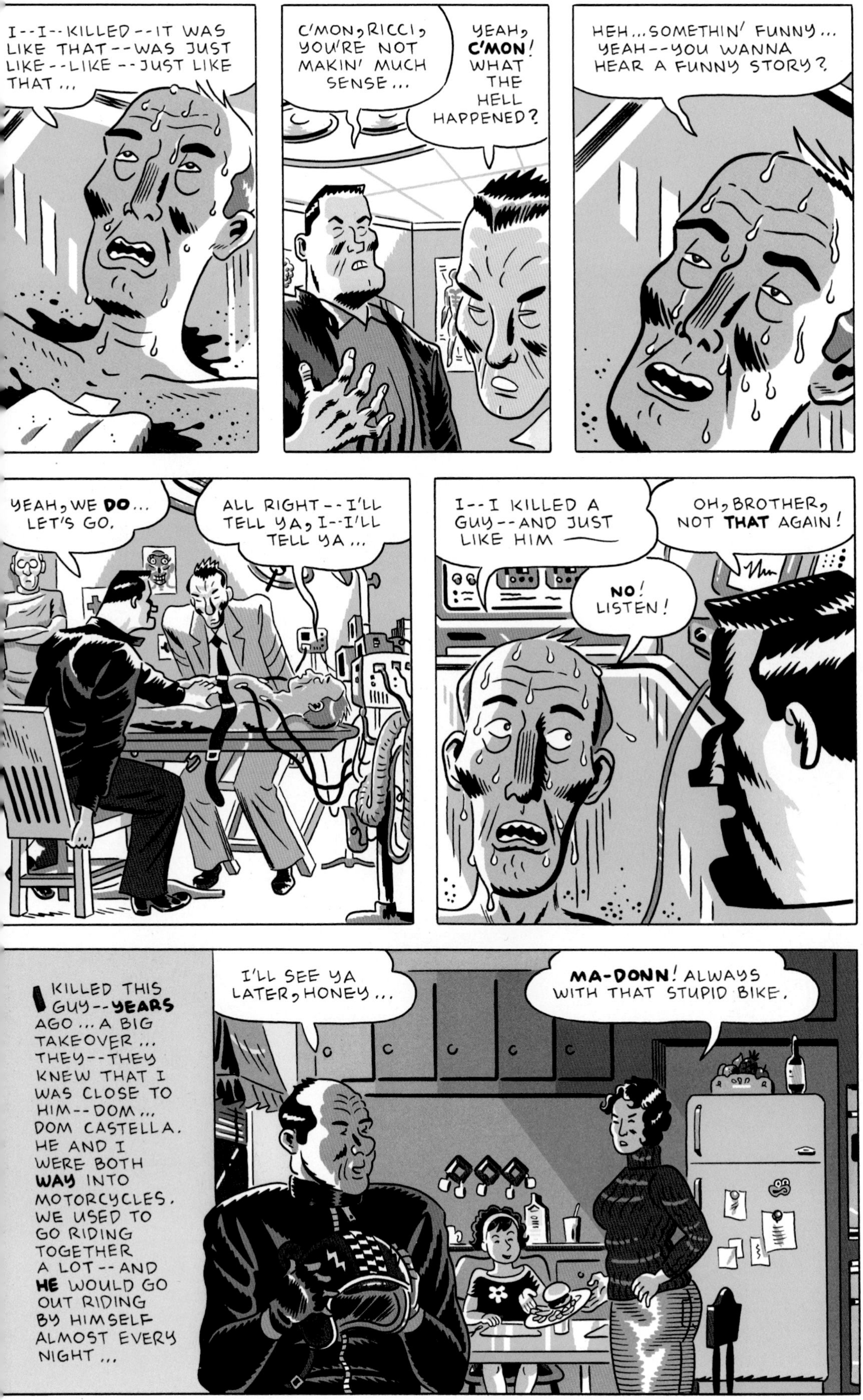
I--I--KILLED--IT WAS LIKE THAT--WAS JUST LIKE--LIKE--JUST LIKE THAT...
C'MON, RICCI, YOU'RE NOT MAKIN' MUCH SENSE...
YEAH, **C'MON**! WHAT THE HELL HAPPENED?
HEH...SOMETHIN' FUNNY... YEAH--YOU WANNA HEAR A FUNNY STORY?
YEAH, WE **DO**... LET'S GO.
ALL RIGHT--I'LL TELL YA, I--I'LL TELL YA...
I--I KILLED A GUY--AND JUST LIKE HIM
OH, BROTHER, NOT **THAT** AGAIN!
NO! LISTEN!
I KILLED THIS GUY--**YEARS** AGO... A BIG TAKEOVER... THEY--THEY KNEW THAT I WAS CLOSE TO HIM--DOM... DOM CASTELLA. HE AND I WERE BOTH **WAY** INTO MOTORCYCLES. WE USED TO GO RIDING TOGETHER A LOT--AND **HE** WOULD GO OUT RIDING BY HIMSELF ALMOST EVERY NIGHT...
I'LL SEE YA LATER, HONEY...
MA-DONN! ALWAYS WITH THAT STUPID BIKE.

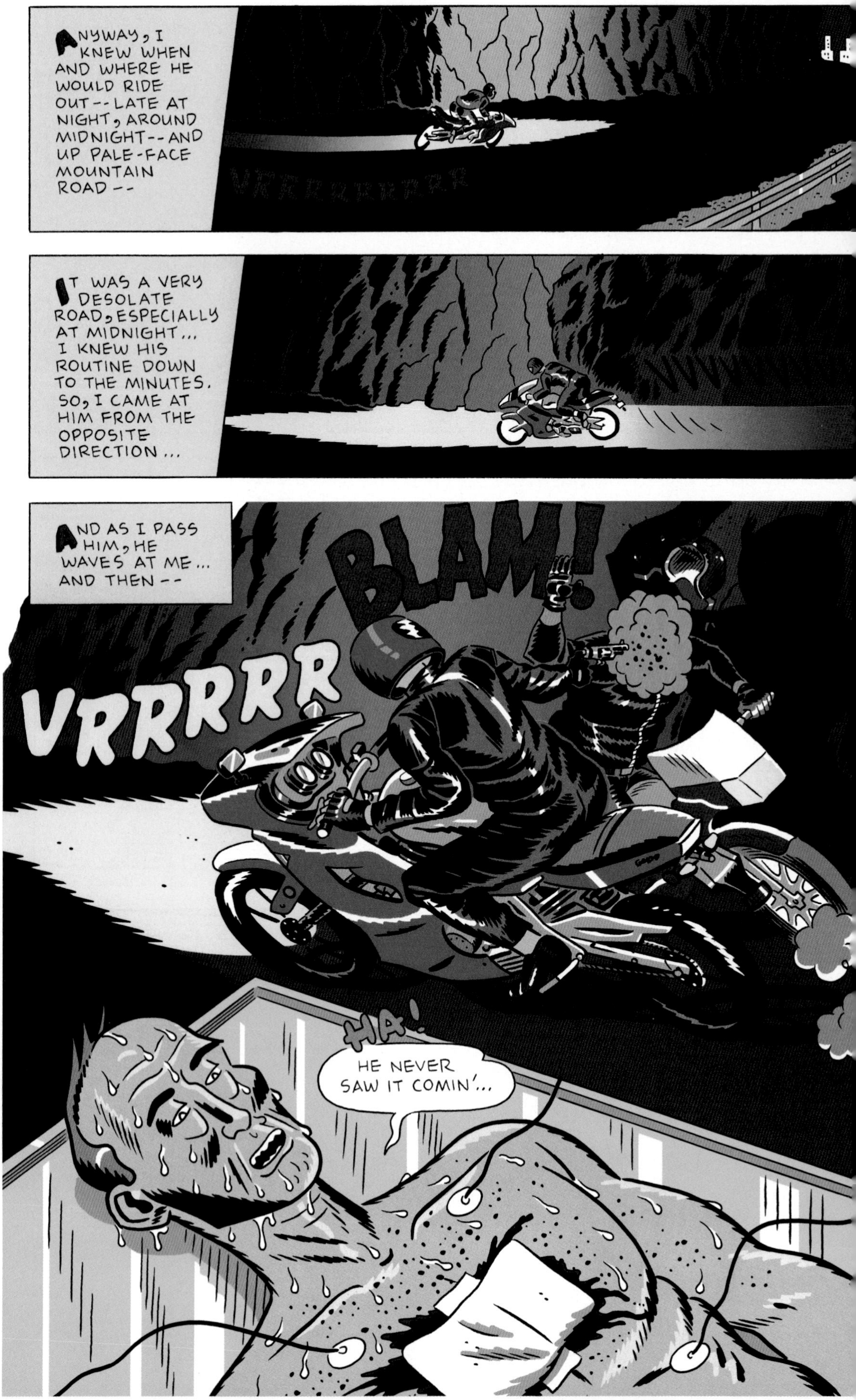
ANYWAY, I KNEW WHEN AND WHERE HE WOULD RIDE OUT--LATE AT NIGHT, AROUND MIDNIGHT--AND UP PALE-FACE MOUNTAIN ROAD--
VRRRRRRRRR
IT WAS A VERY DESOLATE ROAD, ESPECIALLY AT MIDNIGHT... I KNEW HIS ROUTINE DOWN TO THE MINUTES. SO, I CAME AT HIM FROM THE OPPOSITE DIRECTION...
AND AS I PASS HIM, HE WAVES AT ME... AND THEN--
BLAM!
VRRRRR
HA!
HE NEVER SAW IT COMIN'...

THAT'S A BEAUTIFUL STORY, SALVATORE...

YEAH, THANKS FOR YOUR CONFESSION -- WE CAN NOW CLOSE THE BOOK ON **THAT** ONE! PHEW!

WAIT! BUT THAT AIN'T THE PUNCHLINE! -- I'M NOT FINISHED YET!...

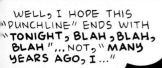

WELL, I HOPE THIS "PUNCHLINE" ENDS WITH "**TONIGHT**, BLAH, BLAH, BLAH"... NOT, "**MANY YEARS AGO**, I..."

IT DOES! JUST -- JUST SIT DOWN AND LISTEN...

NOW -- **TONIGHT** -- IT -- IT HAPPENED AGAIN!...

BUMPED INTO SOME FRIENDS -- THEY -- THEY NEEDED ME 'CAUSE I KNEW OF A FENCE THAT COULD HELP THEM MOVE THESE JEWELS THEY'D JUST... **ACQUIRED**...

OKAY, SAL -- YOU TOOK CARE OF THE JEWELS -- AND THEN?...THE DETECTIVES ARE BEING VERY PATIENT.

I'M GETTIN' THERE, I'M GETTIN' TO IT...

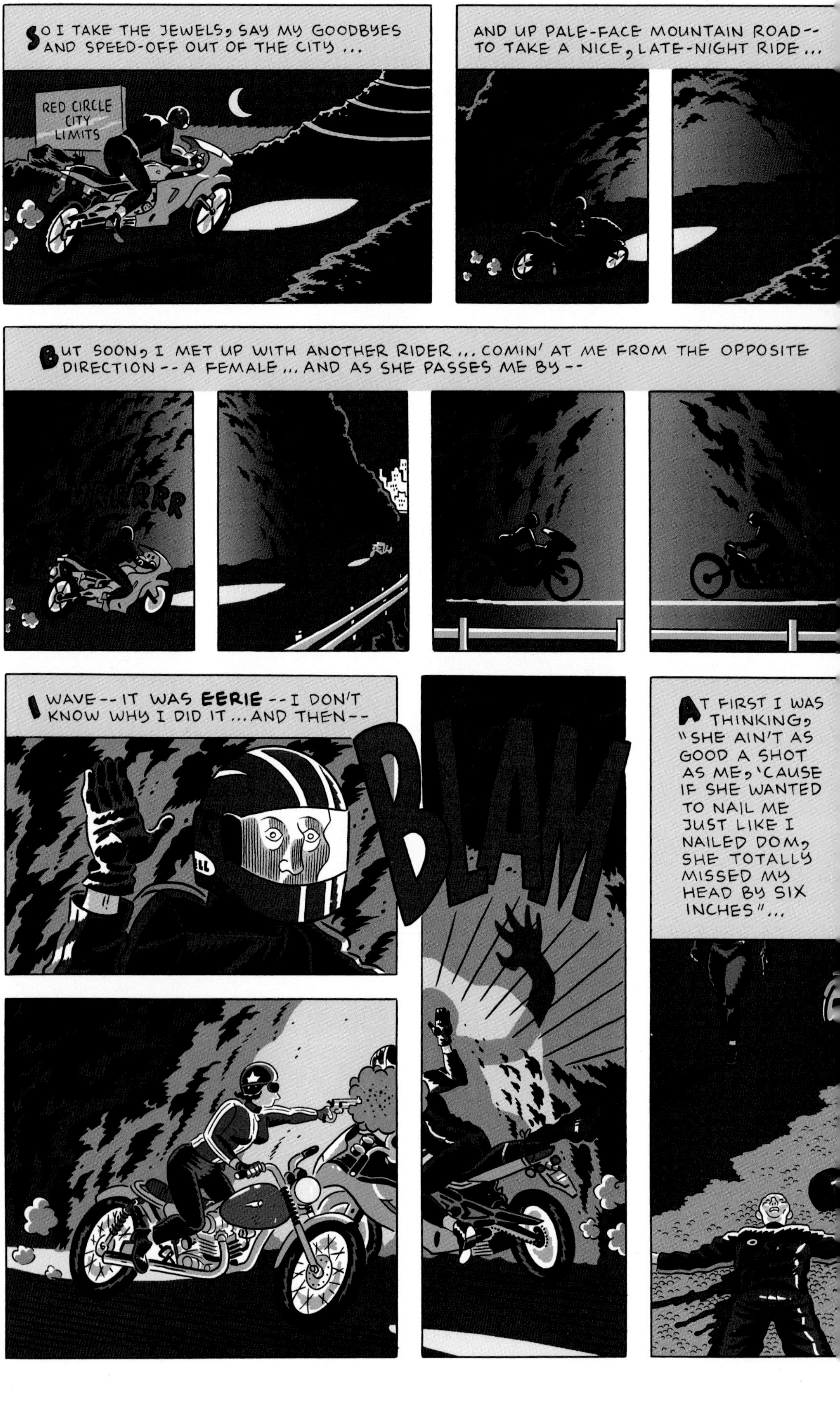
SO I TAKE THE JEWELS, SAY MY GOODBYES AND SPEED-OFF OUT OF THE CITY ...
RED CIRCLE CITY LIMITS
AND UP PALE-FACE MOUNTAIN ROAD-- TO TAKE A NICE, LATE-NIGHT RIDE ...
BUT SOON, I MET UP WITH ANOTHER RIDER ... COMIN' AT ME FROM THE OPPOSITE DIRECTION -- A FEMALE ... AND AS SHE PASSES ME BY --
I WAVE -- IT WAS EERIE -- I DON'T KNOW WHY I DID IT ... AND THEN --
BLAM
AT FIRST I WAS THINKING, "SHE AIN'T AS GOOD A SHOT AS ME, 'CAUSE IF SHE WANTED TO NAIL ME JUST LIKE I NAILED DOM, SHE TOTALLY MISSED MY HEAD BY SIX INCHES" ...

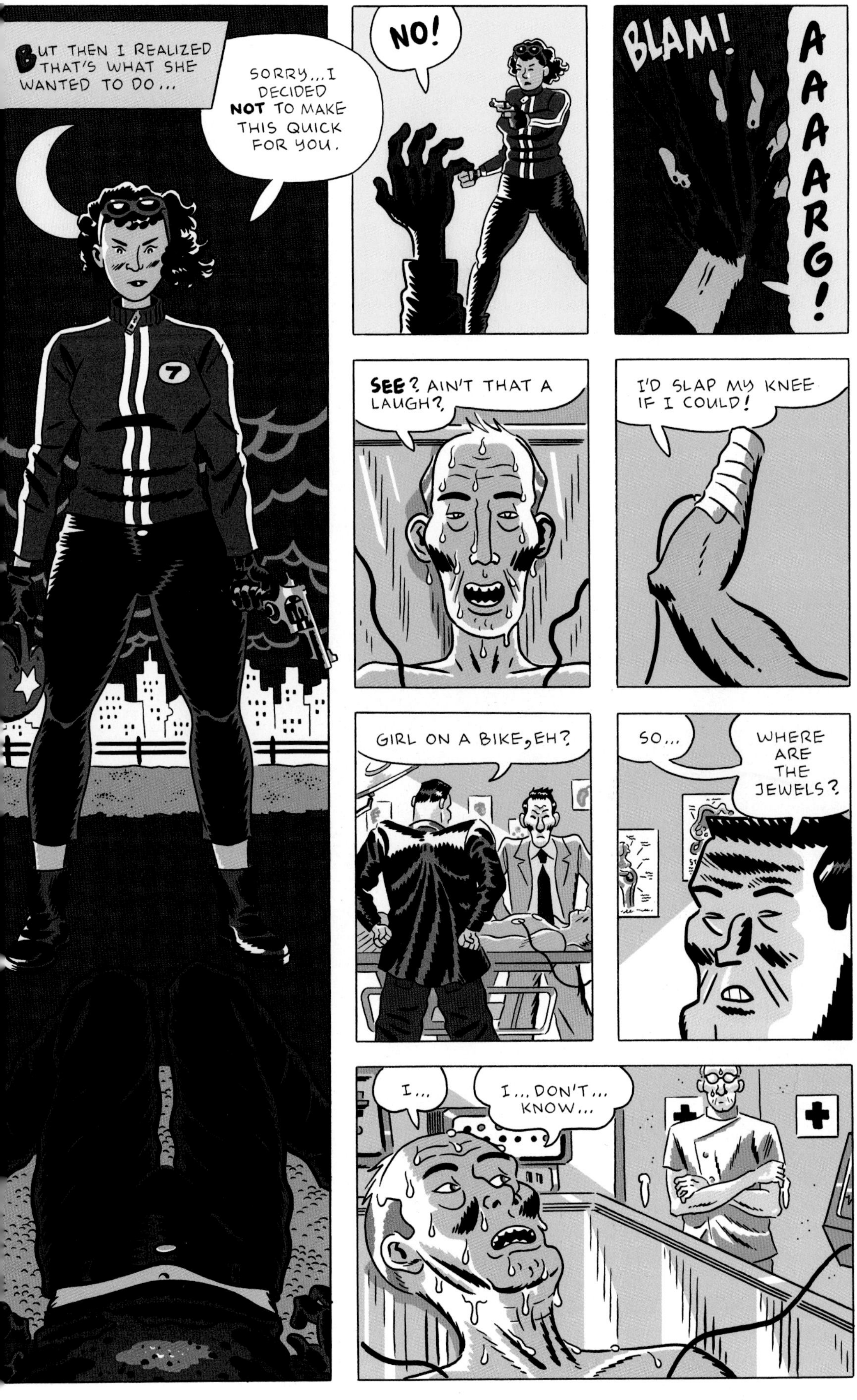

BUT THEN I REALIZED THAT'S WHAT SHE WANTED TO DO...
SORRY... I DECIDED **NOT** TO MAKE THIS QUICK FOR YOU.
NO!
BLAM!
AAAAARG!
SEE? AIN'T THAT A LAUGH?
I'D SLAP MY KNEE IF I COULD!
GIRL ON A BIKE, EH?
SO...
WHERE ARE THE JEWELS?
I...
I... DON'T... KNOW...

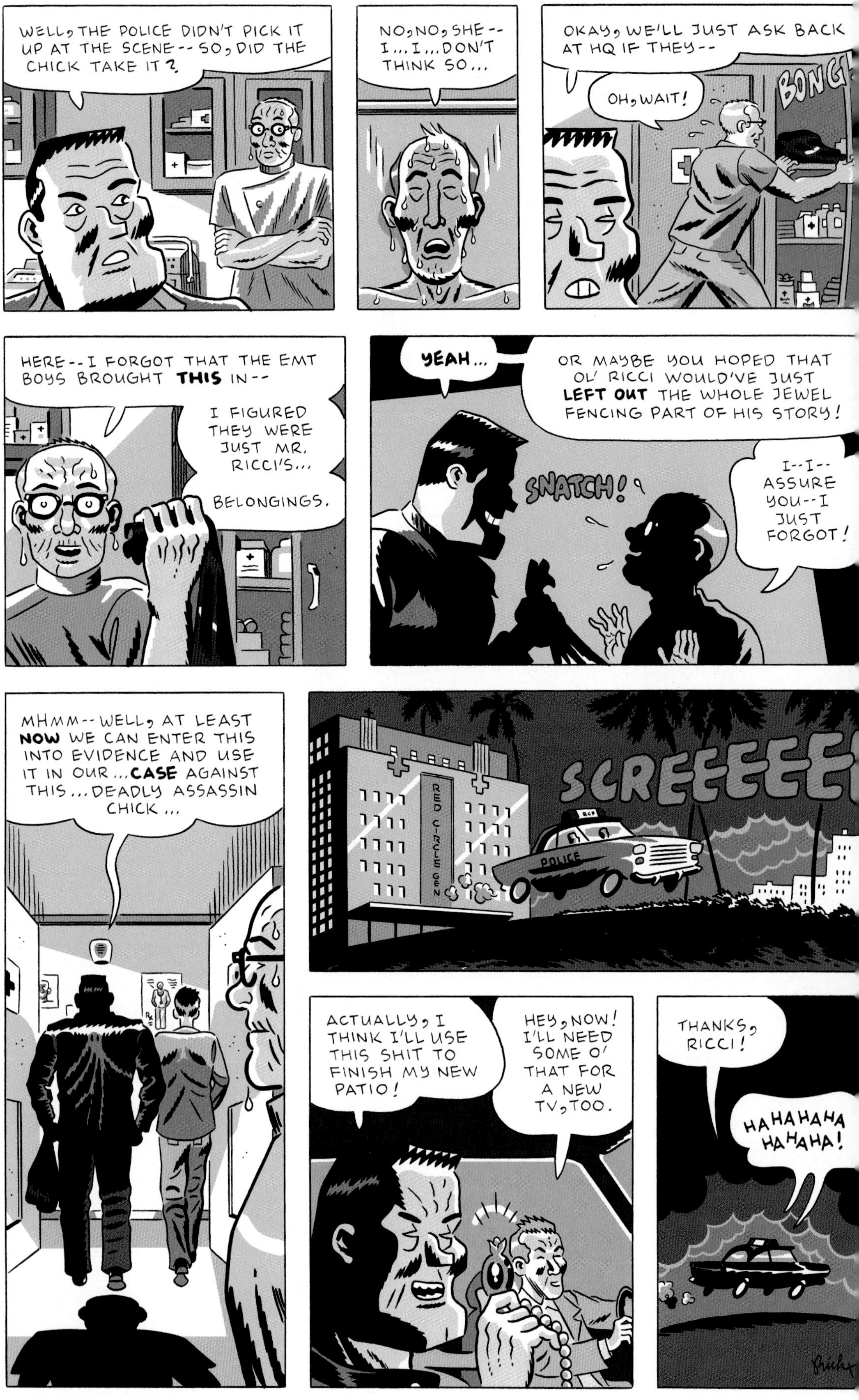

WELL, THE POLICE DIDN'T PICK IT UP AT THE SCENE--SO, DID THE CHICK TAKE IT?
NO, NO, SHE--I...I...DON'T THINK SO...
OKAY, WE'LL JUST ASK BACK AT HQ IF THEY--
OH, WAIT!
BONG!
HERE--I FORGOT THAT THE EMT BOYS BROUGHT THIS IN--
I FIGURED THEY WERE JUST MR. RICCI'S... BELONGINGS.
YEAH...
OR MAYBE YOU HOPED THAT OL' RICCI WOULD'VE JUST LEFT OUT THE WHOLE JEWEL FENCING PART OF HIS STORY!
SNATCH!
I--I--ASSURE YOU--I JUST FORGOT!
MHMM--WELL, AT LEAST NOW WE CAN ENTER THIS INTO EVIDENCE AND USE IT IN OUR...CASE AGAINST THIS...DEADLY ASSASSIN CHICK...
RED CIRCLE GEN
SCREEEEEE
POLICE
ACTUALLY, I THINK I'LL USE THIS SHIT TO FINISH MY NEW PATIO!
HEY, NOW! I'LL NEED SOME O' THAT FOR A NEW TV, TOO.
THANKS, RICCI!
HAHAHAHA HAHAHA!

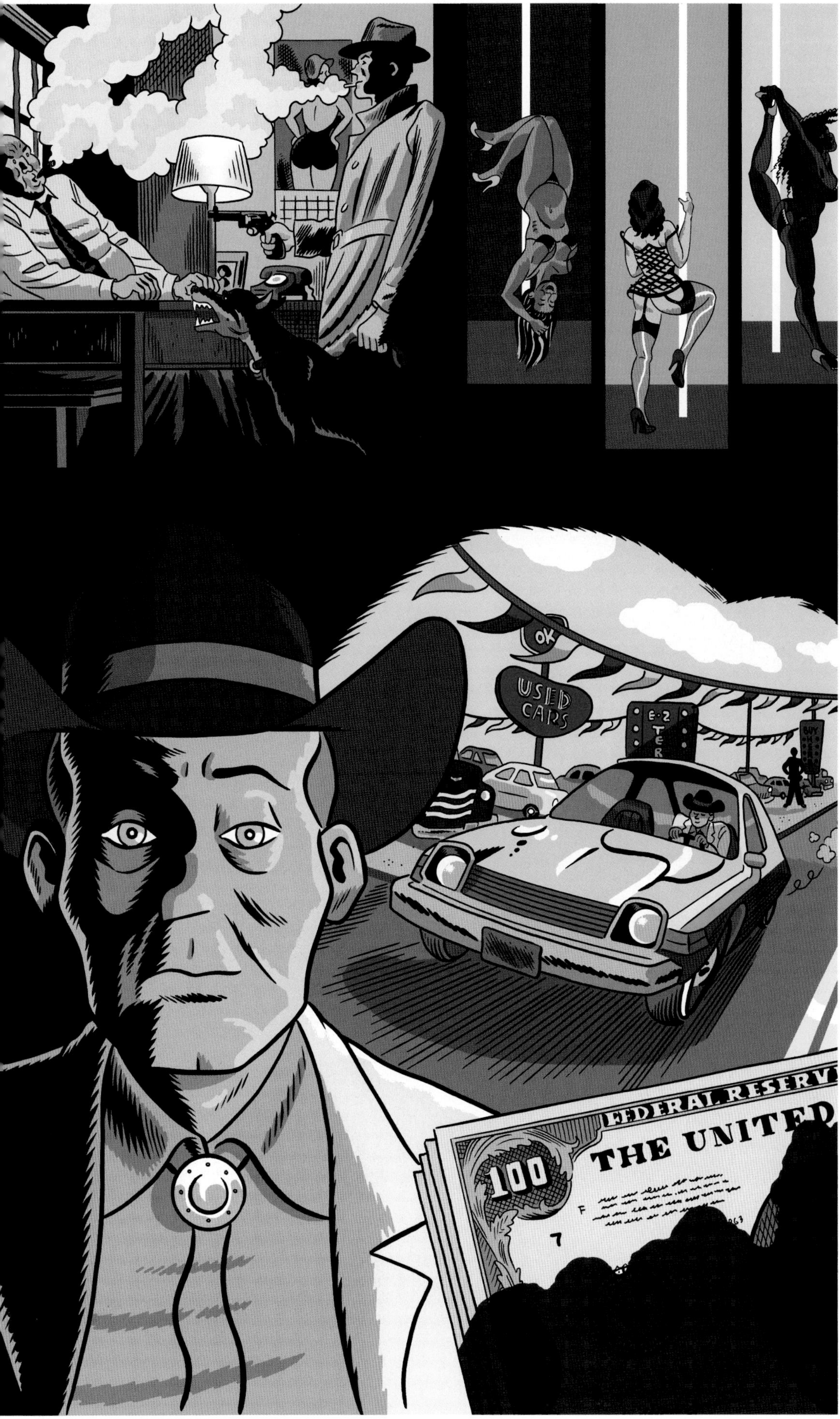
OK
USED CARS
BUY
FEDERAL RESERV
THE UNITED
100

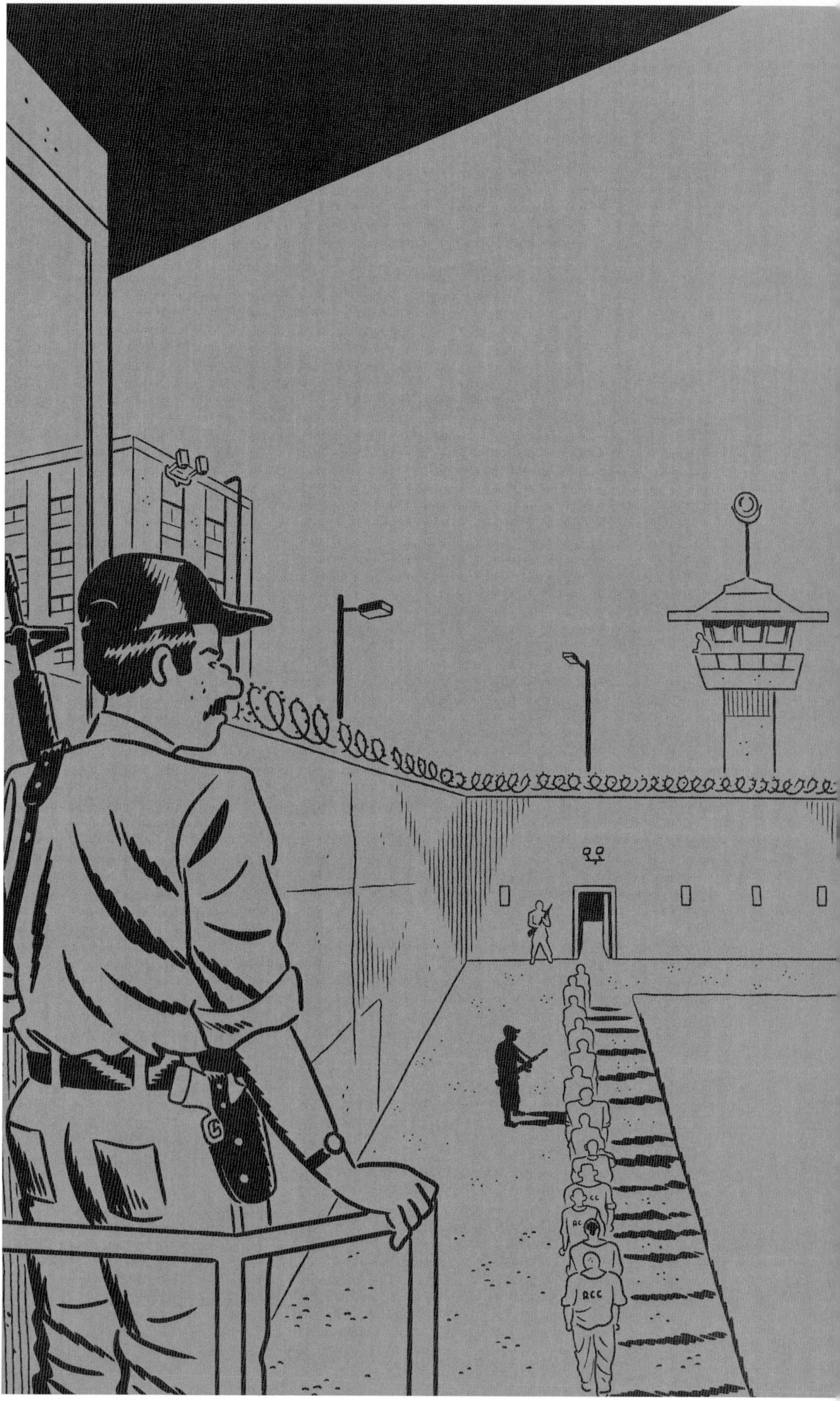

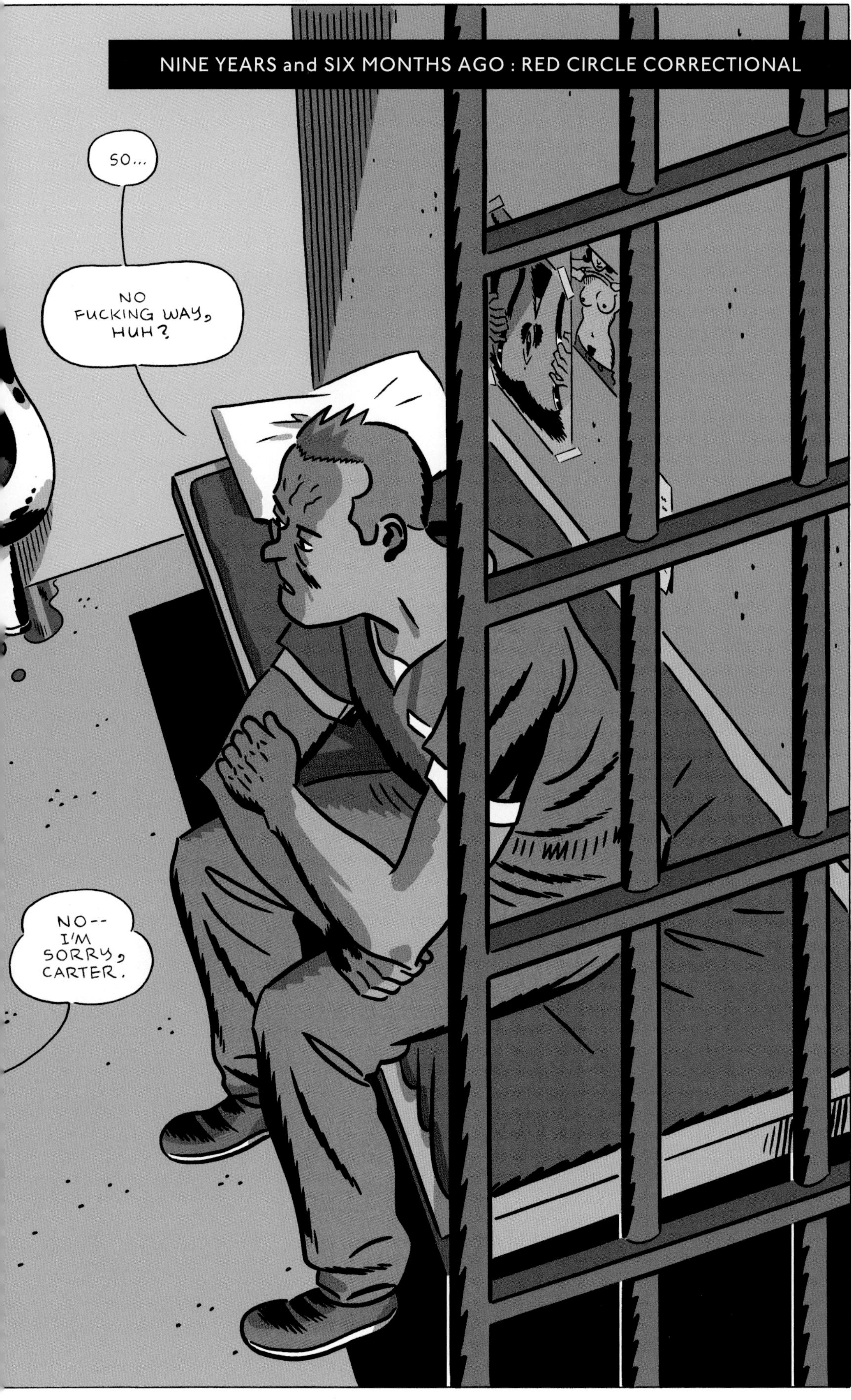
NINE YEARS and SIX MONTHS AGO : RED CIRCLE CORRECTIONAL
SO...
NO FUCKING WAY, HUH?
NO-- I'M SORRY, CARTER.

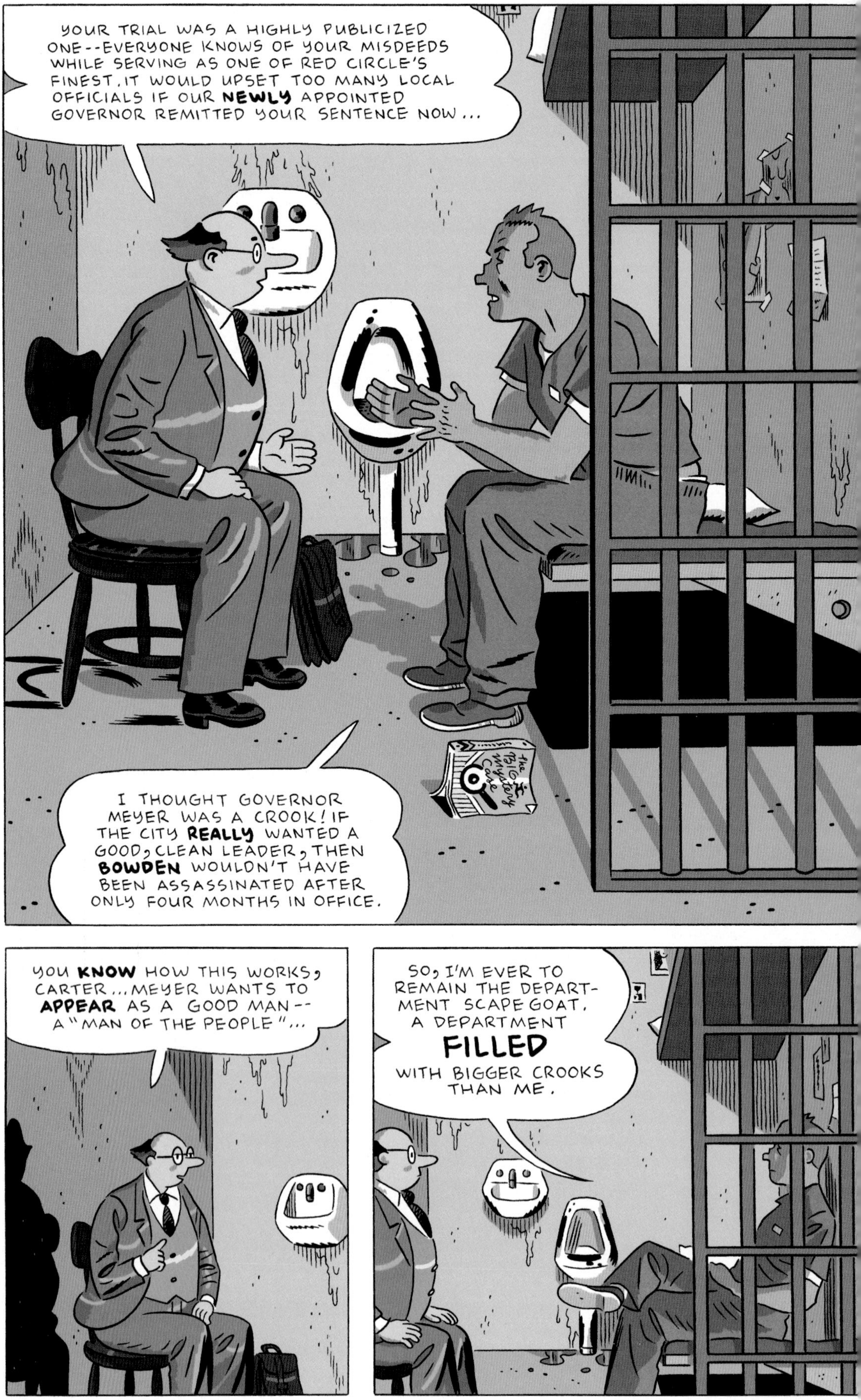
YOUR TRIAL WAS A HIGHLY PUBLICIZED ONE--EVERYONE KNOWS OF YOUR MISDEEDS WHILE SERVING AS ONE OF RED CIRCLE'S FINEST. IT WOULD UPSET TOO MANY LOCAL OFFICIALS IF OUR **NEWLY** APPOINTED GOVERNOR REMITTED YOUR SENTENCE NOW...
the BIG Mystery Case
I THOUGHT GOVERNOR MEYER WAS A CROOK! IF THE CITY **REALLY** WANTED A GOOD, CLEAN LEADER, THEN **BOWDEN** WOULDN'T HAVE BEEN ASSASSINATED AFTER ONLY FOUR MONTHS IN OFFICE.
YOU **KNOW** HOW THIS WORKS, CARTER... MEYER WANTS TO **APPEAR** AS A GOOD MAN-- A "MAN OF THE PEOPLE"...
SO, I'M EVER TO REMAIN THE DEPART-MENT SCAPEGOAT. A DEPARTMENT **FILLED** WITH BIGGER CROOKS THAN ME.

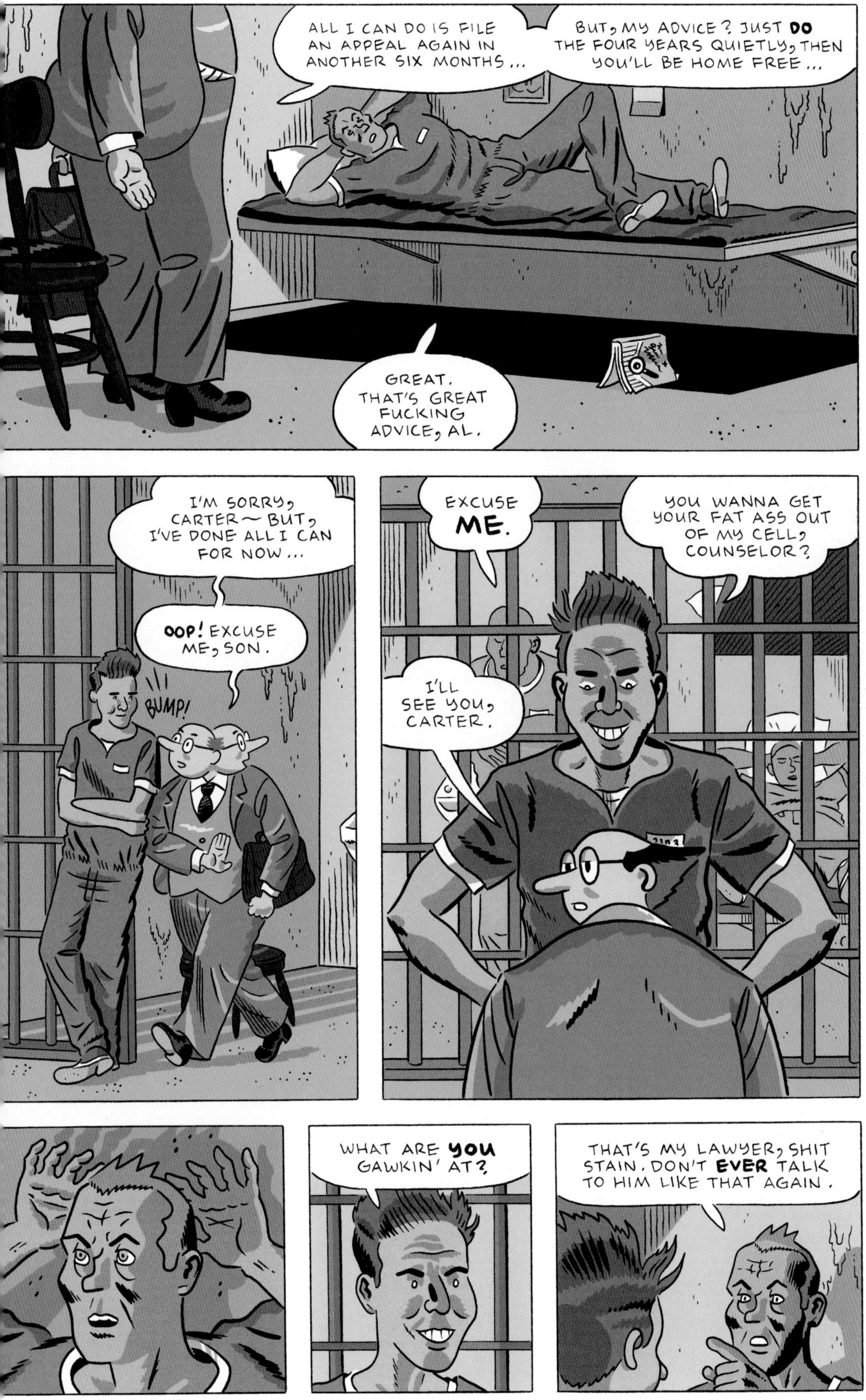
ALL I CAN DO IS FILE AN APPEAL AGAIN IN ANOTHER SIX MONTHS...
BUT, MY ADVICE? JUST **DO** THE FOUR YEARS QUIETLY, THEN YOU'LL BE HOME FREE...
GREAT. THAT'S GREAT FUCKING ADVICE, AL.
I'M SORRY, CARTER ~ BUT, I'VE DONE ALL I CAN FOR NOW...
OOP! EXCUSE ME, SON.
BUMP!
EXCUSE **ME**.
YOU WANNA GET YOUR FAT ASS OUT OF MY CELL, COUNSELOR?
I'LL SEE YOU, CARTER.
WHAT ARE **YOU** GAWKIN' AT?
THAT'S MY LAWYER, SHIT STAIN. DON'T **EVER** TALK TO HIM LIKE THAT AGAIN.

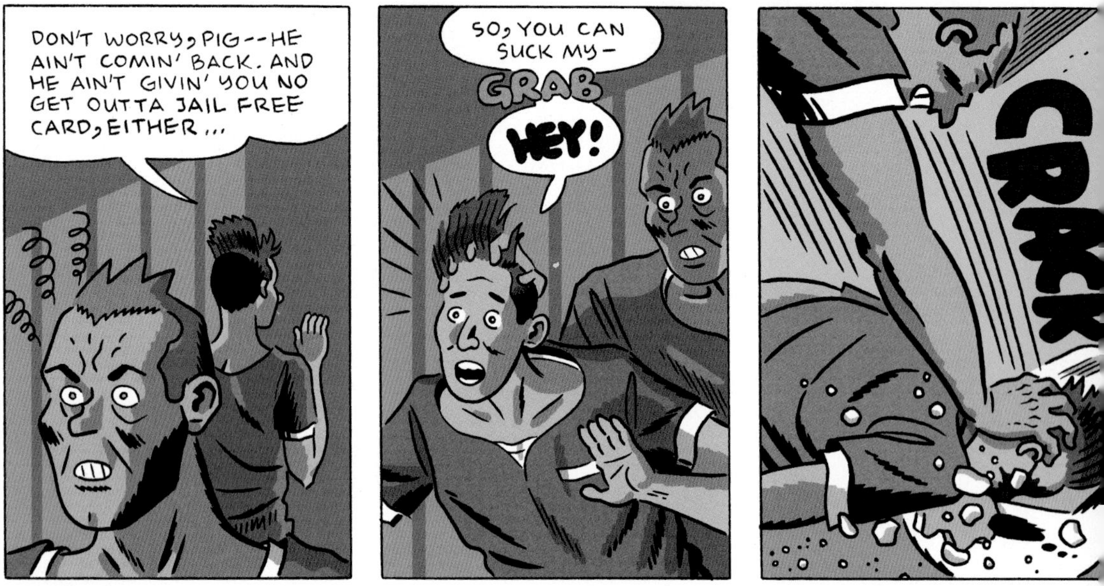
DON'T WORRY, PIG--HE AIN'T COMIN' BACK. AND HE AIN'T GIVIN' YOU NO GET OUTTA JAIL FREE CARD, EITHER...
SO, YOU CAN SUCK MY-
GRAB
HEY!
CRAK

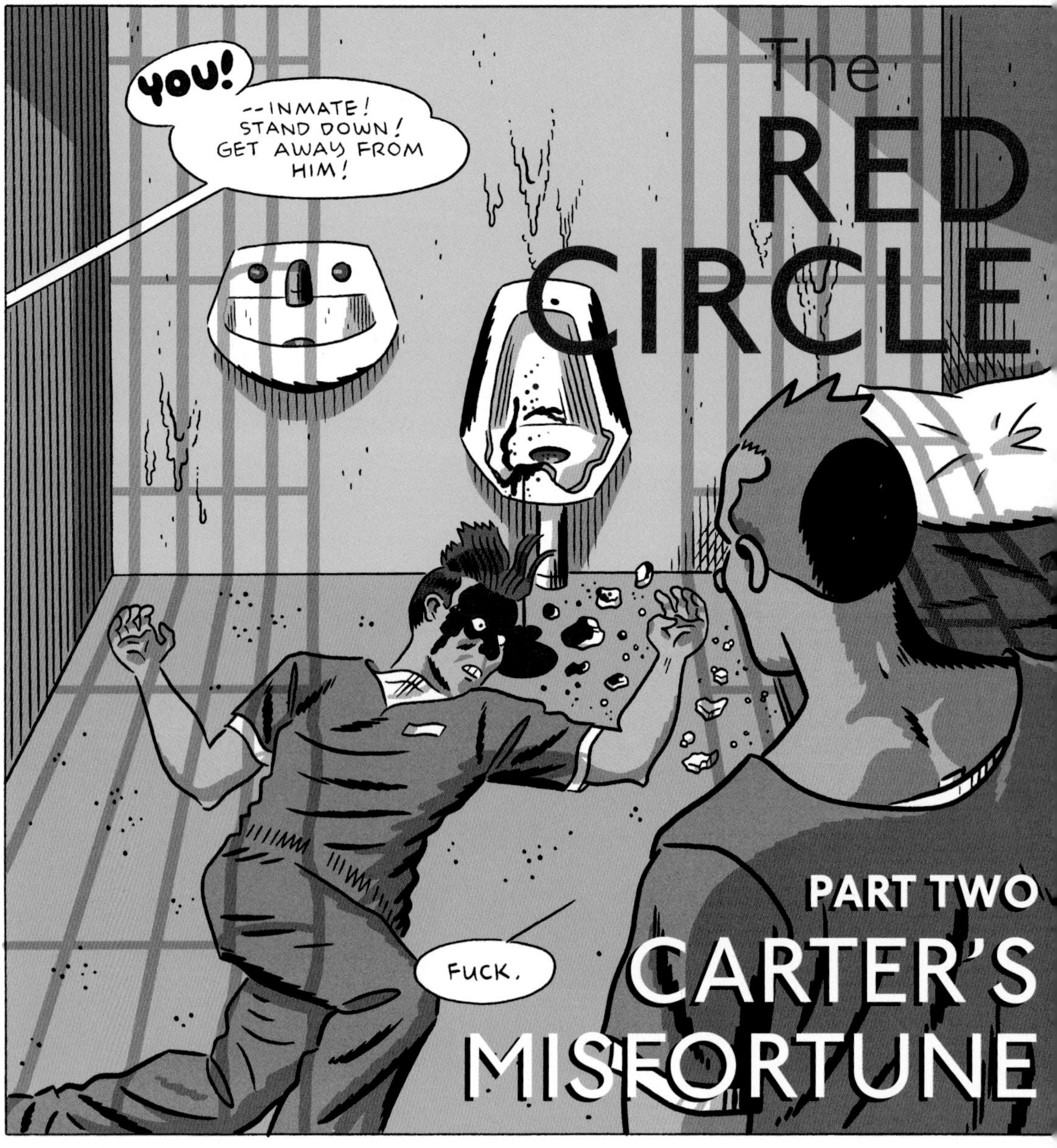
YOU!
--INMATE! STAND DOWN! GET AWAY FROM HIM!
The RED CIRCLE
PART TWO
CARTER'S MISFORTUNE
FUCK.

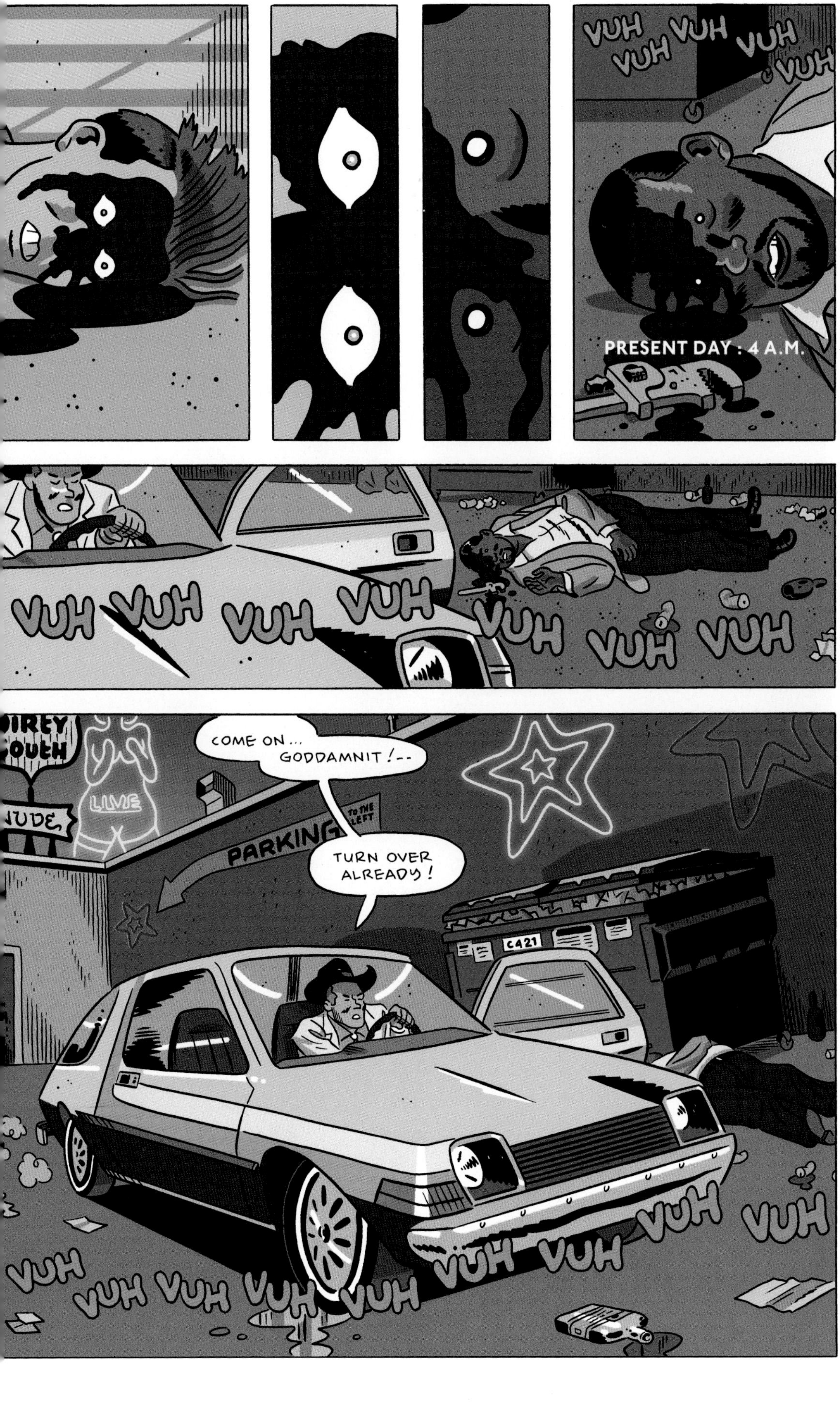
VUH VUH VUH VUH VUH
PRESENT DAY : 4 A.M.
VUH VUH VUH VUH VUH VUH VUH
NUDE
LIVE
PARKING
TO THE LEFT
COME ON... GODDAMNIT!--
TURN OVER ALREADY!
C421
VUH VUH VUH VUH VUH VUH VUH VUH VUH VUH

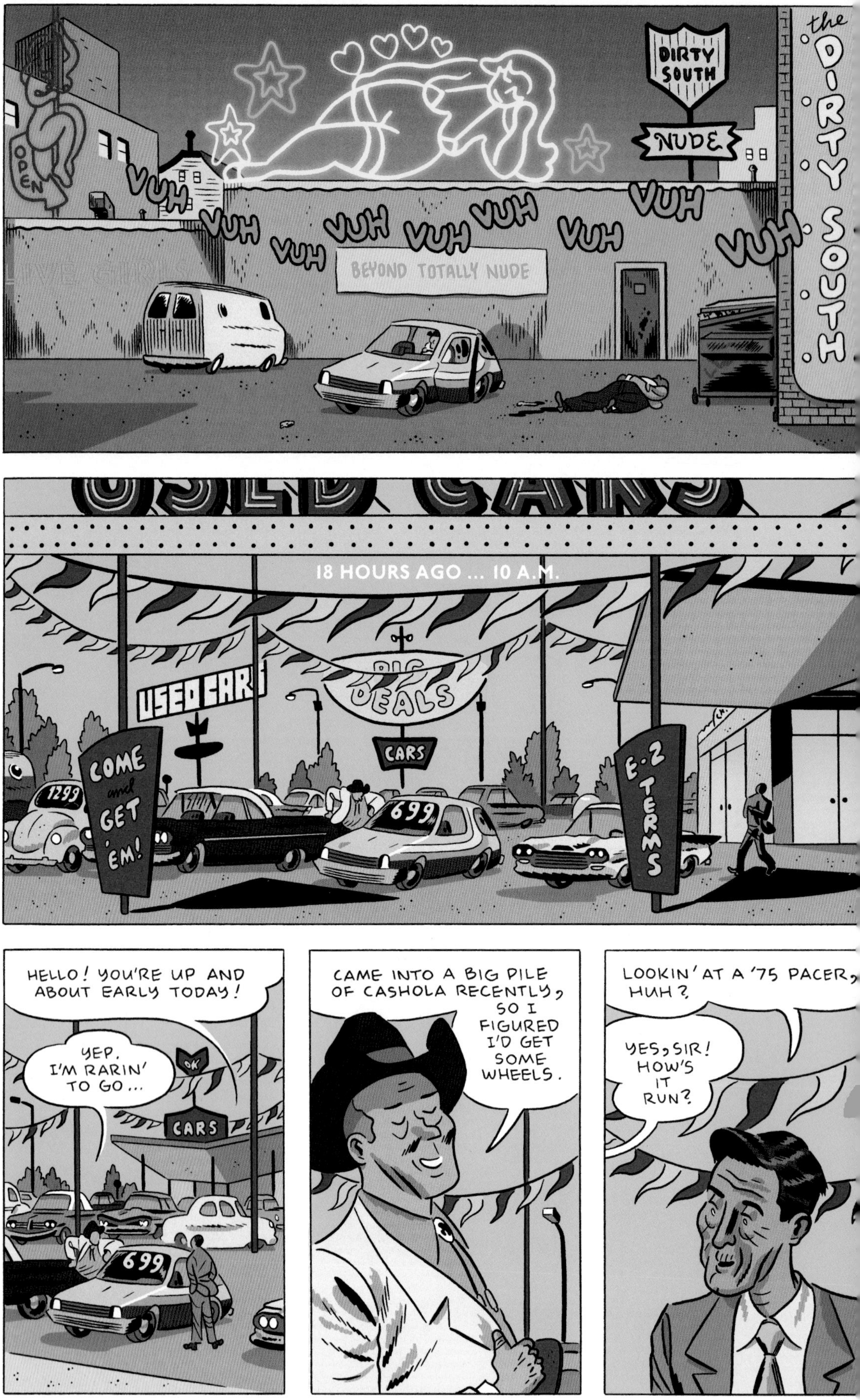

OPEN
VUH VUH VUH VUH VUH VUH VUH VUH VUH
DIRTY SOUTH
NUDE
the DIRTY SOUTH
BEYOND TOTALLY NUDE
USED CARS
18 HOURS AGO ... 10 A.M.
USED CARS
BIG DEALS
CARS
COME and GET 'EM!
1299
699
E-Z TERMS
HELLO! YOU'RE UP AND ABOUT EARLY TODAY!
YEP. I'M RARIN' TO GO...
OK
CARS
699
CAME INTO A BIG PILE OF CASHOLA RECENTLY, SO I FIGURED I'D GET SOME WHEELS.
LOOKIN' AT A '75 PACER, HUH?
YES, SIR! HOW'S IT RUN?

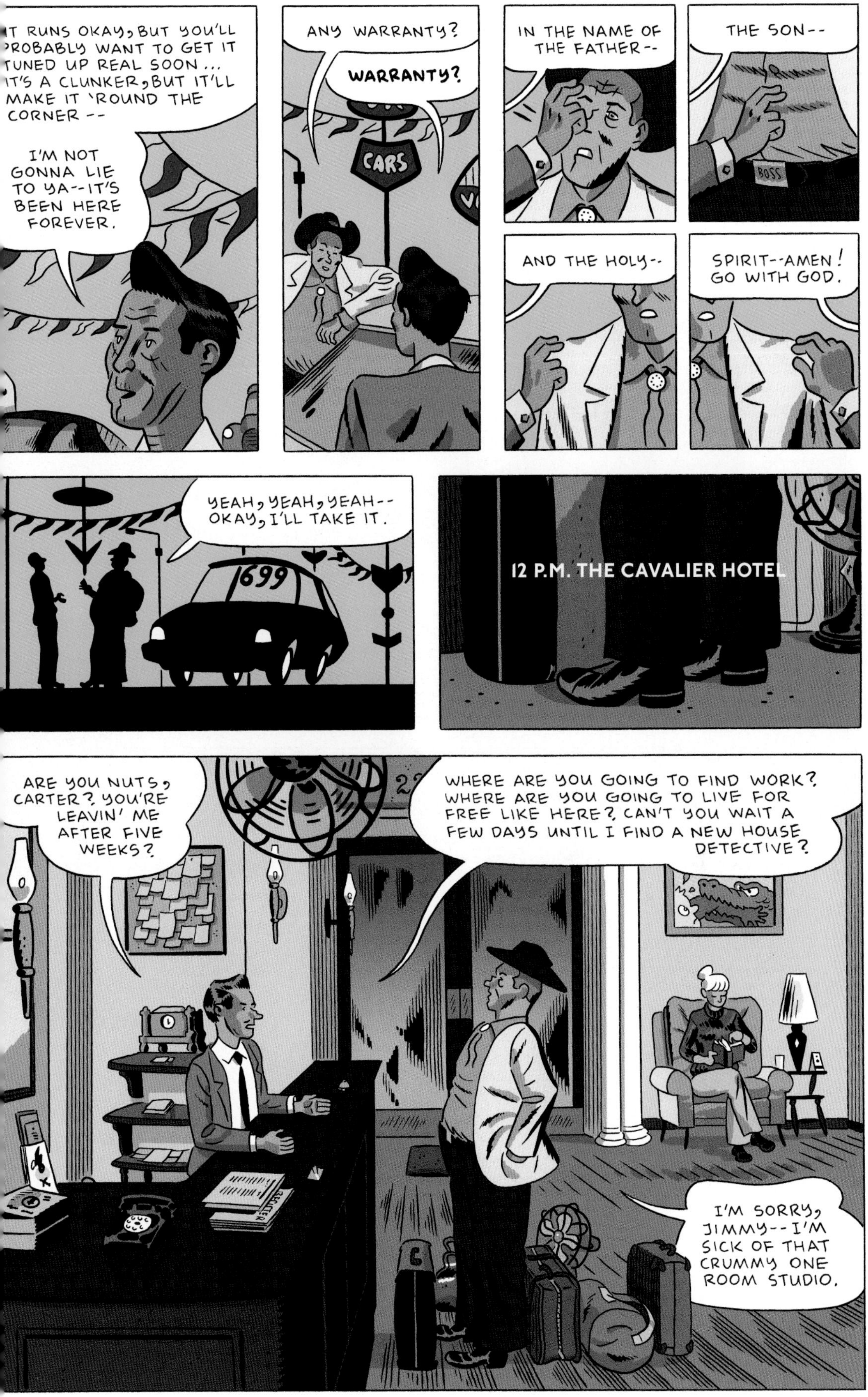

IT RUNS OKAY, BUT YOU'LL PROBABLY WANT TO GET IT TUNED UP REAL SOON... IT'S A CLUNKER, BUT IT'LL MAKE IT 'ROUND THE CORNER --
I'M NOT GONNA LIE TO YA--IT'S BEEN HERE FOREVER.
ANY WARRANTY?
WARRANTY?
CARS
IN THE NAME OF THE FATHER--
THE SON--
BOSS
AND THE HOLY--.
SPIRIT--AMEN! GO WITH GOD.
YEAH, YEAH, YEAH-- OKAY, I'LL TAKE IT.
699
12 P.M. THE CAVALIER HOTEL
ARE YOU NUTS, CARTER? YOU'RE LEAVIN' ME AFTER FIVE WEEKS?
WHERE ARE YOU GOING TO FIND WORK? WHERE ARE YOU GOING TO LIVE FOR FREE LIKE HERE? CAN'T YOU WAIT A FEW DAYS UNTIL I FIND A NEW HOUSE DETECTIVE?
I'M SORRY, JIMMY--I'M SICK OF THAT CRUMMY ONE ROOM STUDIO.

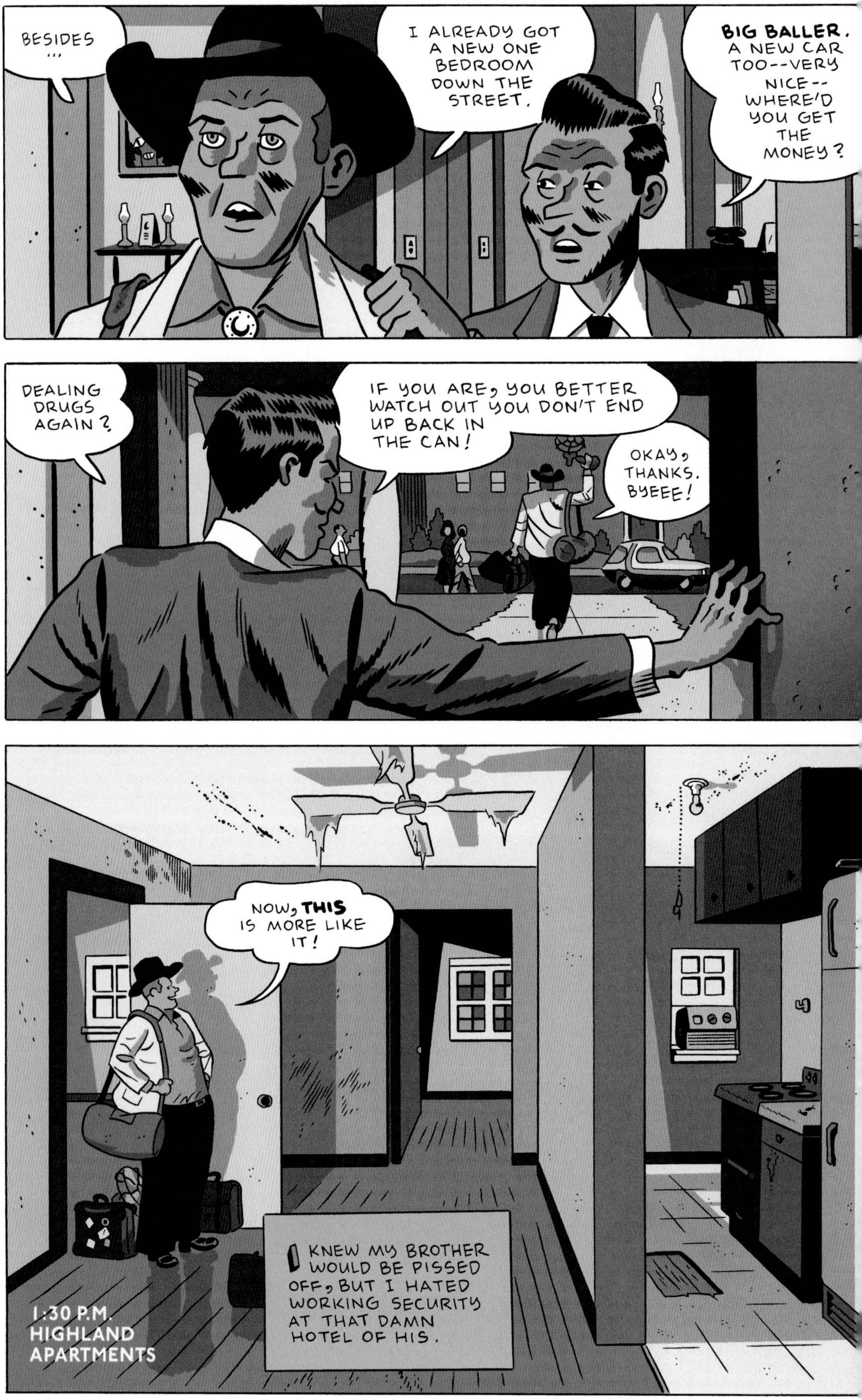
BESIDES ...
I ALREADY GOT A NEW ONE BEDROOM DOWN THE STREET.
BIG BALLER. A NEW CAR TOO--VERY NICE-- WHERE'D YOU GET THE MONEY?
DEALING DRUGS AGAIN?
IF YOU ARE, YOU BETTER WATCH OUT YOU DON'T END UP BACK IN THE CAN!
OKAY, THANKS. BYEEE!
NOW, **THIS** IS MORE LIKE IT!
I KNEW MY BROTHER WOULD BE PISSED OFF, BUT I HATED WORKING SECURITY AT THAT DAMN HOTEL OF HIS.
1:30 P.M. HIGHLAND APARTMENTS

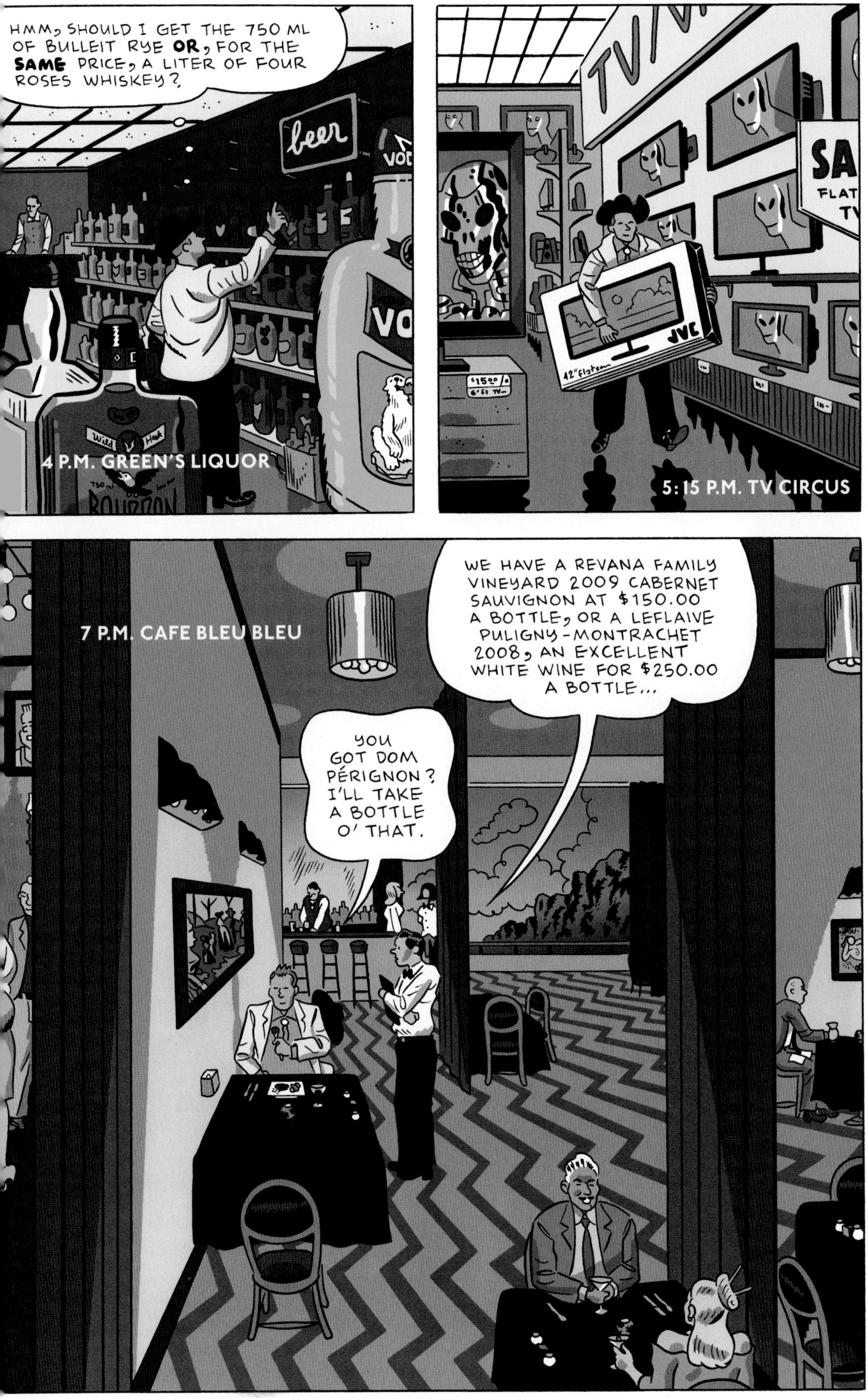
HMM, SHOULD I GET THE 750 ML OF BULLEIT RYE **OR**, FOR THE **SAME** PRICE, A LITER OF FOUR ROSES WHISKEY?
beer
4 P.M. GREEN'S LIQUOR
5:15 P.M. TV CIRCUS
JVC
7 P.M. CAFE BLEU BLEU
WE HAVE A REVANA FAMILY VINEYARD 2009 CABERNET SAUVIGNON AT $150.00 A BOTTLE, OR A LEFLAIVE PULIGNY-MONTRACHET 2008, AN EXCELLENT WHITE WINE FOR $250.00 A BOTTLE...
YOU GOT DOM PÉRIGNON? I'LL TAKE A BOTTLE O' THAT.

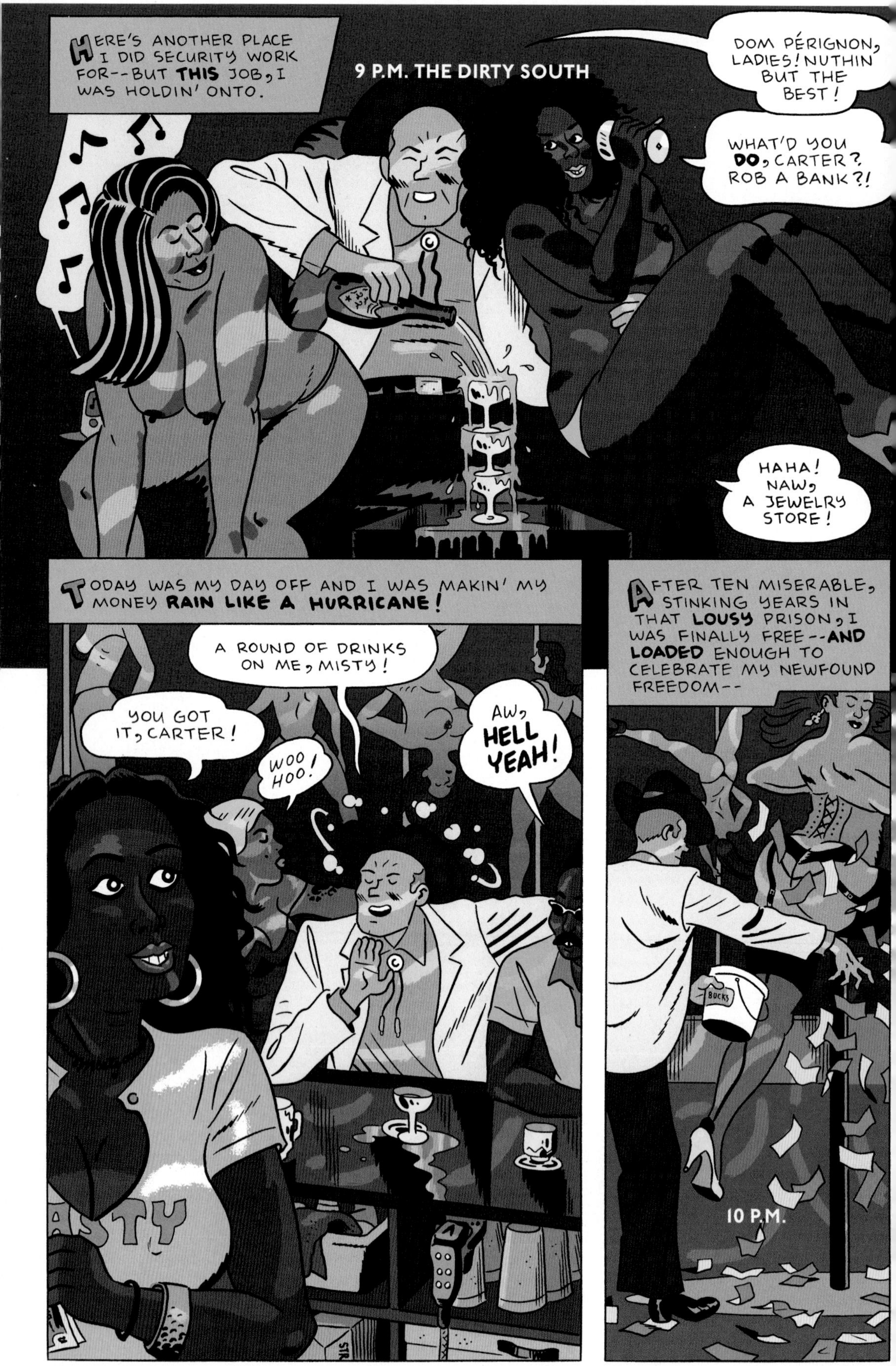
HERE'S ANOTHER PLACE I DID SECURITY WORK FOR--BUT THIS JOB, I WAS HOLDIN' ONTO.
9 P.M. THE DIRTY SOUTH
DOM PÉRIGNON, LADIES! NUTHIN BUT THE BEST!
WHAT'D YOU DO, CARTER? ROB A BANK?!
HAHA! NAW, A JEWELRY STORE!
TODAY WAS MY DAY OFF AND I WAS MAKIN' MY MONEY RAIN LIKE A HURRICANE!
A ROUND OF DRINKS ON ME, MISTY!
YOU GOT IT, CARTER!
WOO HOO!
AW, HELL YEAH!
AFTER TEN MISERABLE, STINKING YEARS IN THAT LOUSY PRISON, I WAS FINALLY FREE--AND LOADED ENOUGH TO CELEBRATE MY NEWFOUND FREEDOM--
BUCKS
10 P.M.

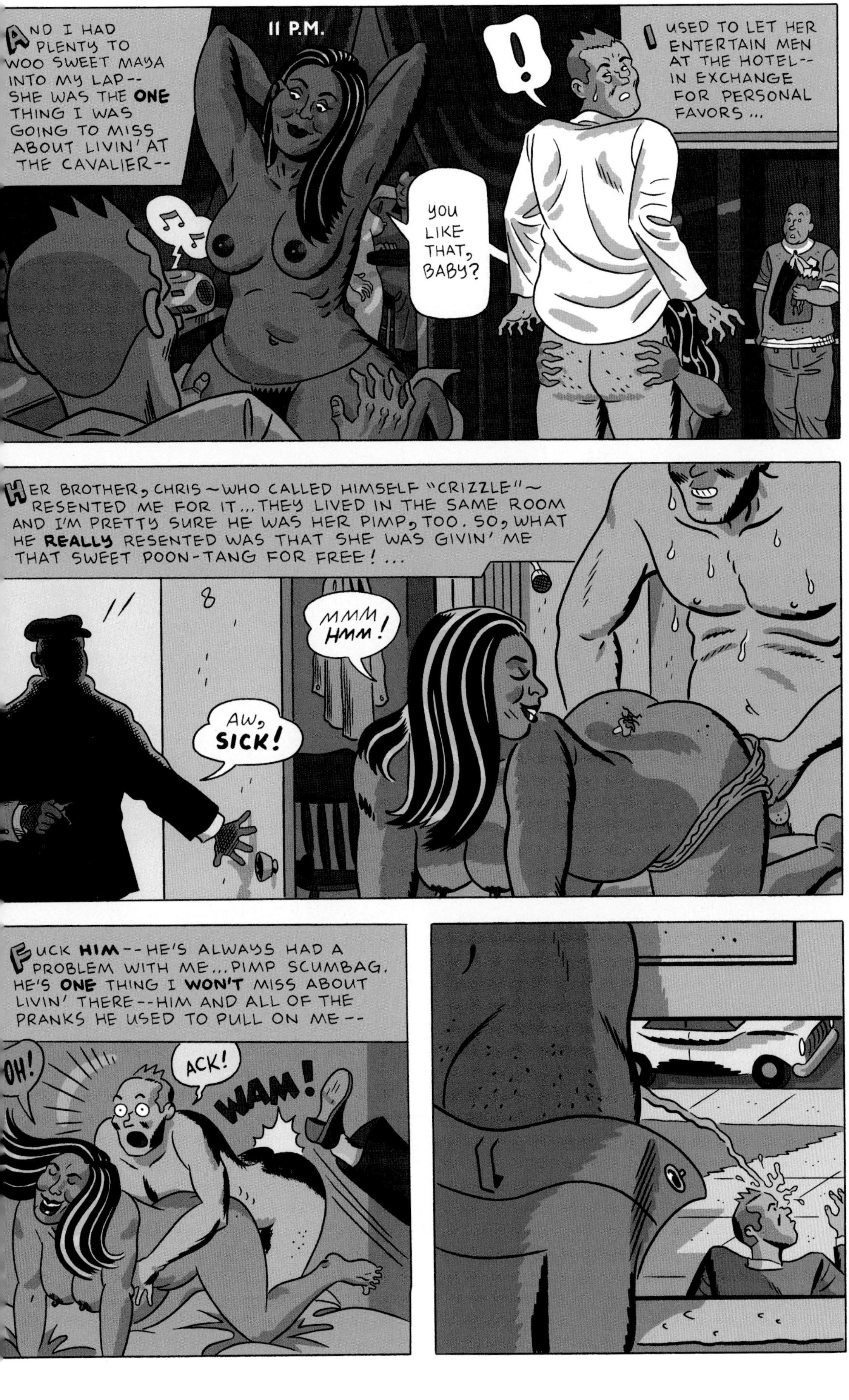

AND I HAD PLENTY TO WOO SWEET MAYA INTO MY LAP-- SHE WAS THE **ONE** THING I WAS GOING TO MISS ABOUT LIVIN' AT THE CAVALIER--
11 P.M.
!
I USED TO LET HER ENTERTAIN MEN AT THE HOTEL-- IN EXCHANGE FOR PERSONAL FAVORS...
YOU LIKE THAT, BABY?
HER BROTHER, CHRIS~WHO CALLED HIMSELF "CRIZZLE"~ RESENTED ME FOR IT... THEY LIVED IN THE SAME ROOM AND I'M PRETTY SURE HE WAS HER PIMP, TOO. SO, WHAT HE **REALLY** RESENTED WAS THAT SHE WAS GIVIN' ME THAT SWEET POON-TANG FOR FREE!...
8
MMM HMM!
AW, **SICK!**
FUCK **HIM**--HE'S ALWAYS HAD A PROBLEM WITH ME... PIMP SCUMBAG. HE'S **ONE** THING I **WON'T** MISS ABOUT LIVIN' THERE--HIM AND ALL OF THE PRANKS HE USED TO PULL ON ME--
OH!
ACK!
WAM!

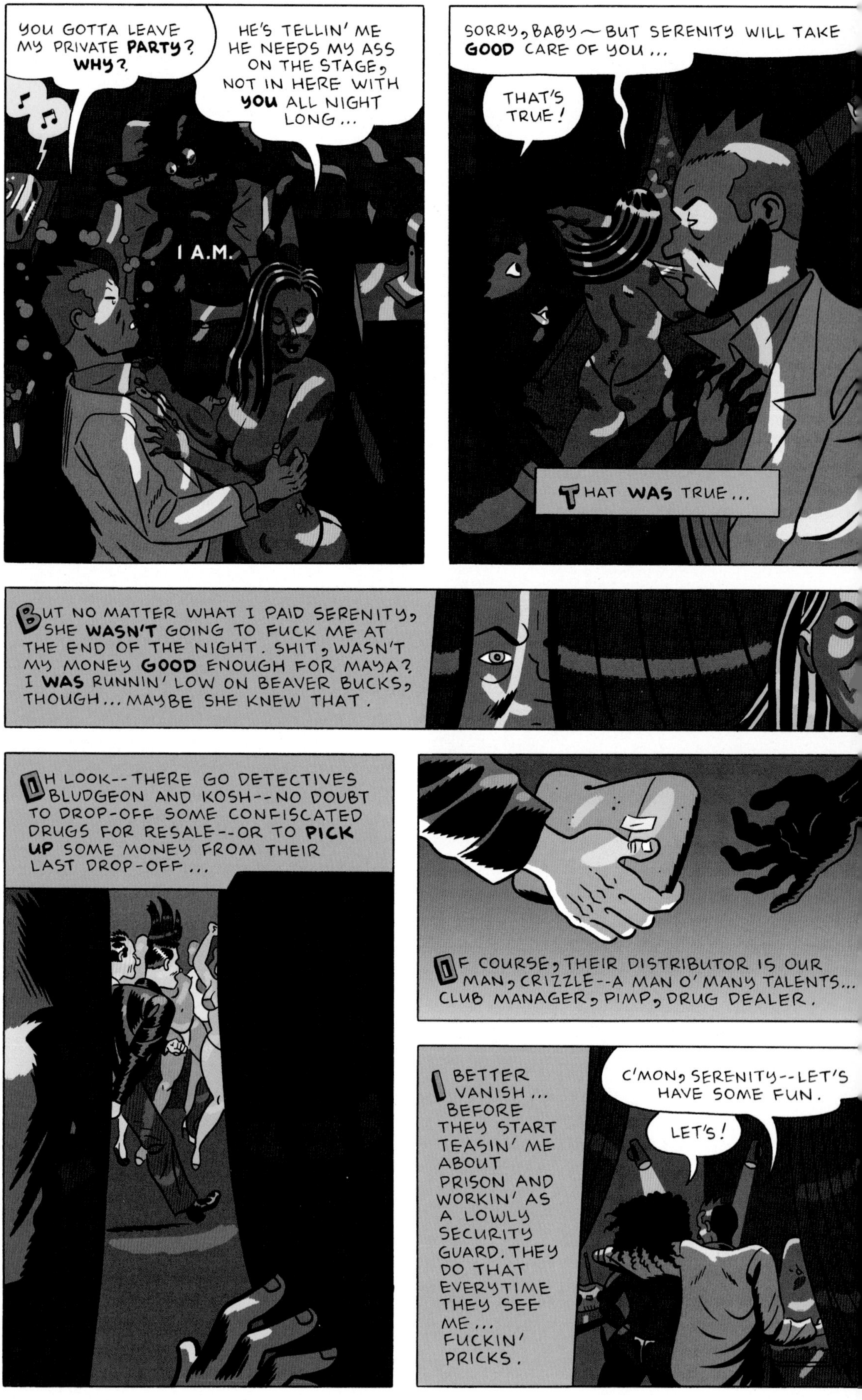

YOU GOTTA LEAVE MY PRIVATE **PARTY**? **WHY**?
HE'S TELLIN' ME HE NEEDS MY ASS ON THE STAGE, NOT IN HERE WITH **YOU** ALL NIGHT LONG...
I A.M.
SORRY, BABY~ BUT SERENITY WILL TAKE **GOOD** CARE OF YOU...
THAT'S TRUE!
THAT **WAS** TRUE...
BUT NO MATTER WHAT I PAID SERENITY, SHE **WASN'T** GOING TO FUCK ME AT THE END OF THE NIGHT. SHIT, WASN'T MY MONEY **GOOD** ENOUGH FOR MAYA? I **WAS** RUNNIN' LOW ON BEAVER BUCKS, THOUGH... MAYBE SHE KNEW THAT.
OH LOOK--THERE GO DETECTIVES BLUDGEON AND KOSH--NO DOUBT TO DROP-OFF SOME CONFISCATED DRUGS FOR RESALE--OR TO **PICK UP** SOME MONEY FROM THEIR LAST DROP-OFF...
OF COURSE, THEIR DISTRIBUTOR IS OUR MAN, CRIZZLE--A MAN O' MANY TALENTS... CLUB MANAGER, PIMP, DRUG DEALER.
I BETTER VANISH... BEFORE THEY START TEASIN' ME ABOUT PRISON AND WORKIN' AS A LOWLY SECURITY GUARD. THEY DO THAT EVERYTIME THEY SEE ME... FUCKIN' PRICKS.
C'MON, SERENITY--LET'S HAVE SOME FUN.
LET'S!

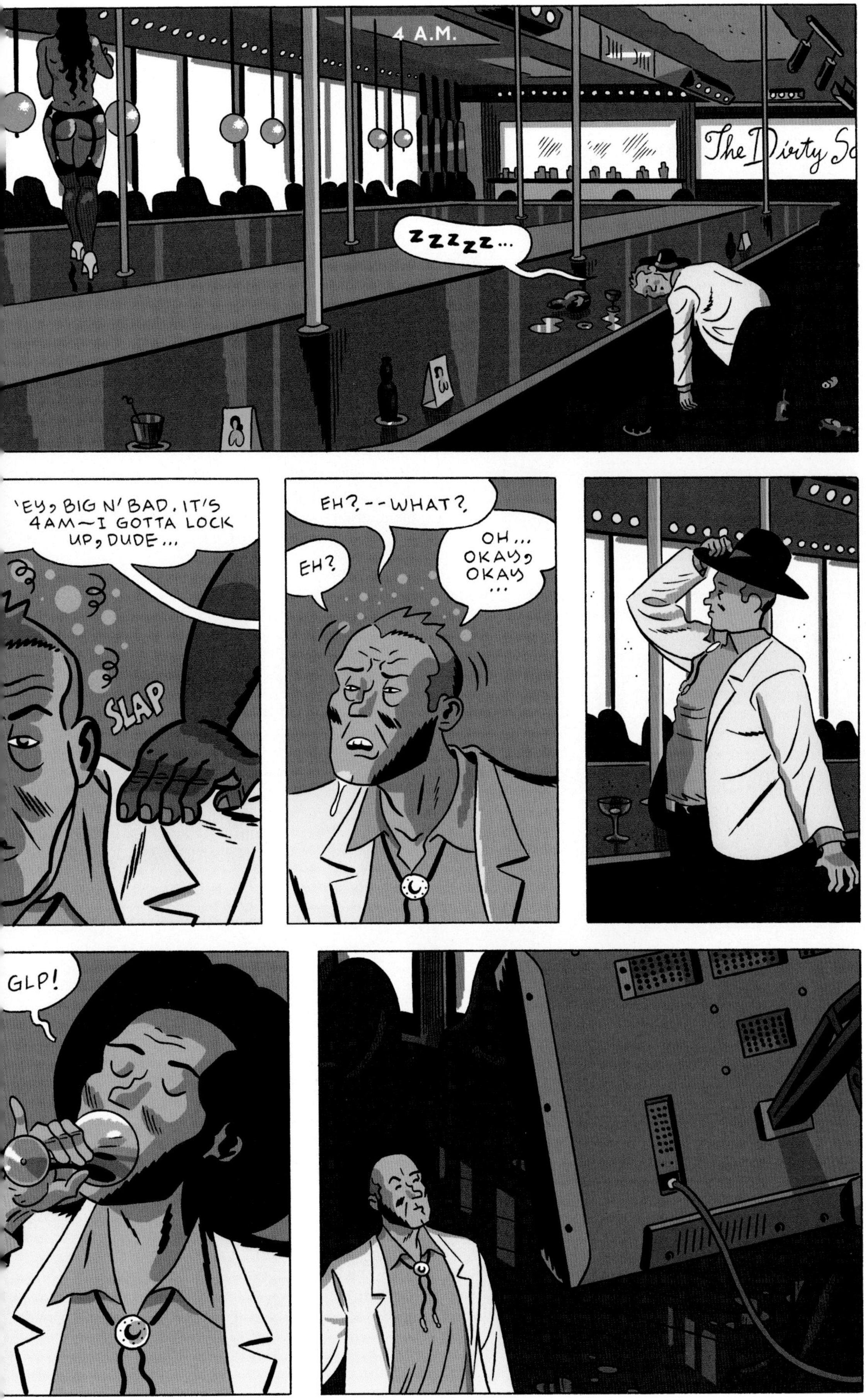
4 A.M.
The Dirty So
ZZZZZ...
'EY, BIG N' BAD. IT'S 4AM~I GOTTA LOCK UP, DUDE...
SLAP
EH?--WHAT?
EH?
OH... OKAY, OKAY...
GLP!

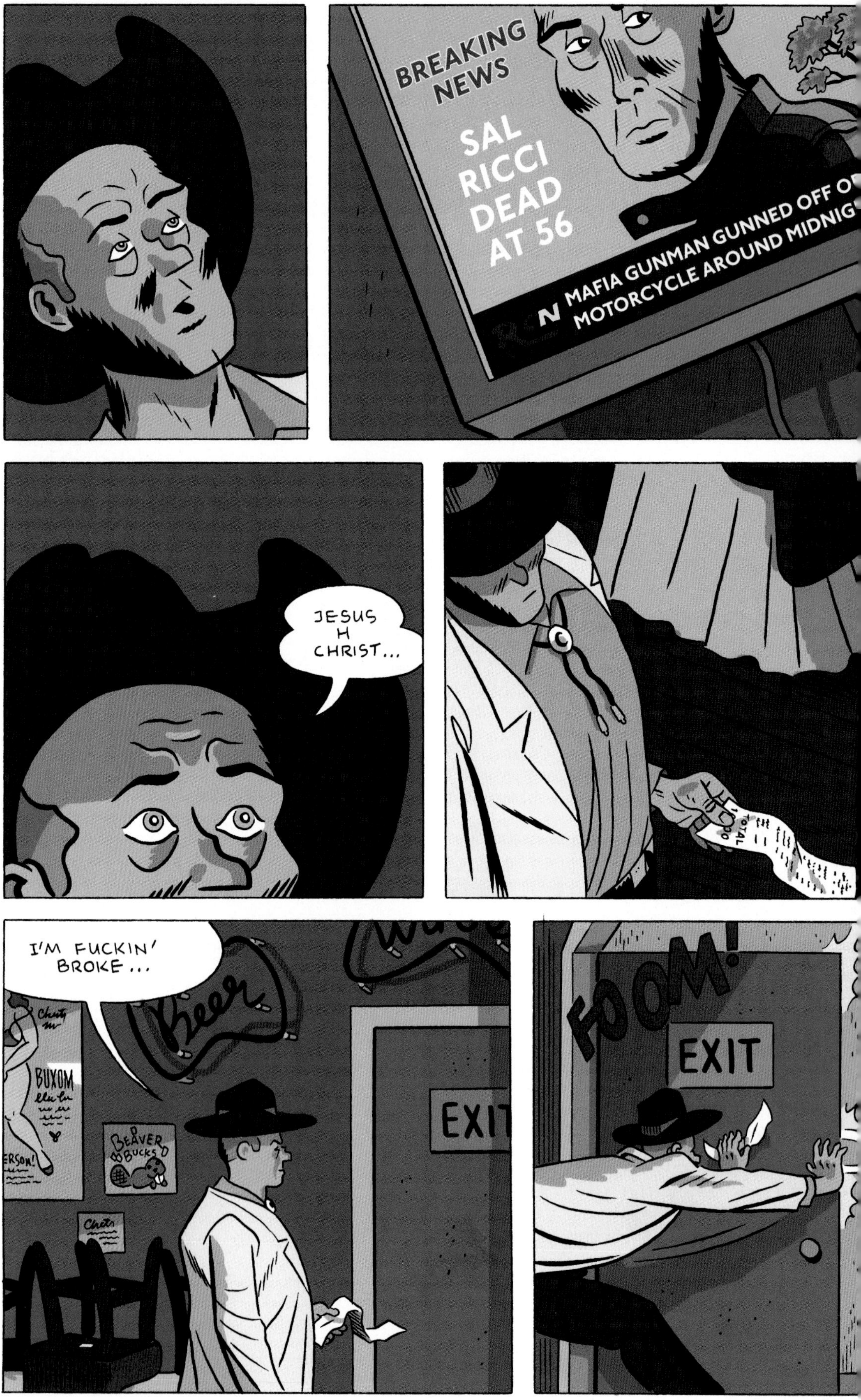

BREAKING NEWS
SAL RICCI DEAD AT 56
N
MAFIA GUNMAN GUNNED OFF O
MOTORCYCLE AROUND MIDNIG
JESUS H CHRIST...
TOTAL
I'M FUCKIN' BROKE...
Beer
BUXOM
BEAVER BUCKS
EXIT
FOOM!
EXIT

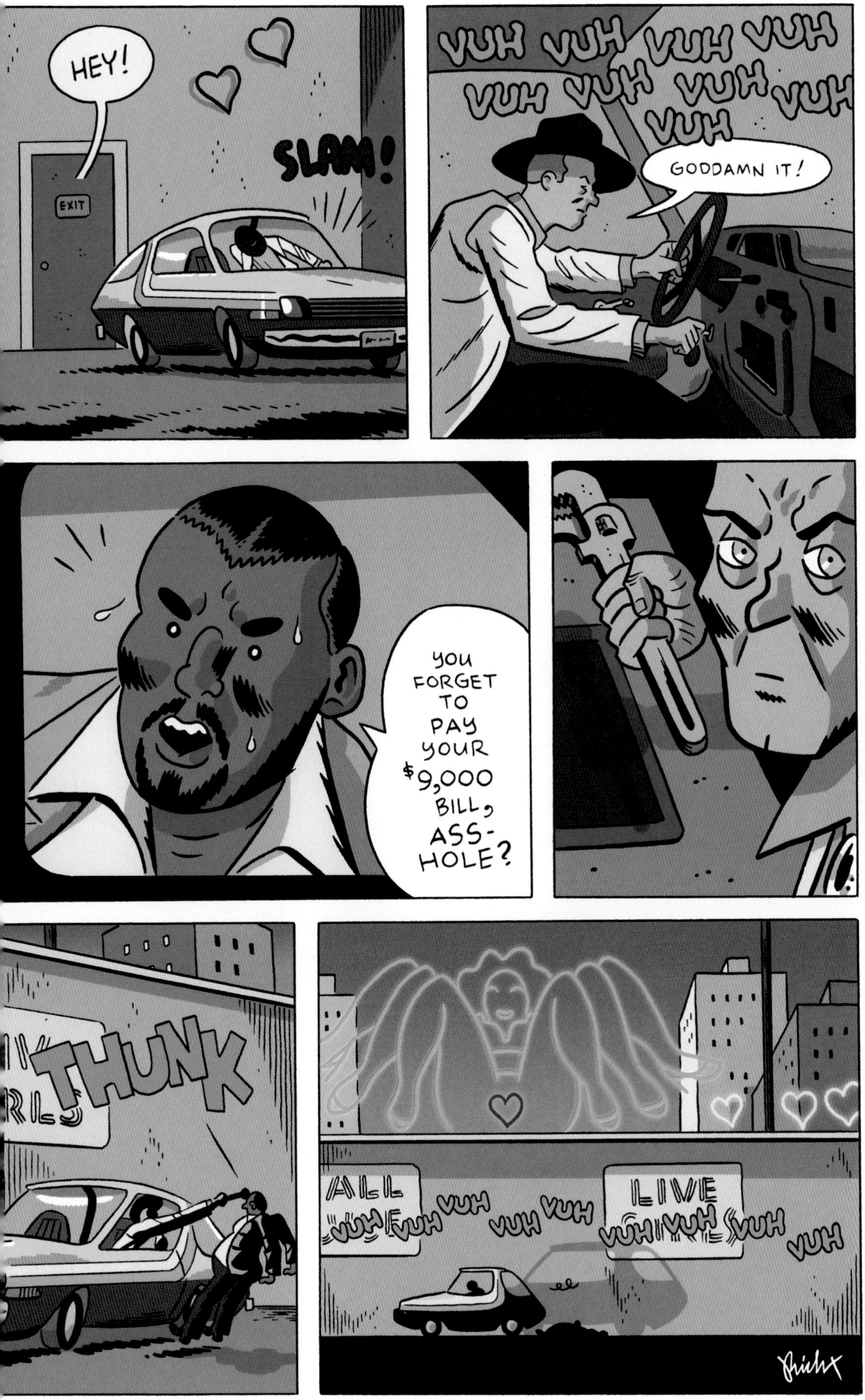

HEY!
EXIT
SLAM!
VUH VUH VUH VUH VUH VUH VUH VUH VUH
GODDAMN IT!
YOU FORGET TO PAY YOUR $9,000 BILL, ASS-HOLE?
THUNK
LIVE
VUH VUH VUH VUH VUH VUH VUH VUH VUH

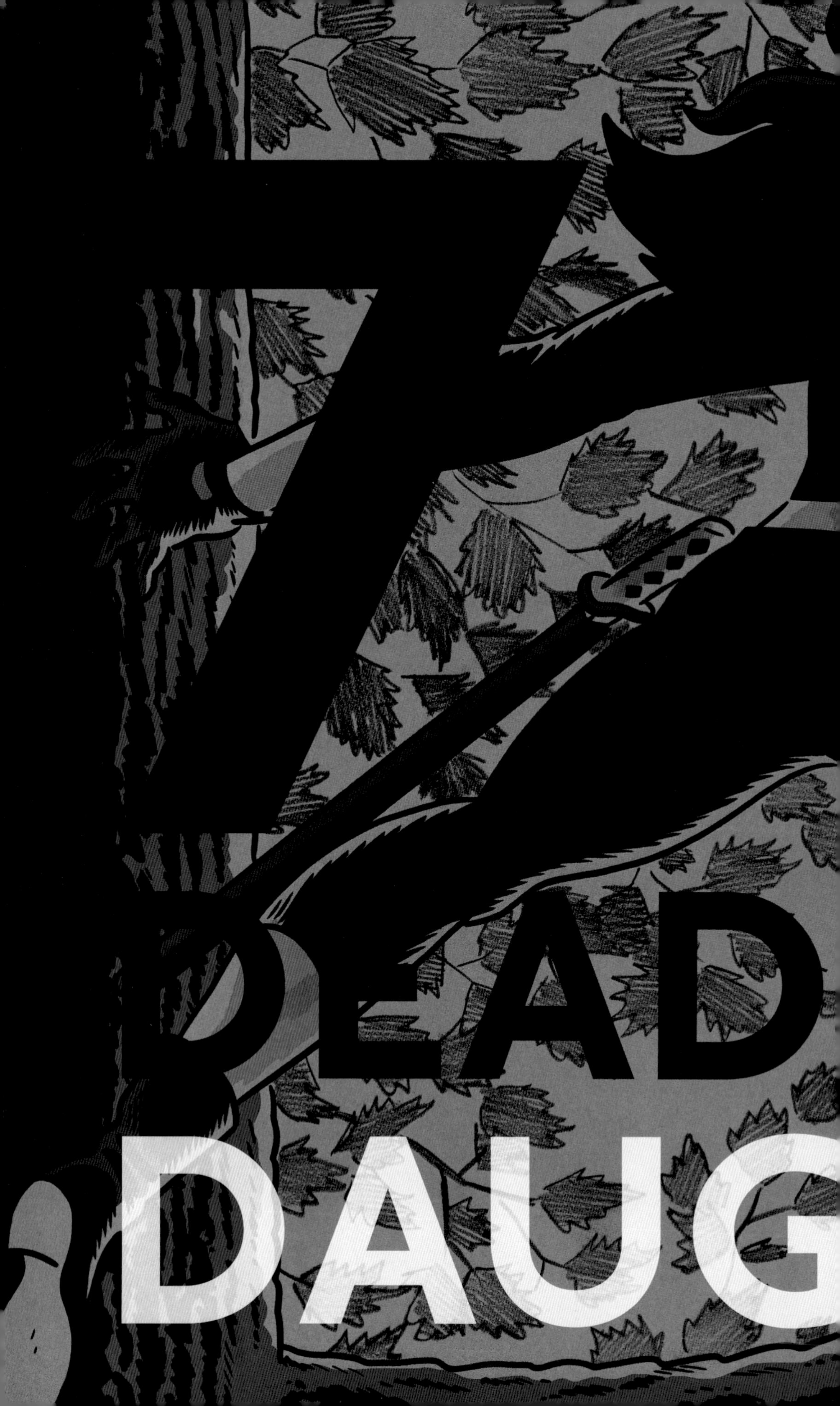

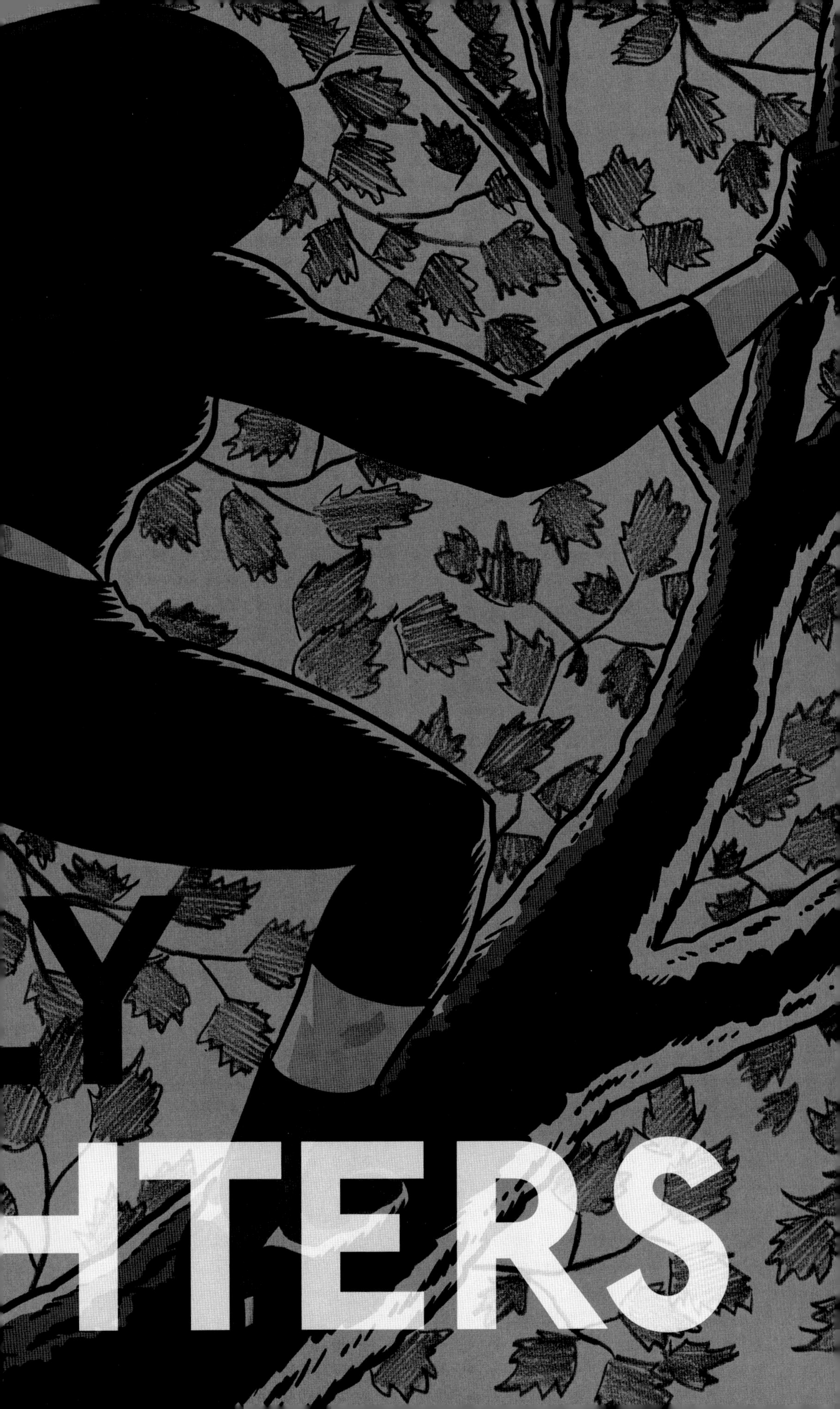
Y
HTERS

GREATEST HITS VOLUME TWO: NICOLE BRECCIA

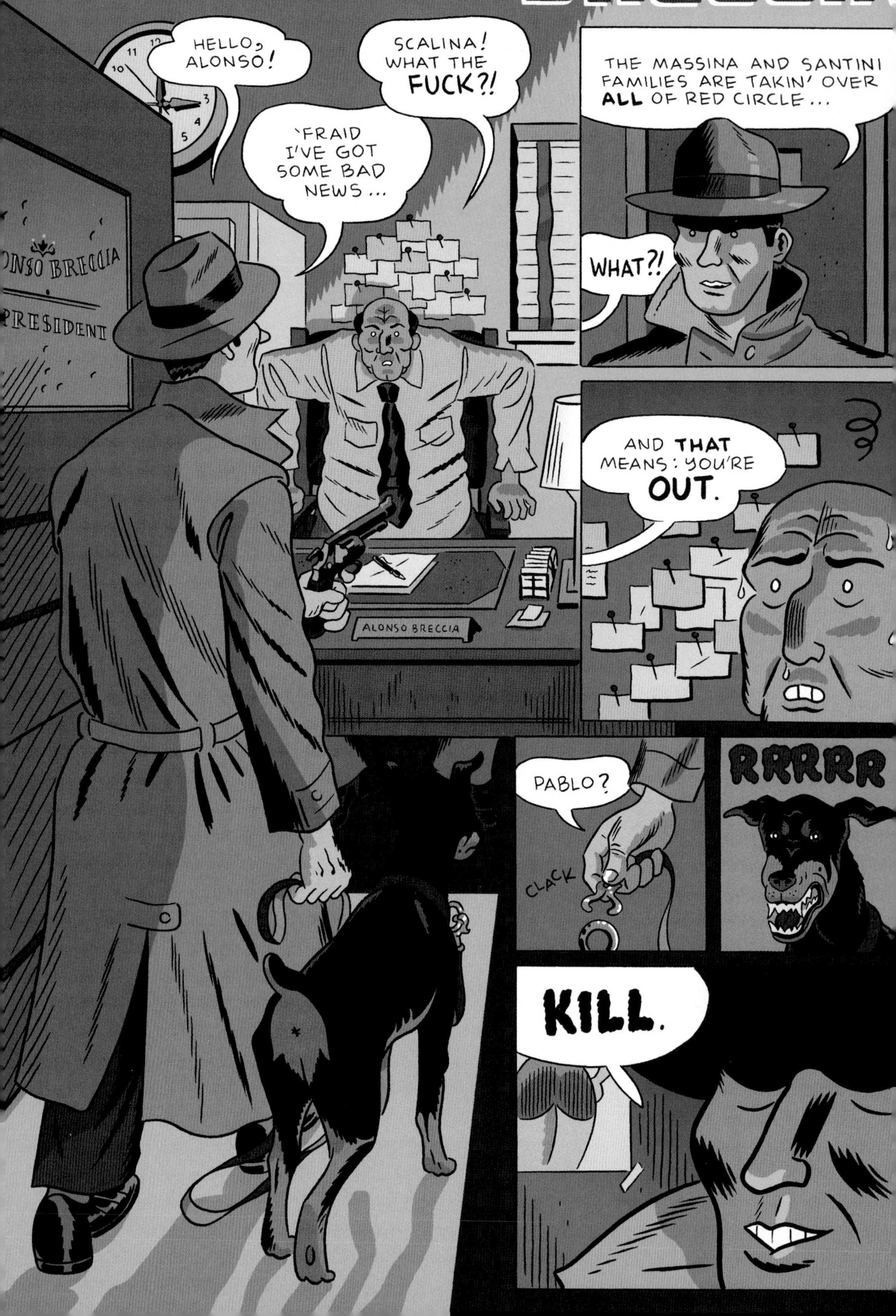

HELLO, ALONSO!
SCALINA! WHAT THE FUCK?!
'FRAID I'VE GOT SOME BAD NEWS...
ONSO BRECCIA
PRESIDENT
ALONSO BRECCIA
THE MASSINA AND SANTINI FAMILIES ARE TAKIN' OVER ALL OF RED CIRCLE...
WHAT?!
AND THAT MEANS: YOU'RE OUT.
PABLO?
CLACK
RRRRR
KILL.

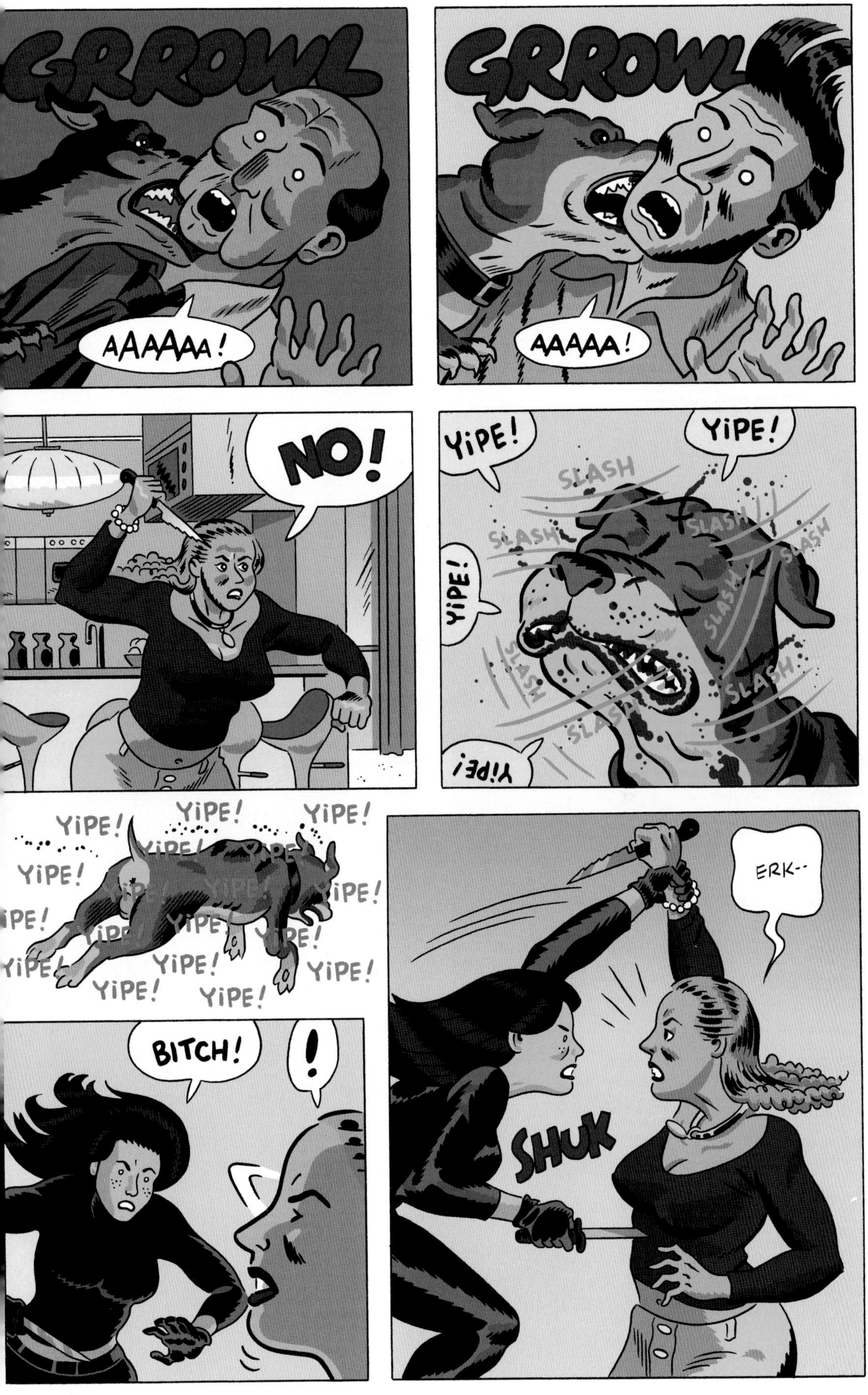
GRROWL
AAAAAA!
GRROWL
AAAAA!
NO!
YIPE!
YIPE!
SLASH
SLASH
SLASH
SLASH
YIPE!
SLASH
SLASH
SLASH
SLASH
YIPE!
YIPE!
YIPE!
YIPE!
YIPE!
YIPE!
YIPE!
YIPE!
YIPE!
YIPE!
BITCH!
!
ERK--
SHUK

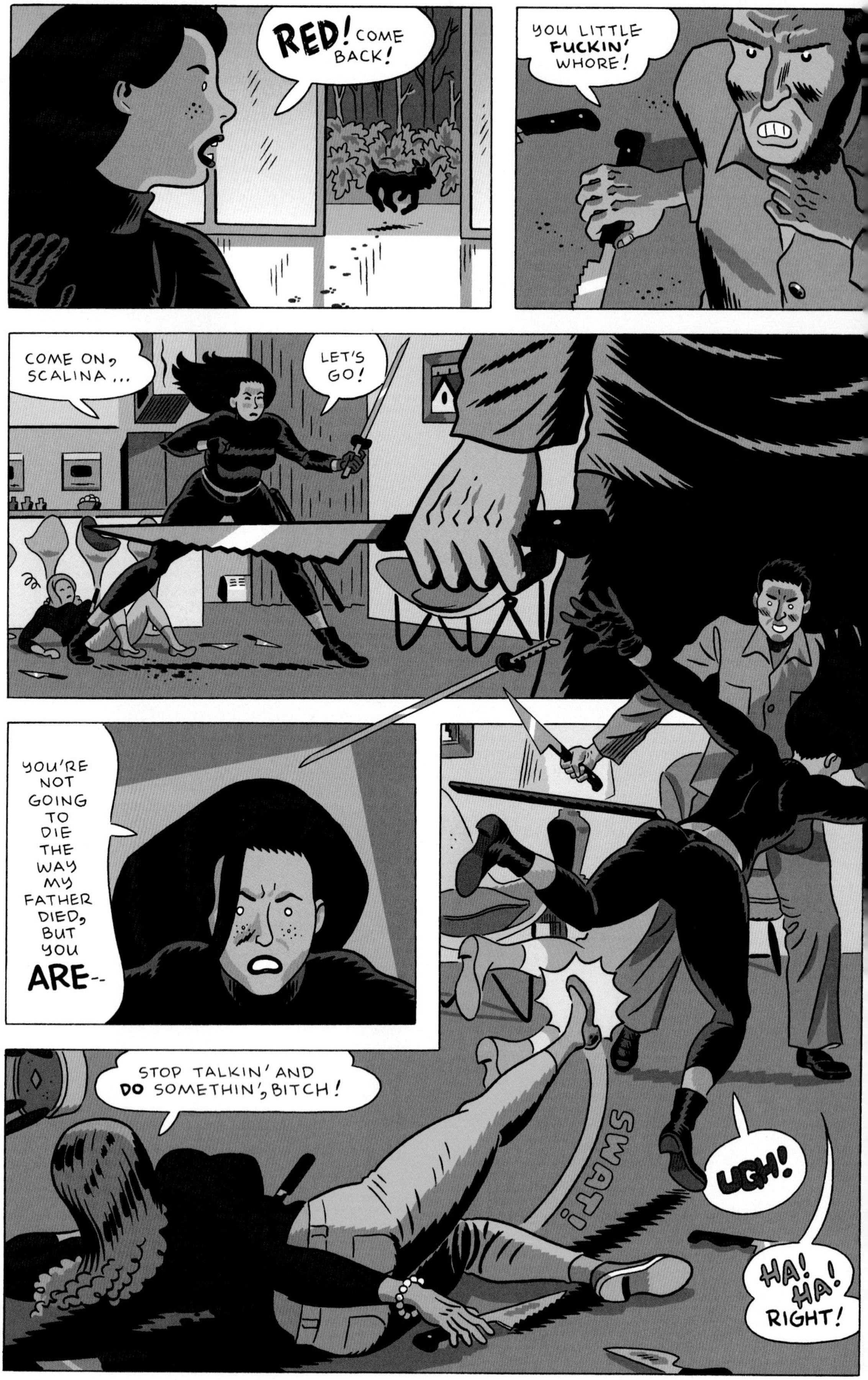

RED! COME BACK!
YOU LITTLE FUCKIN' WHORE!
COME ON, SCALINA...
LET'S GO!
YOU'RE NOT GOING TO DIE THE WAY MY FATHER DIED, BUT YOU ARE--
STOP TALKIN' AND DO SOMETHIN', BITCH!
SWAT!
UGH!
HA! HA! RIGHT!

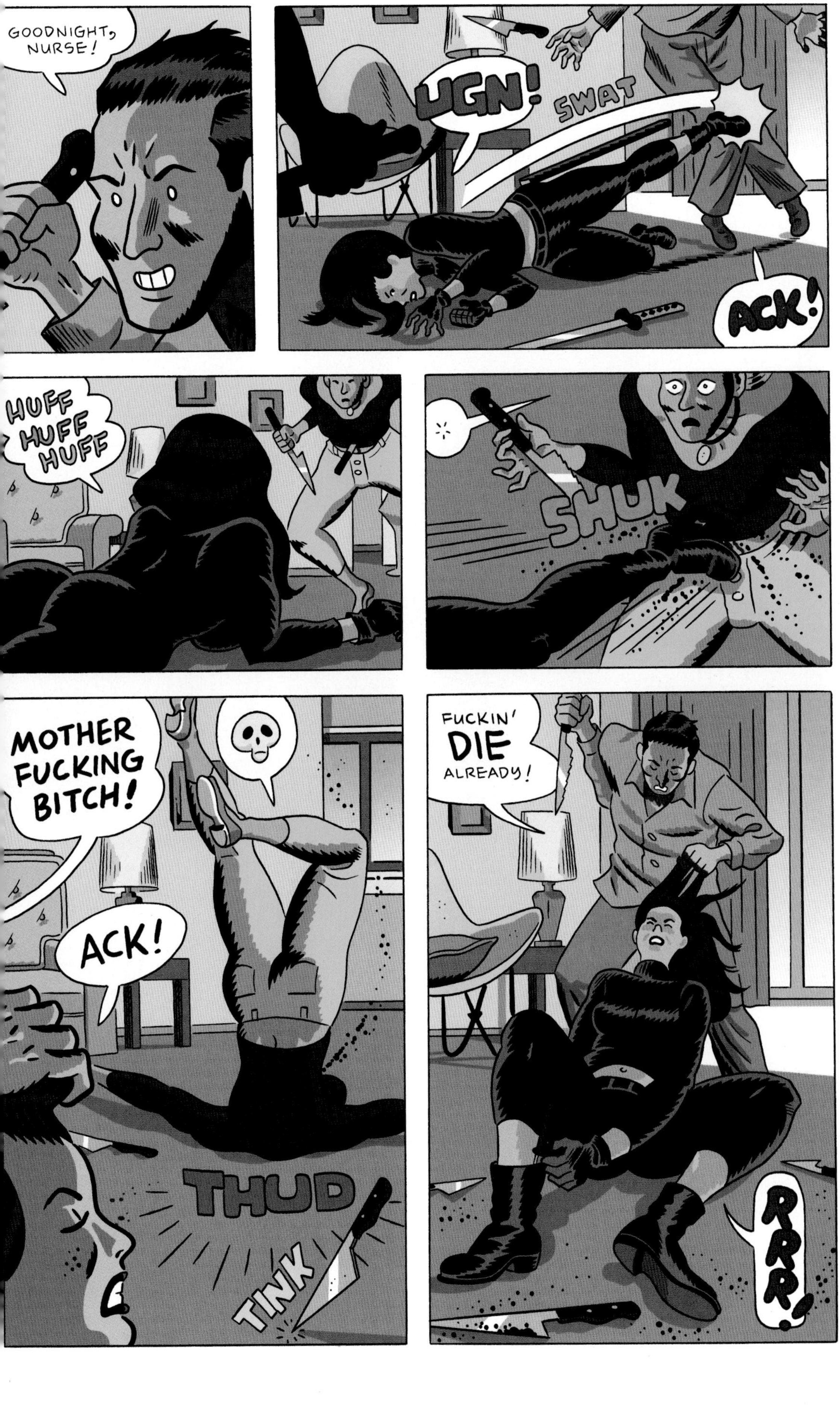

GOODNIGHT, NURSE!
UGN!
SWAT
ACK!
HUFF HUFF HUFF
SHUK
MOTHER FUCKING BITCH!
ACK!
THUD
TINK
FUCKIN' DIE ALREADY!
RRR!

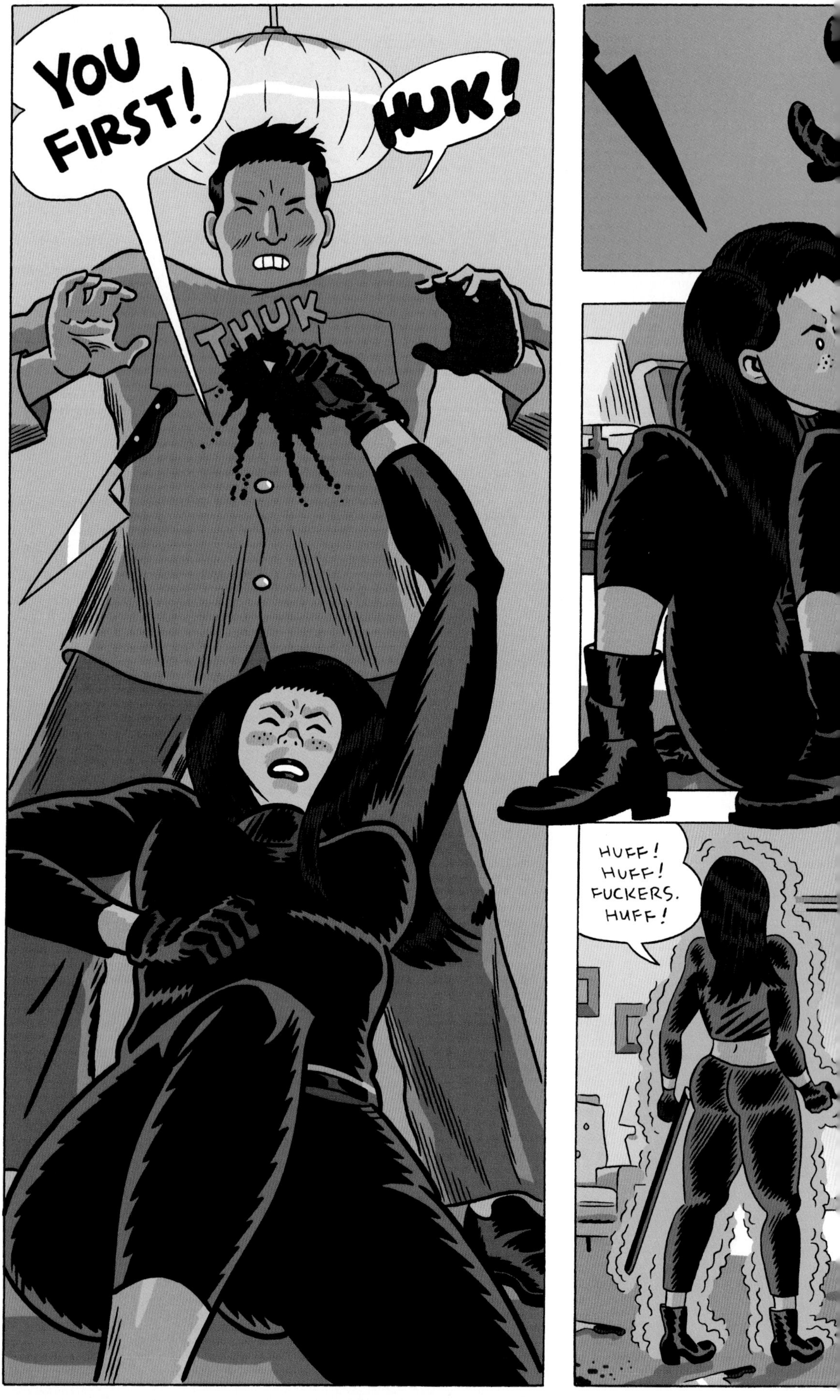
YOU FIRST!
HUK!
THUK
HUFF! HUFF! FUCKERS. HUFF!

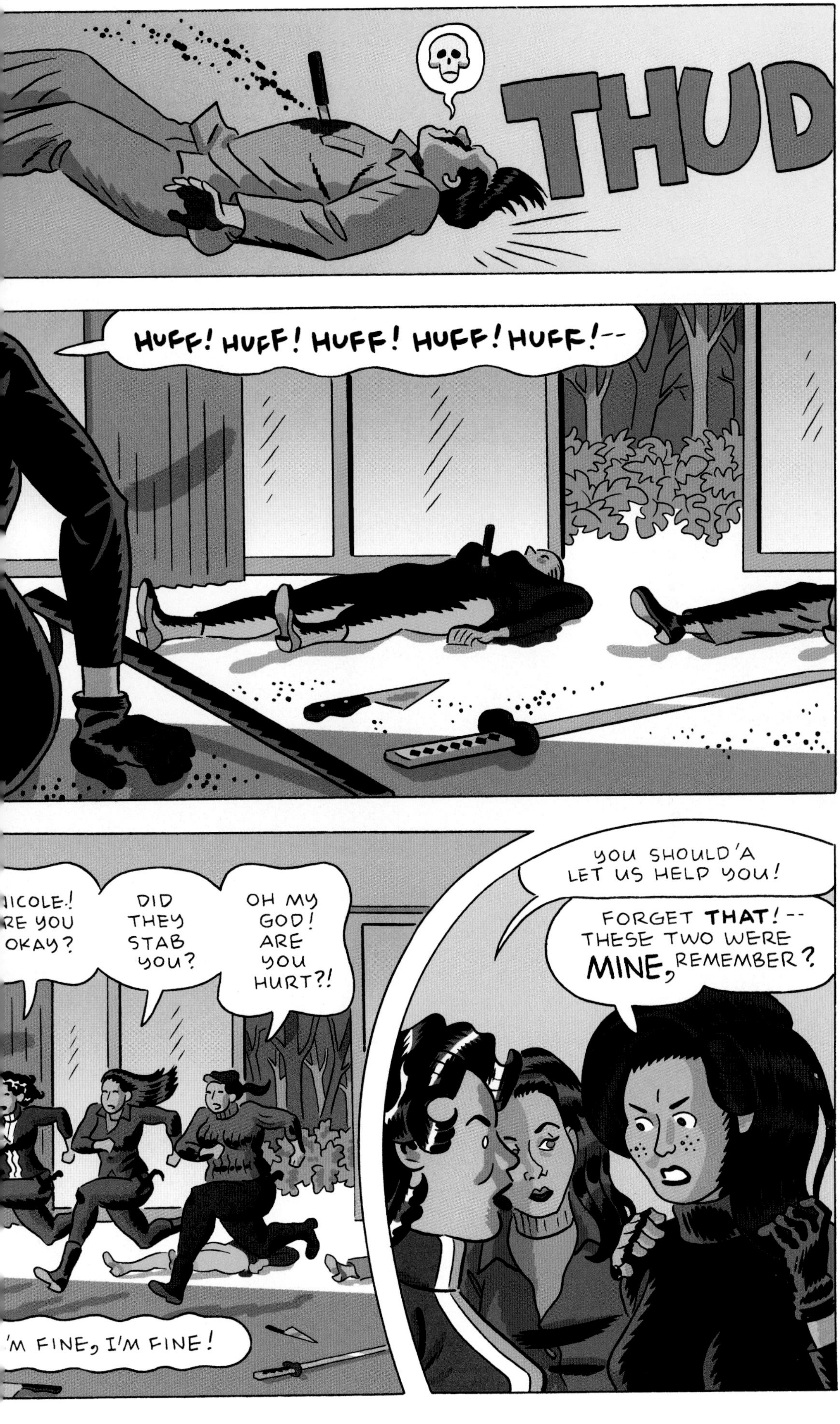
THUD
HUFF! HUFF! HUFF! HUFF! HUFF!--
ICOLE! RE YOU OKAY?
DID THEY STAB YOU?
OH MY GOD! ARE YOU HURT?!
'M FINE, I'M FINE!
YOU SHOULD'A LET US HELP YOU!
FORGET THAT! -- THESE TWO WERE MINE, REMEMBER?

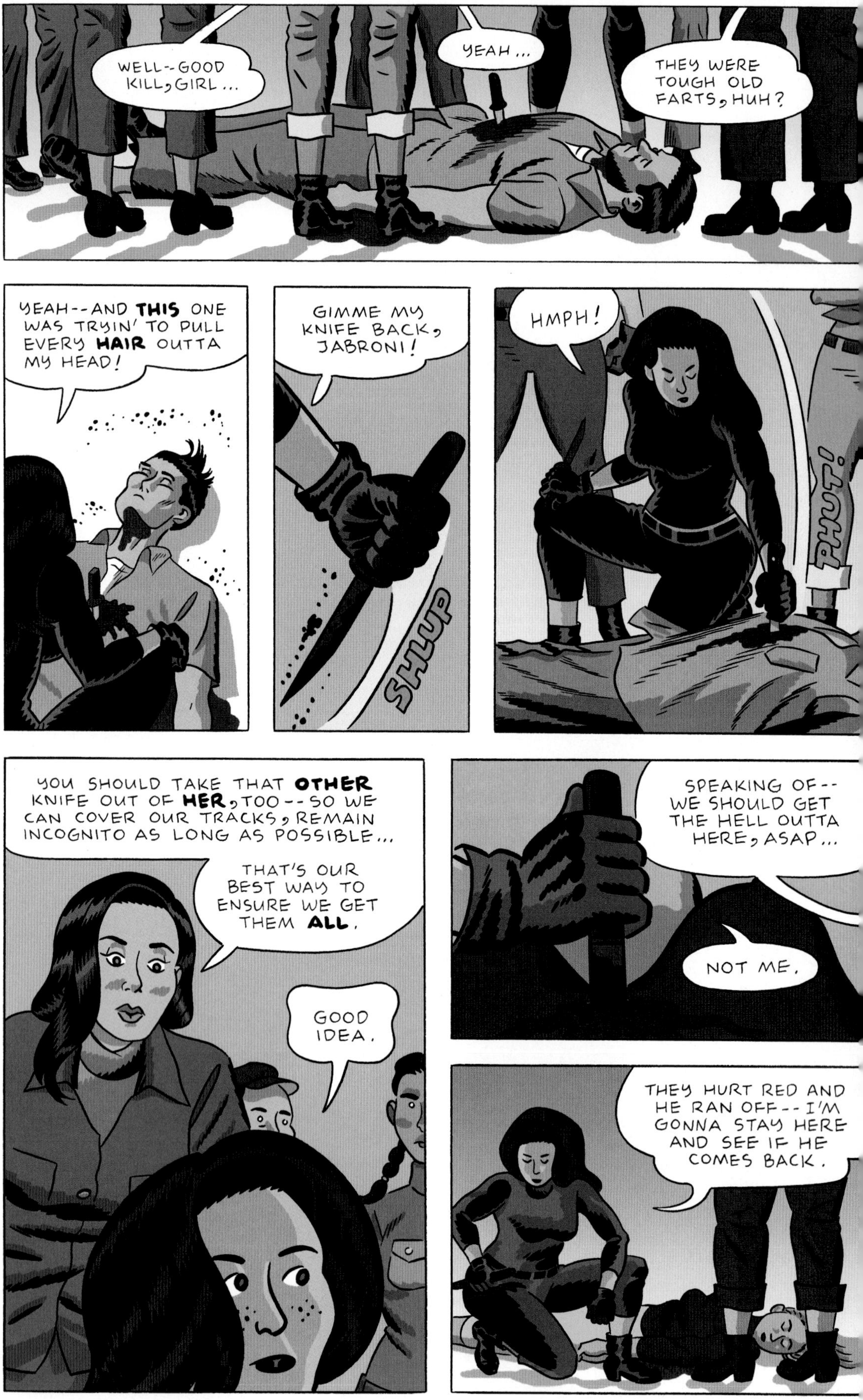

WELL--GOOD KILL, GIRL...
YEAH...
THEY WERE TOUGH OLD FARTS, HUH?
YEAH--AND THIS ONE WAS TRYIN' TO PULL EVERY HAIR OUTTA MY HEAD!
GIMME MY KNIFE BACK, JABRONI!
SHLUP
HMPH!
PHUT!
YOU SHOULD TAKE THAT OTHER KNIFE OUT OF HER, TOO--SO WE CAN COVER OUR TRACKS, REMAIN INCOGNITO AS LONG AS POSSIBLE...
THAT'S OUR BEST WAY TO ENSURE WE GET THEM ALL.
GOOD IDEA.
SPEAKING OF--WE SHOULD GET THE HELL OUTTA HERE, ASAP...
NOT ME.
THEY HURT RED AND HE RAN OFF--I'M GONNA STAY HERE AND SEE IF HE COMES BACK.

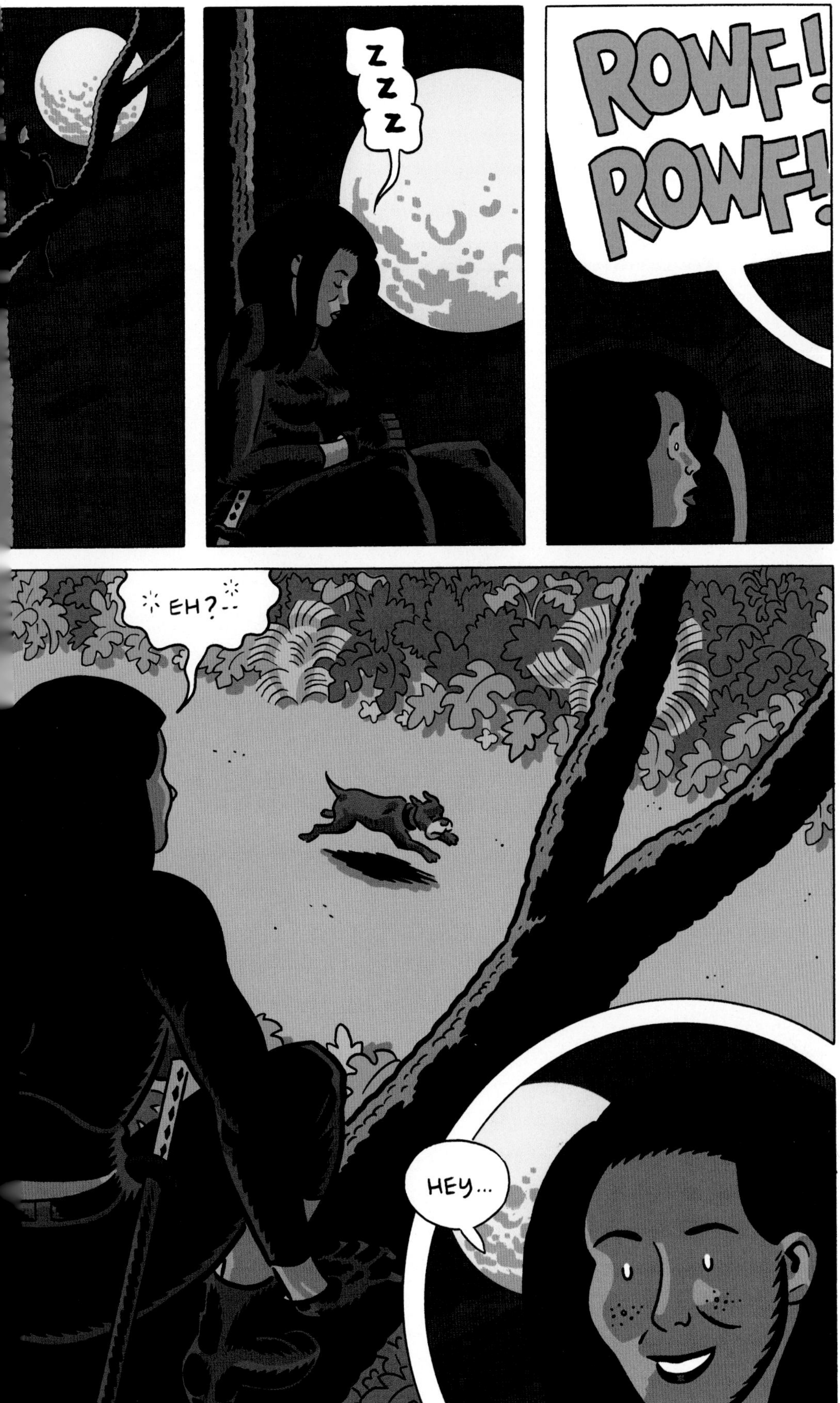
Z Z Z
ROWF! ROWF!
EH?--
HEY...

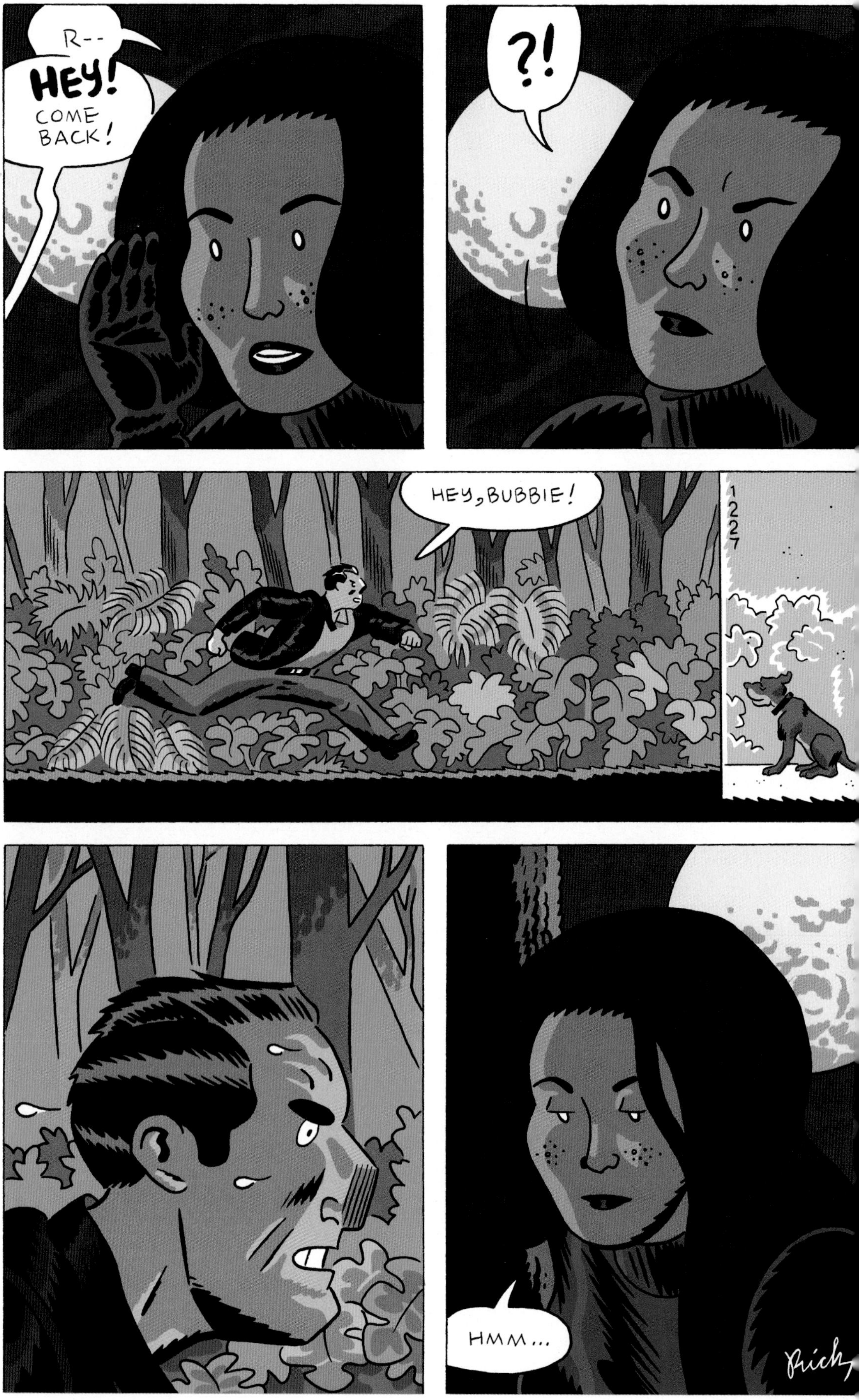
R--
HEY! COME BACK!
?!
HEY, BUBBIE!
1227
HMM...
Rich

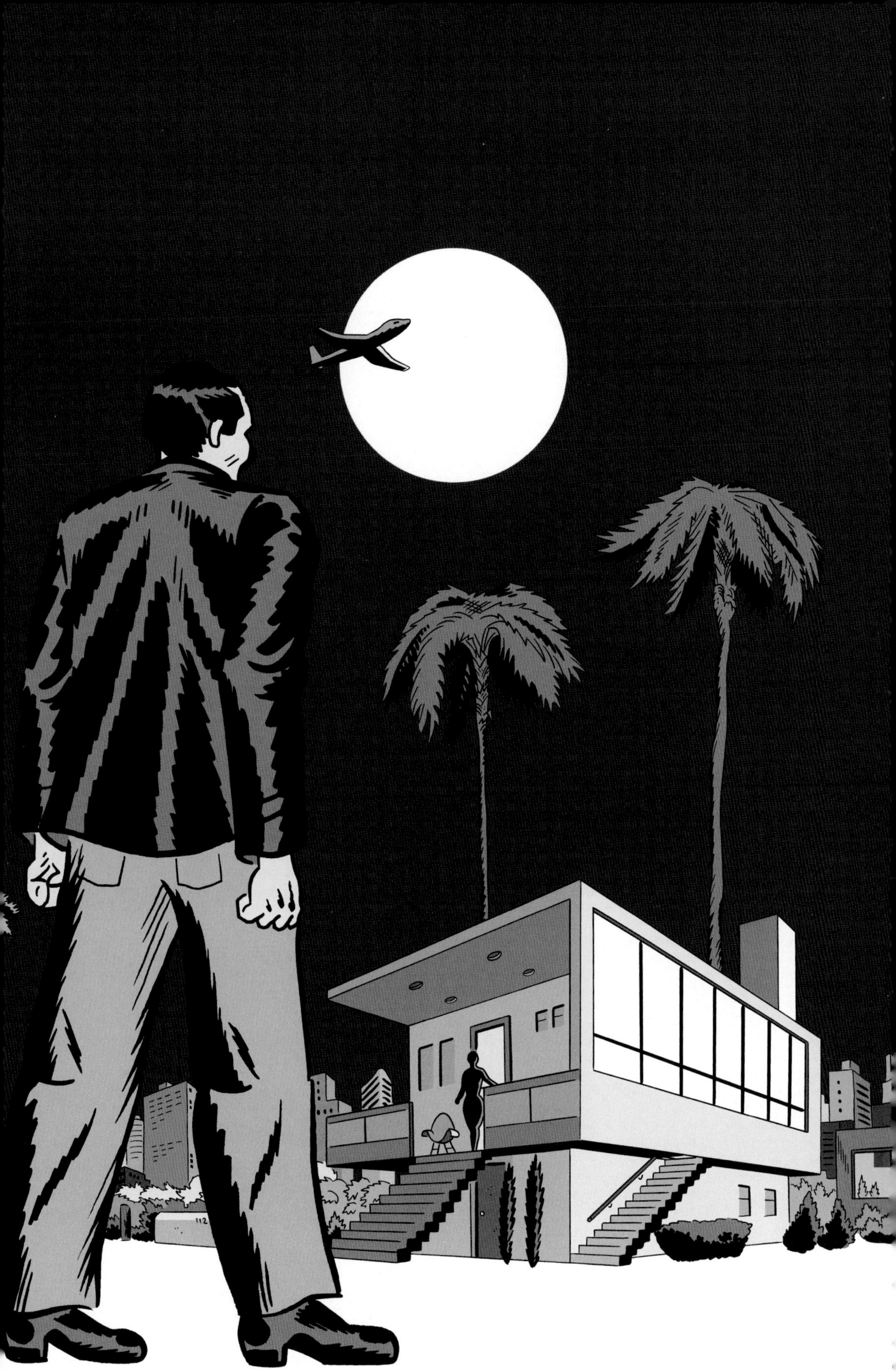

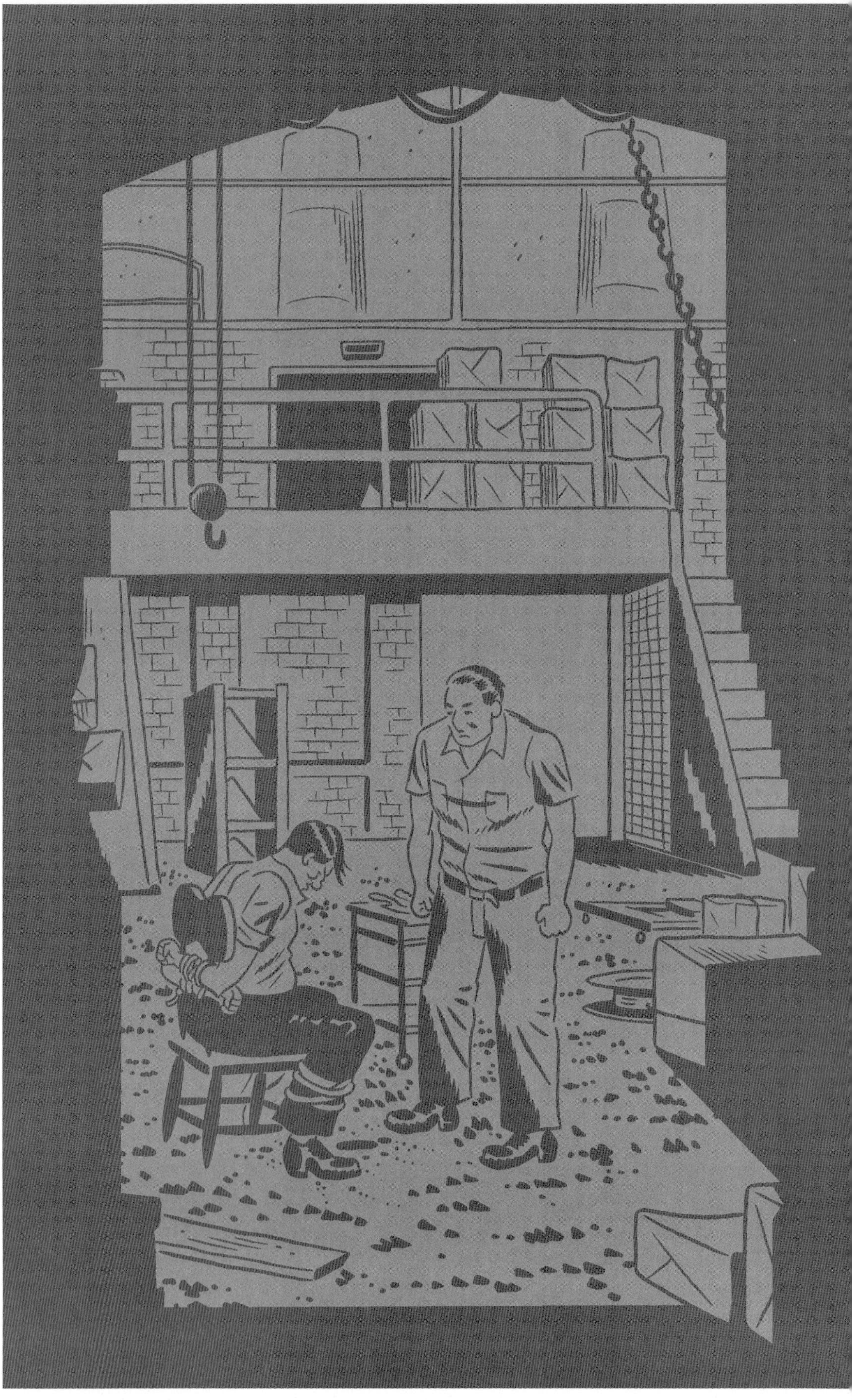

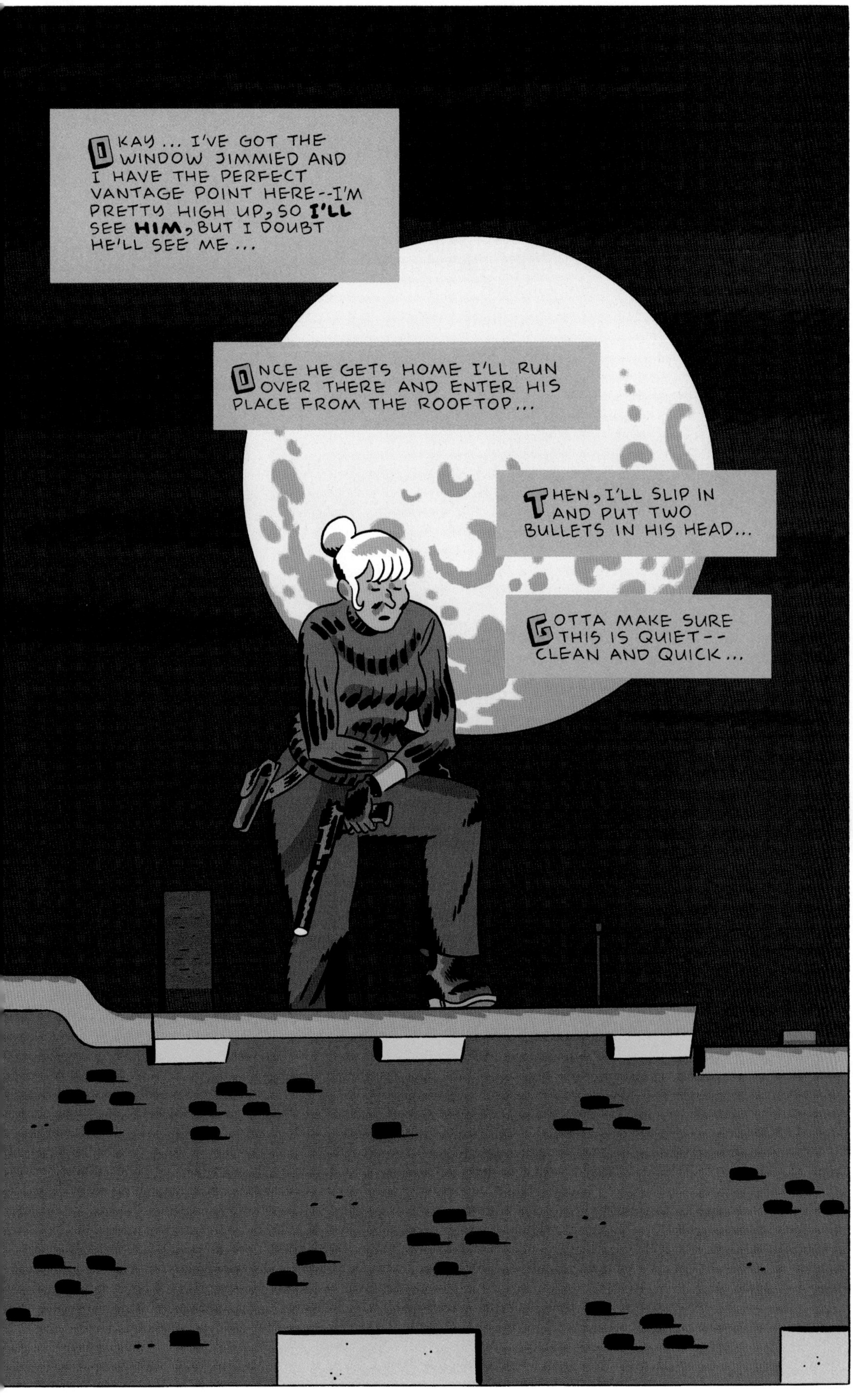
OKAY... I'VE GOT THE WINDOW JIMMIED AND I HAVE THE PERFECT VANTAGE POINT HERE--I'M PRETTY HIGH UP, SO I'LL SEE HIM, BUT I DOUBT HE'LL SEE ME...
ONCE HE GETS HOME I'LL RUN OVER THERE AND ENTER HIS PLACE FROM THE ROOFTOP...
THEN, I'LL SLIP IN AND PUT TWO BULLETS IN HIS HEAD...
GOTTA MAKE SURE THIS IS QUIET--CLEAN AND QUICK...

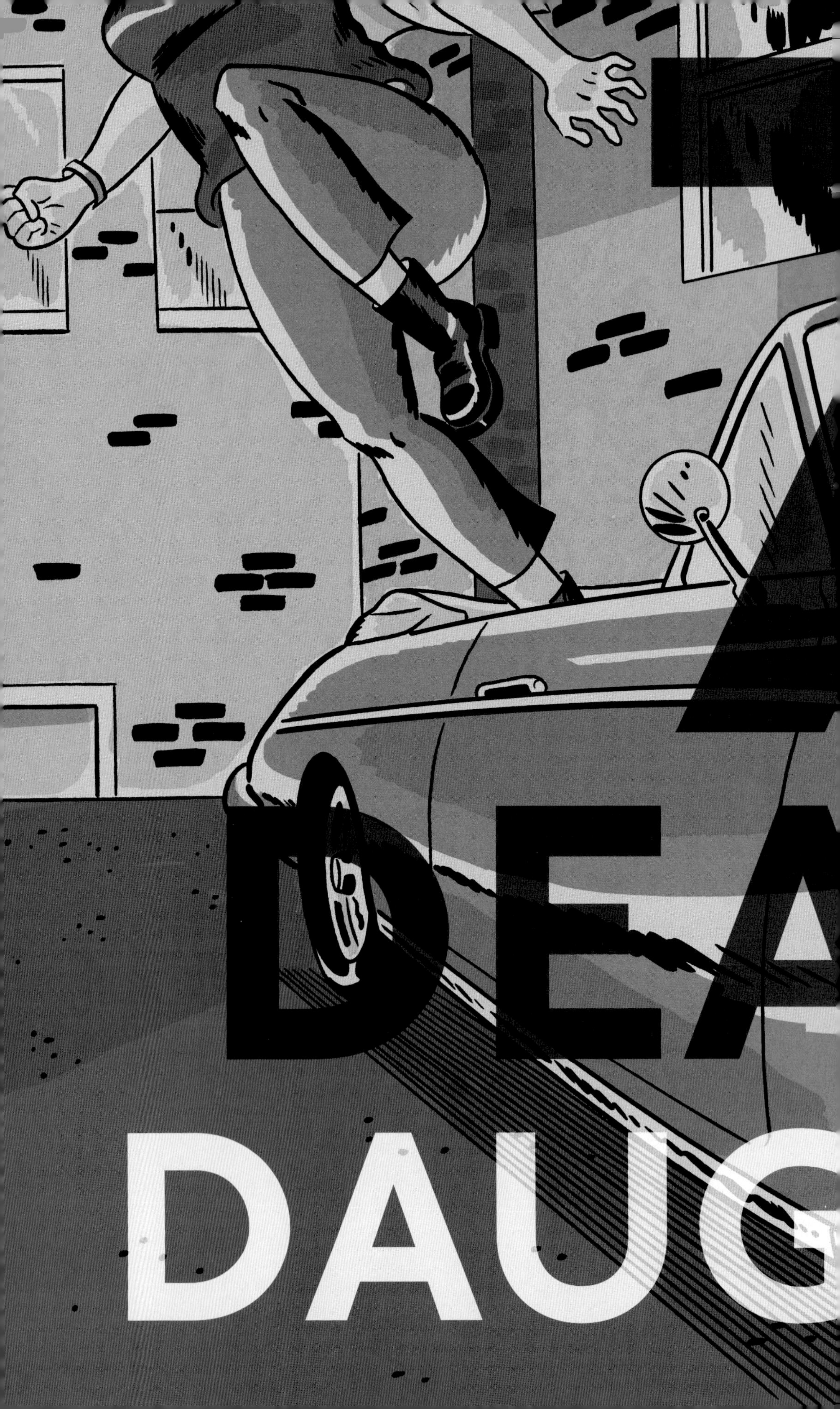
DEA
DAUG

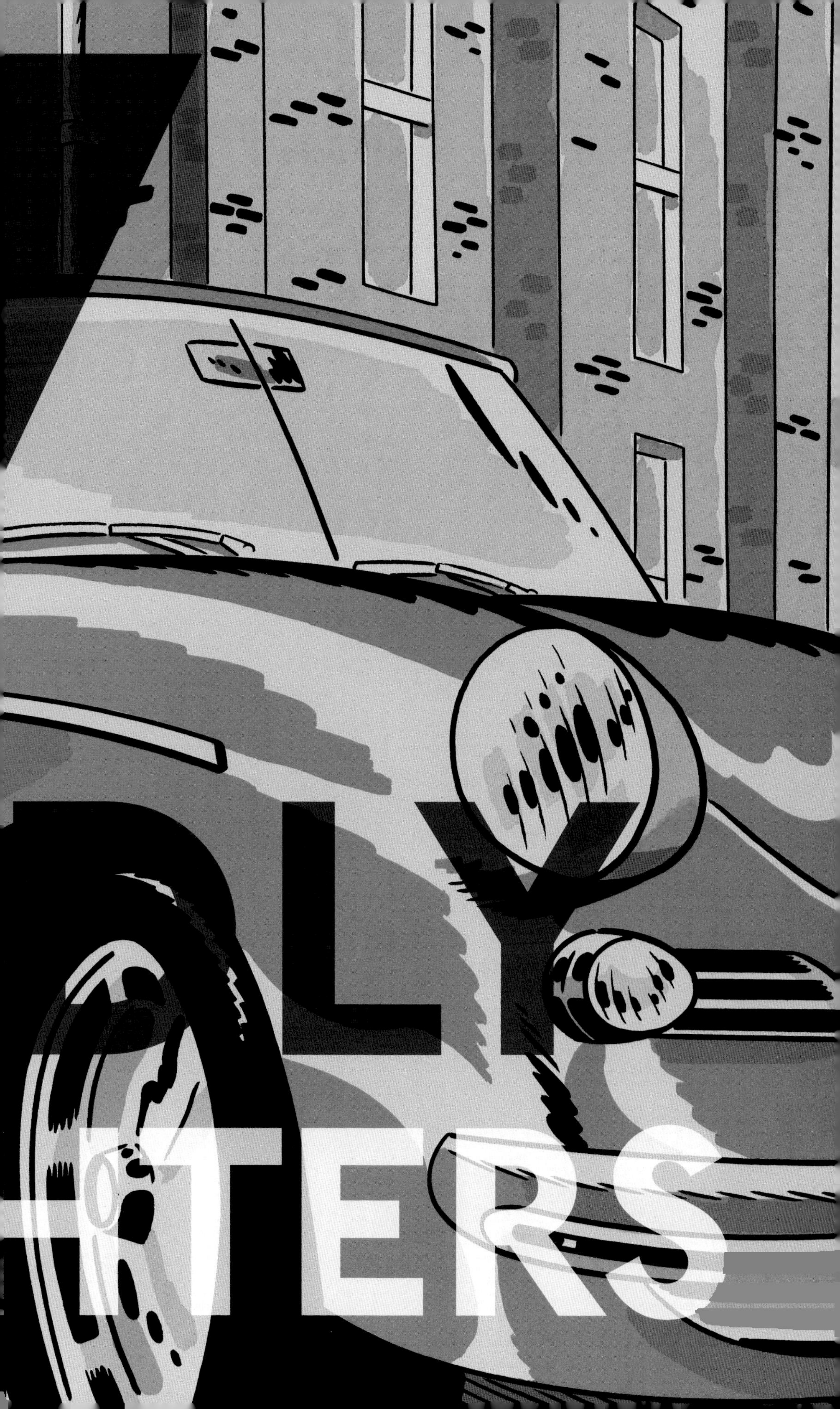
LY
TERS

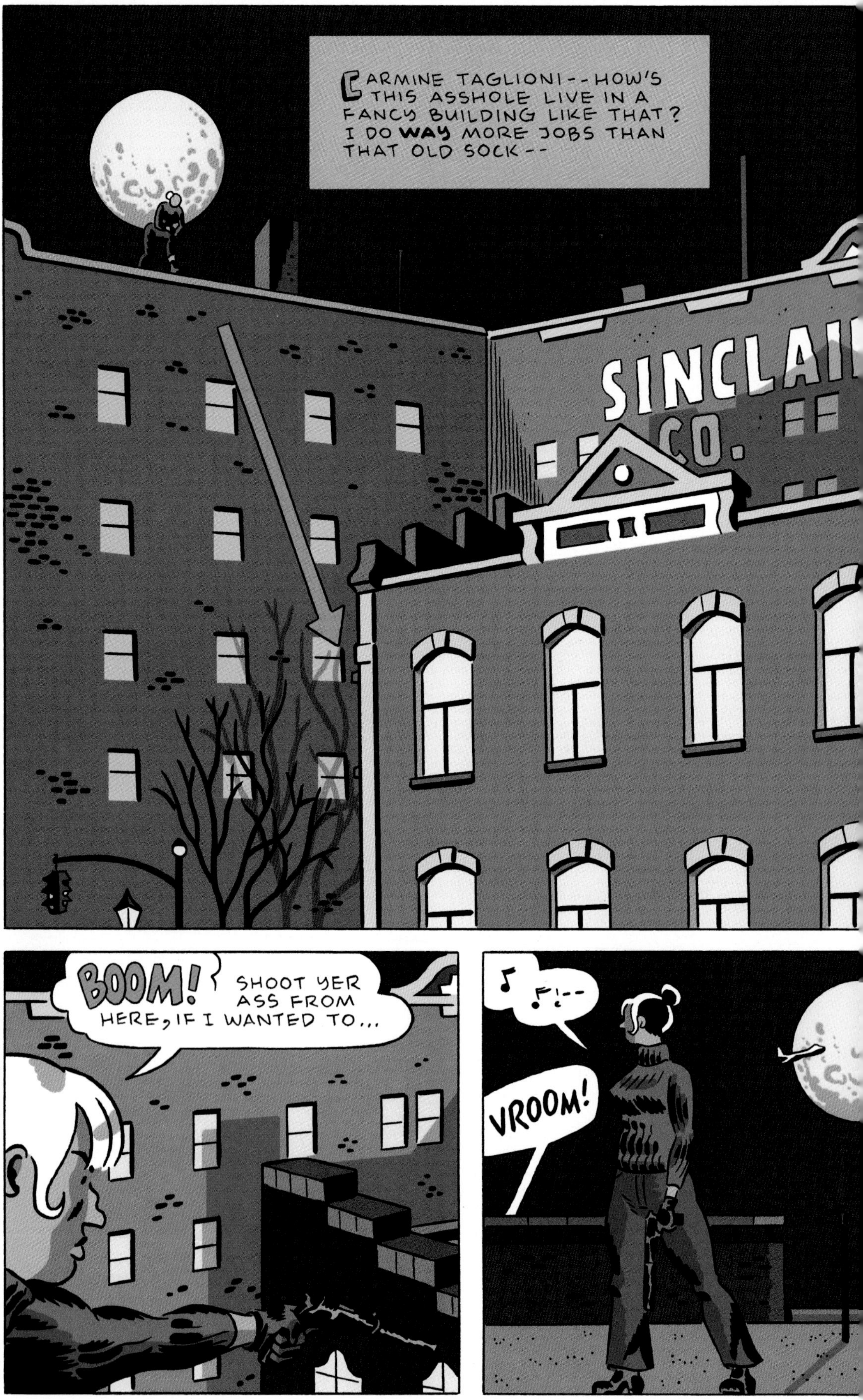
CARMINE TAGLIONI--HOW'S THIS ASSHOLE LIVE IN A FANCY BUILDING LIKE THAT? I DO WAY MORE JOBS THAN THAT OLD SOCK--
SINCLAI
CO.
BOOM! SHOOT YER ASS FROM HERE, IF I WANTED TO...
F!--
VROOM!

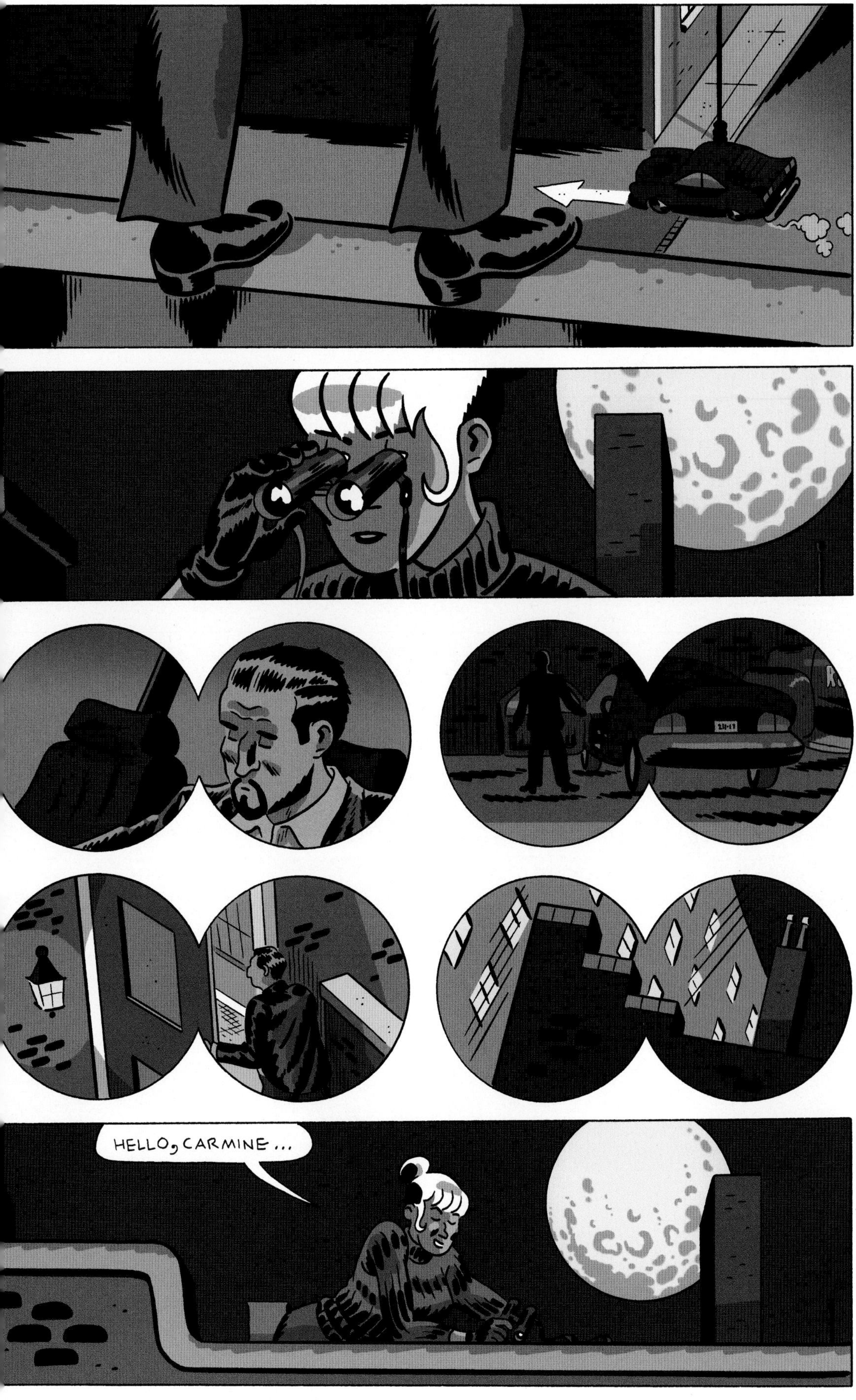
HELLO, CARMINE...

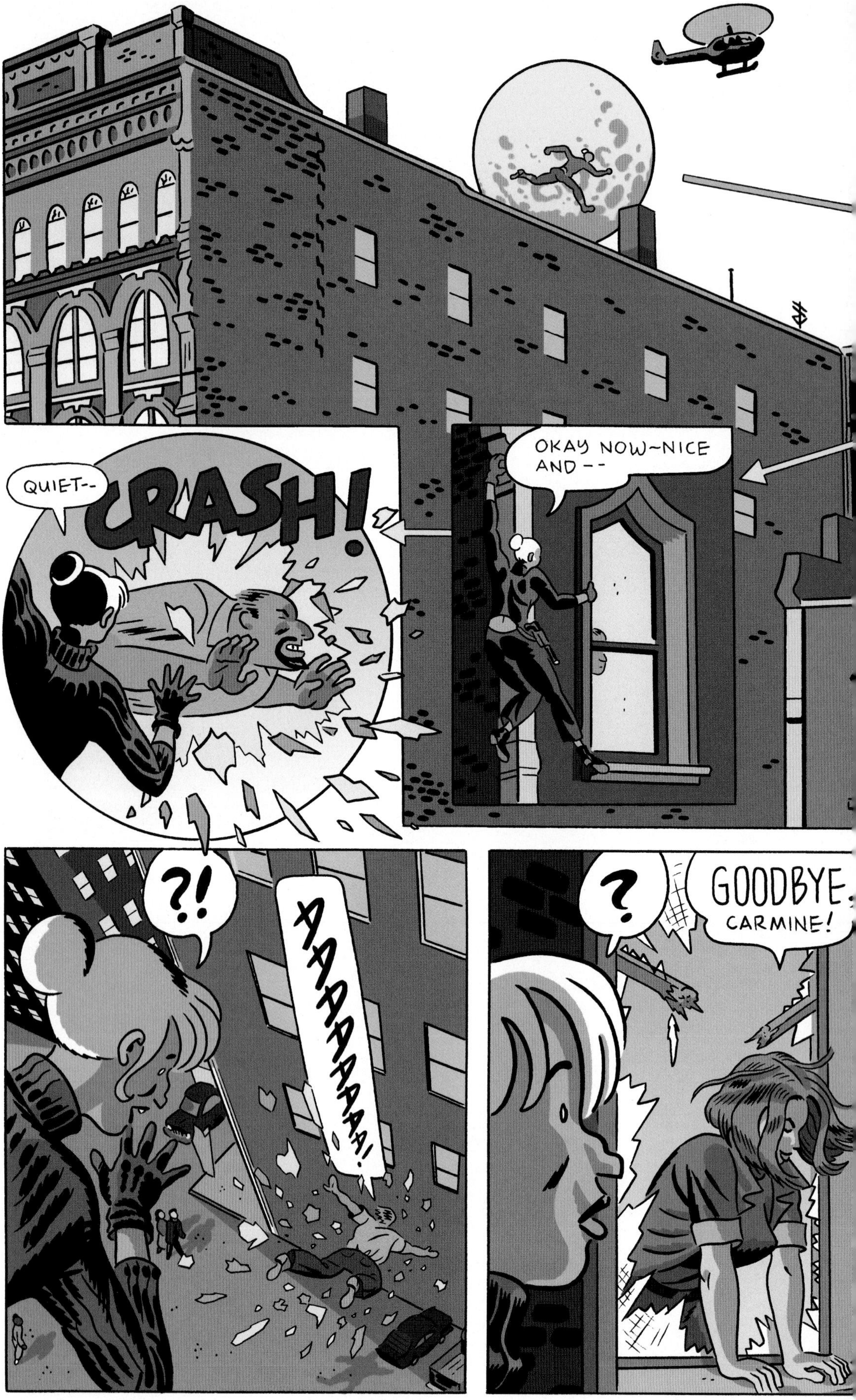
OKAY NOW~NICE AND --
QUIET--
CRASH!
?!
AAAAAAAAAA!
?
GOODBYE CARMINE!

GREATEST HITS

VOLUME THREE:

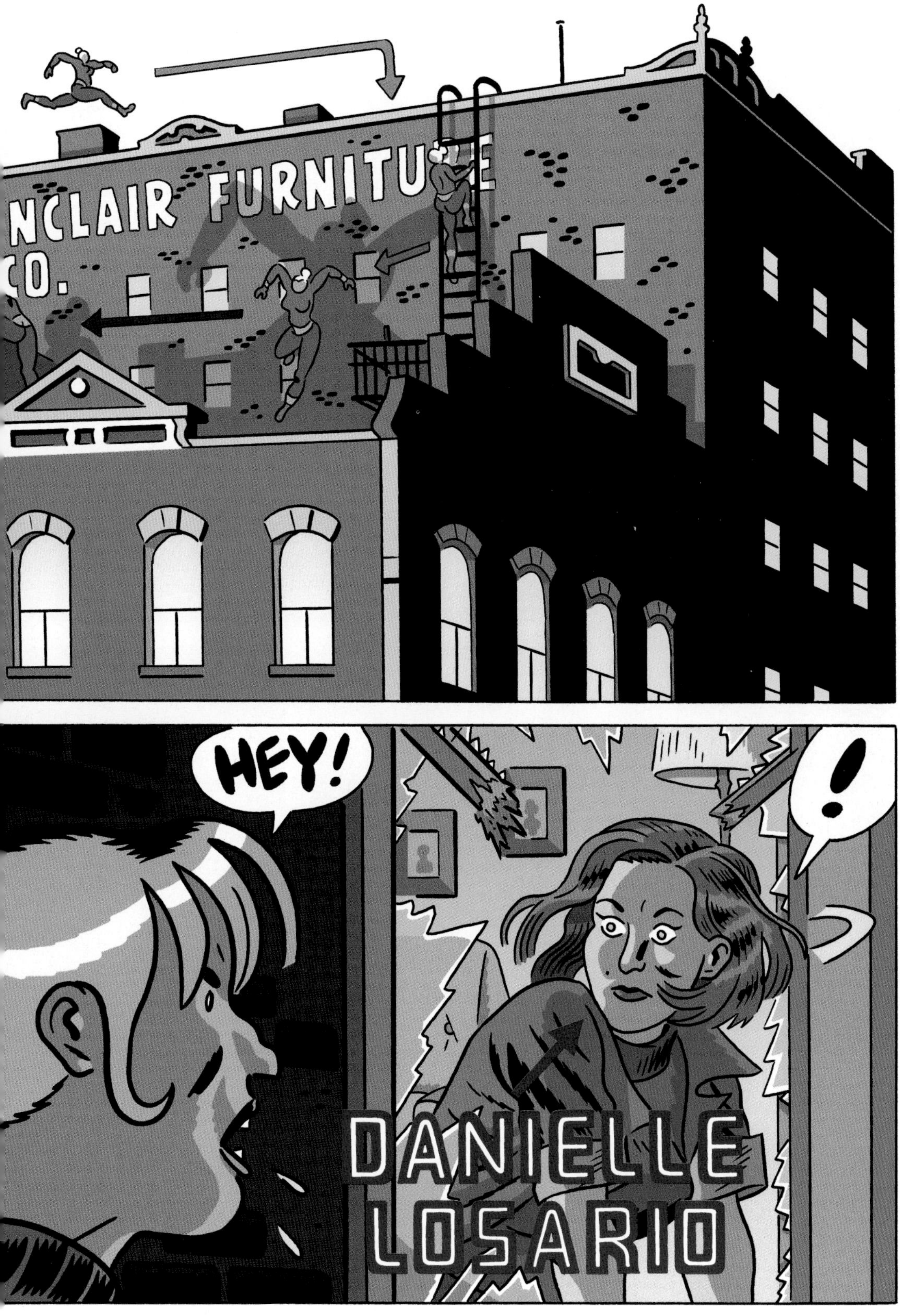
NCLAIR FURNITURE
CO.
HEY!
!
DANIELLE
LOSARIO

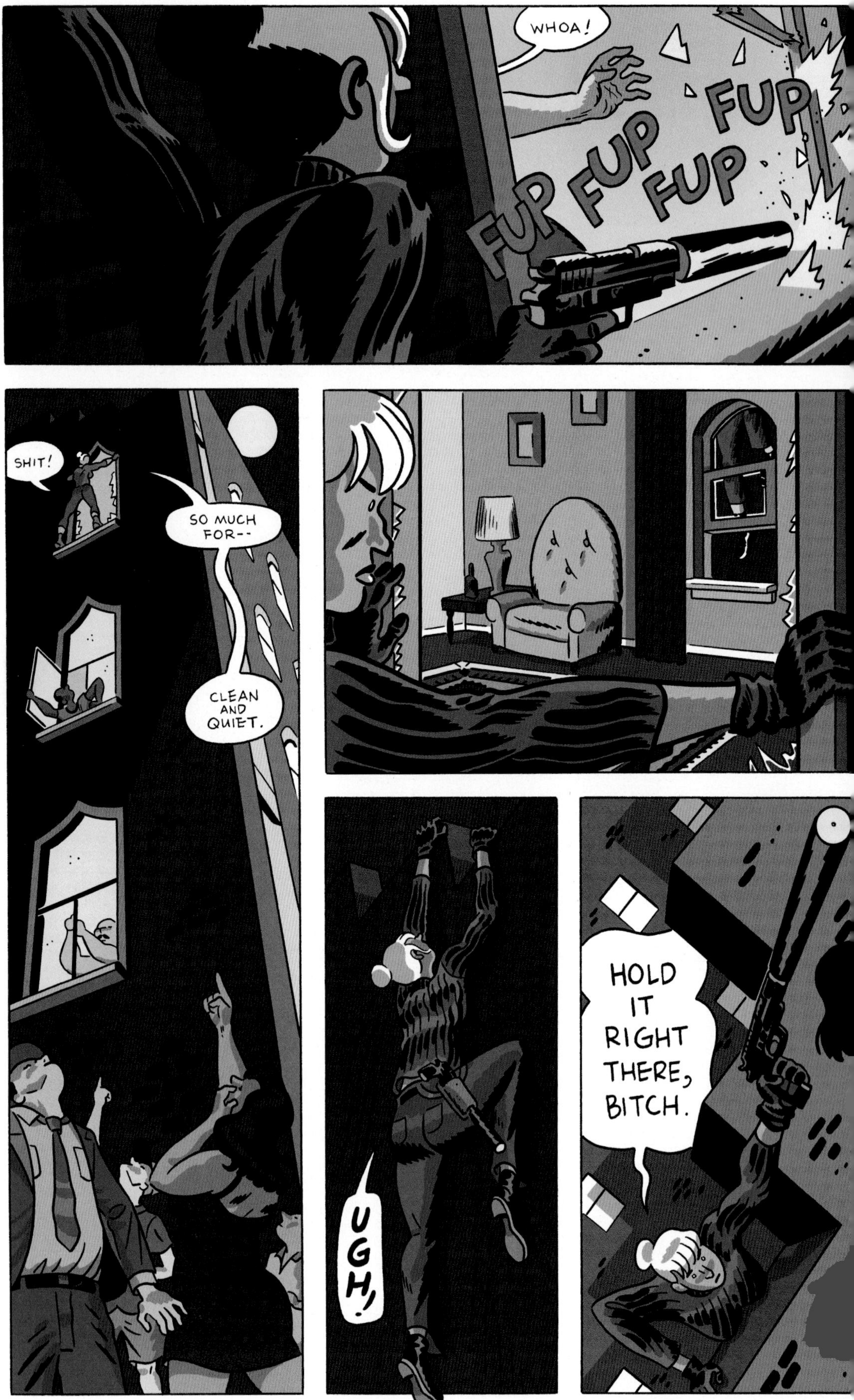
WHOA!
FUP FUP FUP FUP
SHIT!
SO MUCH FOR--
CLEAN AND QUIET.
UGH!
HOLD IT RIGHT THERE, BITCH.

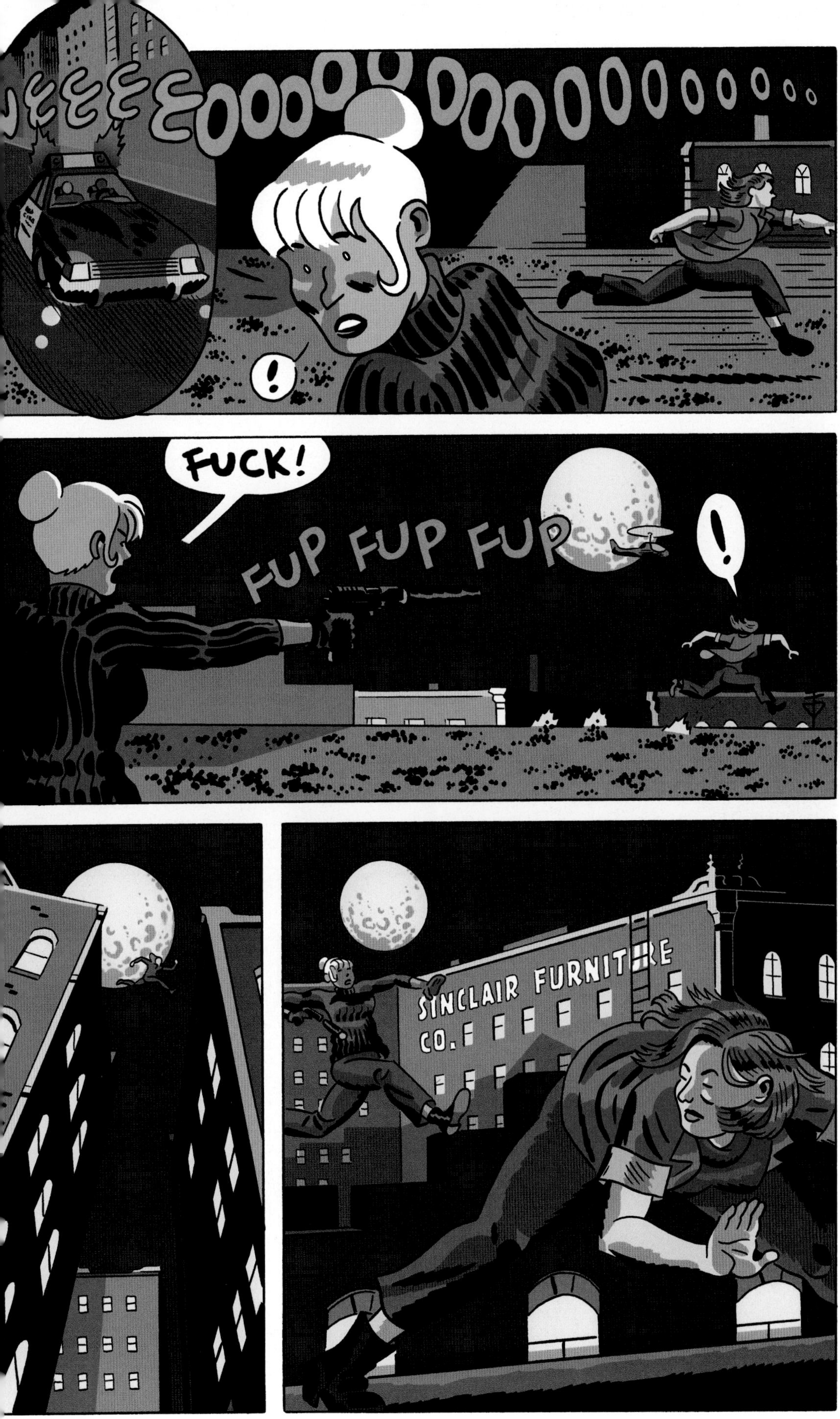

WEEEEEOOOOOOOOOOOOOOOO...
!
FUCK!
FUP FUP FUP FUP
!
SINCLAIR FURNITURE
CO.

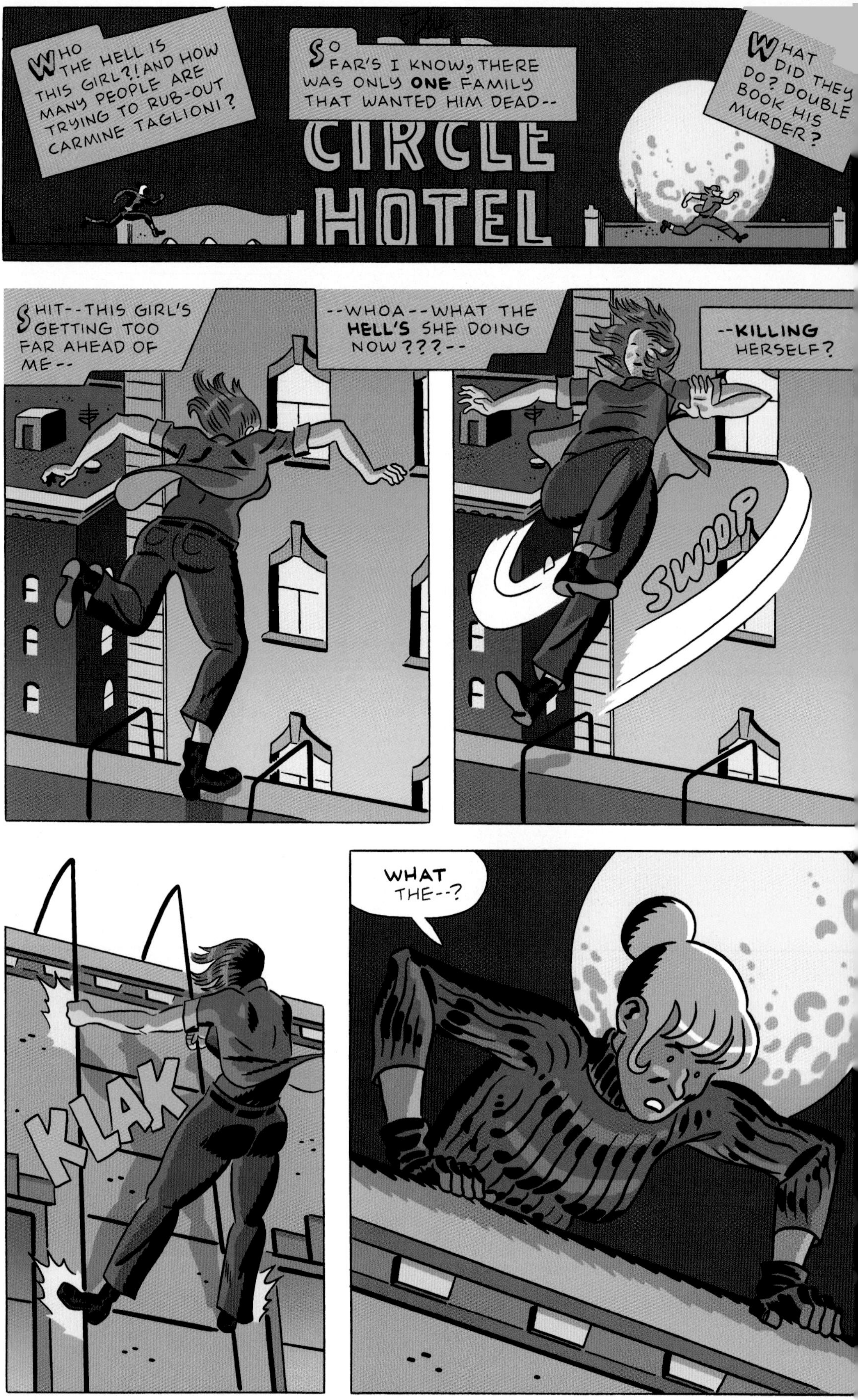
WHO THE HELL IS THIS GIRL?! AND HOW MANY PEOPLE ARE TRYING TO RUB-OUT CARMINE TAGLIONI?
SO FAR'S I KNOW, THERE WAS ONLY ONE FAMILY THAT WANTED HIM DEAD--
CIRCLE HOTEL
WHAT DID THEY DO? DOUBLE BOOK HIS MURDER?
SHIT--THIS GIRL'S GETTING TOO FAR AHEAD OF ME--
--WHOA--WHAT THE HELL'S SHE DOING NOW???--
--KILLING HERSELF?
SWOOP
KLAK
WHAT THE--?

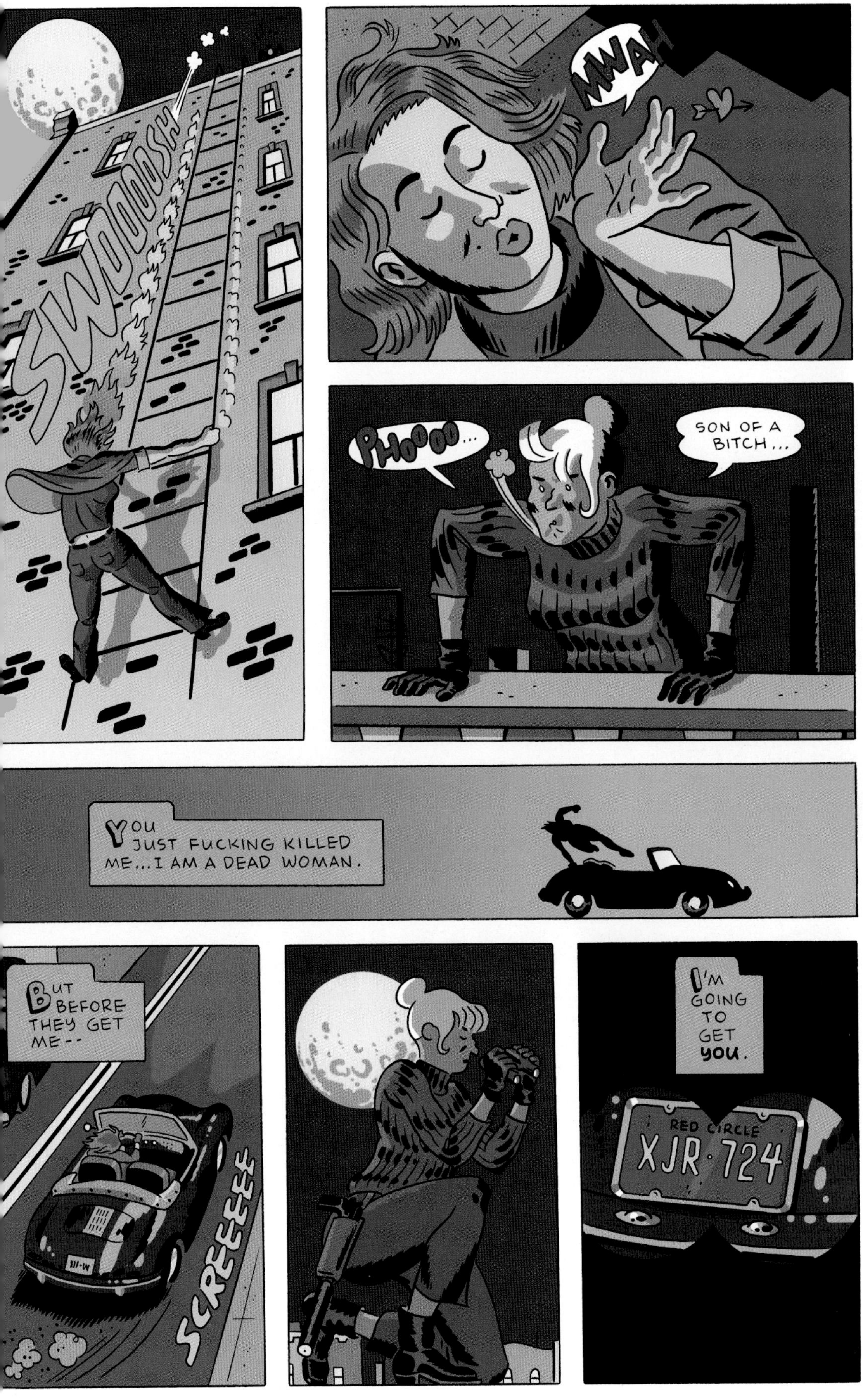
SWOOOOSH
MWAH
PHOOOOO...
SON OF A BITCH...
YOU JUST FUCKING KILLED ME...I AM A DEAD WOMAN.
BUT BEFORE THEY GET ME--
SCREEEEEE
I'M GOING TO GET YOU.
RED CIRCLE
XJR·724

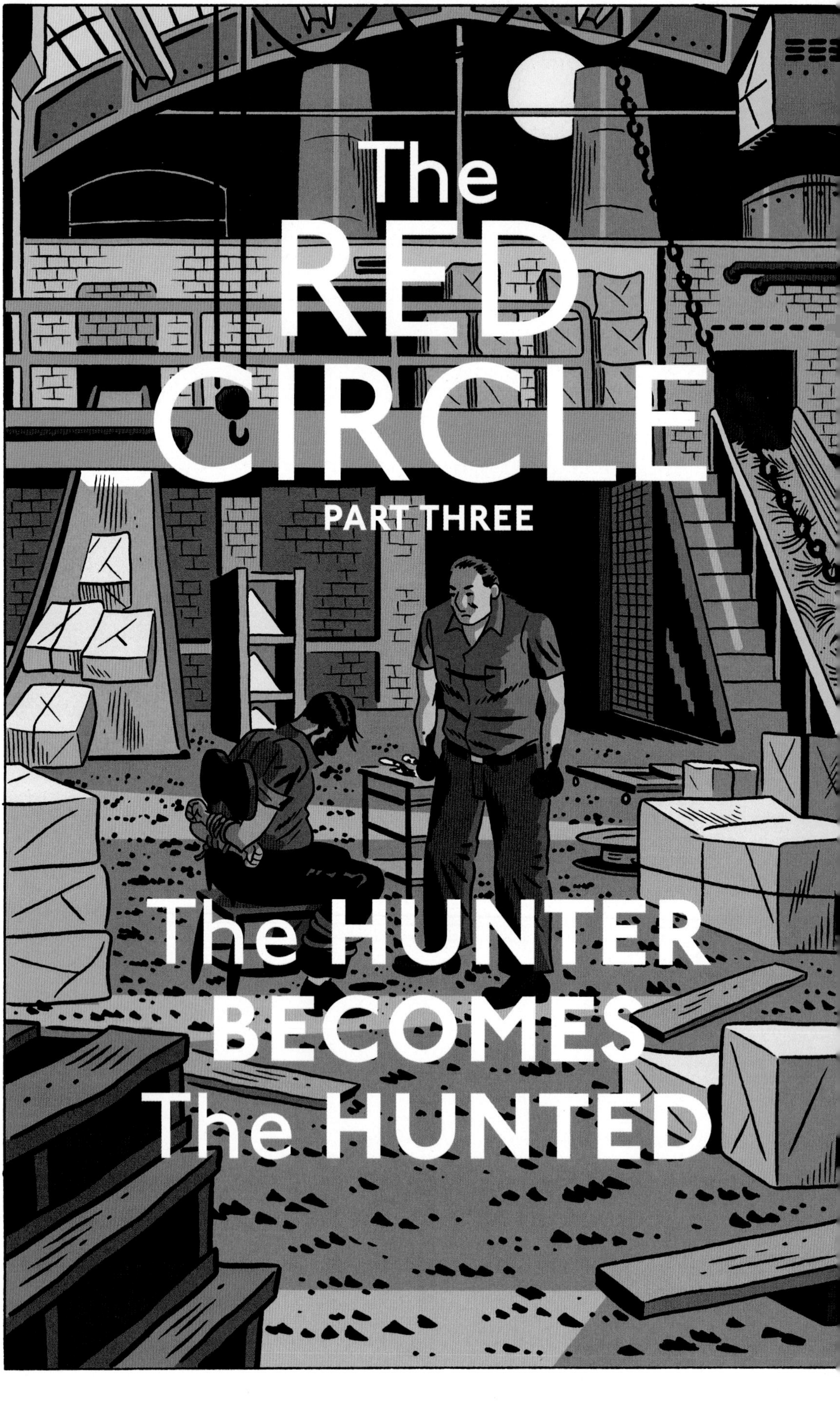
The RED CIRCLE
PART THREE
The HUNTER BECOMES The HUNTED

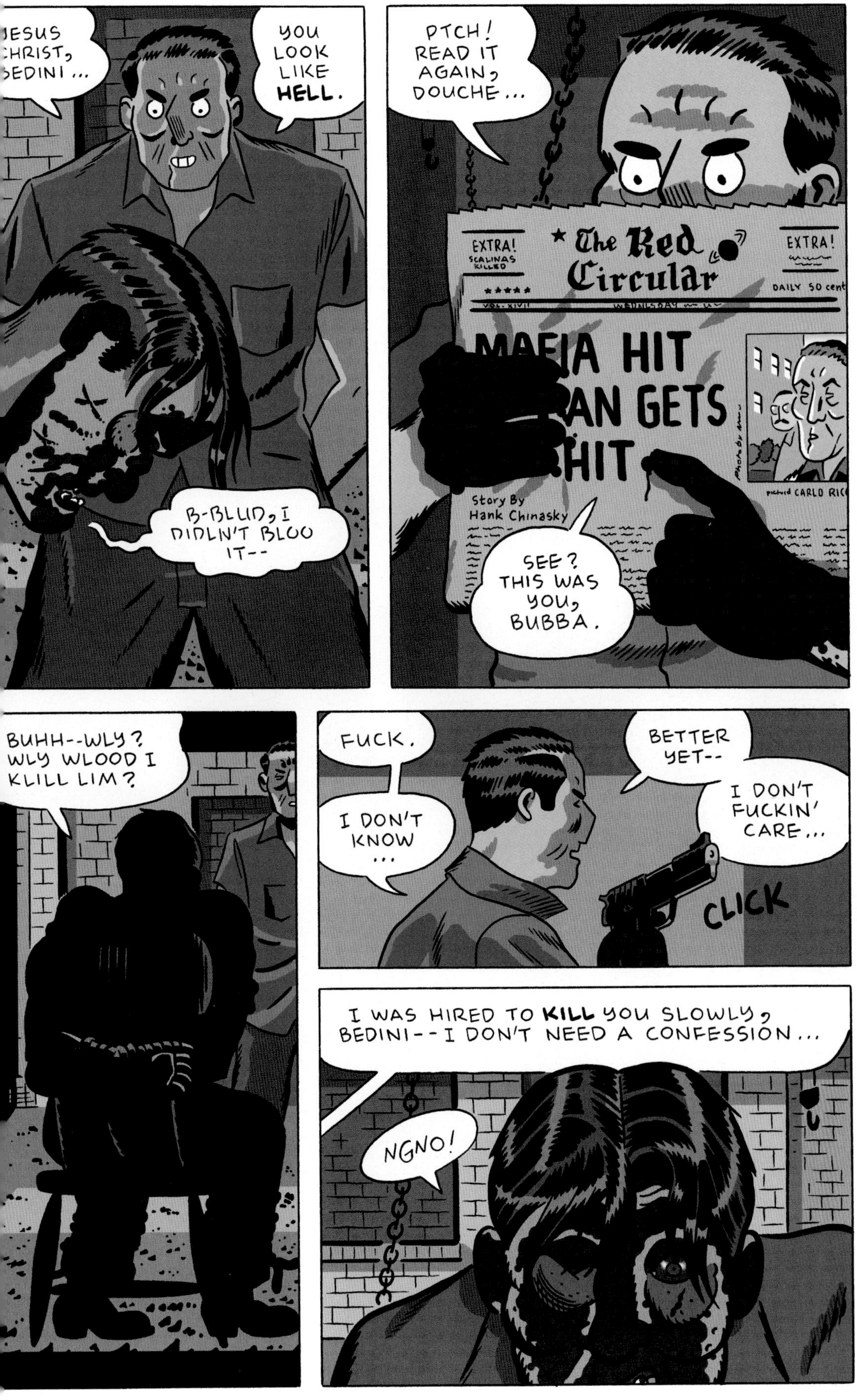
JESUS CHRIST, BEDINI...
YOU LOOK LIKE **HELL**.
B-BLUD, I DIDLN'T BLOO IT--
PTCH! READ IT AGAIN, DOUCHE...
EXTRA!
The Red Circular
EXTRA!
DAILY 50 cent
Story By Hank Chinasky
SEE? THIS WAS YOU, BUBBA.
BUHH--WLY? WLY WLOOD I KLILL LIM?
FUCK.
I DON'T KNOW...
BETTER YET--
I DON'T FUCKIN' CARE...
CLICK
I WAS HIRED TO **KILL** YOU SLOWLY, BEDINI--I DON'T NEED A CONFESSION...
NGNO!

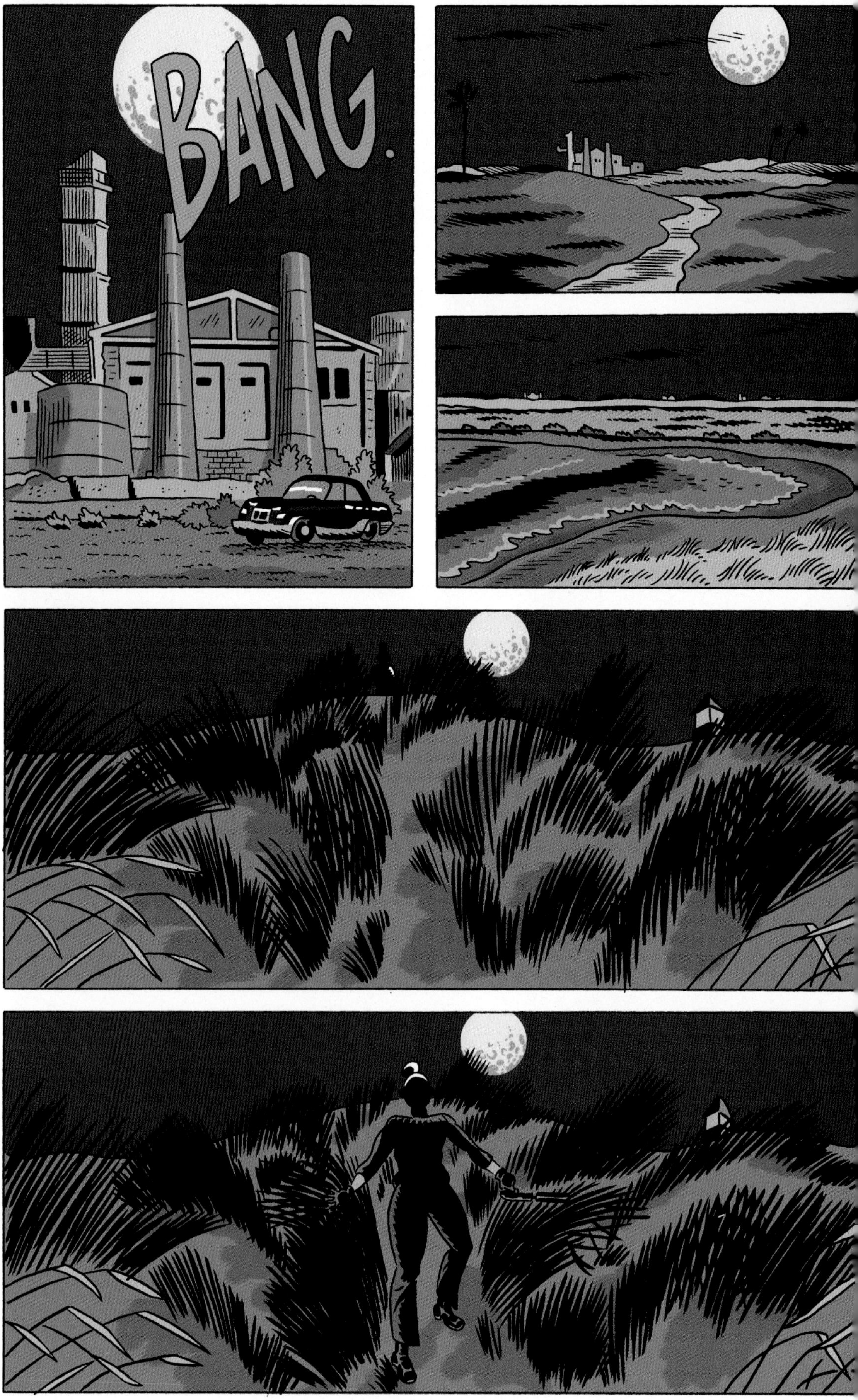
BANG.

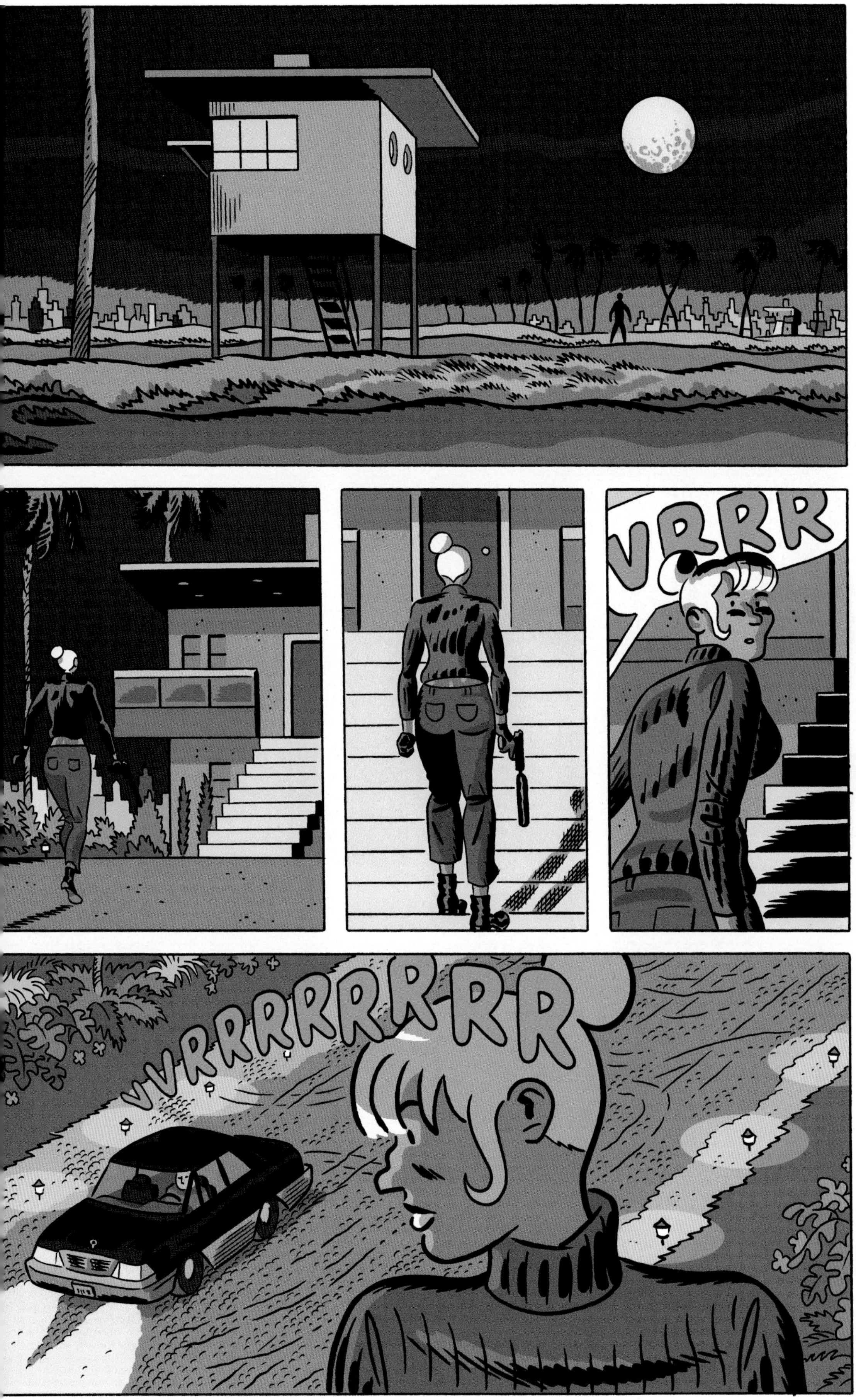
VRRR
VVRRRRRRRR

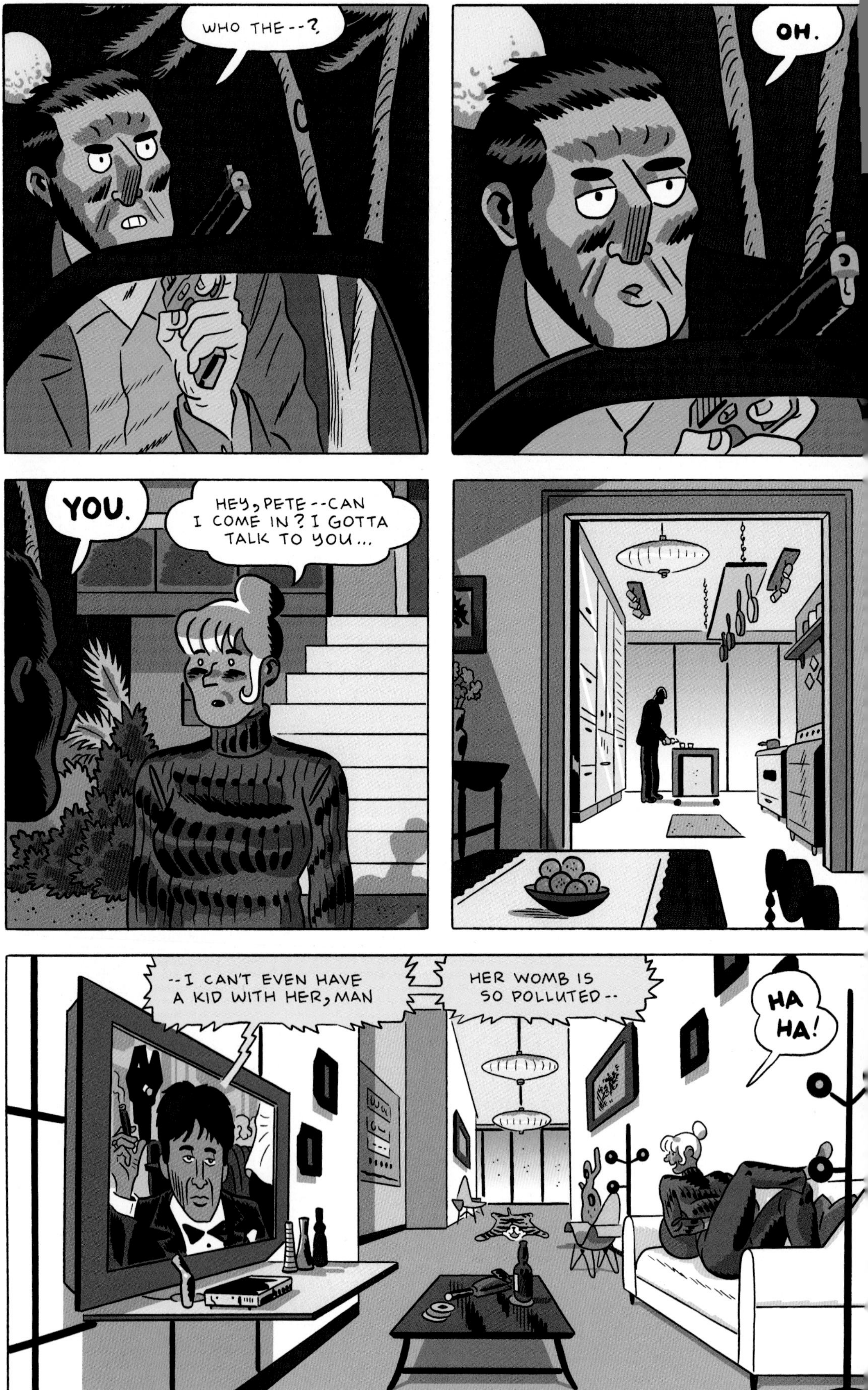
WHO THE--?
OH.
YOU.
HEY, PETE--CAN I COME IN? I GOTTA TALK TO YOU...
--I CAN'T EVEN HAVE A KID WITH HER, MAN
HER WOMB IS SO POLLUTED--
HA HA!

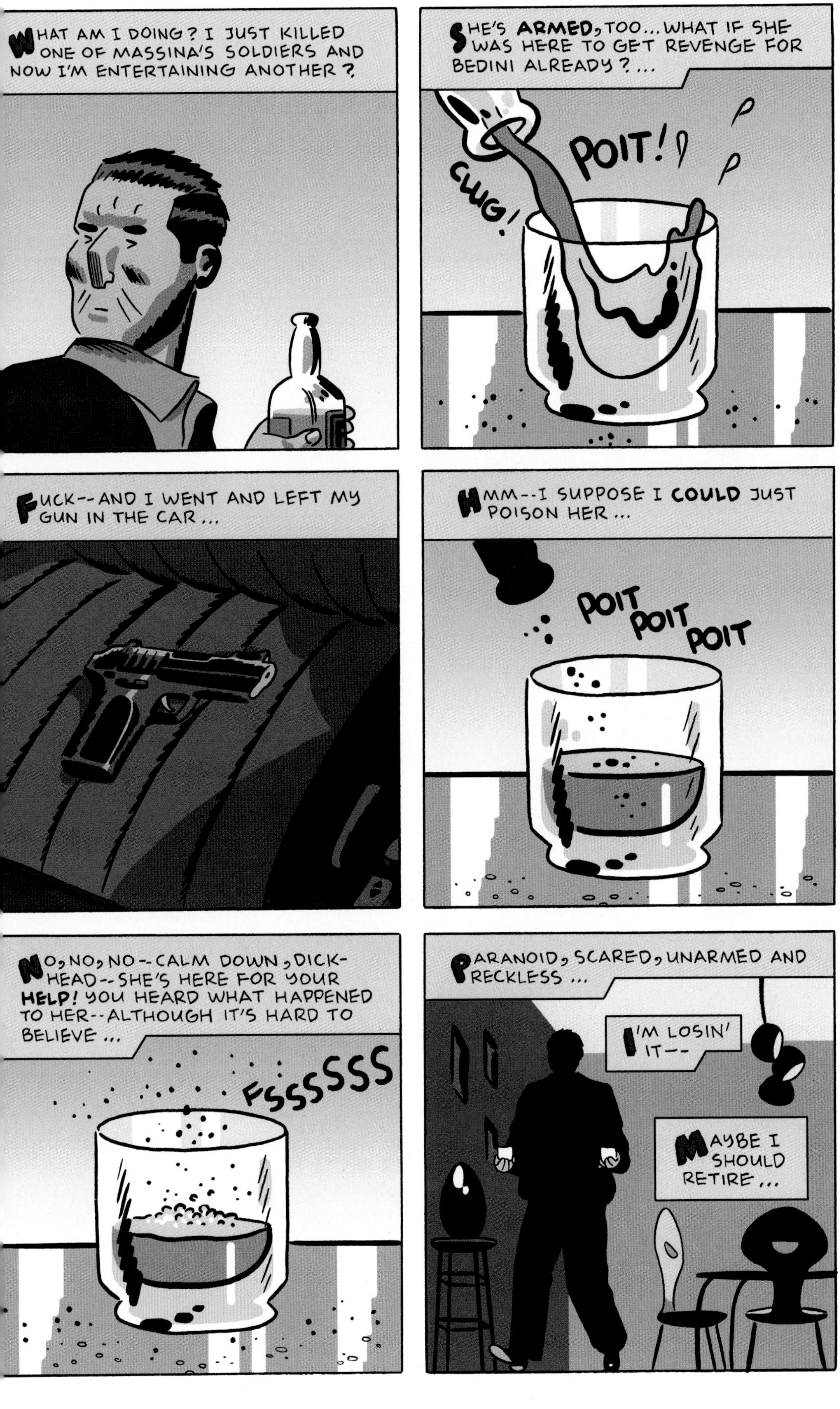
WHAT AM I DOING? I JUST KILLED ONE OF MASSINA'S SOLDIERS AND NOW I'M ENTERTAINING ANOTHER?
SHE'S ARMED, TOO... WHAT IF SHE WAS HERE TO GET REVENGE FOR BEDINI ALREADY?...
CLUG!
POIT!
FUCK--AND I WENT AND LEFT MY GUN IN THE CAR...
HMM--I SUPPOSE I COULD JUST POISON HER...
POIT POIT POIT
NO, NO, NO--CALM DOWN, DICK-HEAD--SHE'S HERE FOR YOUR HELP! YOU HEARD WHAT HAPPENED TO HER--ALTHOUGH IT'S HARD TO BELIEVE...
FSSSSSS
PARANOID, SCARED, UNARMED AND RECKLESS...
I'M LOSIN' IT--
MAYBE I SHOULD RETIRE...

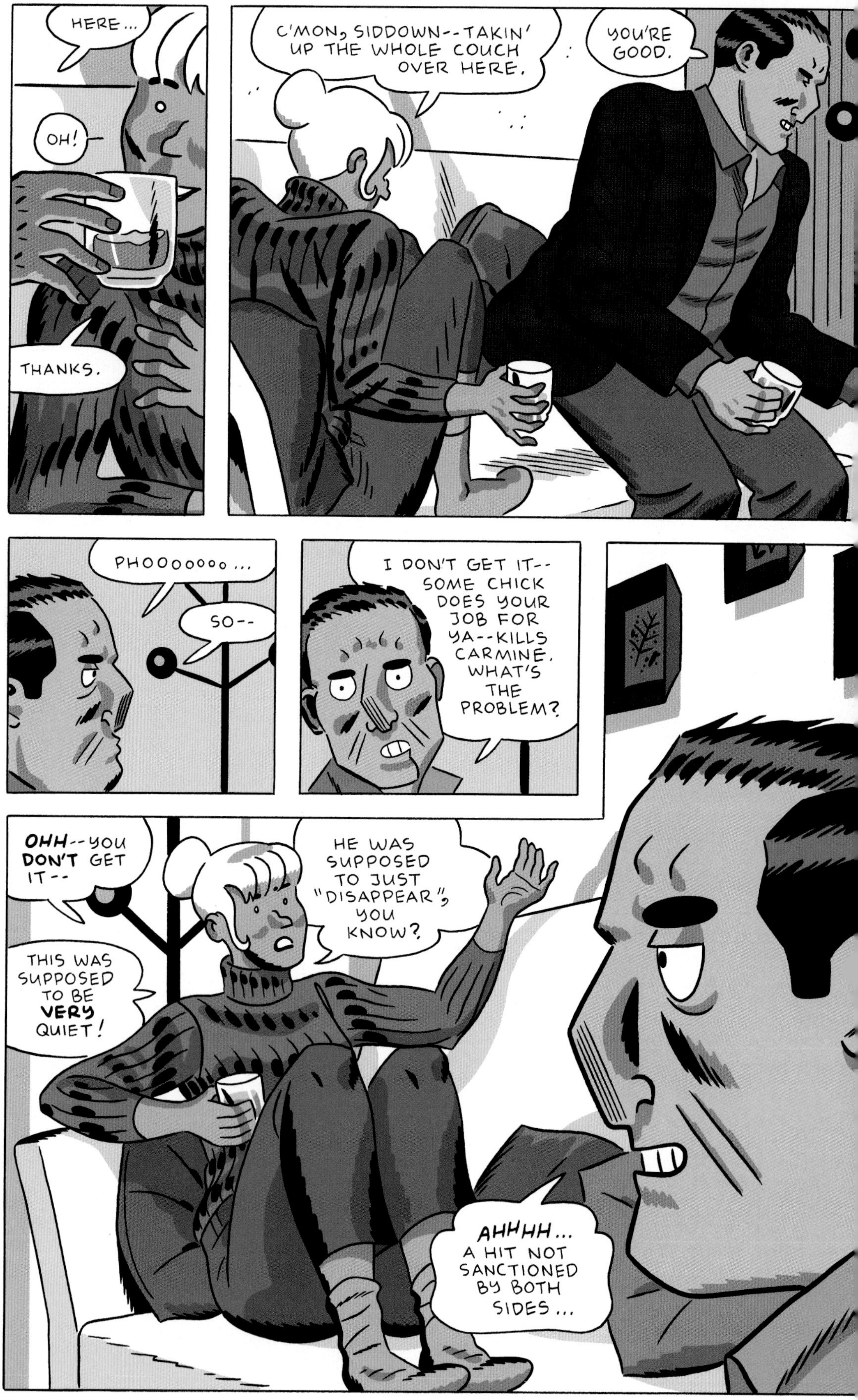
HERE...
OH!
THANKS.
C'MON, SIDDOWN--TAKIN' UP THE WHOLE COUCH OVER HERE.
YOU'RE GOOD.
PHOOOOOOO...
SO--
I DON'T GET IT--SOME CHICK DOES YOUR JOB FOR YA--KILLS CARMINE. WHAT'S THE PROBLEM?
OHH--YOU DON'T GET IT--
THIS WAS SUPPOSED TO BE VERY QUIET!
HE WAS SUPPOSED TO JUST "DISAPPEAR", YOU KNOW?
AHHHH... A HIT NOT SANCTIONED BY BOTH SIDES...

PRECISELY ... MASSINA'S GONNA **KILL** ME NOW--THIS WAS SUPPOSED TO BE A QUIET RETALIATION ON THE SANTINI MOB--FOR THE SCALINAS' KILLINGS ...

WHAT? ... THE SCALINAS? SANTINI ORDERED THAT?--

THAT'S WHAT MASSINA BELIEVES. HE THINKS IT'S THE RESULT OF A LONG-TIME DISPUTE OVER THE AMOUNT OF CONTROL THE SCALINAS HELD OVER THE CITY'S GAMBLING RACKETS ...

HE **THINKS?**

SAY GOODBYE TO THE BAD GUY!--

IT'S BEEN A **BONE** OF CONTENTION FOR **YEARS** BETWEEN THE TWO FAMILIES. BIGGER THAN ANY OTHER DISPUTES THEY'VE HAD...

SO I WAS HIRED TO WHACK CARMINE, WHO WAS THE **MOST** VOCAL ABOUT THAT INBALANCE OF POWER ...BUT MASSINA DIDN'T WAIT TO HAVE A SIT DOWN WITH SANTINI AND THE CAPTAINS--HE WAS TOO ANGRY ...

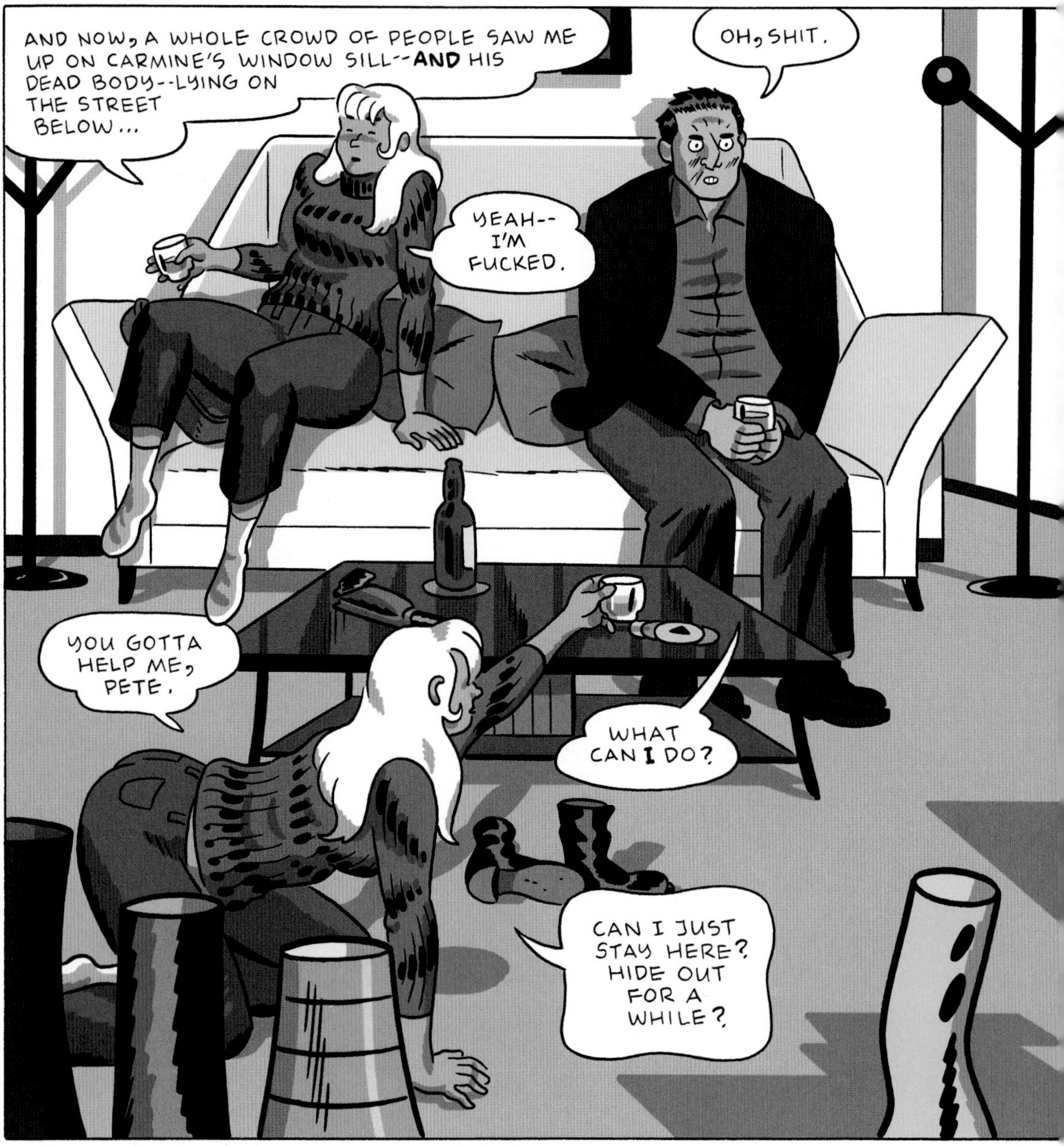
AND NOW, A WHOLE CROWD OF PEOPLE SAW ME UP ON CARMINE'S WINDOW SILL--**AND** HIS DEAD BODY--LYING ON THE STREET BELOW...
OH, SHIT.
YEAH-- I'M FUCKED.
YOU GOTTA HELP ME, PETE.
WHAT CAN **I** DO?
CAN I JUST STAY HERE? HIDE OUT FOR A WHILE?

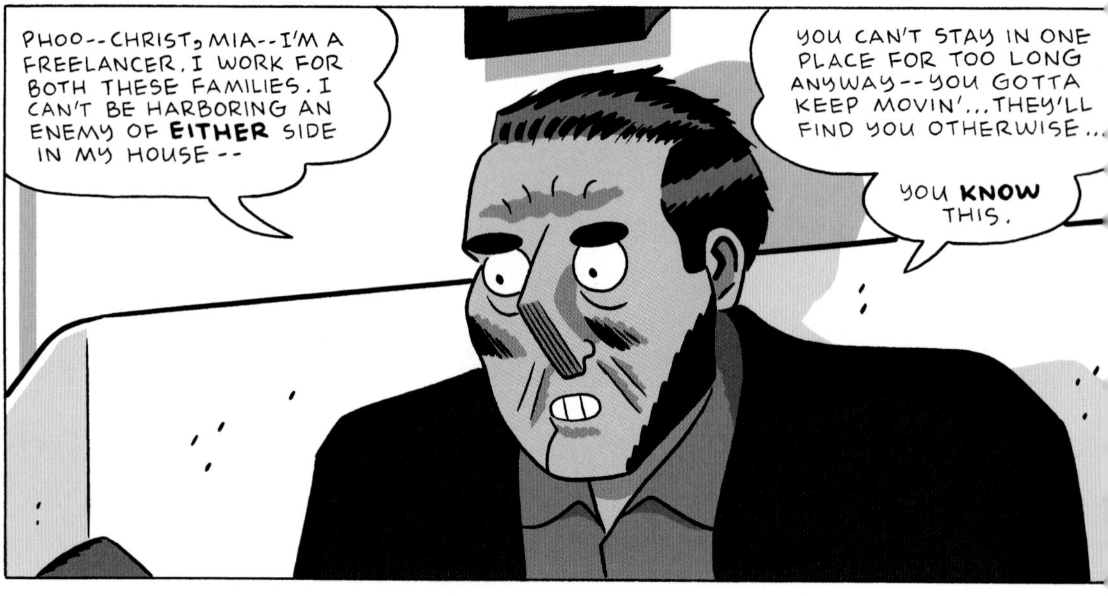
PHOO--CHRIST, MIA--I'M A FREELANCER. I WORK FOR BOTH THESE FAMILIES. I CAN'T BE HARBORING AN ENEMY OF **EITHER** SIDE IN MY HOUSE--
YOU CAN'T STAY IN ONE PLACE FOR TOO LONG ANYWAY--YOU GOTTA KEEP MOVIN'...THEY'LL FIND YOU OTHERWISE...
YOU **KNOW** THIS.

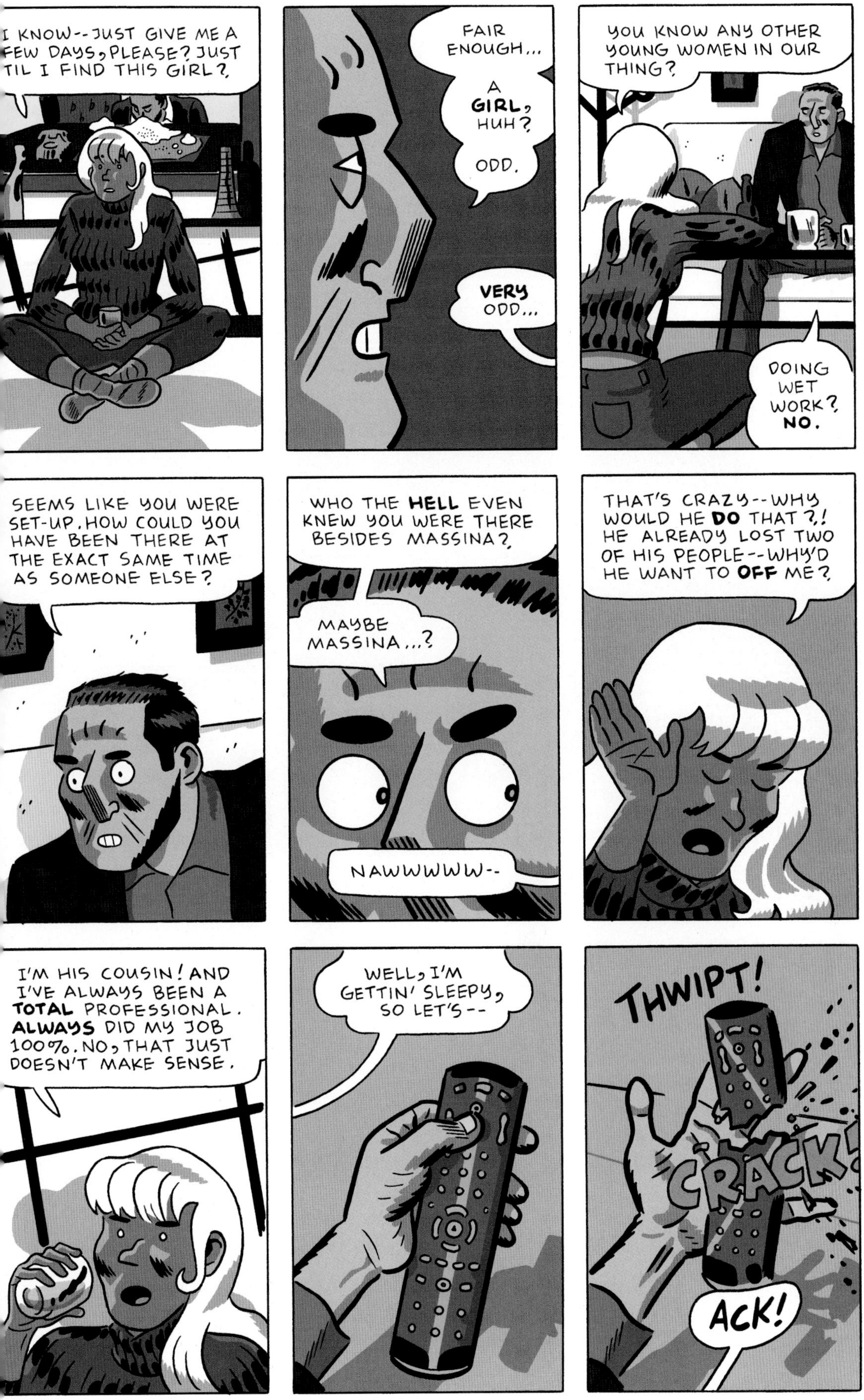

I KNOW--JUST GIVE ME A FEW DAYS, PLEASE? JUST TIL I FIND THIS GIRL?
FAIR ENOUGH...
A GIRL, HUH?
ODD.
VERY ODD...
YOU KNOW ANY OTHER YOUNG WOMEN IN OUR THING?
DOING WET WORK? NO.
SEEMS LIKE YOU WERE SET-UP. HOW COULD YOU HAVE BEEN THERE AT THE EXACT SAME TIME AS SOMEONE ELSE?
WHO THE HELL EVEN KNEW YOU WERE THERE BESIDES MASSINA?
MAYBE MASSINA...?
NAWWWWWW--
THAT'S CRAZY--WHY WOULD HE DO THAT?! HE ALREADY LOST TWO OF HIS PEOPLE--WHY'D HE WANT TO OFF ME?
I'M HIS COUSIN! AND I'VE ALWAYS BEEN A TOTAL PROFESSIONAL. ALWAYS DID MY JOB 100%. NO, THAT JUST DOESN'T MAKE SENSE.
WELL, I'M GETTIN' SLEEPY, SO LET'S--
THWIPT!
CRACK!
ACK!

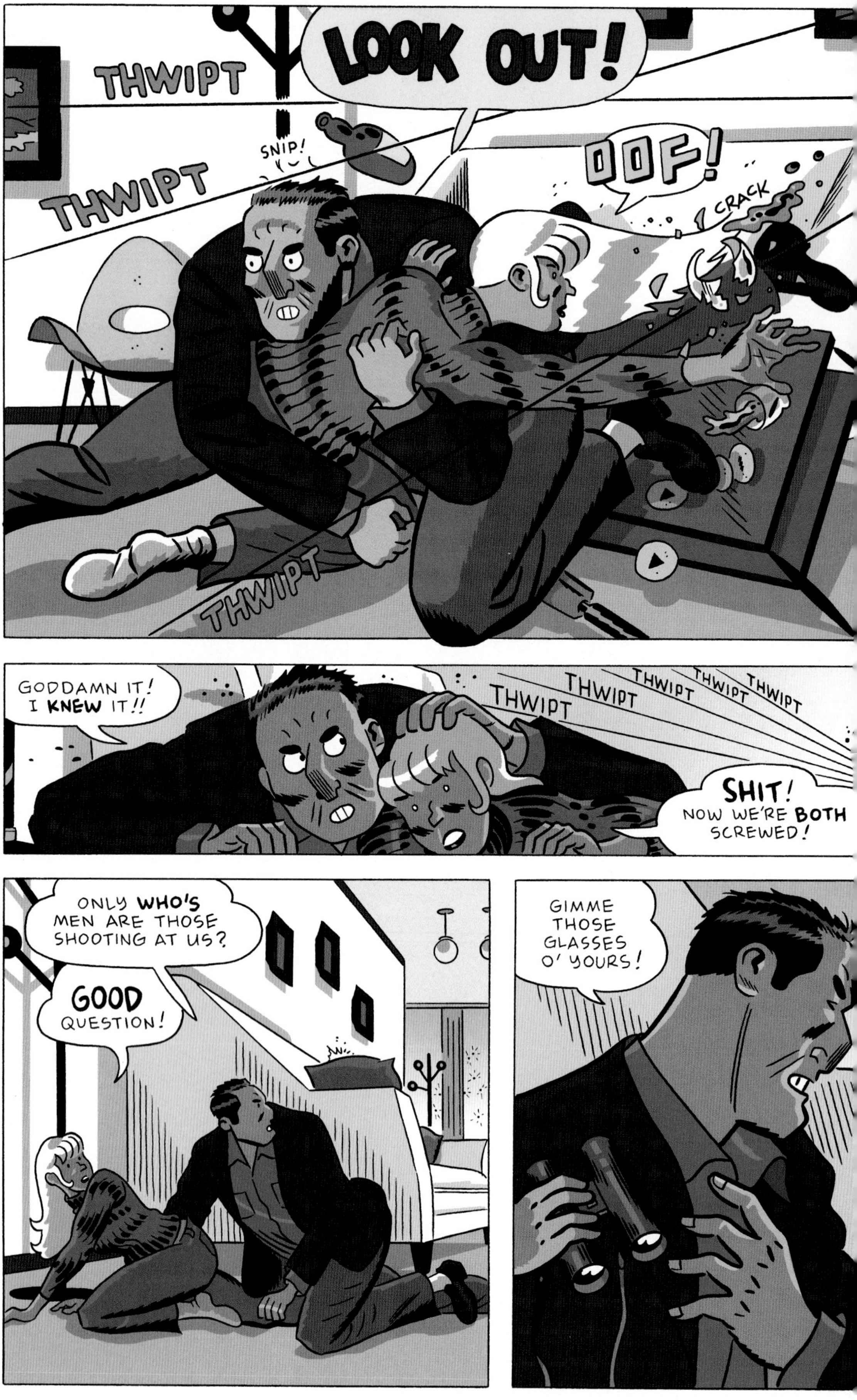
THWIPT
LOOK OUT!
SNIP!
THWIPT
OOF!
CRACK
THWIPT
GODDAMN IT! I KNEW IT!!
THWIPT
THWIPT
THWIPT
THWIPT
THWIPT
SHIT! NOW WE'RE BOTH SCREWED!
ONLY WHO'S MEN ARE THOSE SHOOTING AT US?
GOOD QUESTION!
GIMME THOSE GLASSES O' YOURS!

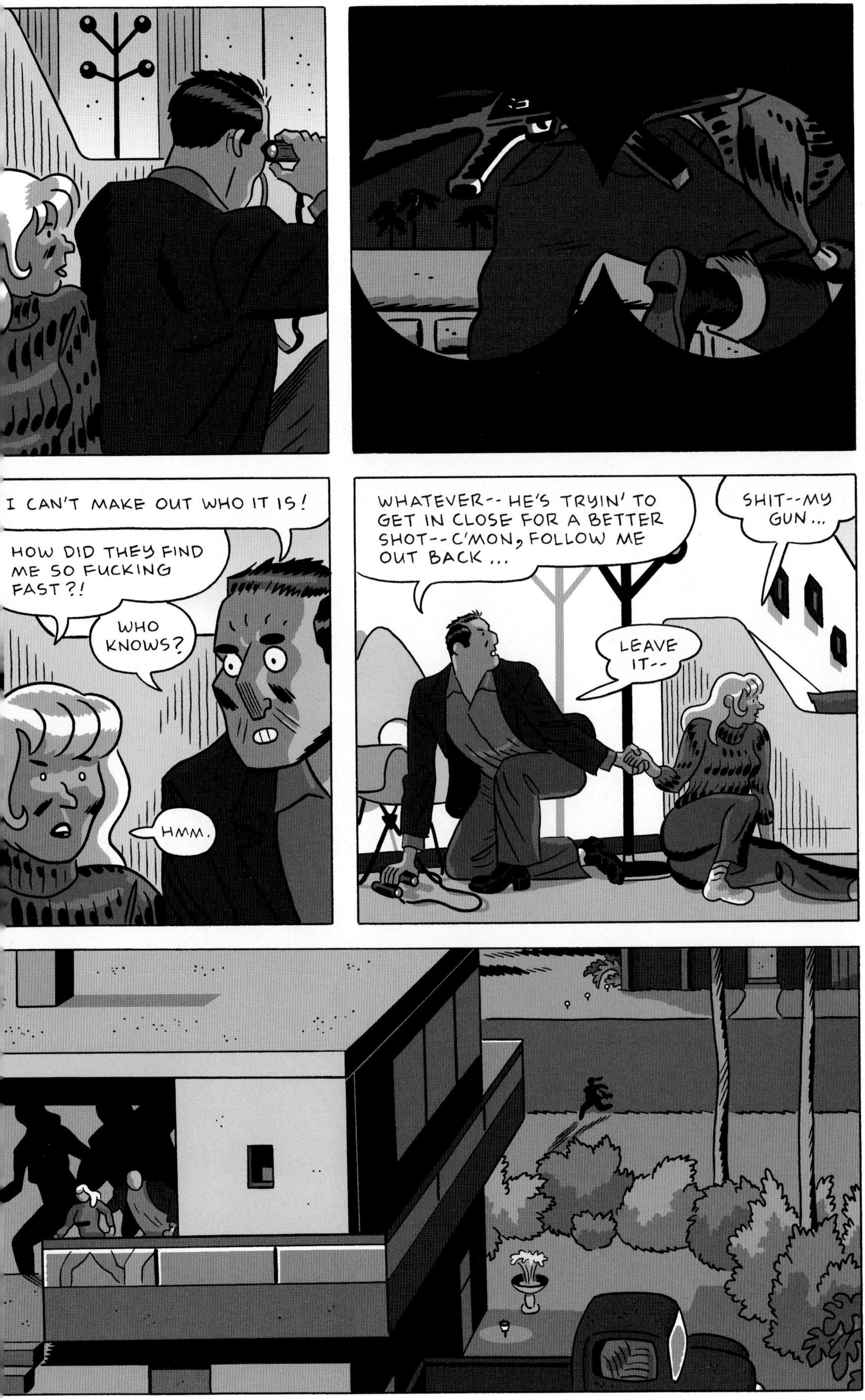
I CAN'T MAKE OUT WHO IT IS!
HOW DID THEY FIND ME SO FUCKING FAST?!
WHO KNOWS?
HMM.
WHATEVER-- HE'S TRYIN' TO GET IN CLOSE FOR A BETTER SHOT-- C'MON, FOLLOW ME OUT BACK...
SHIT--MY GUN...
LEAVE IT--

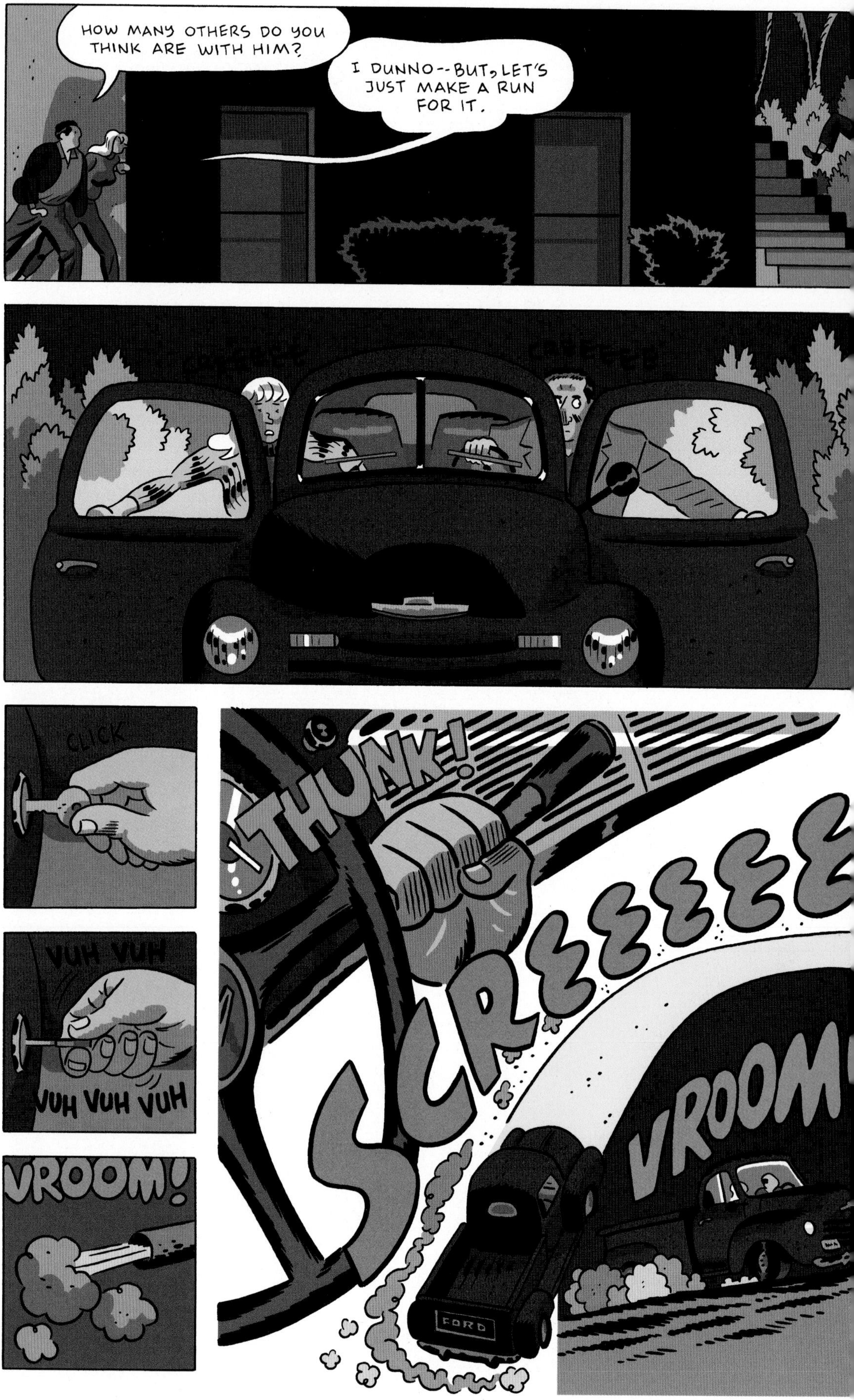
HOW MANY OTHERS DO YOU THINK ARE WITH HIM?
I DUNNO--BUT, LET'S JUST MAKE A RUN FOR IT.
CLICK
VUH VUH
VUH VUH VUH
VROOM!
THUNK!
SCREEEEEE
VROOM
FORD

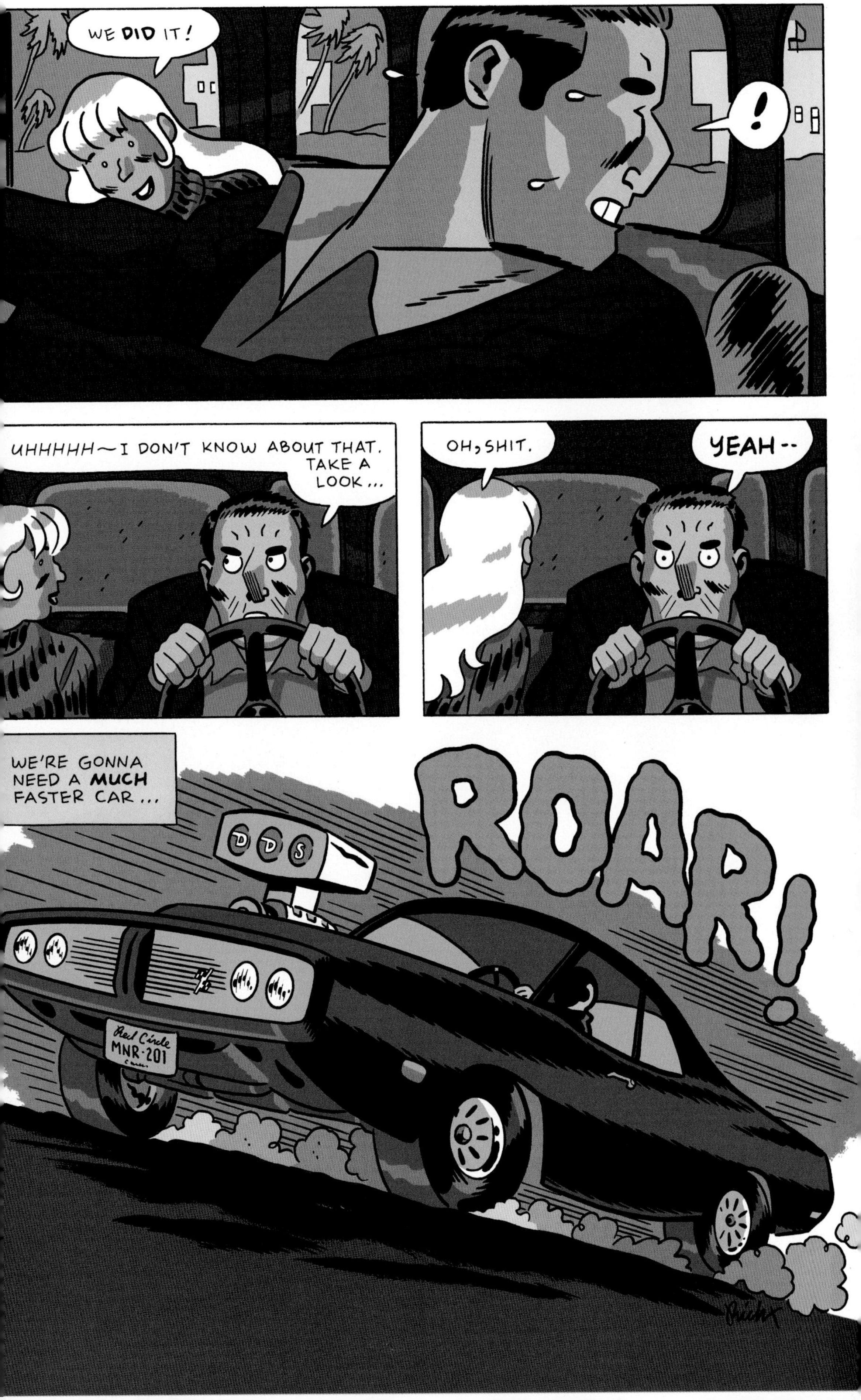

WE DID IT!
!
UHHHHH~I DON'T KNOW ABOUT THAT. TAKE A LOOK...
OH, SHIT.
YEAH--
WE'RE GONNA NEED A MUCH FASTER CAR...
ROAR!
Red Circle
MNR-201

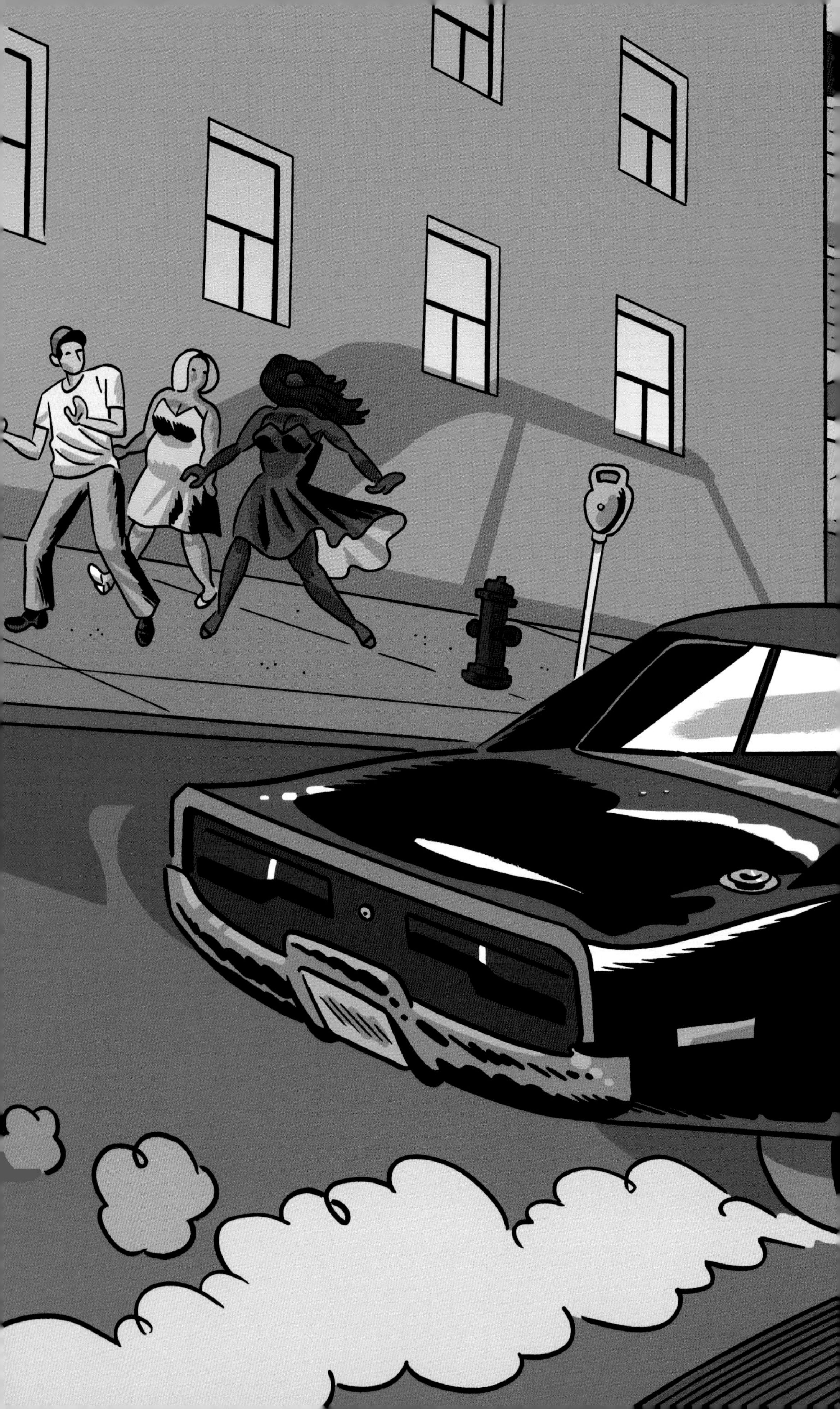

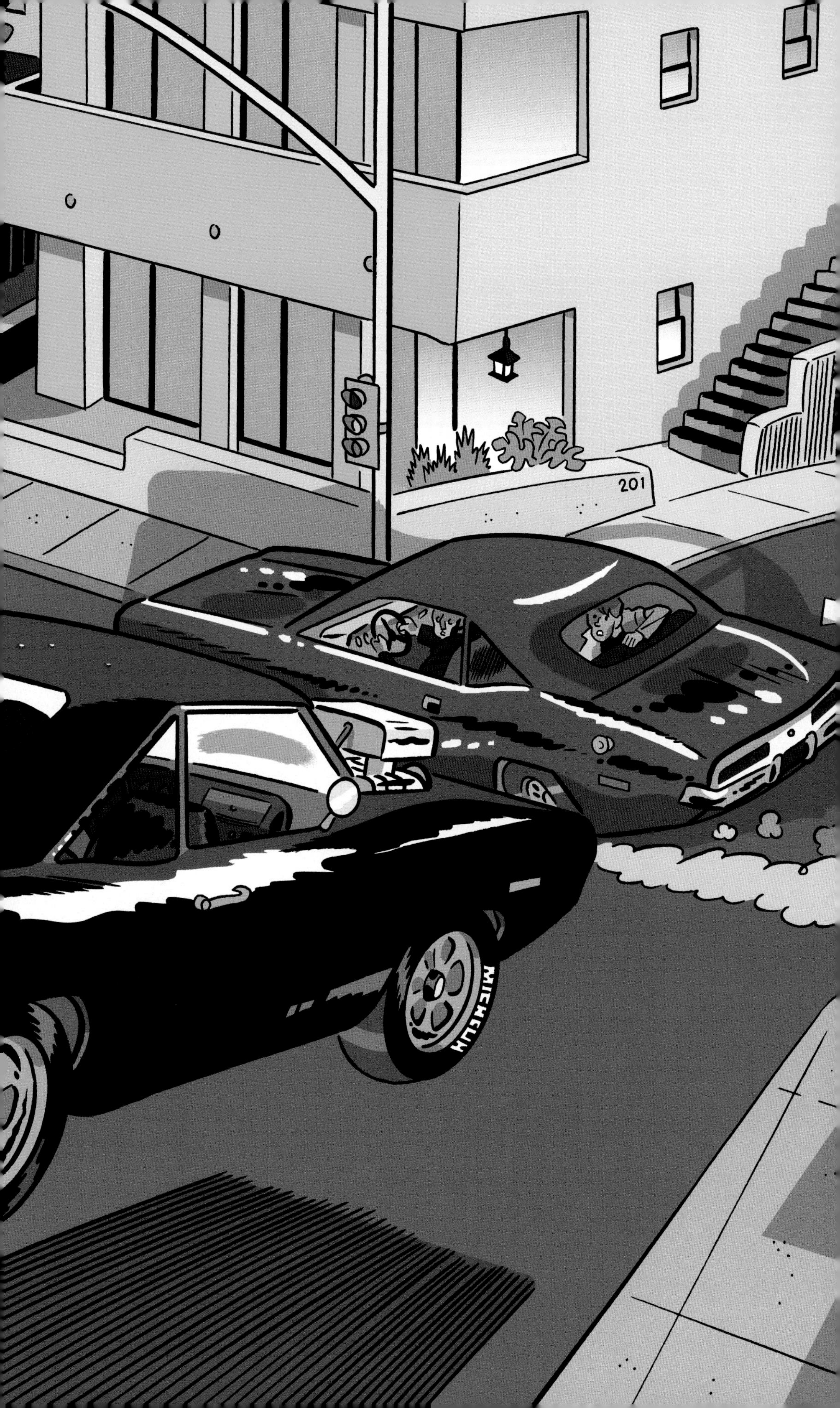
201
MICHELIN

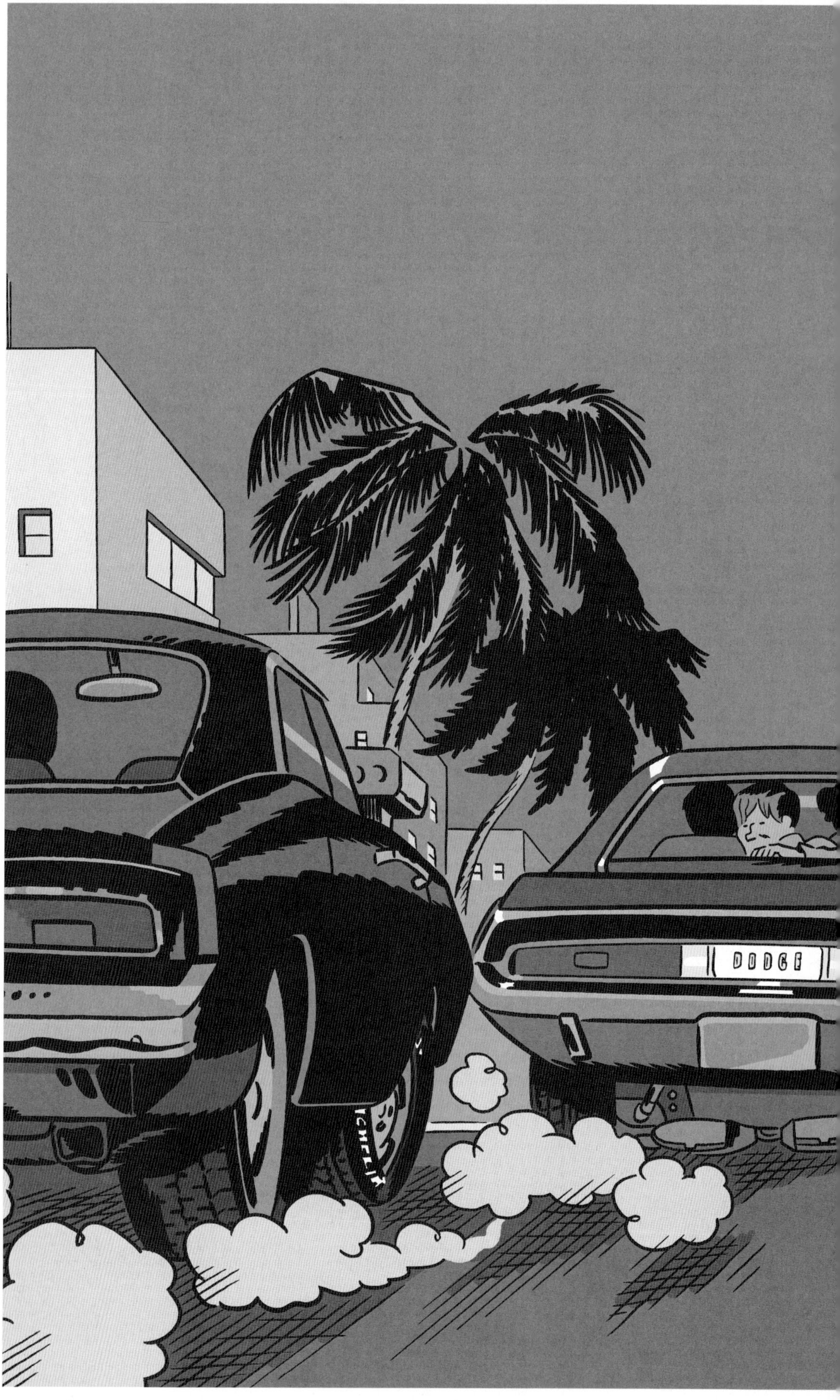
DODGE

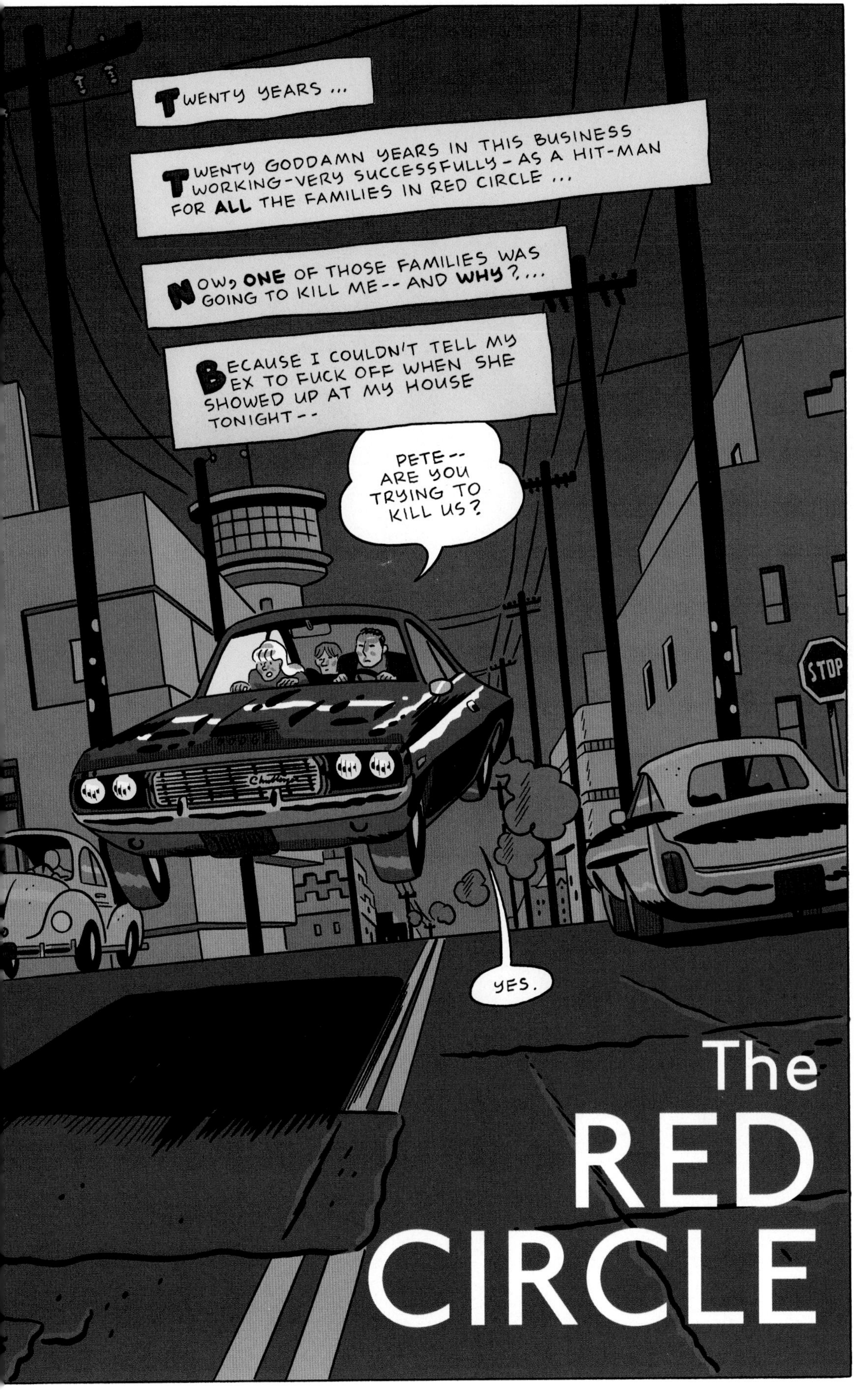
TWENTY YEARS ...
TWENTY GODDAMN YEARS IN THIS BUSINESS WORKING--VERY SUCCESSFULLY--AS A HIT-MAN FOR **ALL** THE FAMILIES IN RED CIRCLE ...
NOW, **ONE** OF THOSE FAMILIES WAS GOING TO KILL ME-- AND **WHY**?...
BECAUSE I COULDN'T TELL MY EX TO FUCK OFF WHEN SHE SHOWED UP AT MY HOUSE TONIGHT--
PETE-- ARE YOU TRYING TO KILL US?
STOP
YES.
The RED CIRCLE

PART FOUR
BLOW OUT

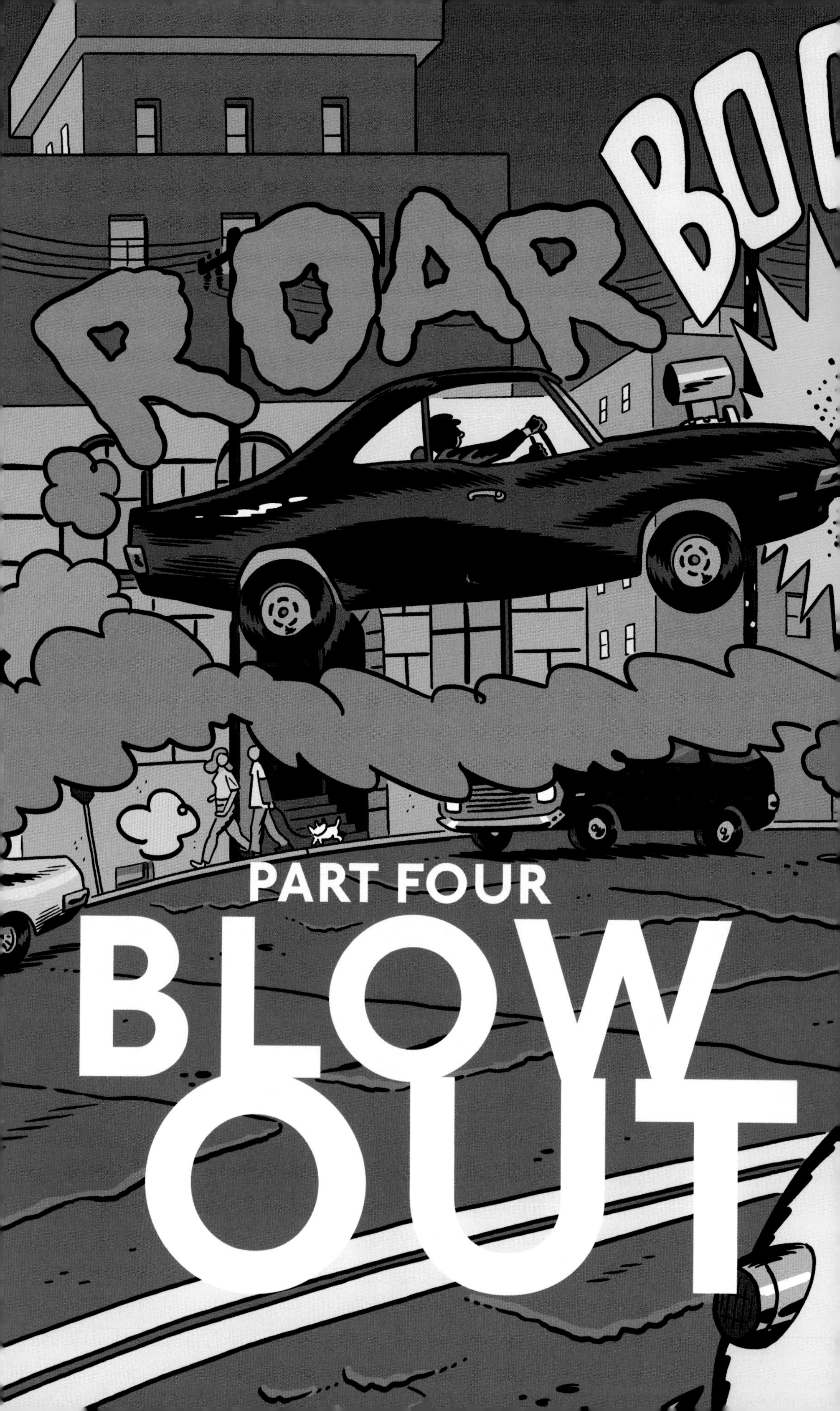
ROAR

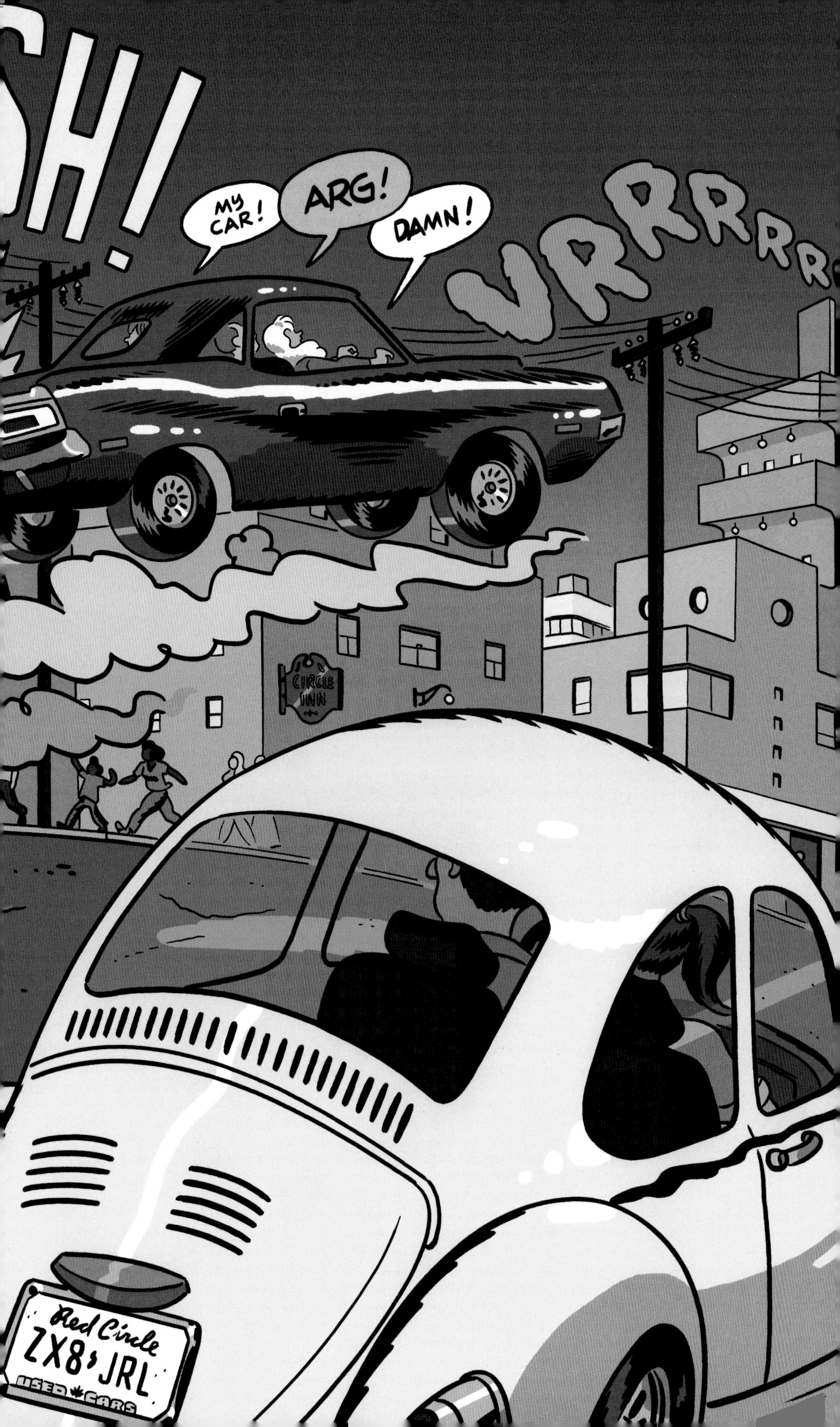
SH!
MY CAR!
ARG!
DAMN!
VRRRRR
CIRCLE INN
Red Circle
ZX8 JRL
USED CARS

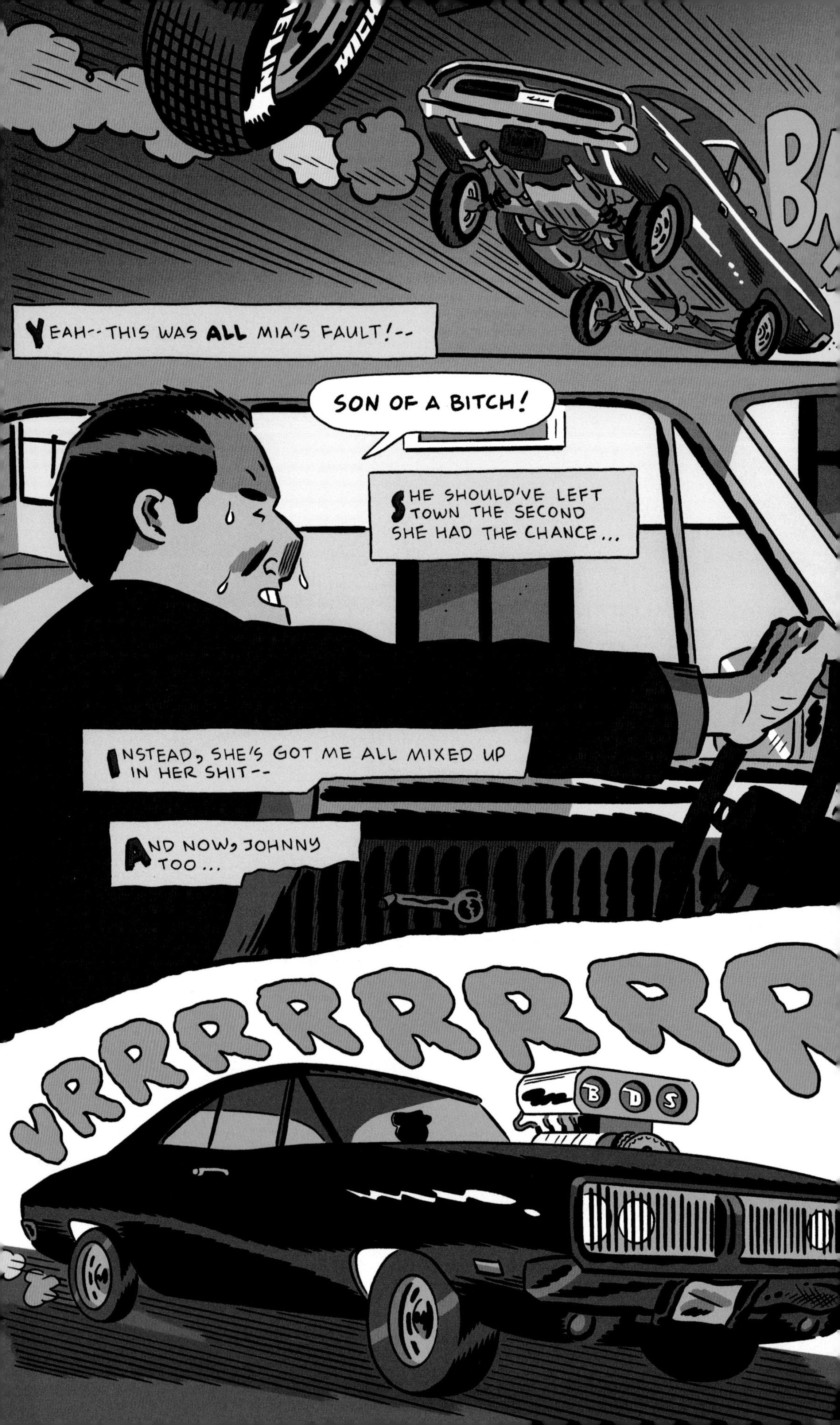
B
YEAH--THIS WAS ALL MIA'S FAULT!--
SON OF A BITCH!
SHE SHOULD'VE LEFT TOWN THE SECOND SHE HAD THE CHANCE...
INSTEAD, SHE'S GOT ME ALL MIXED UP IN HER SHIT--
AND NOW, JOHNNY TOO...
VRRRRRRRRR
BDS

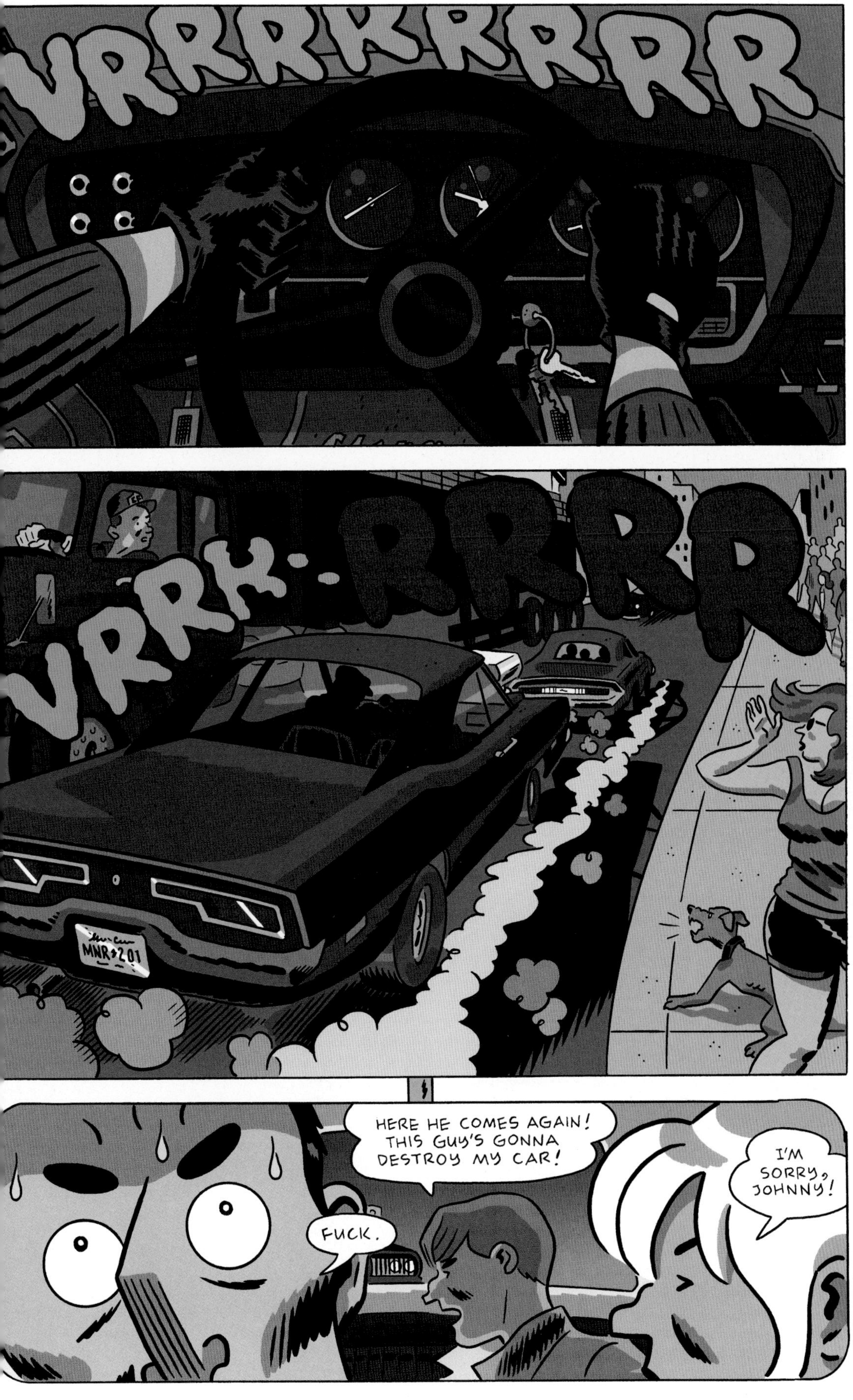
VRRRKRRRRR
VRRK-RRRR
MNR•201
HERE HE COMES AGAIN! THIS GUY'S GONNA DESTROY MY CAR!
FUCK.
I'M SORRY, JOHNNY!

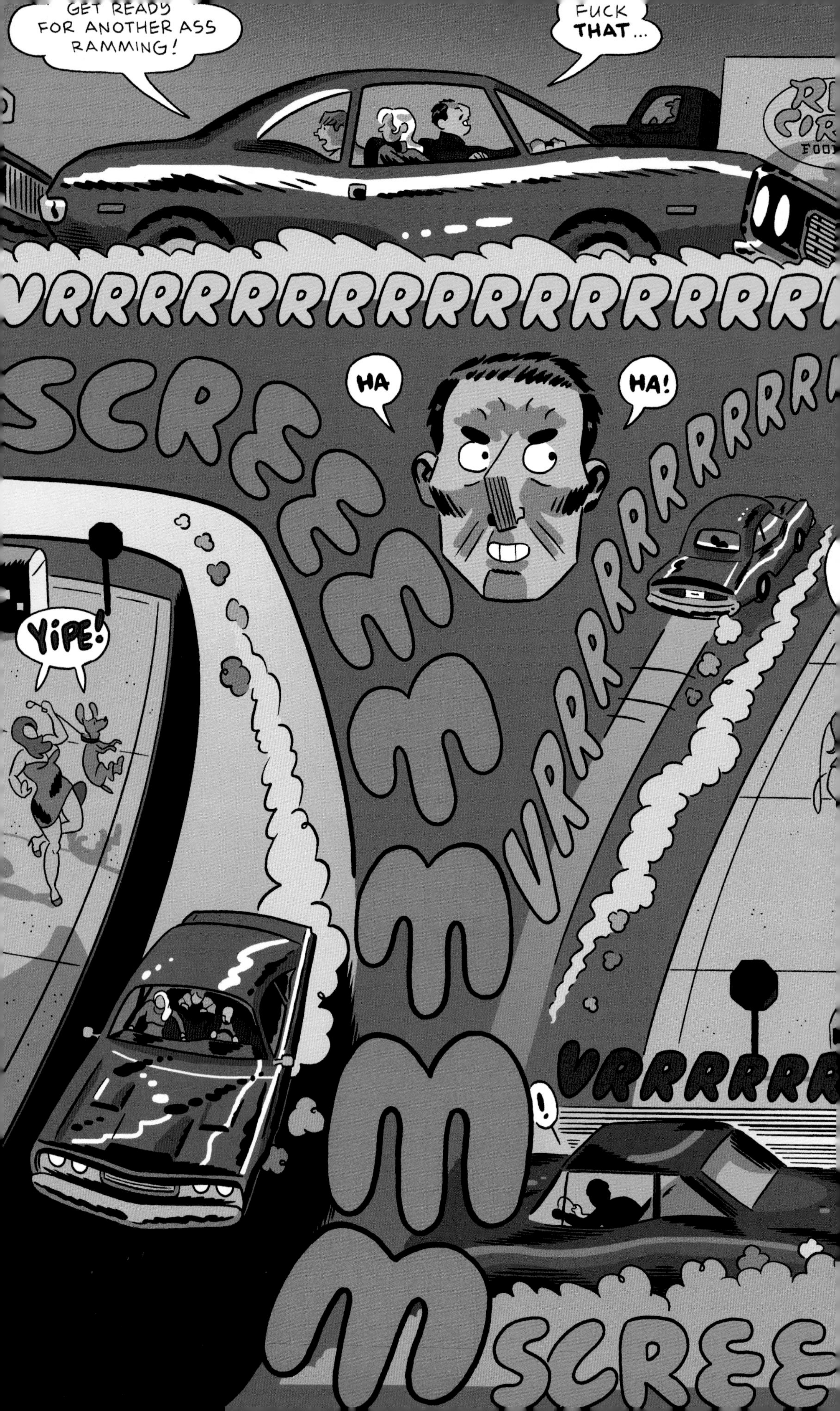

GET READY FOR ANOTHER ASS RAMMING!
FUCK THAT...
VRRRRRRRRRRRRRRRR
SCREEEMMMM
HA
HA!
VRRRRRRRRRRRRRRR
YIPE!
VRRRRRRR
!
SCREE

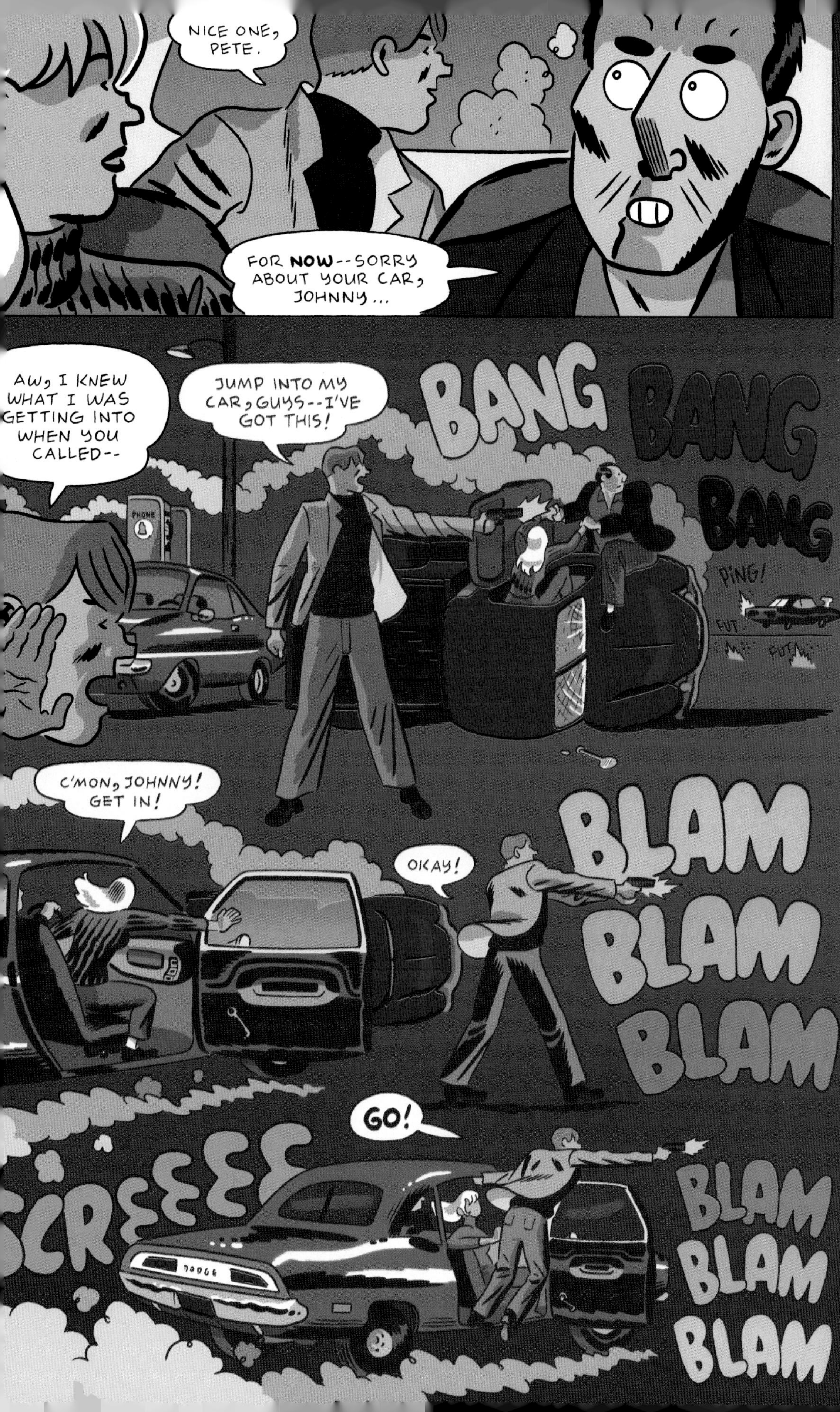
NICE ONE, PETE.
FOR NOW--SORRY ABOUT YOUR CAR, JOHNNY...
AW, I KNEW WHAT I WAS GETTING INTO WHEN YOU CALLED--
JUMP INTO MY CAR, GUYS--I'VE GOT THIS!
BANG
BANG
BANG
PING!
FUT
FUT
PHONE
C'MON, JOHNNY! GET IN!
OKAY!
BLAM
BLAM
BLAM
GO!
SCREEEE
DODGE
BLAM
BLAM
BLAM

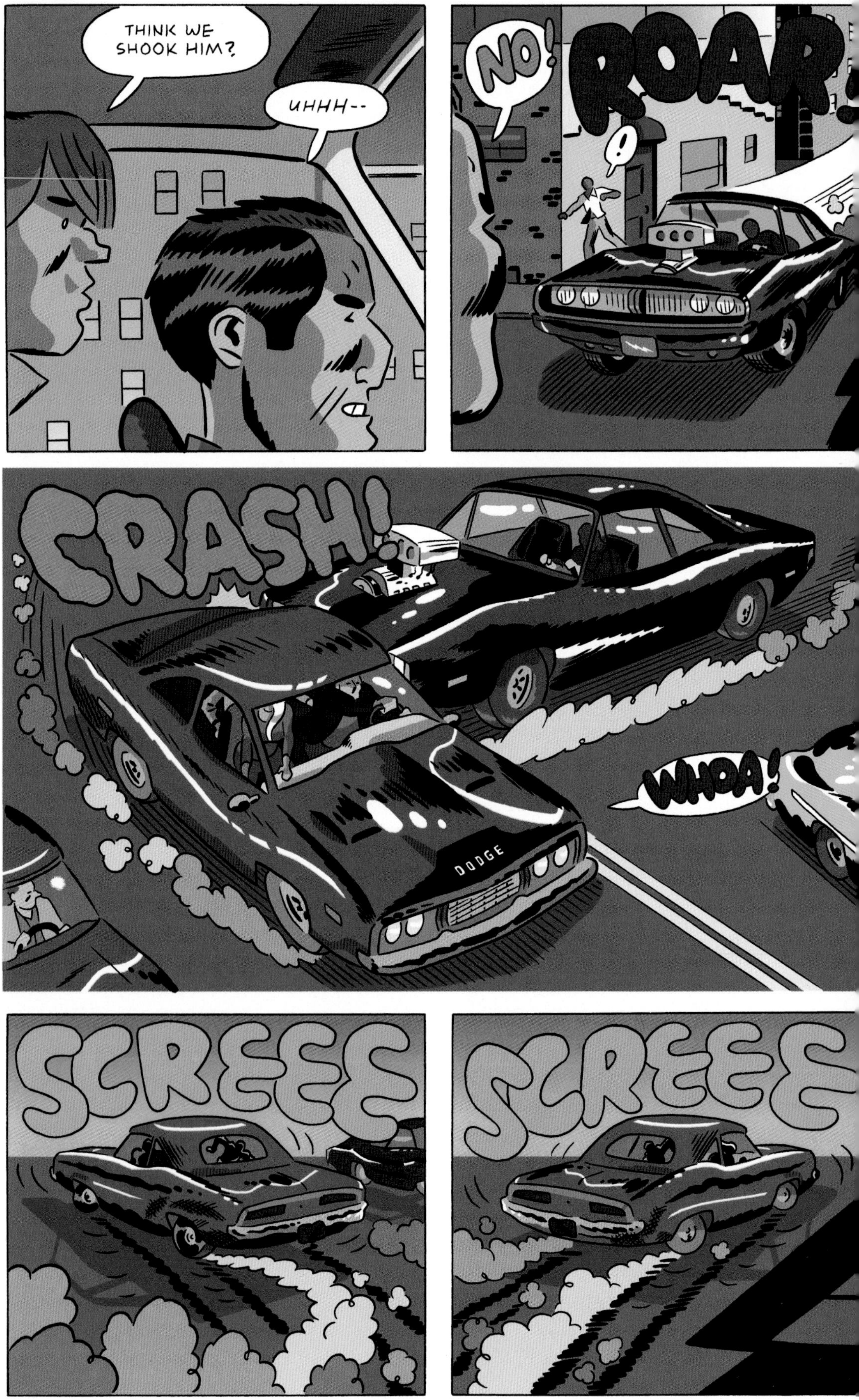
THINK WE SHOOK HIM?
UHHH--
NO!
ROAR!
!
CRASH!
DODGE
WHOA!
SCREEE
SCREEE

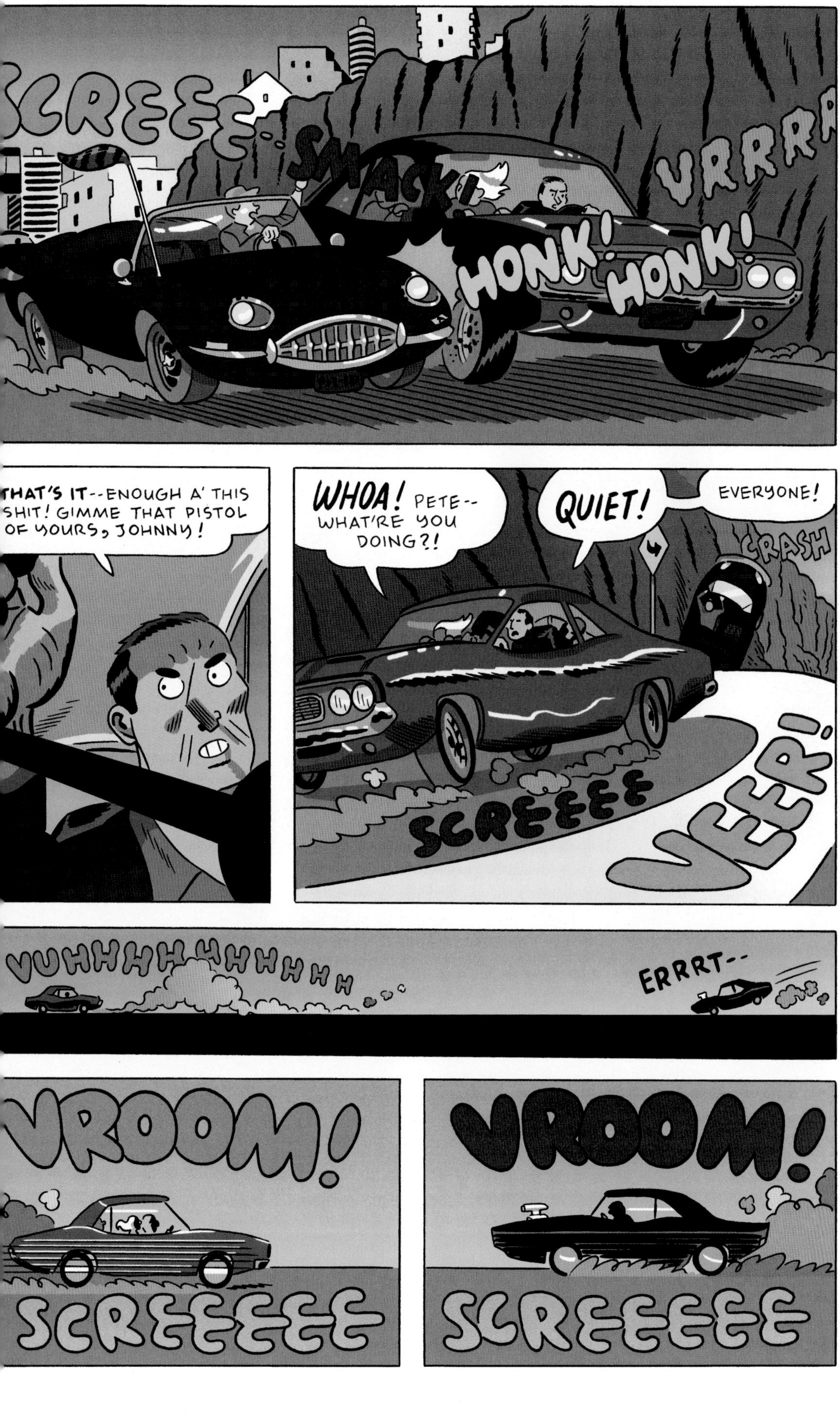
SCREEE--SMACK!
VRRRR
HONK! HONK!
THAT'S IT--ENOUGH A' THIS SHIT! GIMME THAT PISTOL OF YOURS, JOHNNY!
WHOA! PETE--WHAT'RE YOU DOING?!
QUIET!
EVERYONE!
CRASH
SCREEEE
VEER!
VUHHHHHHHHHHHH
ERRRT--
VROOM!
SCREEEEEE
VROOM!
SCREEEEEE

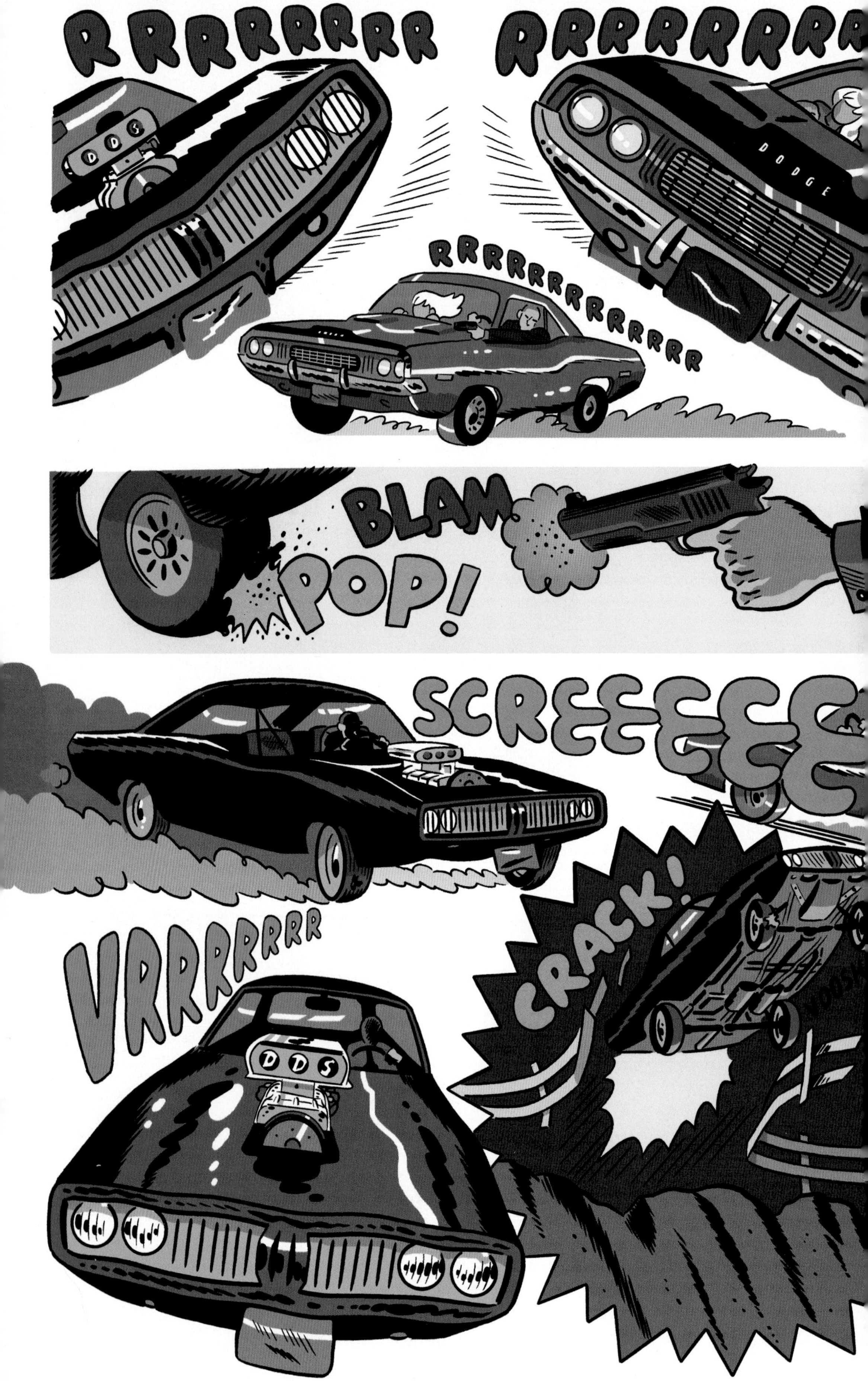
RRRRRRRRR
RRRRRRRR
DDS
DODGE
RRRRRRRRRRRRRRRRRR
BLAM
POP!
SCREEEEE
CRACK!
VRRRRRRR
DDS

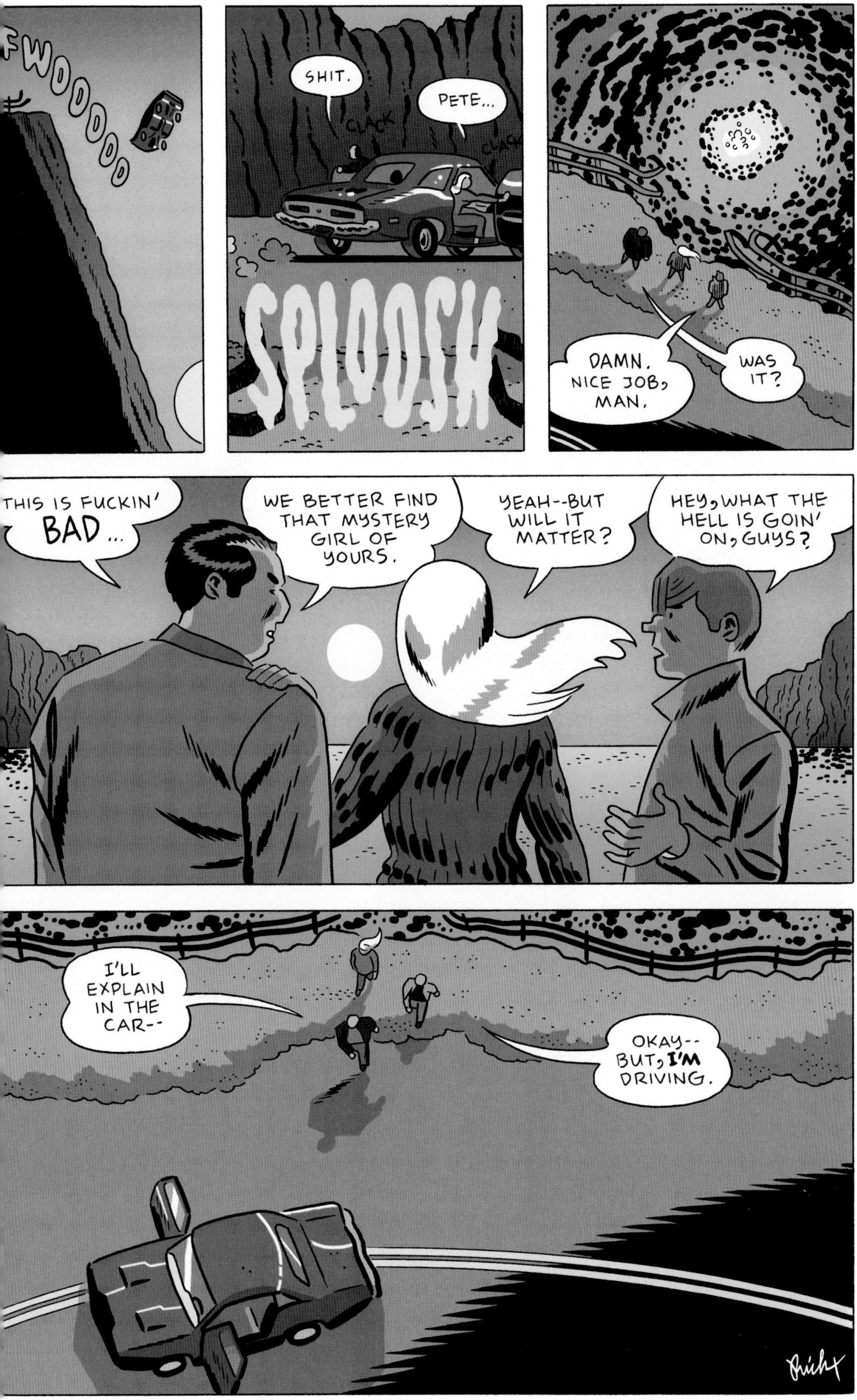
FWOOOOOOO
SHIT.
PETE...
CLACK
CLACK
SPLOOSH
DAMN. NICE JOB, MAN.
WAS IT?
THIS IS FUCKIN' BAD...
WE BETTER FIND THAT MYSTERY GIRL OF YOURS.
YEAH--BUT WILL IT MATTER?
HEY, WHAT THE HELL IS GOIN' ON, GUYS?
I'LL EXPLAIN IN THE CAR--
OKAY-- BUT, I'M DRIVING.

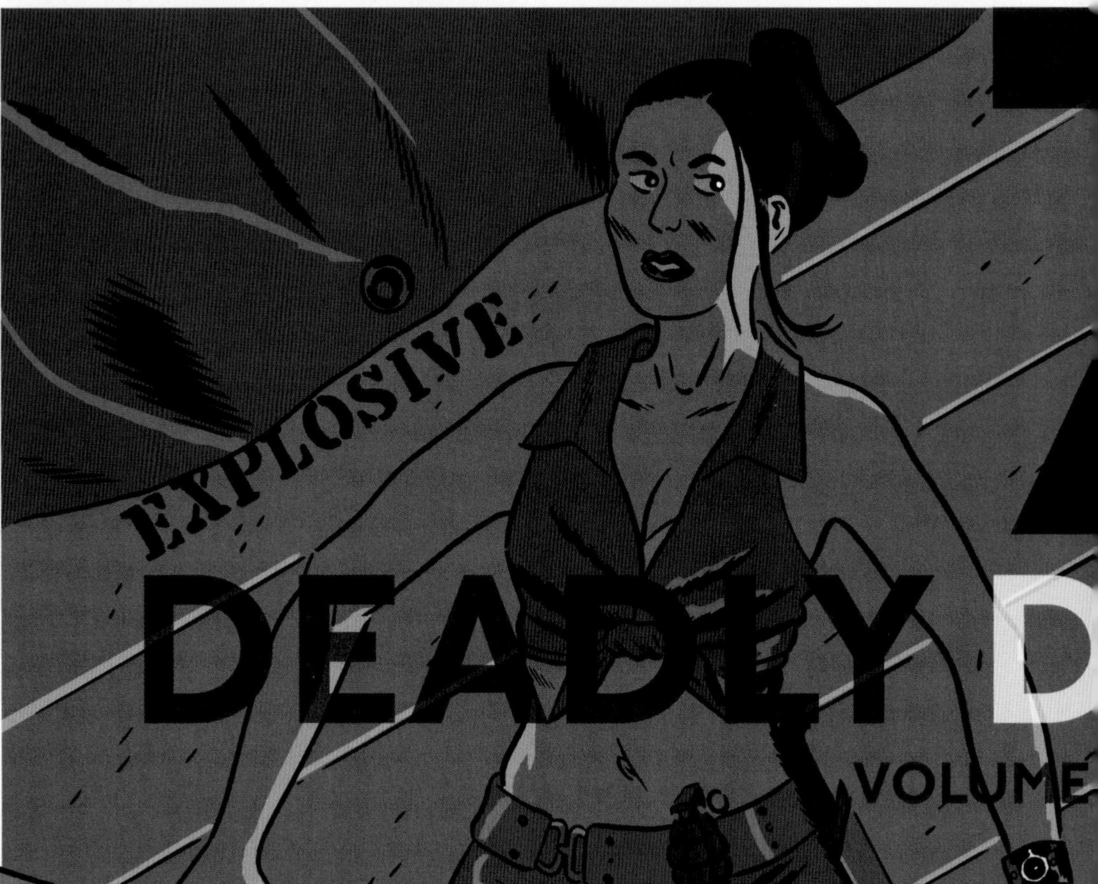
EXPLOSIVE
DEADLY D
VOLUME
PATRICIA
FRANCO

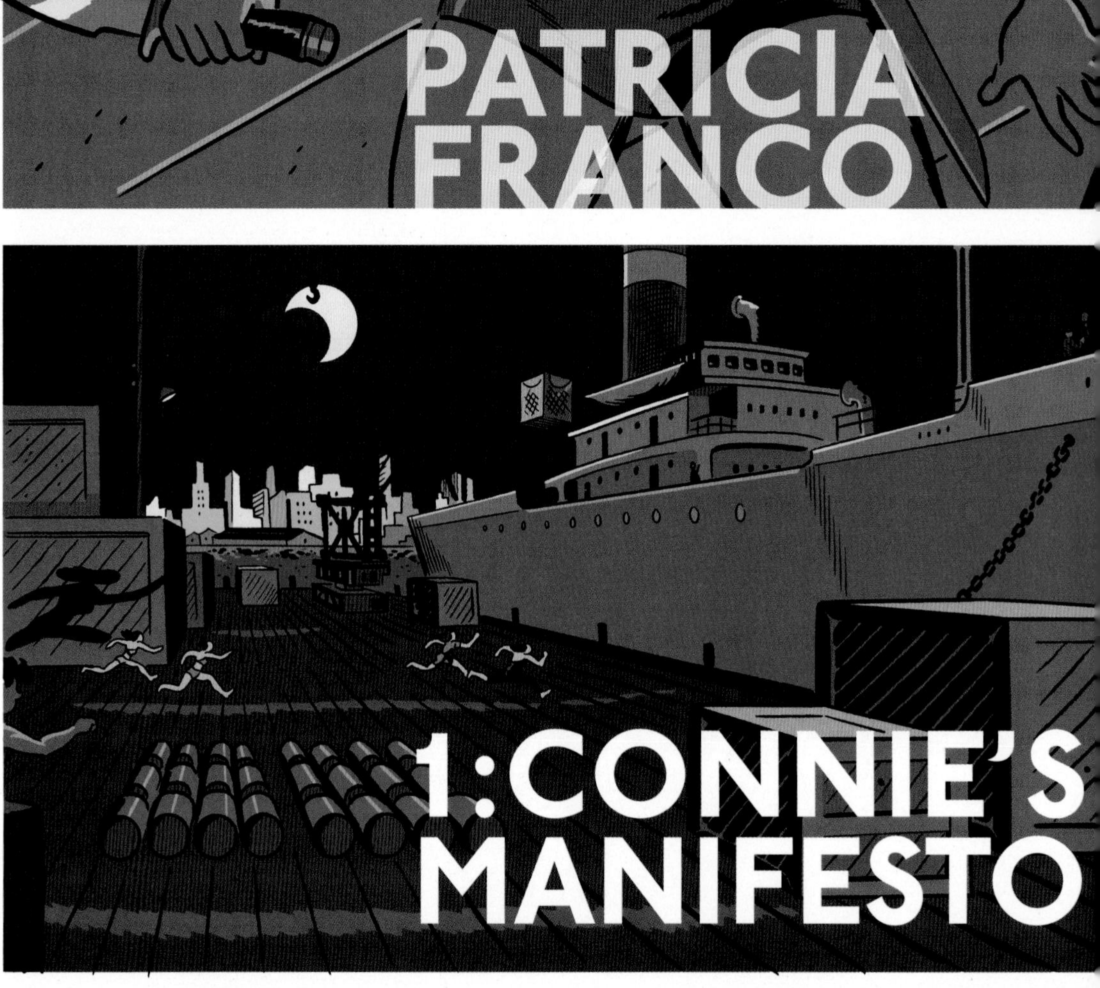
1:CONNIE'S
MANIFESTO

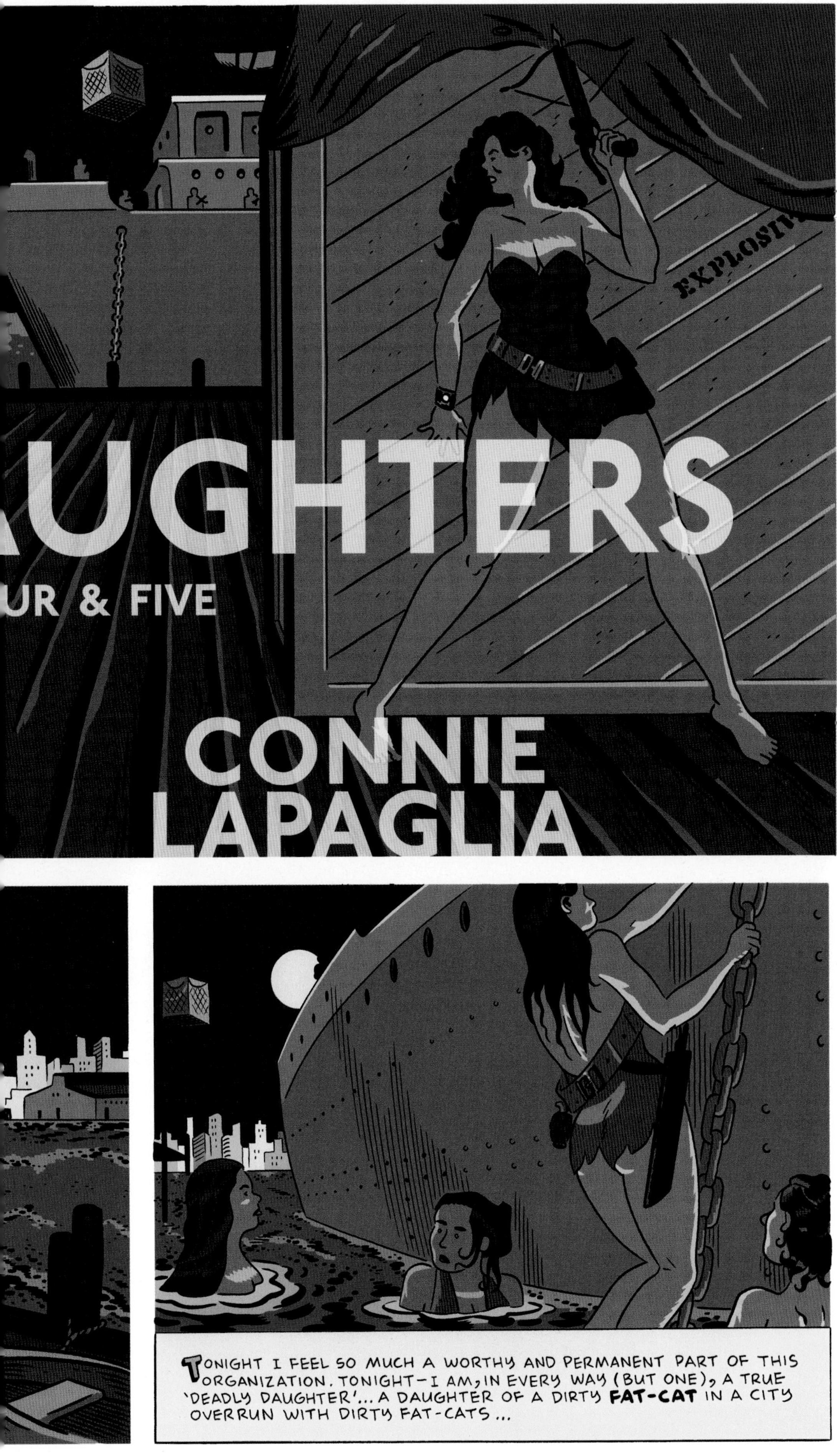
UGHTERS
UR & FIVE
CONNIE
LAPAGLIA
EXPLOSIV
TONIGHT I FEEL SO MUCH A WORTHY AND PERMANENT PART OF THIS ORGANIZATION. TONIGHT—I AM, IN EVERY WAY (BUT ONE), A TRUE 'DEADLY DAUGHTER'... A DAUGHTER OF A DIRTY **FAT-CAT** IN A CITY OVERRUN WITH DIRTY FAT-CATS...

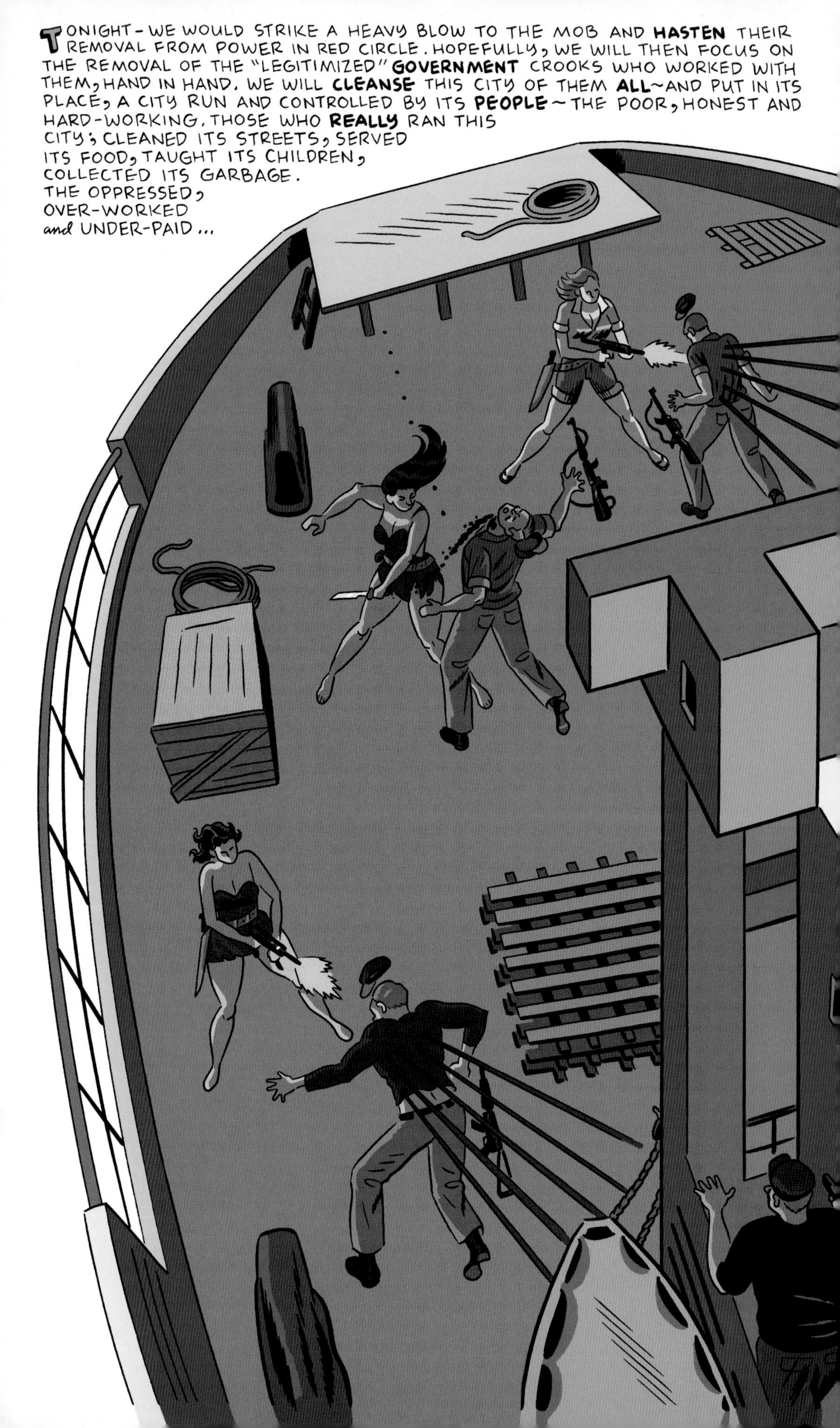
TONIGHT - WE WOULD STRIKE A HEAVY BLOW TO THE MOB AND **HASTEN** THEIR REMOVAL FROM POWER IN RED CIRCLE. HOPEFULLY, WE WILL THEN FOCUS ON THE REMOVAL OF THE "LEGITIMIZED" **GOVERNMENT** CROOKS WHO WORKED WITH THEM, HAND IN HAND. WE WILL **CLEANSE** THIS CITY OF THEM **ALL**~AND PUT IN ITS PLACE, A CITY RUN AND CONTROLLED BY ITS **PEOPLE**~THE POOR, HONEST AND HARD-WORKING. THOSE WHO **REALLY** RAN THIS CITY; CLEANED ITS STREETS, SERVED ITS FOOD, TAUGHT ITS CHILDREN, COLLECTED ITS GARBAGE. THE OPPRESSED, OVER-WORKED and UNDER-PAID...

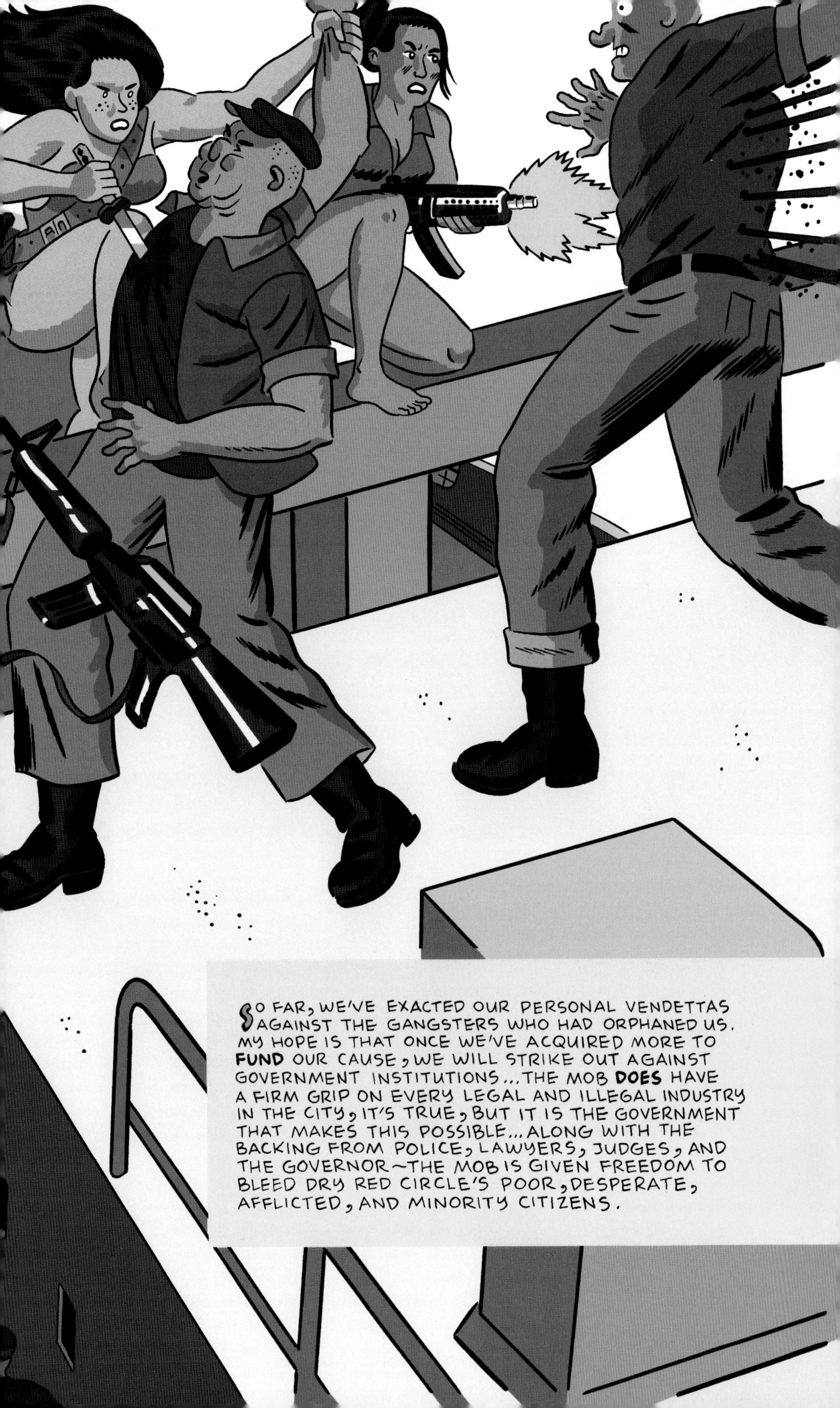
SO FAR, WE'VE EXACTED OUR PERSONAL VENDETTAS AGAINST THE GANGSTERS WHO HAD ORPHANED US. MY HOPE IS THAT ONCE WE'VE ACQUIRED MORE TO FUND OUR CAUSE, WE WILL STRIKE OUT AGAINST GOVERNMENT INSTITUTIONS... THE MOB DOES HAVE A FIRM GRIP ON EVERY LEGAL AND ILLEGAL INDUSTRY IN THE CITY, IT'S TRUE, BUT IT IS THE GOVERNMENT THAT MAKES THIS POSSIBLE... ALONG WITH THE BACKING FROM POLICE, LAWYERS, JUDGES, AND THE GOVERNOR~THE MOB IS GIVEN FREEDOM TO BLEED DRY RED CIRCLE'S POOR, DESPERATE, AFFLICTED, AND MINORITY CITIZENS.

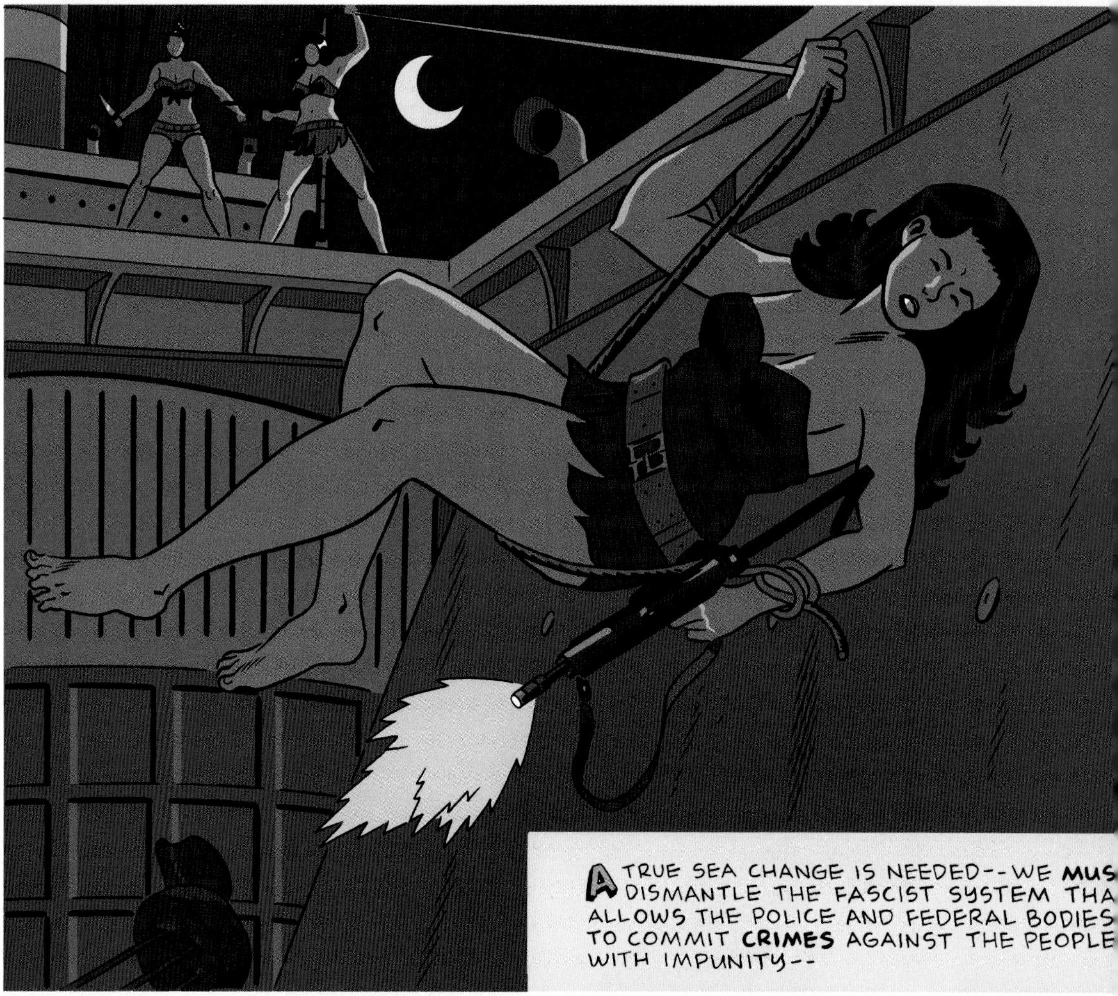
A TRUE SEA CHANGE IS NEEDED--WE MUS DISMANTLE THE FASCIST SYSTEM THA ALLOWS THE POLICE AND FEDERAL BODIES TO COMMIT CRIMES AGAINST THE PEOPLE WITH IMPUNITY--

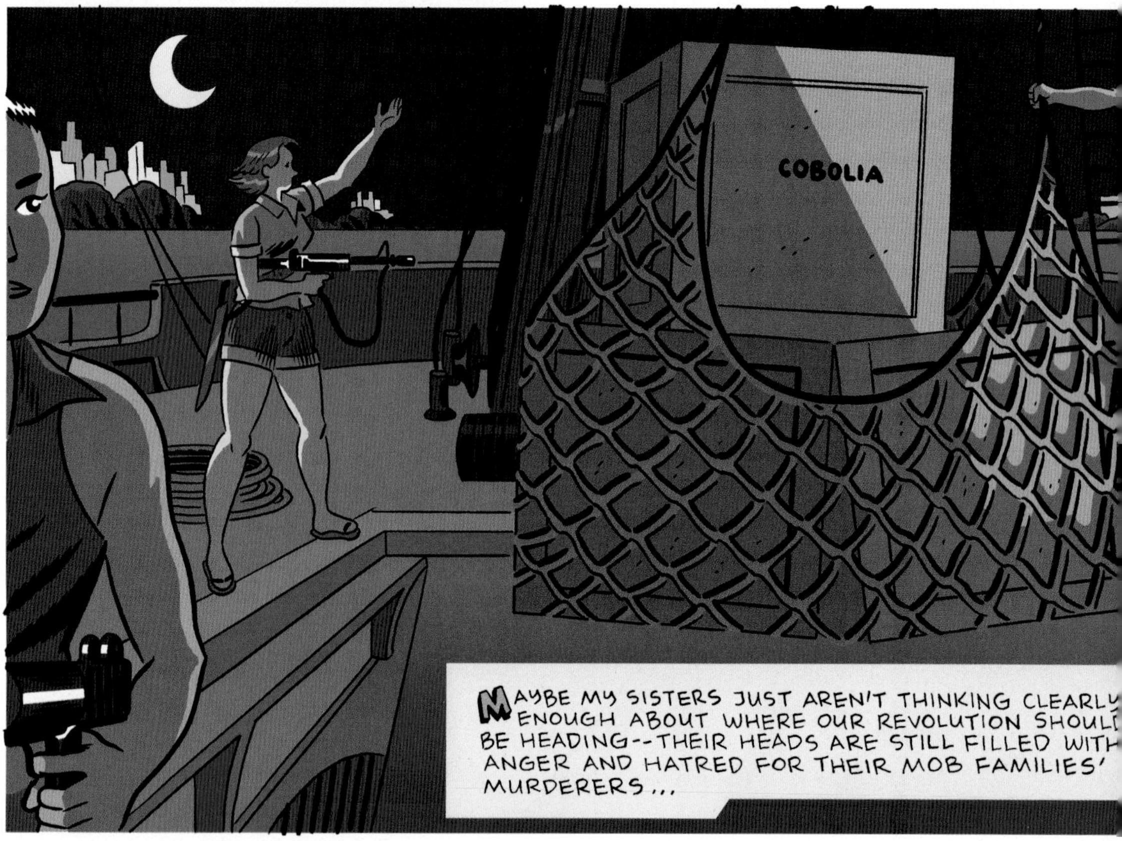
COBOLIA
MAYBE MY SISTERS JUST AREN'T THINKING CLEARLY ENOUGH ABOUT WHERE OUR REVOLUTION SHOULI BE HEADING--THEIR HEADS ARE STILL FILLED WITH ANGER AND HATRED FOR THEIR MOB FAMILIES' MURDERERS...

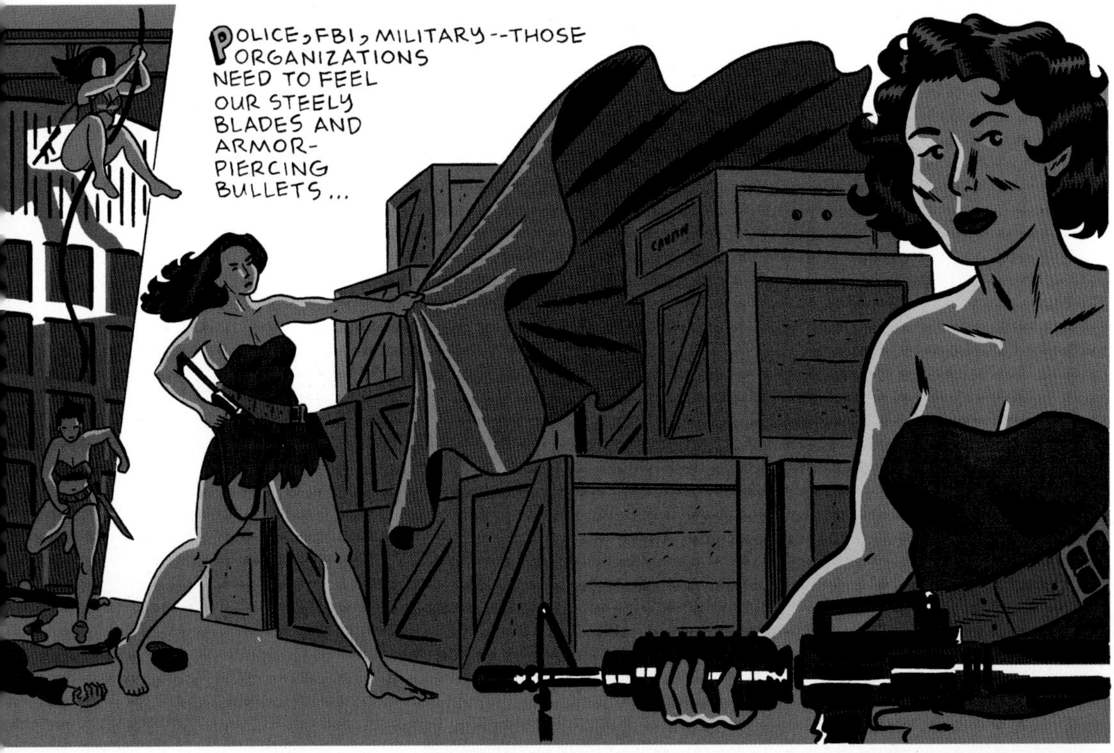
POLICE, FBI, MILITARY--THOSE ORGANIZATIONS NEED TO FEEL OUR STEELY BLADES AND ARMOR-PIERCING BULLETS...

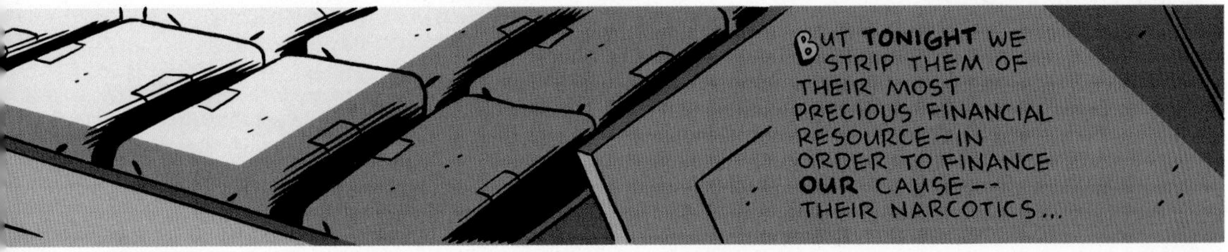
BUT TONIGHT WE STRIP THEM OF THEIR MOST PRECIOUS FINANCIAL RESOURCE~IN ORDER TO FINANCE OUR CAUSE-- THEIR NARCOTICS...

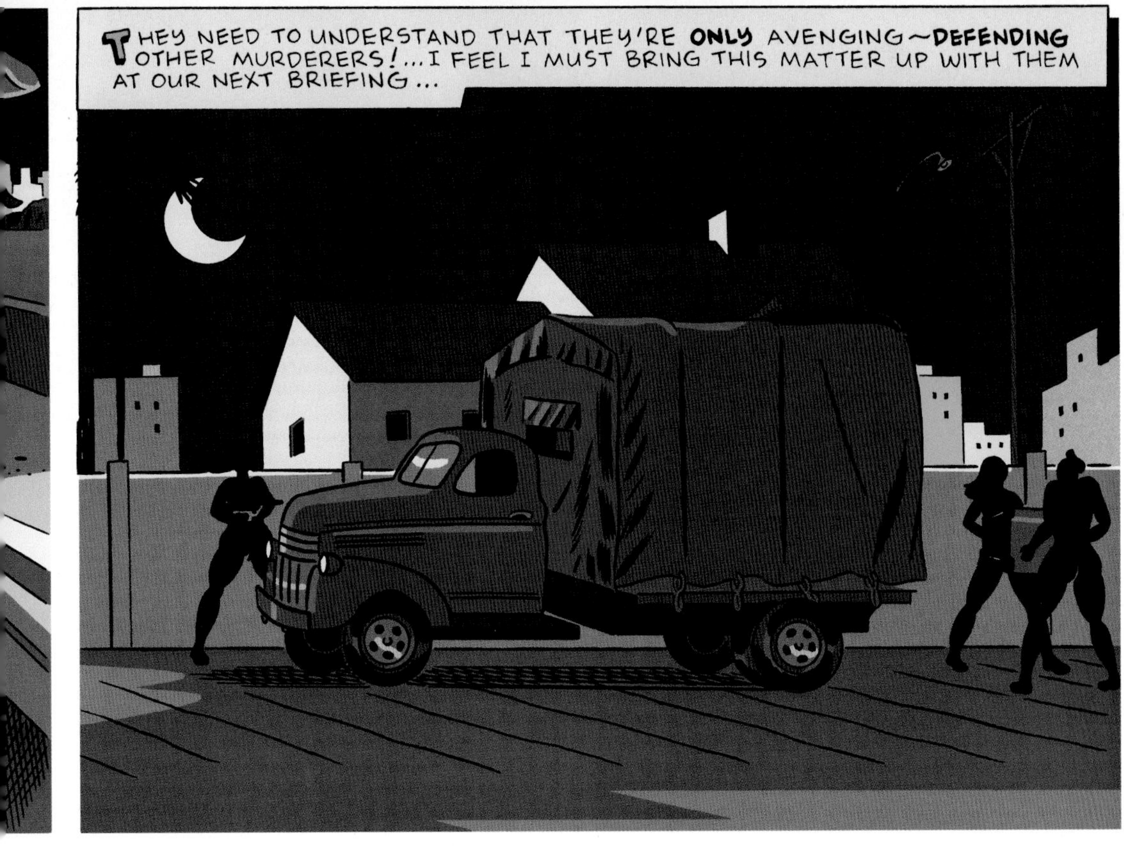
THEY NEED TO UNDERSTAND THAT THEY'RE ONLY AVENGING~DEFENDING OTHER MURDERERS!...I FEEL I MUST BRING THIS MATTER UP WITH THEM AT OUR NEXT BRIEFING...

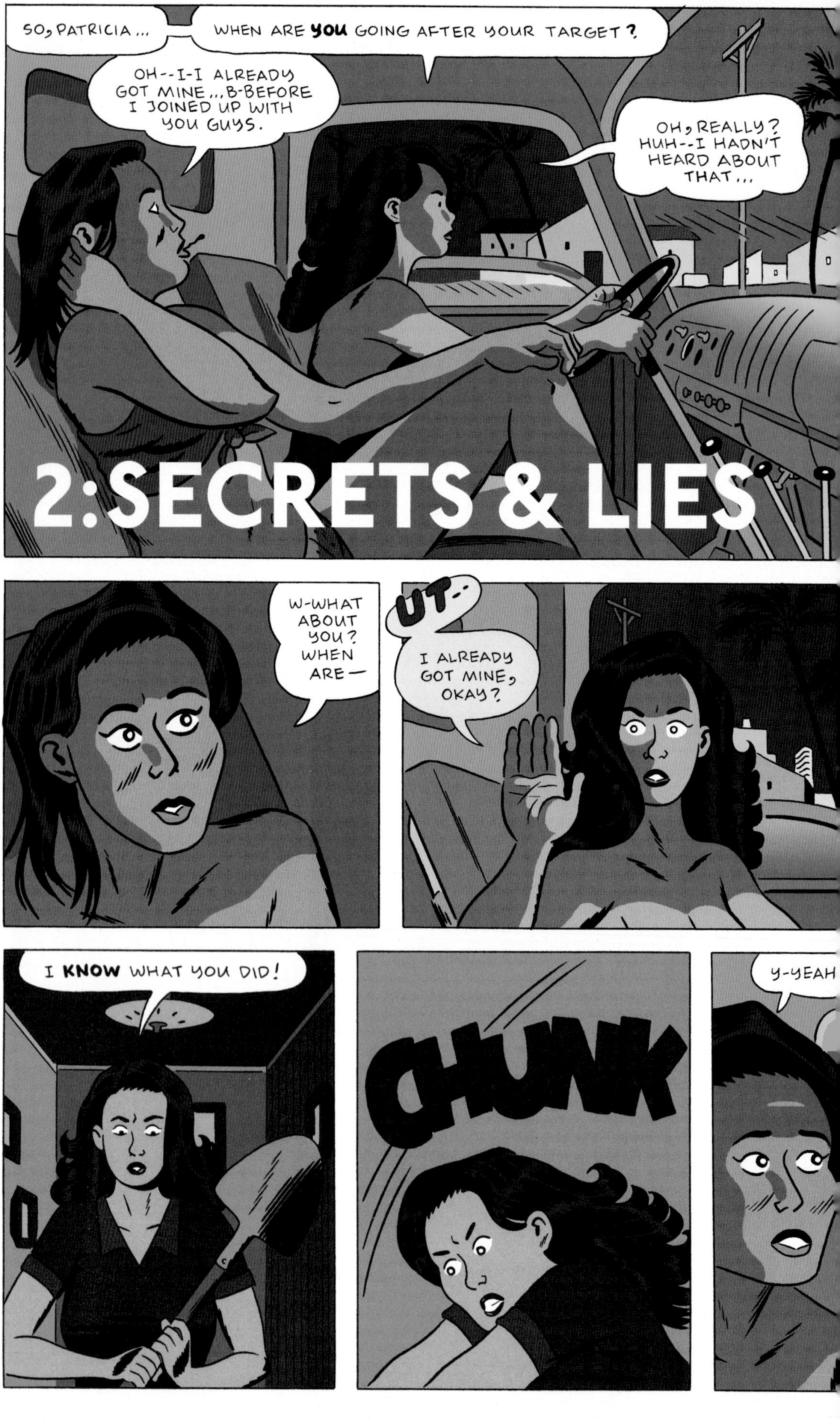

SO, PATRICIA...
WHEN ARE YOU GOING AFTER YOUR TARGET?
OH--I-I ALREADY GOT MINE... B-BEFORE I JOINED UP WITH YOU GUYS.
OH, REALLY? HUH--I HADN'T HEARD ABOUT THAT...
2:SECRETS & LIES
W-WHAT ABOUT YOU? WHEN ARE—
UT-
I ALREADY GOT MINE, OKAY?
I KNOW WHAT YOU DID!
CHUNK
Y-YEAH

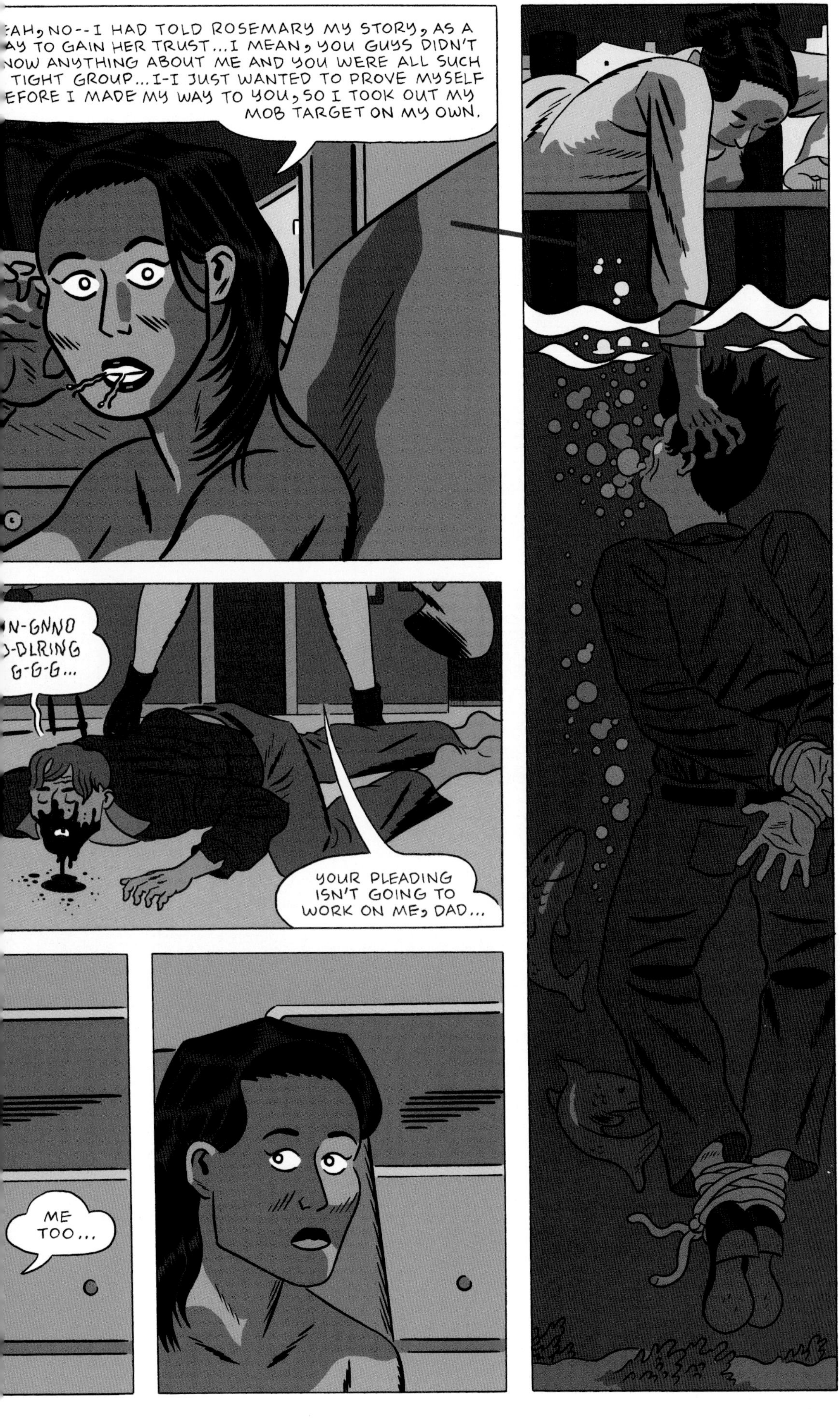
EAH, NO--I HAD TOLD ROSEMARY MY STORY, AS A
AY TO GAIN HER TRUST... I MEAN, YOU GUYS DIDN'T
NOW ANYTHING ABOUT ME AND YOU WERE ALL SUCH
TIGHT GROUP... I-I JUST WANTED TO PROVE MYSELF
EFORE I MADE MY WAY TO YOU, SO I TOOK OUT MY
MOB TARGET ON MY OWN.
N-GNNO
-DLRING
G-G-G...
YOUR PLEADING ISN'T GOING TO WORK ON ME, DAD...
ME TOO...

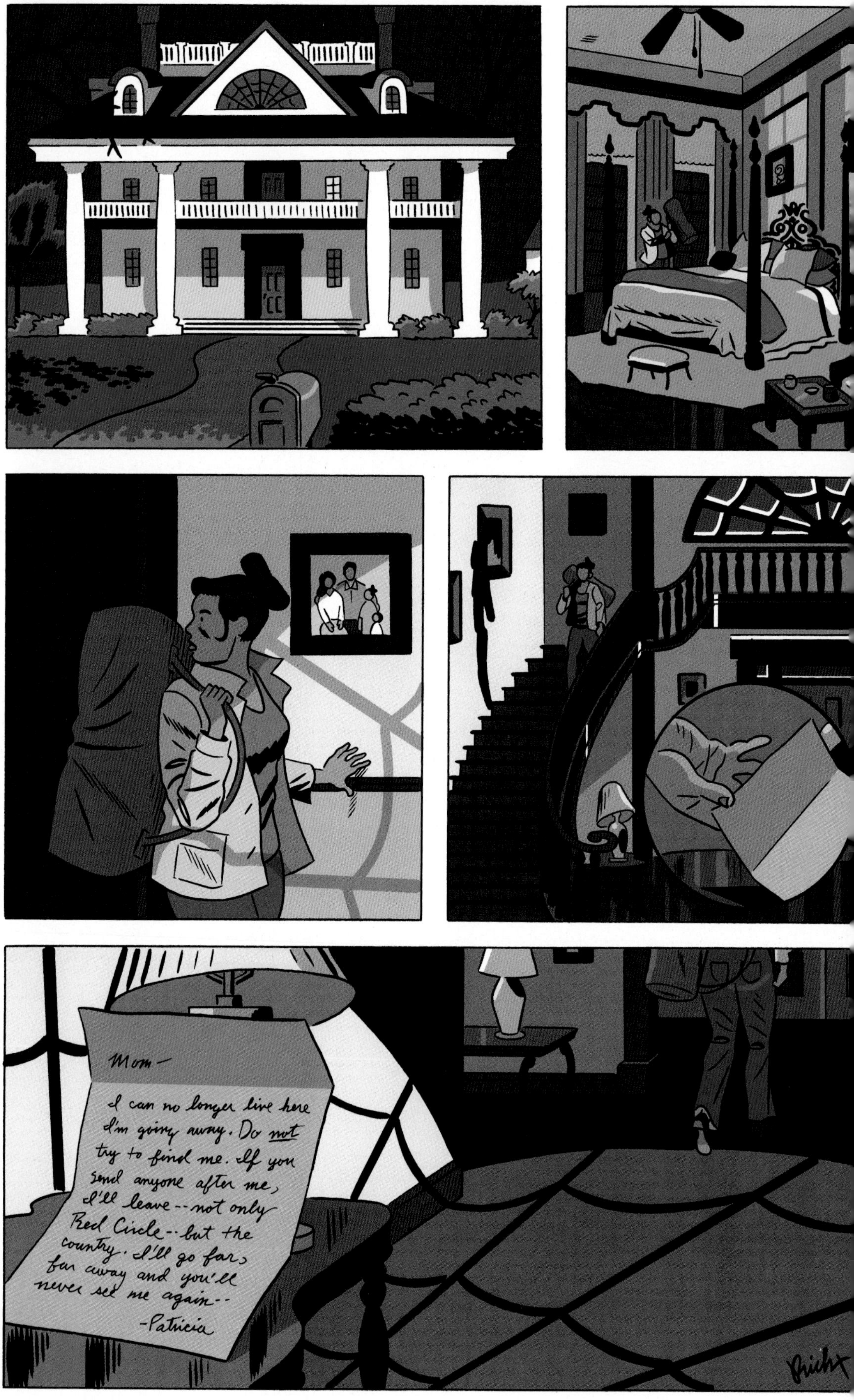
Mom—
I can no longer live here
I'm going away. Do not
try to find me. If you
send anyone after me,
I'll leave--not only
Red Circle--but the
country. I'll go far,
far away and you'll
never see me again--
-Patricia

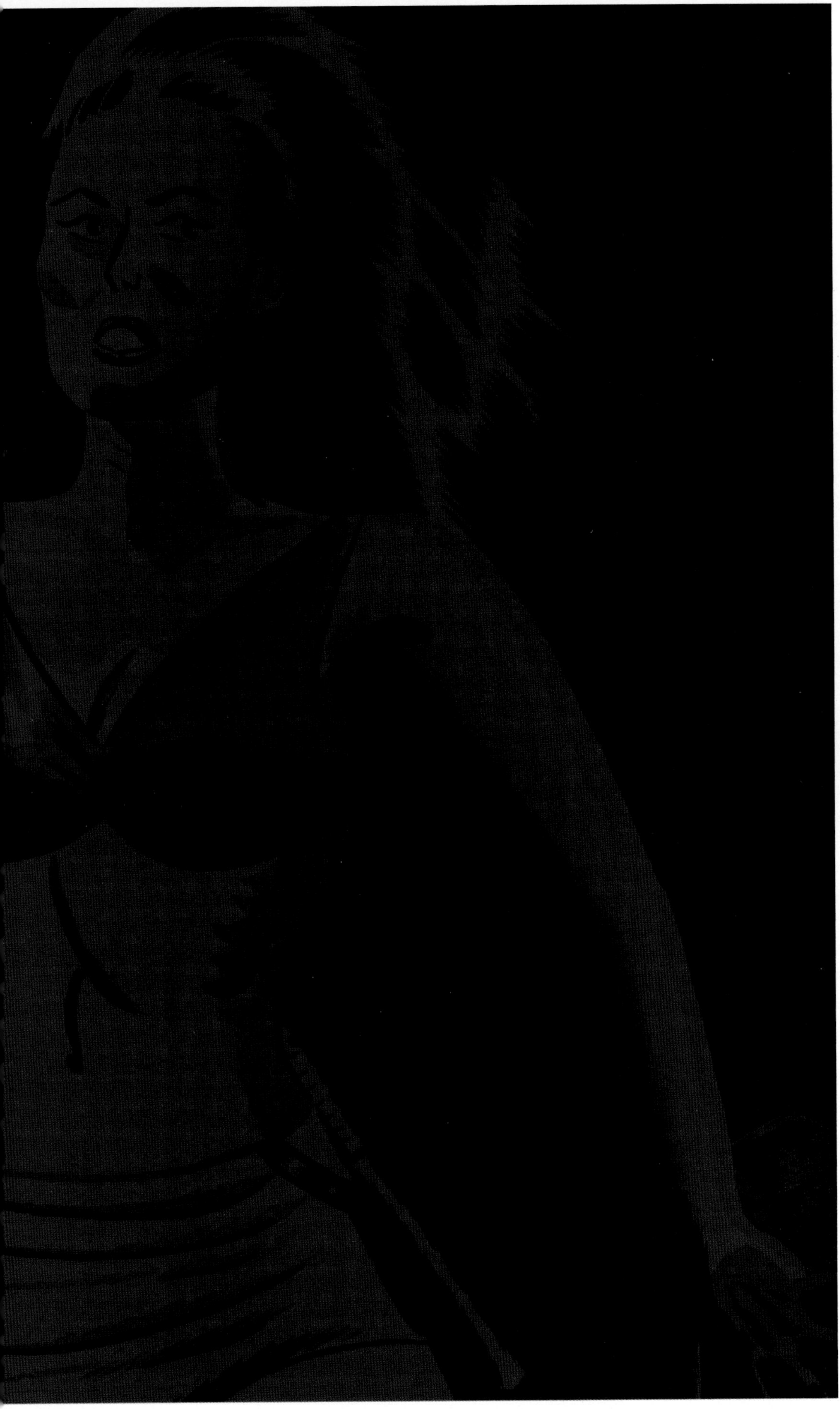

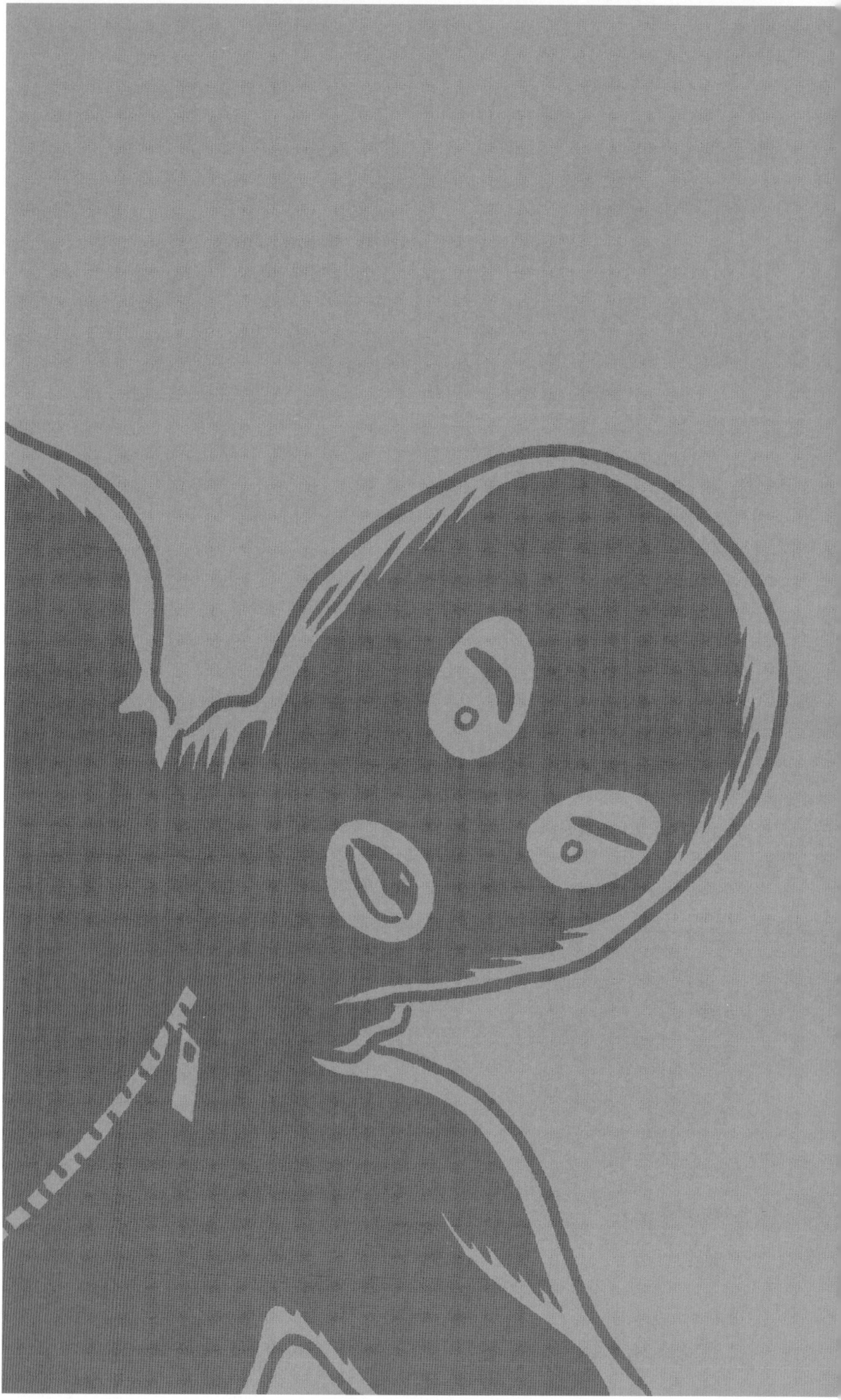

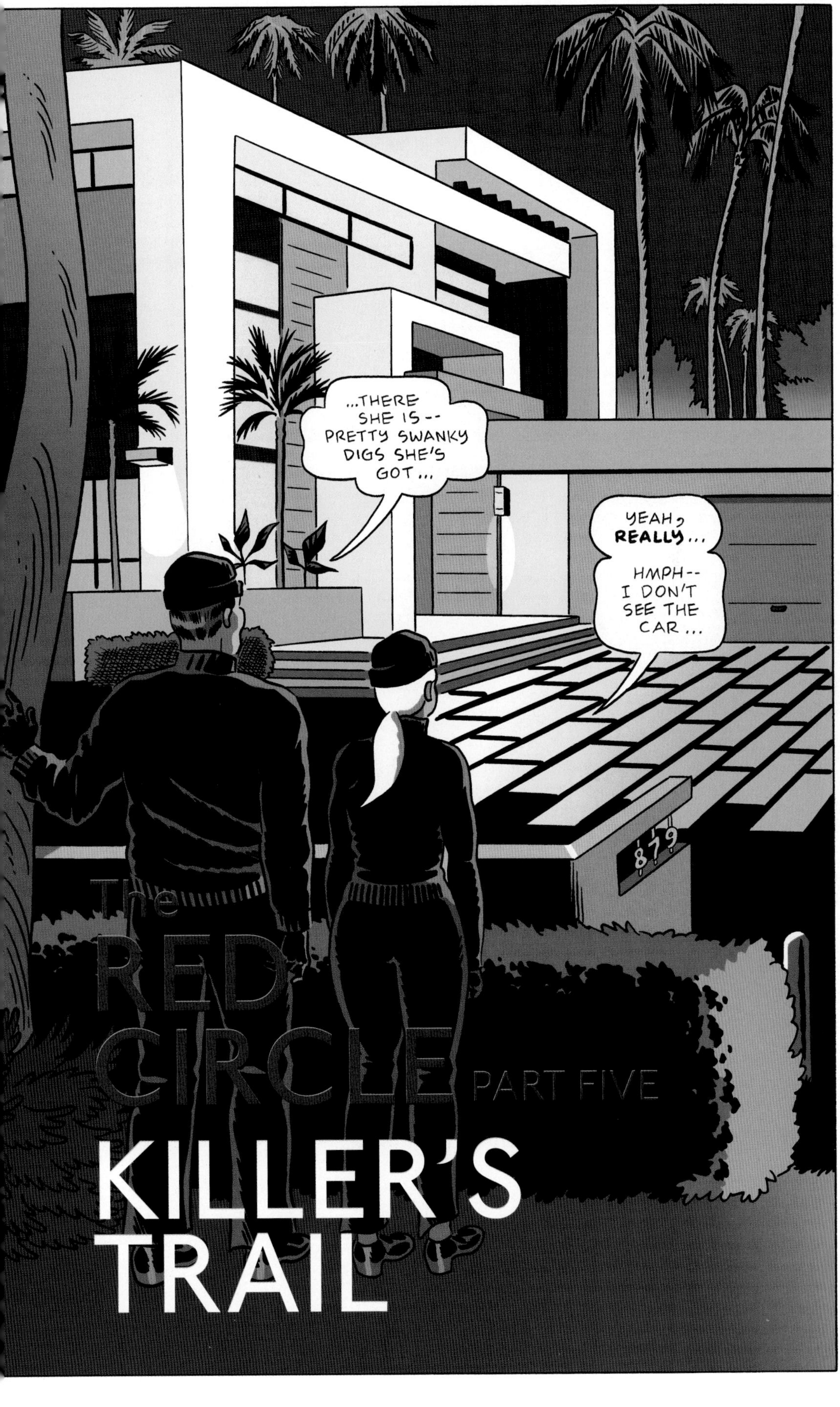

...THERE SHE IS -- PRETTY SWANKY DIGS SHE'S GOT...
YEAH, **REALLY**...
HMPH-- I DON'T SEE THE CAR...
879
The RED CIRCLE PART FIVE
KILLER'S TRAIL

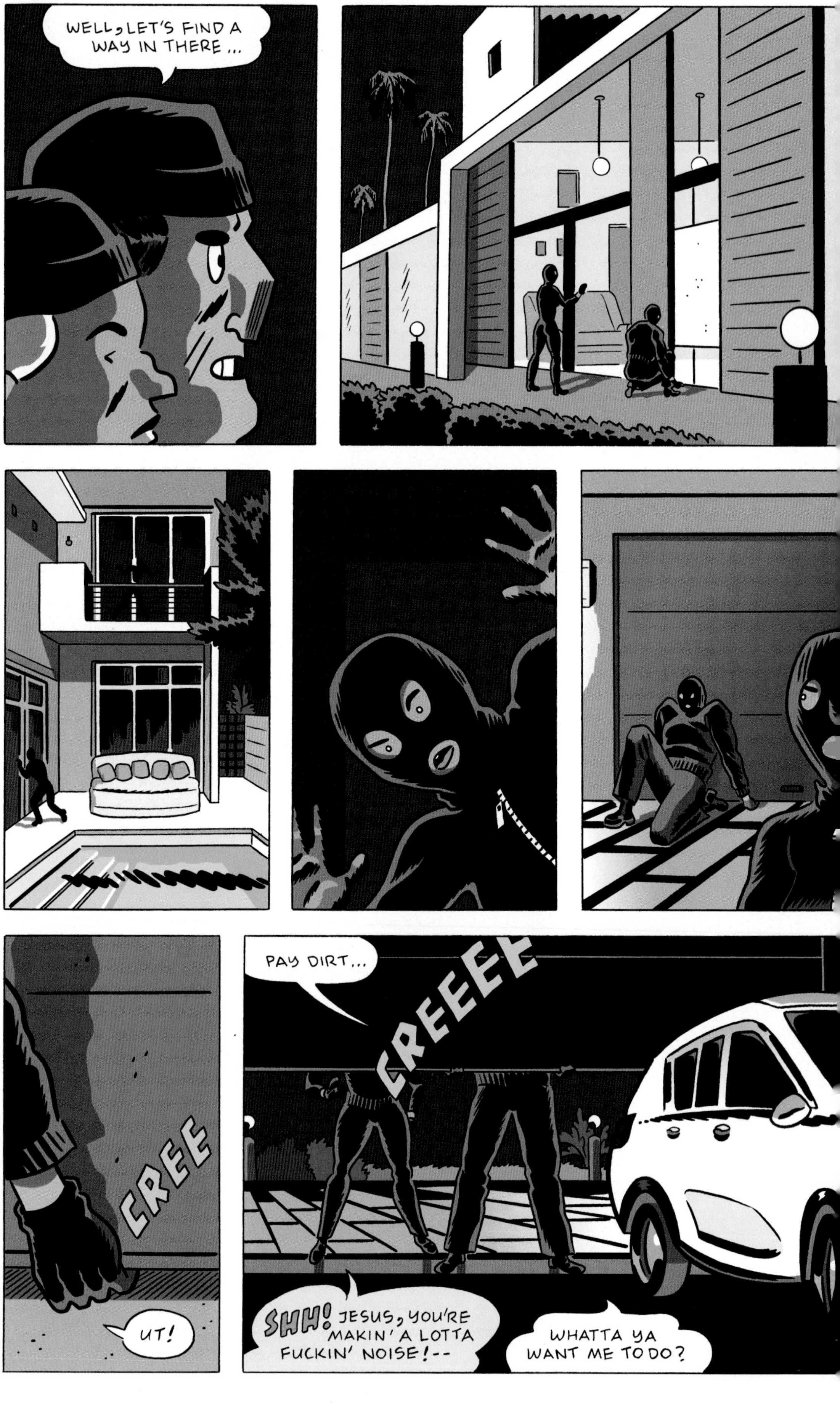
WELL, LET'S FIND A WAY IN THERE...
PAY DIRT...
CREEE
CREEEEE
UT!
SHH! JESUS, YOU'RE MAKIN' A LOTTA FUCKIN' NOISE!--
WHATTA YA WANT ME TO DO?

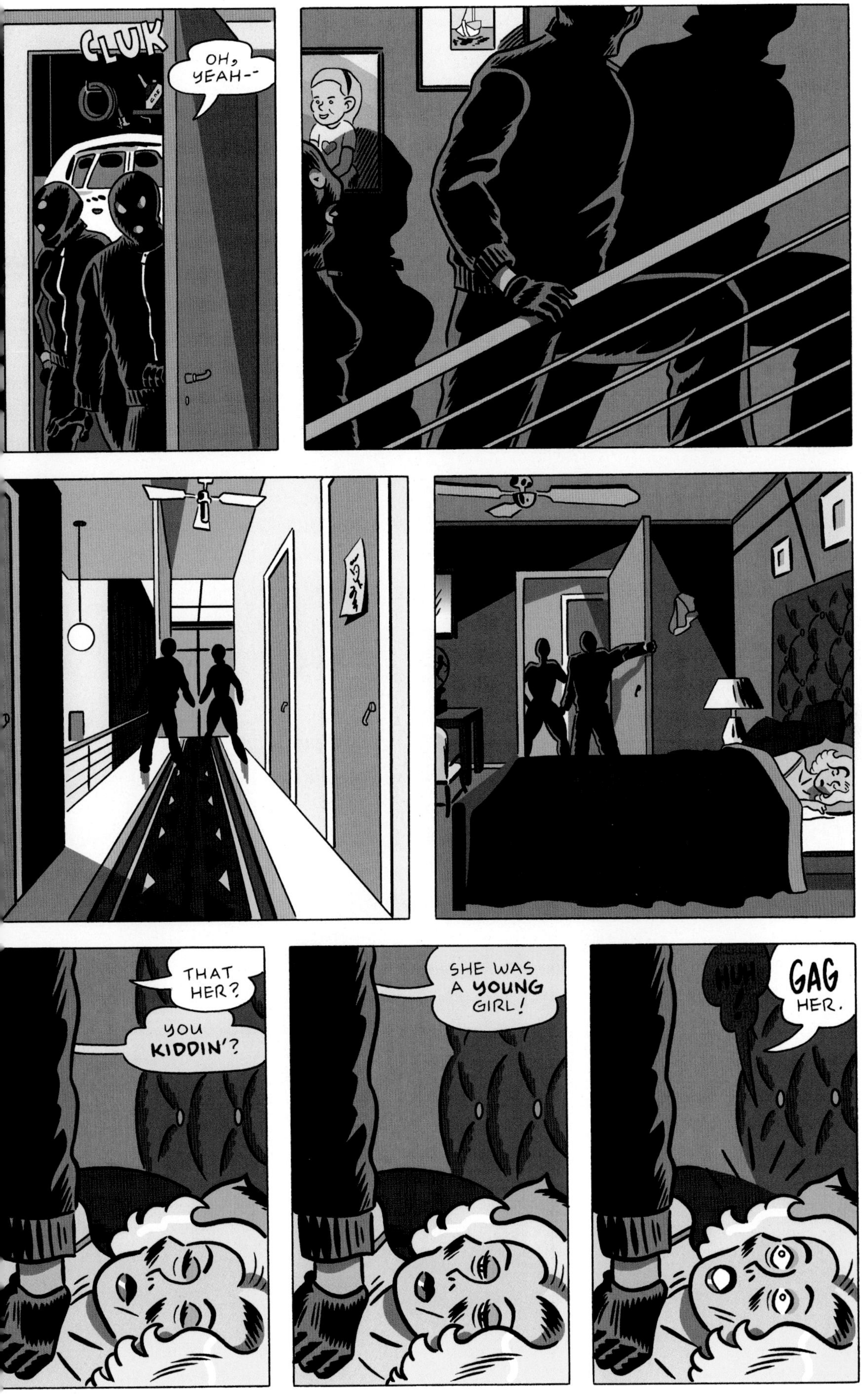
CLUK
OH, YEAH--
THAT HER?
YOU KIDDIN'?
SHE WAS A YOUNG GIRL!
HUH
GAG HER.

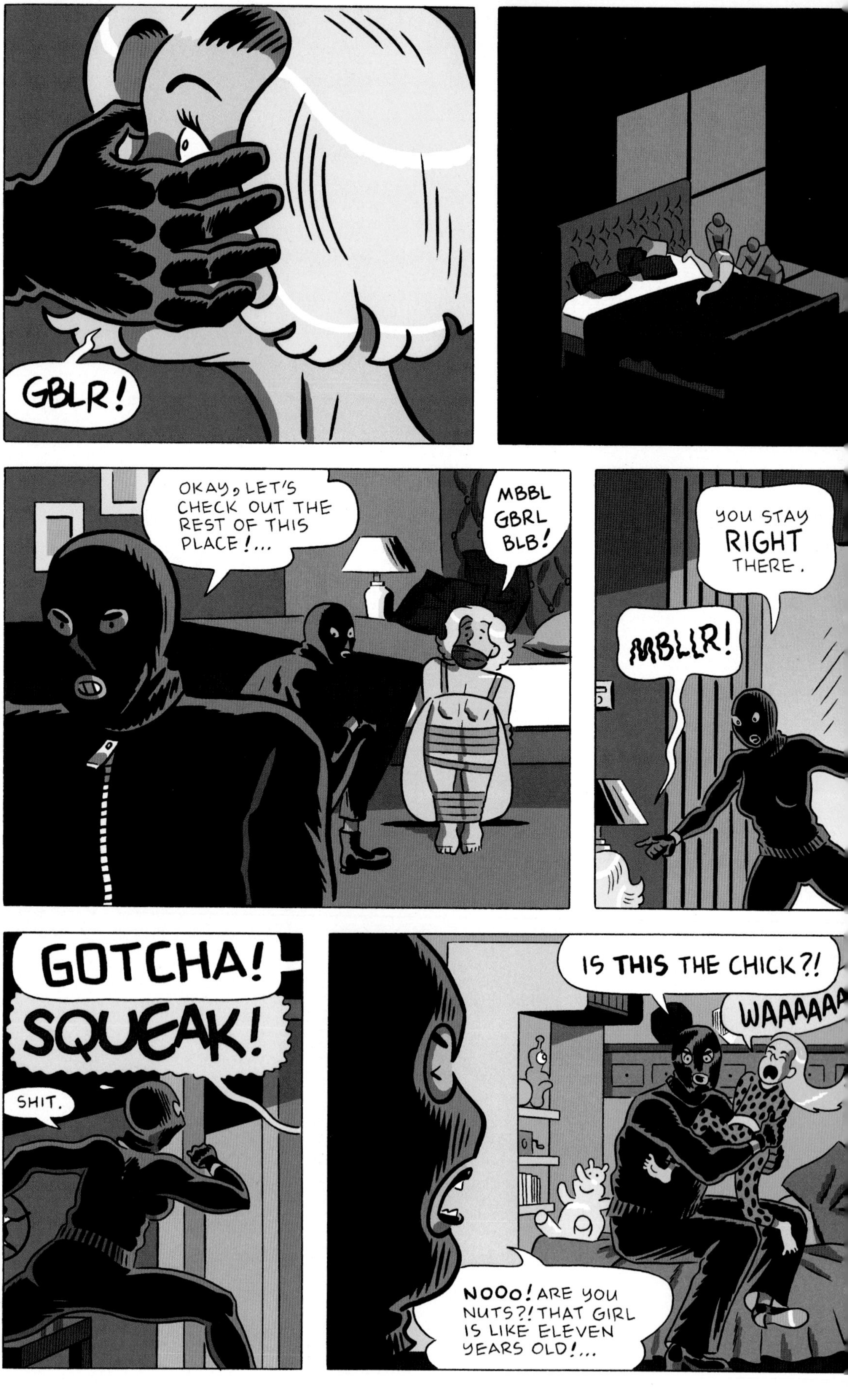
GBLR!
OKAY, LET'S CHECK OUT THE REST OF THIS PLACE!...
MBBL GBRL BLB!
YOU STAY RIGHT THERE.
MBLLR!
GOTCHA!
SQUEAK!
SHIT.
IS THIS THE CHICK?!
WAAAAAA
NOOO! ARE YOU NUTS?! THAT GIRL IS LIKE ELEVEN YEARS OLD!...

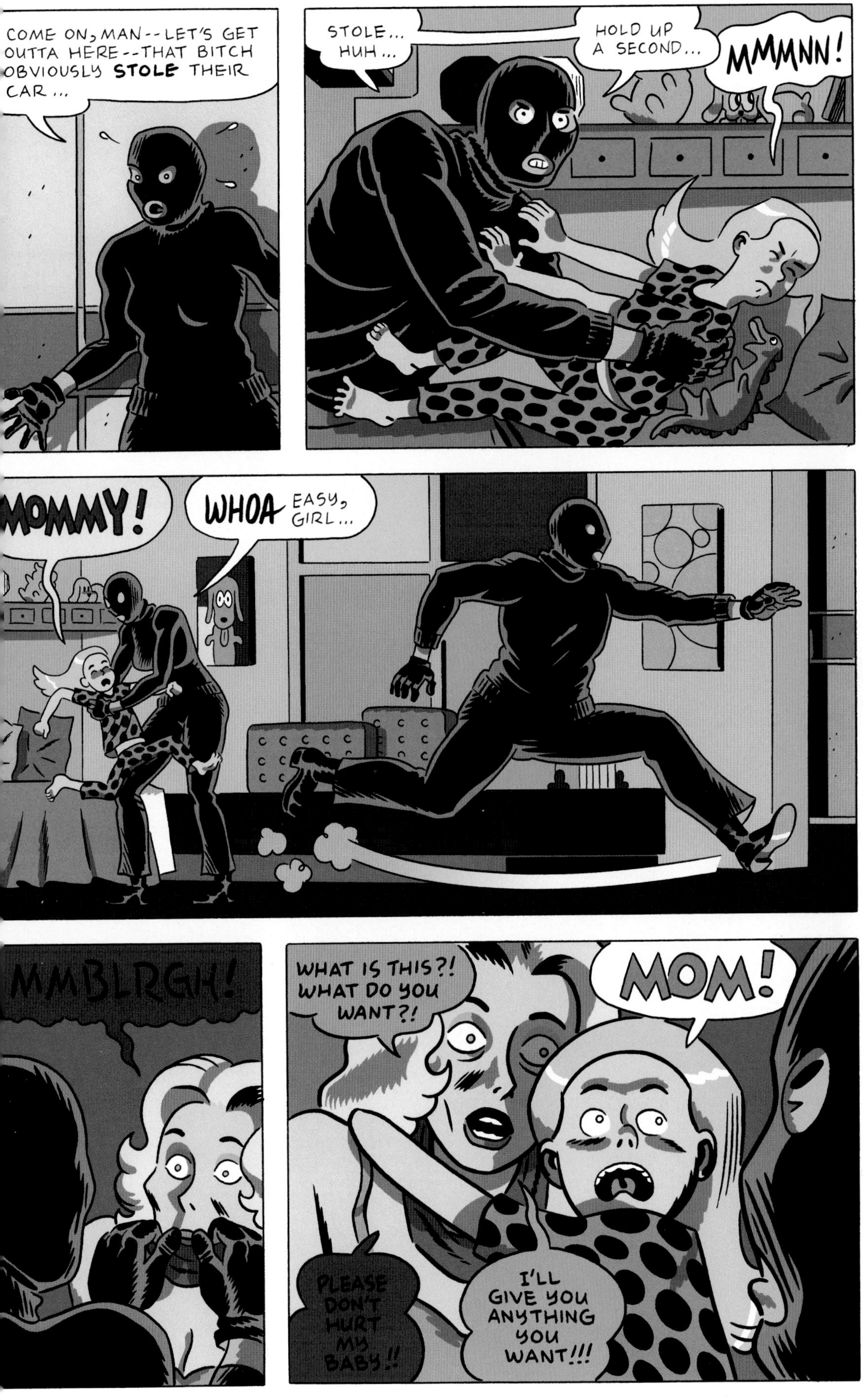
COME ON, MAN--LET'S GET OUTTA HERE--THAT BITCH OBVIOUSLY STOLE THEIR CAR...
STOLE... HUH...
HOLD UP A SECOND...
MMMNN!
MOMMY!
WHOA EASY, GIRL...
MMBLRGH!
WHAT IS THIS?! WHAT DO YOU WANT?!
MOM!
PLEASE DON'T HURT MY BABY!!
I'LL GIVE YOU ANYTHING YOU WANT!!!

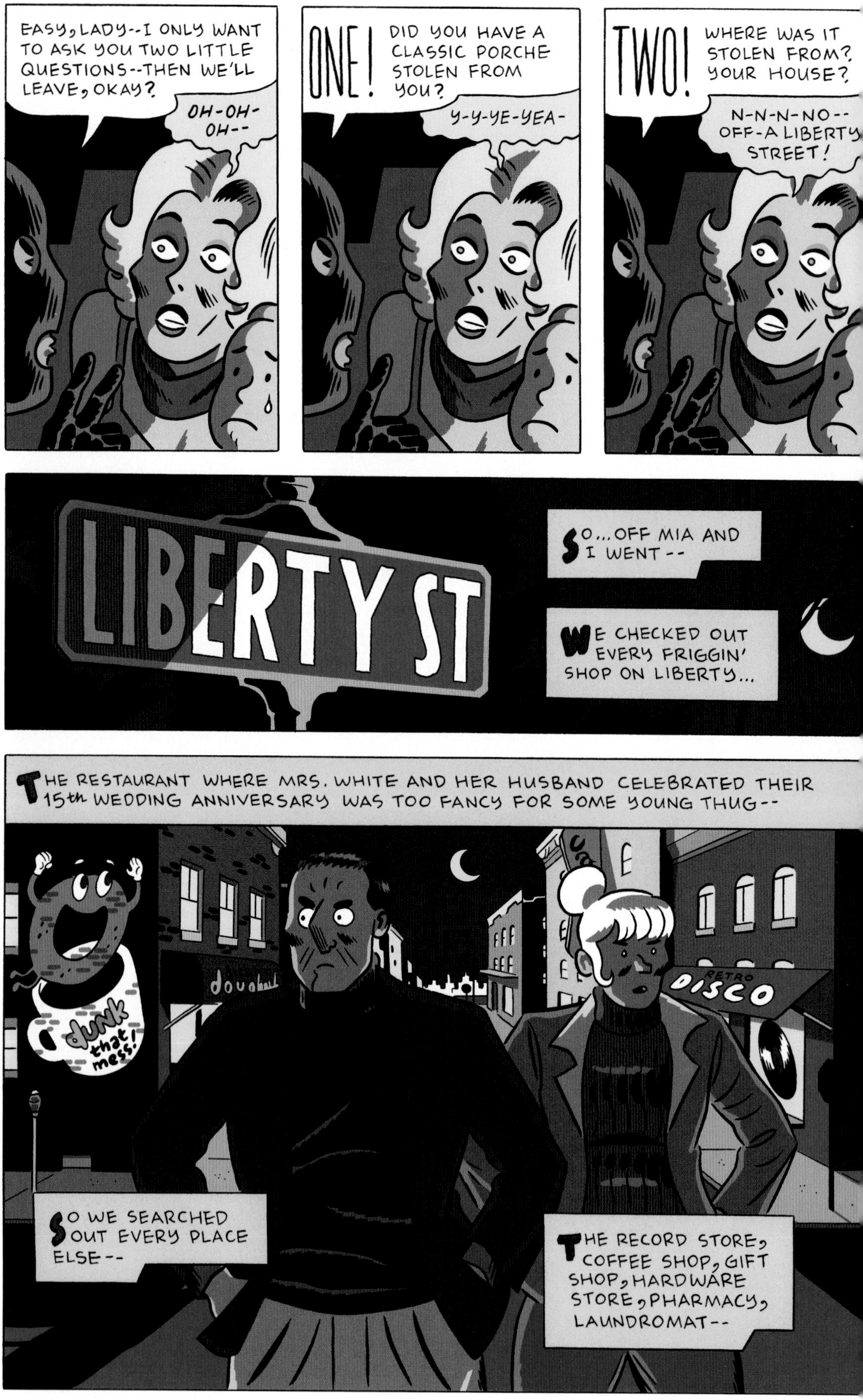

EASY, LADY--I ONLY WANT TO ASK YOU TWO LITTLE QUESTIONS--THEN WE'LL LEAVE, OKAY?
OH-OH-OH--
ONE!
DID YOU HAVE A CLASSIC PORCHE STOLEN FROM YOU?
Y-Y-YE-YEA-
TWO!
WHERE WAS IT STOLEN FROM? YOUR HOUSE?
N-N-N-NO--OFF-A LIBERTY STREET!
LIBERTY ST
SO...OFF MIA AND I WENT--
WE CHECKED OUT EVERY FRIGGIN' SHOP ON LIBERTY...
THE RESTAURANT WHERE MRS. WHITE AND HER HUSBAND CELEBRATED THEIR 15th WEDDING ANNIVERSARY WAS TOO FANCY FOR SOME YOUNG THUG--
dunk that mess!
RETRO DISCO
SO WE SEARCHED OUT EVERY PLACE ELSE--
THE RECORD STORE, COFFEE SHOP, GIFT SHOP, HARDWARE STORE, PHARMACY, LAUNDROMAT--

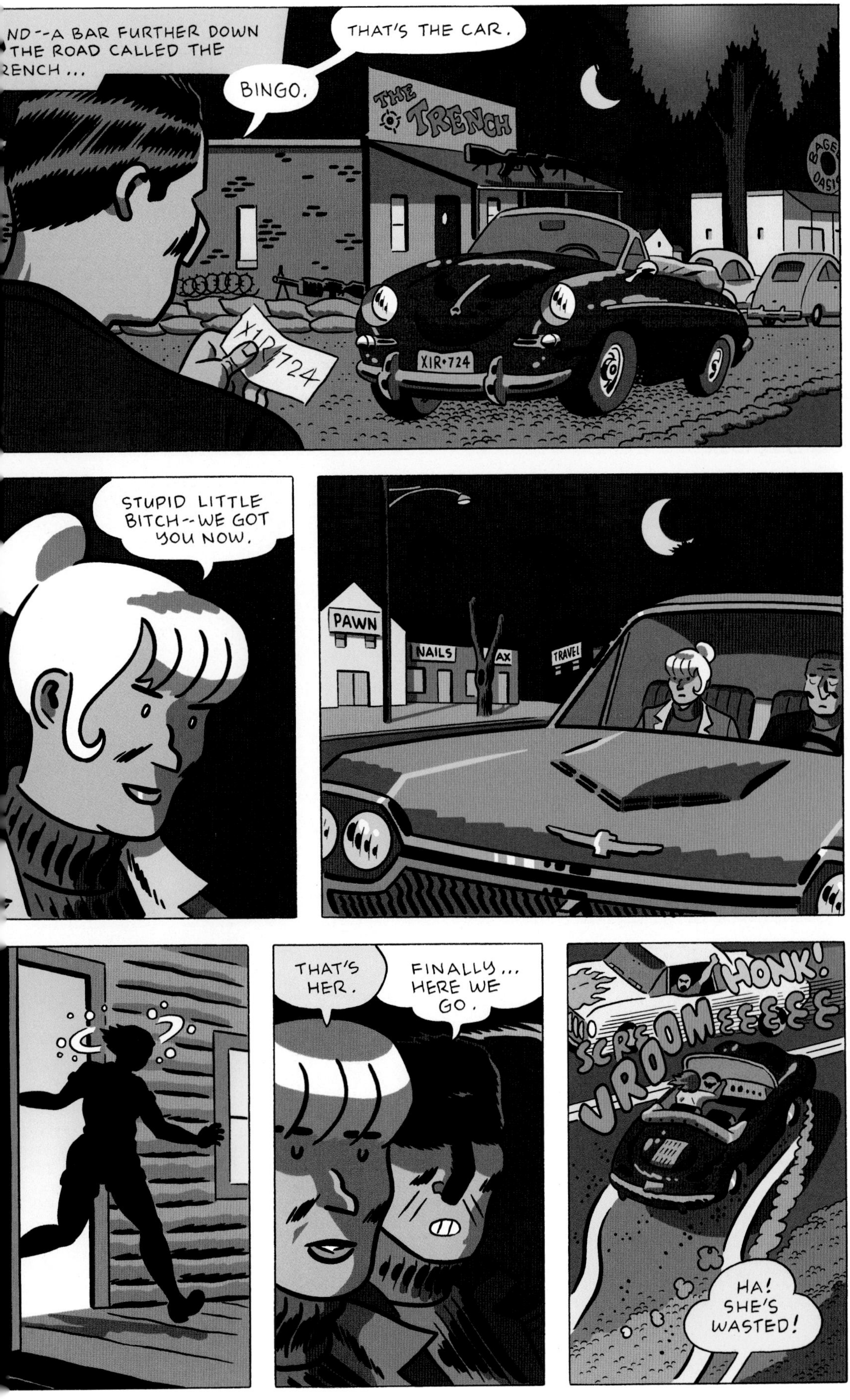
ND--A BAR FURTHER DOWN THE ROAD CALLED THE RENCH...
THAT'S THE CAR.
BINGO.
THE TRENCH
BAGEL OASIS
XIR 724
XIR•724
STUPID LITTLE BITCH--WE GOT YOU NOW.
PAWN
NAILS
AX
TRAVEL
THAT'S HER.
FINALLY... HERE WE GO.
HONK!
SCREE
VROOMEEEEE
HA! SHE'S WASTED!

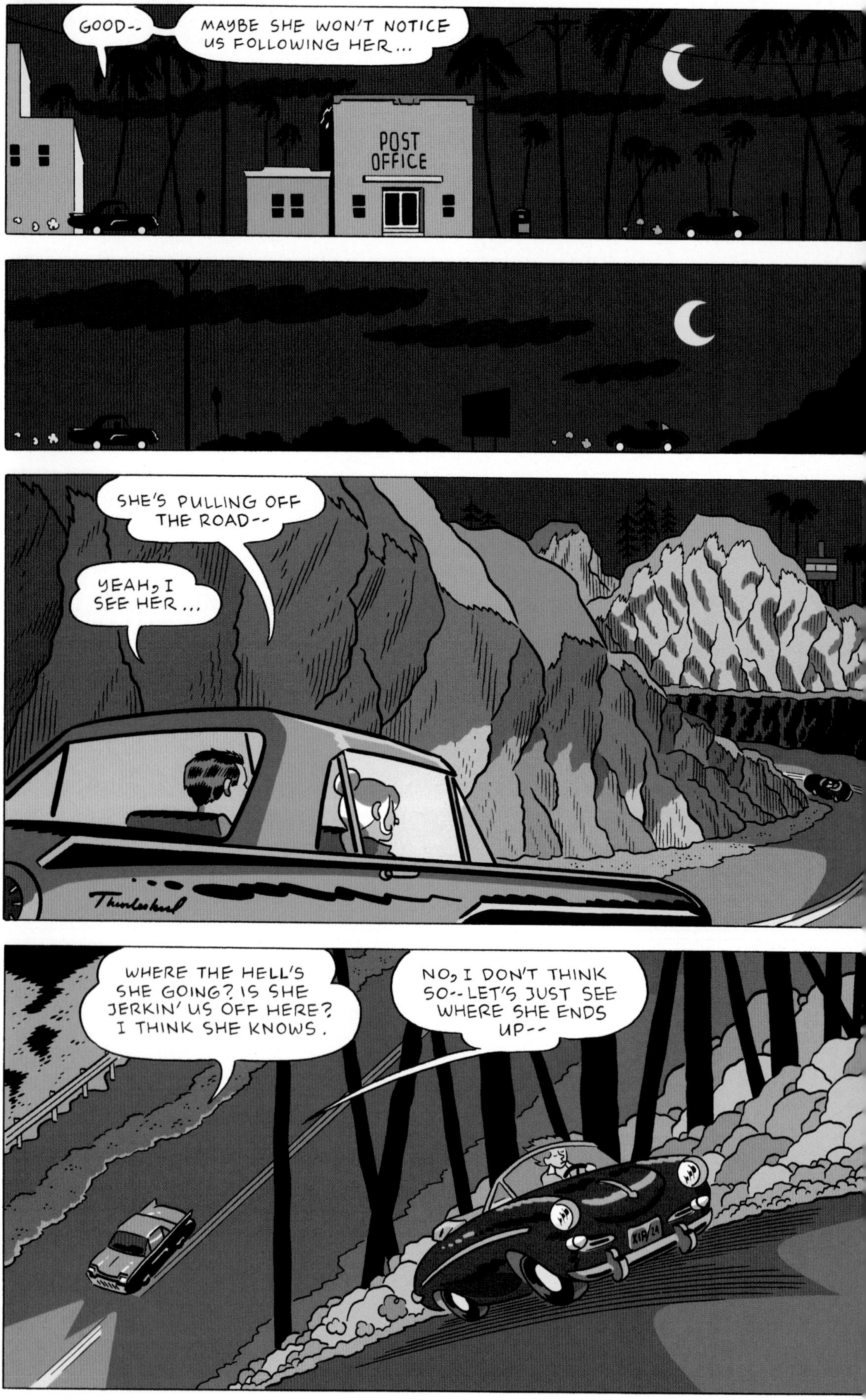
GOOD--
MAYBE SHE WON'T NOTICE US FOLLOWING HER...
POST OFFICE
SHE'S PULLING OFF THE ROAD--
YEAH, I SEE HER...
Thunderbird
WHERE THE HELL'S SHE GOING? IS SHE JERKIN' US OFF HERE? I THINK SHE KNOWS.
NO, I DON'T THINK SO--LET'S JUST SEE WHERE SHE ENDS UP--

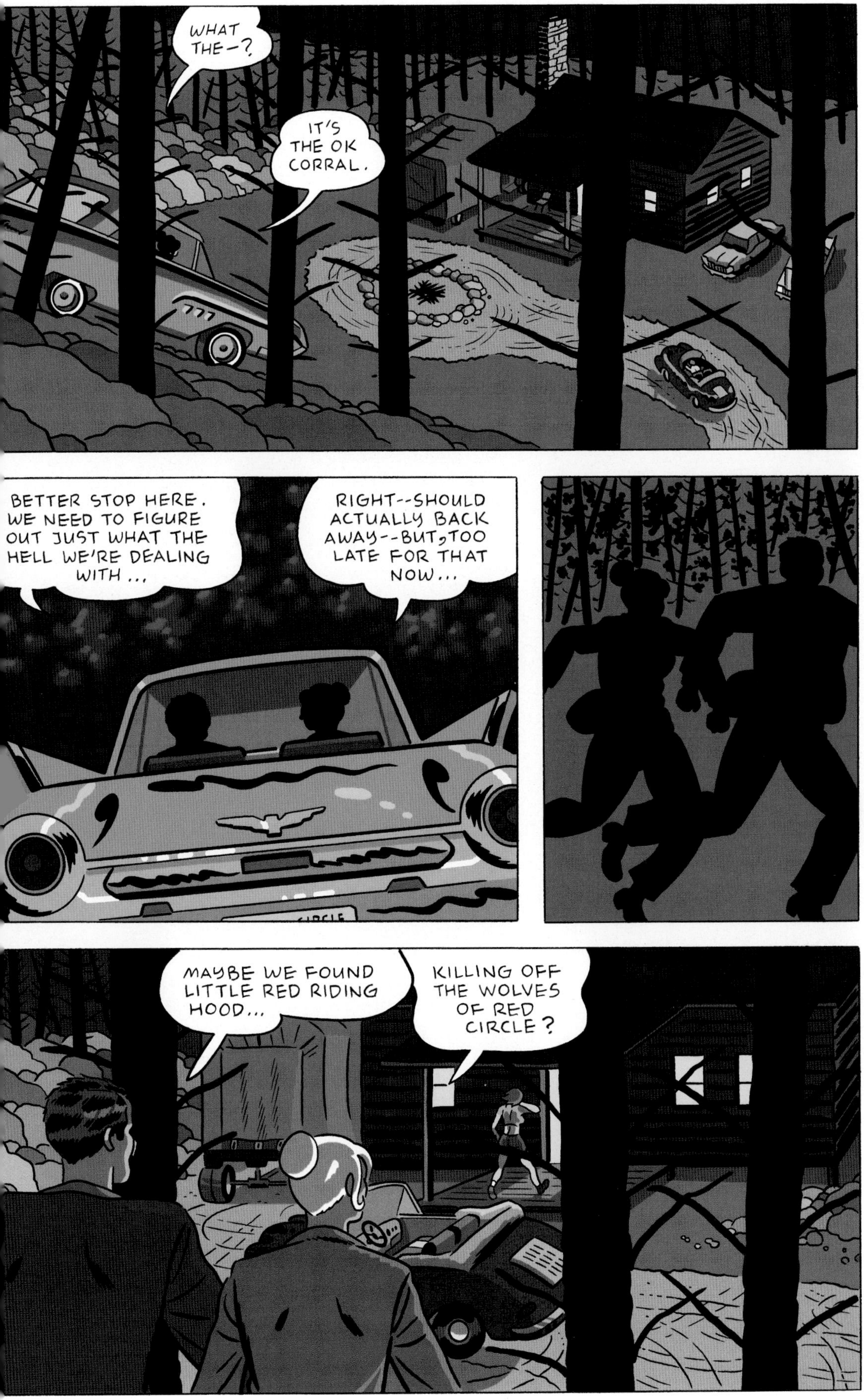
WHAT THE–?
IT'S THE OK CORRAL.
BETTER STOP HERE. WE NEED TO FIGURE OUT JUST WHAT THE HELL WE'RE DEALING WITH...
RIGHT--SHOULD ACTUALLY BACK AWAY--BUT, TOO LATE FOR THAT NOW...
MAYBE WE FOUND LITTLE RED RIDING HOOD...
KILLING OFF THE WOLVES OF RED CIRCLE?

WHAT'RE YOU DOING HERE, DANIELLE?

'EY, DON'T YELL AT **ME**-- GUY NEVER SHOWED UP!

HE NEVER **SHOWED**?! DID YOU **CALL** HIM?

'BOUT SIX TIMES!

THIS IS NOT GOOD.

GREAT...

NO SHIT, CONNIE.

FUCK OFF.

WHERE'S CRIZZLE?! WE'VE GOT **TONS** OF STOLEN DRUGS ON OUR HANDS AND NOW WE LOSE OUR ONLY CONNECTION?

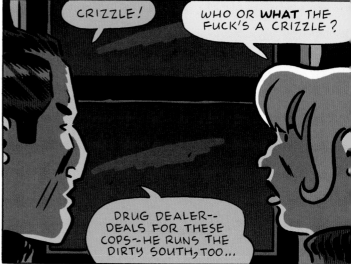

CRIZZLE!

WHO OR **WHAT** THE FUCK'S A CRIZZLE?

DRUG DEALER-- DEALS FOR THESE COPS--HE RUNS THE DIRTY SOUTH, TOO...

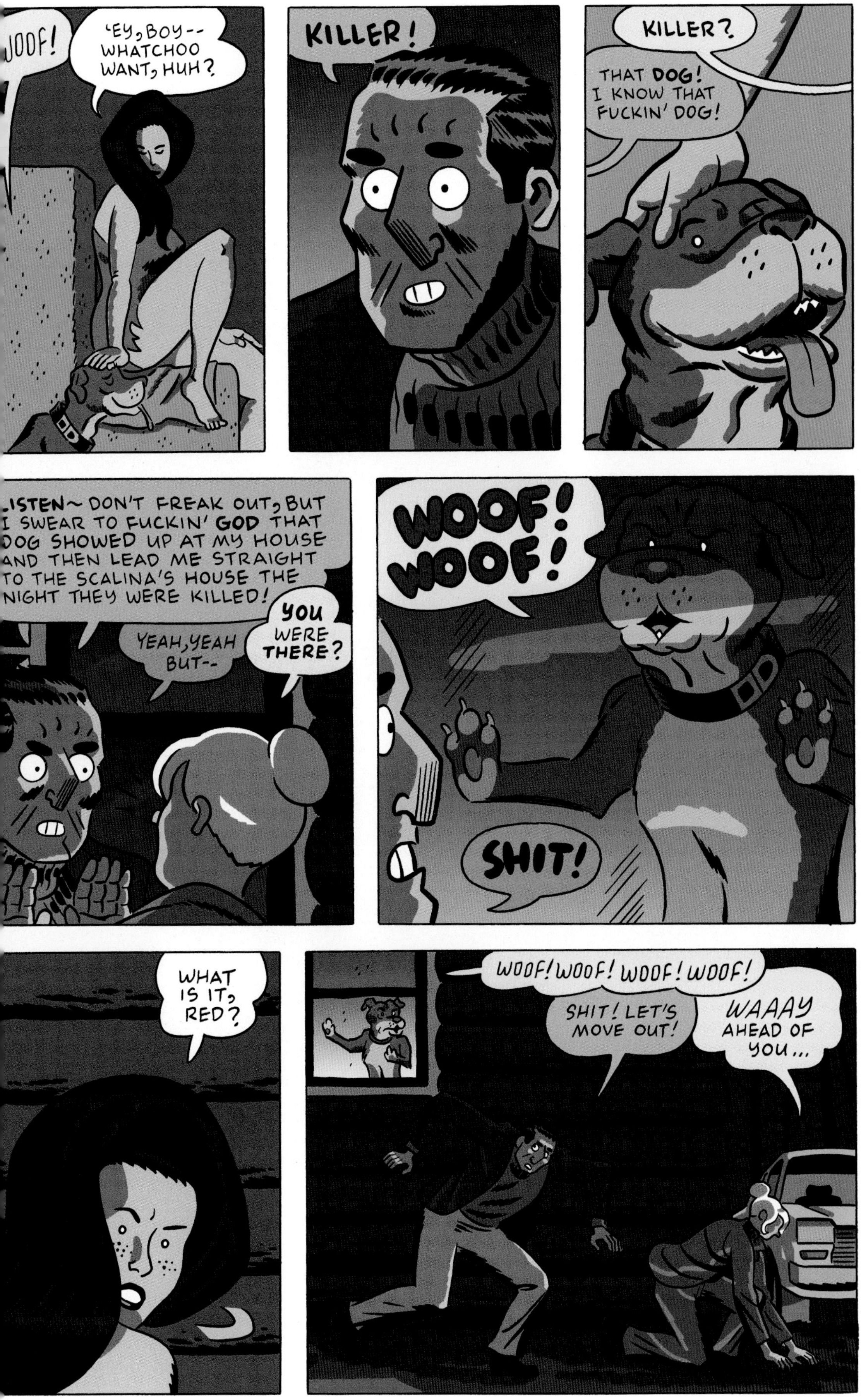

WOOF!
'EY, BOY-- WHATCHOO WANT, HUH?
KILLER!
KILLER?
THAT DOG! I KNOW THAT FUCKIN' DOG!
LISTEN~ DON'T FREAK OUT, BUT I SWEAR TO FUCKIN' GOD THAT DOG SHOWED UP AT MY HOUSE AND THEN LEAD ME STRAIGHT TO THE SCALINA'S HOUSE THE NIGHT THEY WERE KILLED!
YEAH, YEAH BUT--
YOU WERE THERE?
WOOF! WOOF!
SHIT!
WHAT IS IT, RED?
WOOF! WOOF! WOOF! WOOF!
SHIT! LET'S MOVE OUT!
WAAAY AHEAD OF YOU...

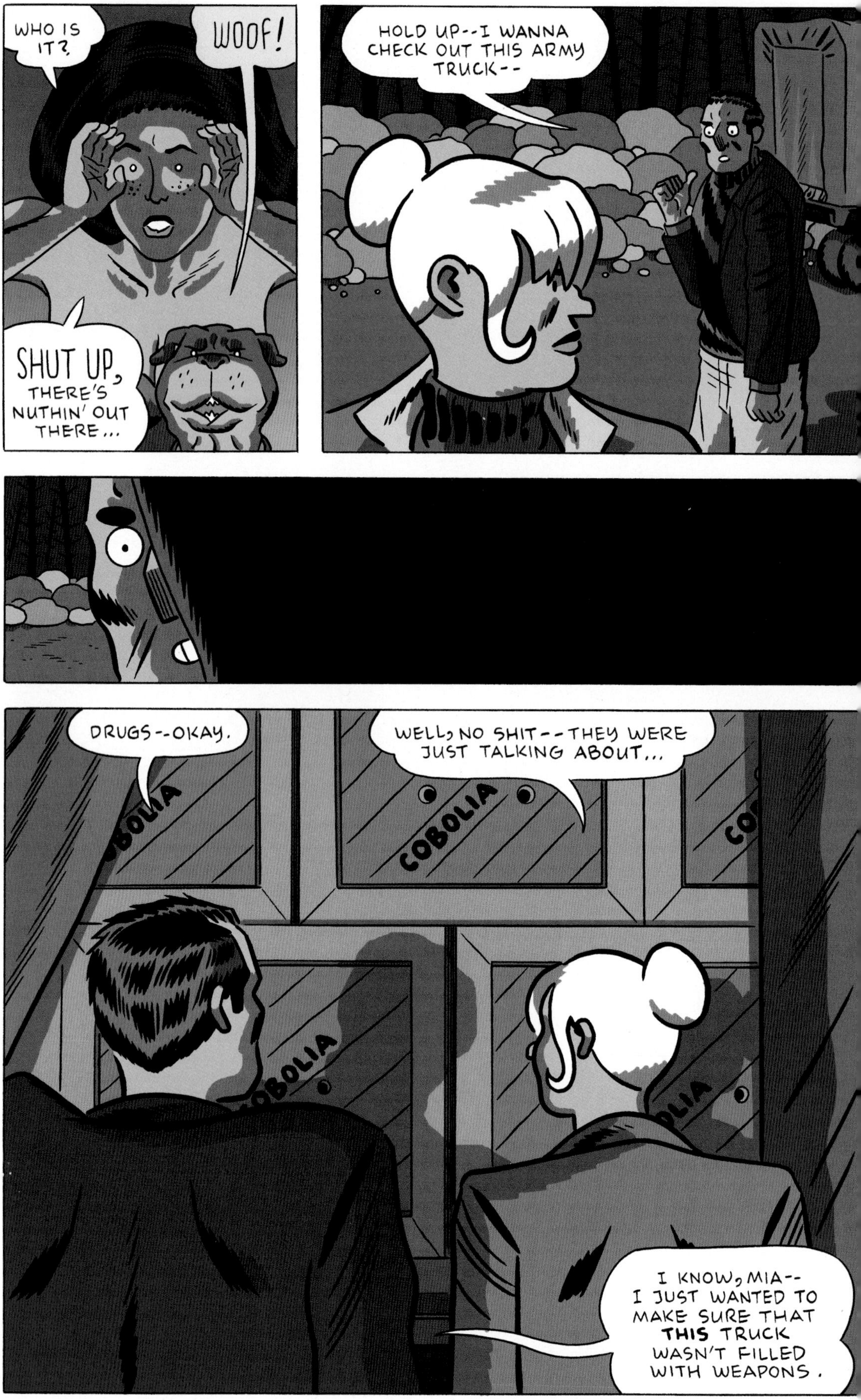
WHO IS IT?
WOOF!
SHUT UP, THERE'S NUTHIN' OUT THERE...
HOLD UP--I WANNA CHECK OUT THIS ARMY TRUCK--
DRUGS--OKAY.
WELL, NO SHIT--THEY WERE JUST TALKING ABOUT...
COBOLIA
I KNOW, MIA--I JUST WANTED TO MAKE SURE THAT THIS TRUCK WASN'T FILLED WITH WEAPONS.

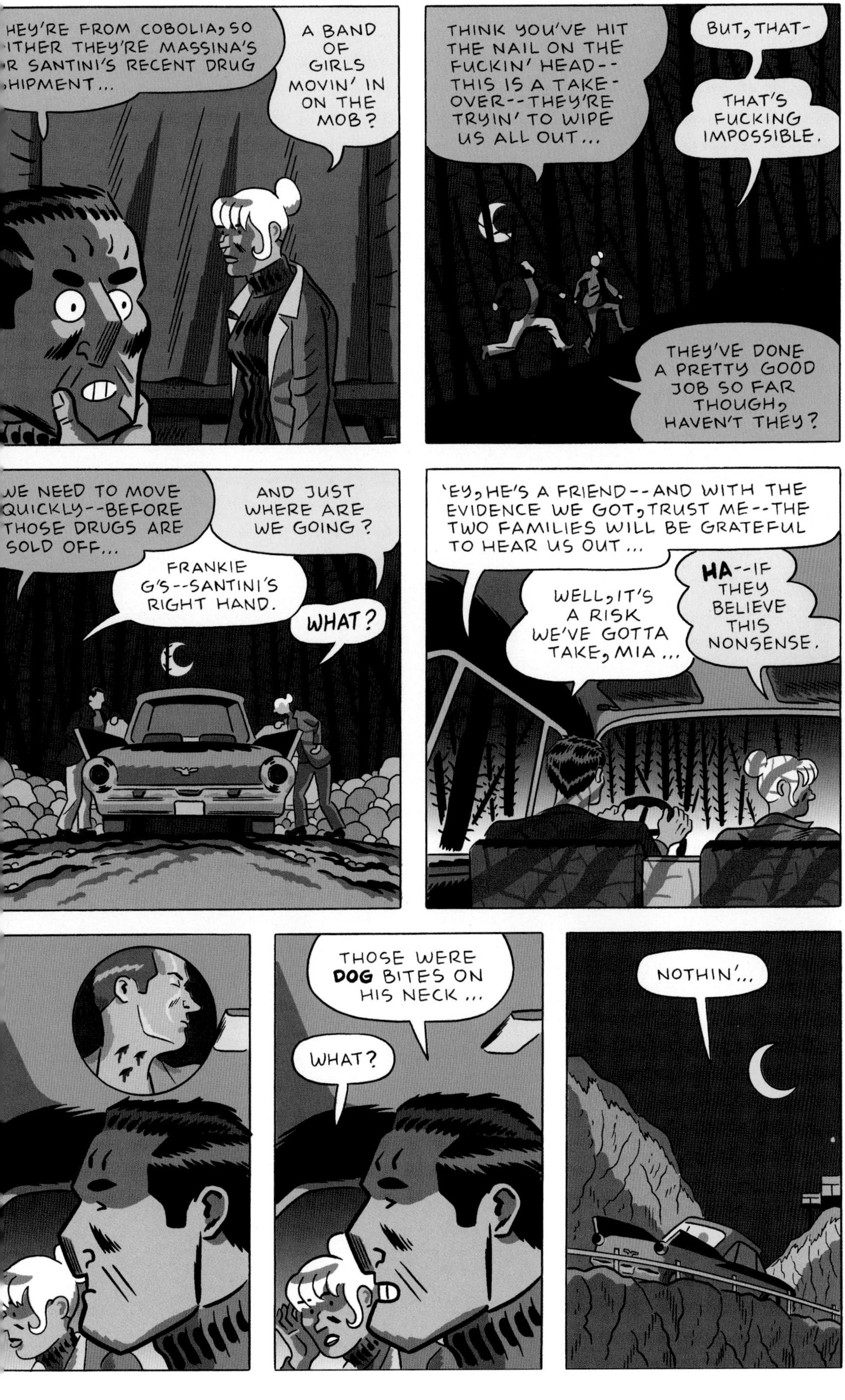

HEY'RE FROM COBOLIA, SO ITHER THEY'RE MASSINA'S R SANTINI'S RECENT DRUG HIPMENT...
A BAND OF GIRLS MOVIN' IN ON THE MOB?
THINK YOU'VE HIT THE NAIL ON THE FUCKIN' HEAD-- THIS IS A TAKE-OVER--THEY'RE TRYIN' TO WIPE US ALL OUT...
BUT, THAT-
THAT'S FUCKING IMPOSSIBLE.
THEY'VE DONE A PRETTY GOOD JOB SO FAR THOUGH, HAVEN'T THEY?
WE NEED TO MOVE QUICKLY--BEFORE THOSE DRUGS ARE SOLD OFF...
AND JUST WHERE ARE WE GOING?
FRANKIE G'S--SANTINI'S RIGHT HAND.
WHAT?
'EY, HE'S A FRIEND--AND WITH THE EVIDENCE WE GOT, TRUST ME--THE TWO FAMILIES WILL BE GRATEFUL TO HEAR US OUT...
WELL, IT'S A RISK WE'VE GOTTA TAKE, MIA...
HA--IF THEY BELIEVE THIS NONSENSE.
THOSE WERE DOG BITES ON HIS NECK...
WHAT?
NOTHIN'...

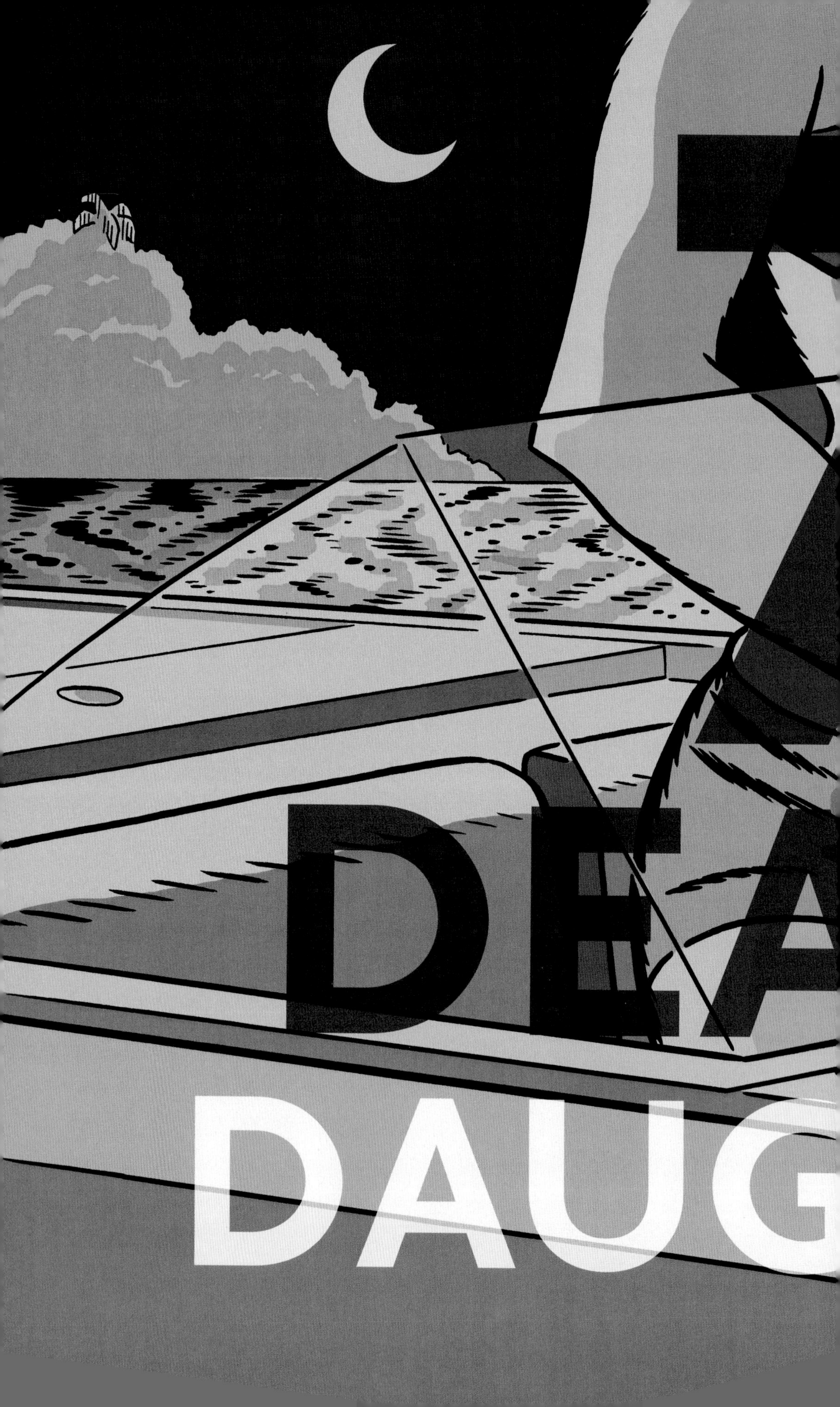
DEA
DAUG

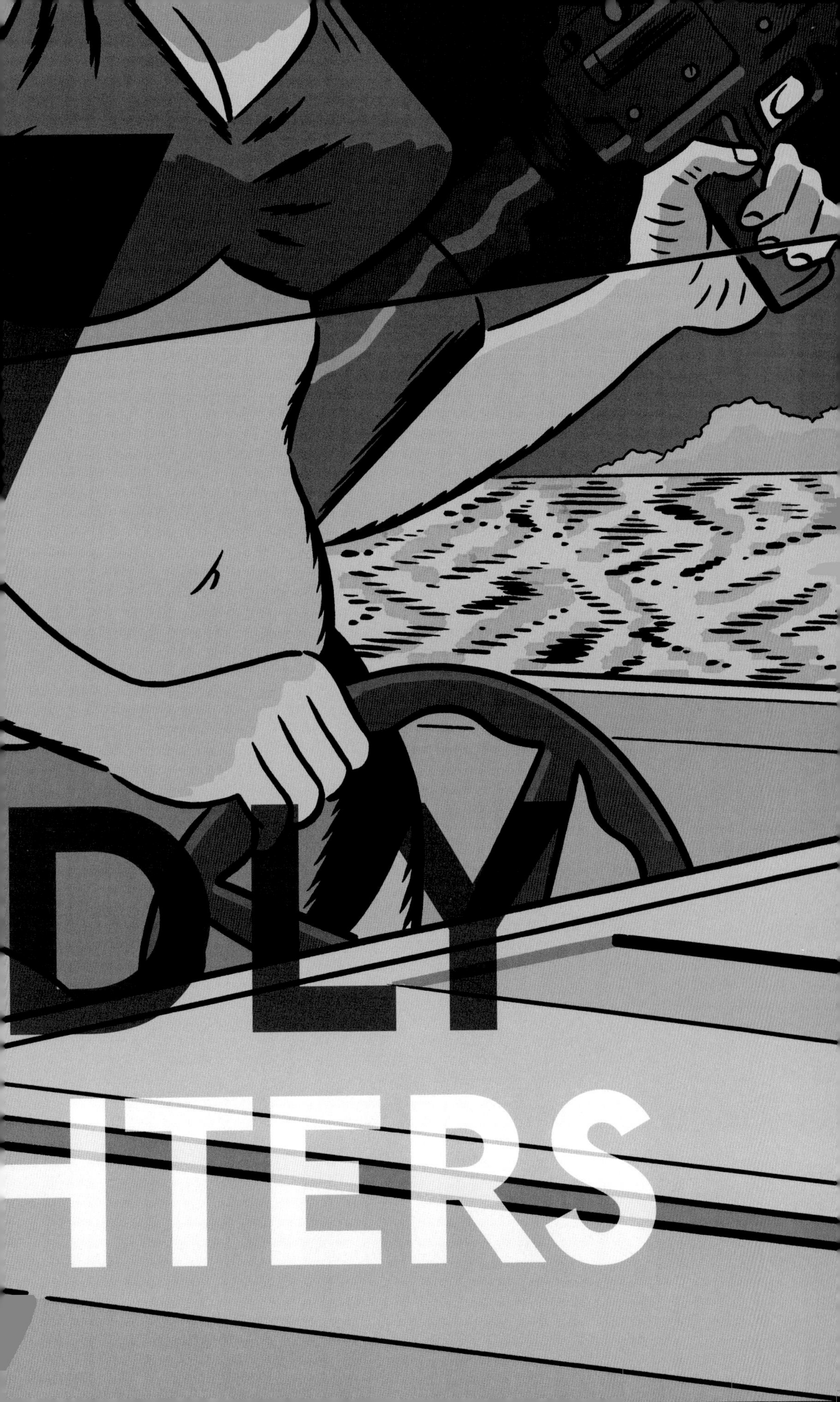

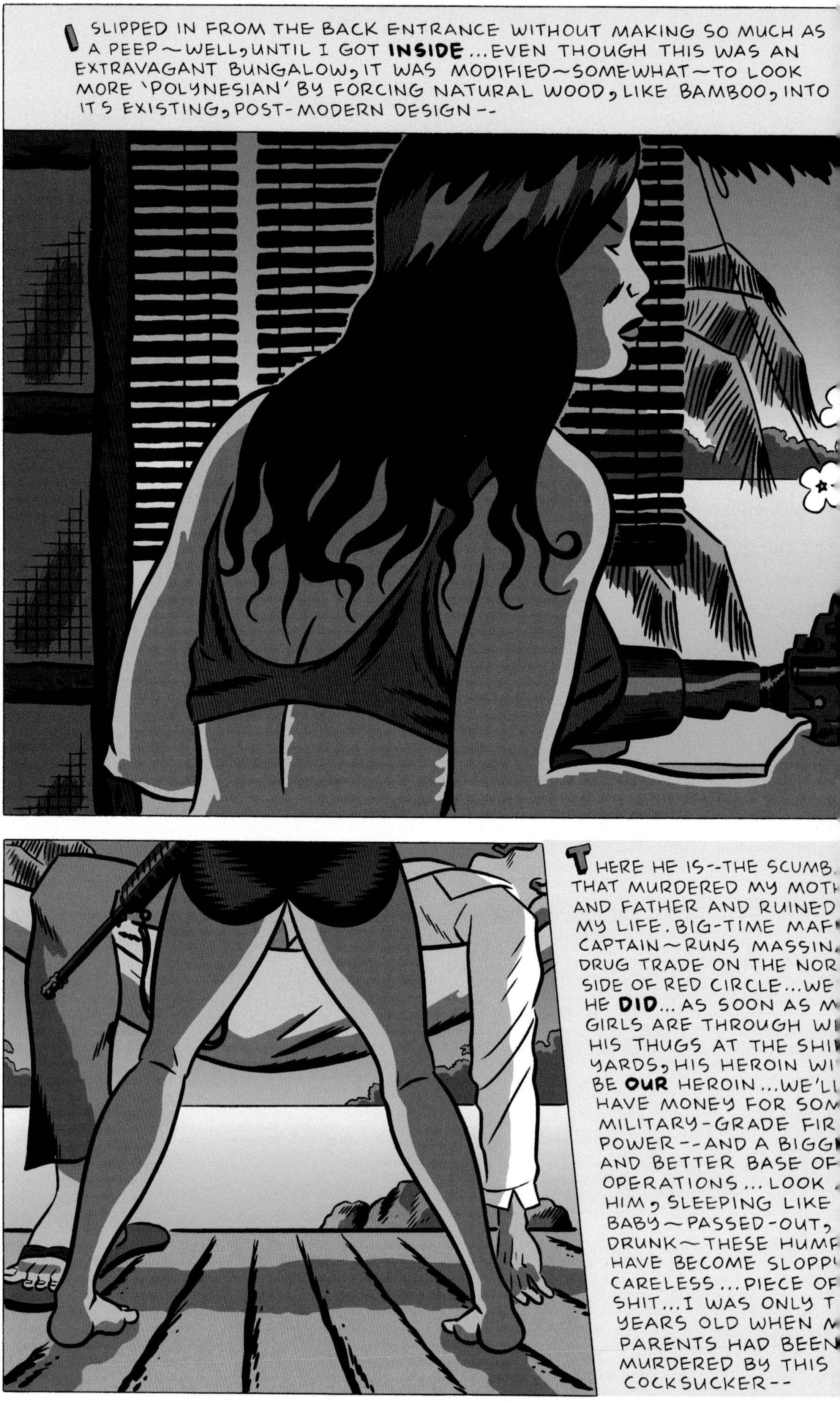
I SLIPPED IN FROM THE BACK ENTRANCE WITHOUT MAKING SO MUCH AS A PEEP~WELL, UNTIL I GOT **INSIDE**...EVEN THOUGH THIS WAS AN EXTRAVAGANT BUNGALOW, IT WAS MODIFIED~SOMEWHAT~TO LOOK MORE 'POLYNESIAN' BY FORCING NATURAL WOOD, LIKE BAMBOO, INTO ITS EXISTING, POST-MODERN DESIGN--
THERE HE IS--THE SCUMB
THAT MURDERED MY MOTH
AND FATHER AND RUINED
MY LIFE. BIG-TIME MAF
CAPTAIN~RUNS MASSIN
DRUG TRADE ON THE NOR
SIDE OF RED CIRCLE...WE
HE **DID**... AS SOON AS M
GIRLS ARE THROUGH WI
HIS THUGS AT THE SHI
YARDS, HIS HEROIN WI
BE **OUR** HEROIN...WE'LI
HAVE MONEY FOR SOM
MILITARY-GRADE FIR
POWER--AND A BIGG
AND BETTER BASE OF
OPERATIONS...LOOK
HIM, SLEEPING LIKE
BABY~PASSED-OUT,
DRUNK~THESE HUMP
HAVE BECOME SLOPP
CARELESS...PIECE OF
SHIT...I WAS ONLY T
YEARS OLD WHEN M
PARENTS HAD BEEN
MURDERED BY THIS
COCKSUCKER--

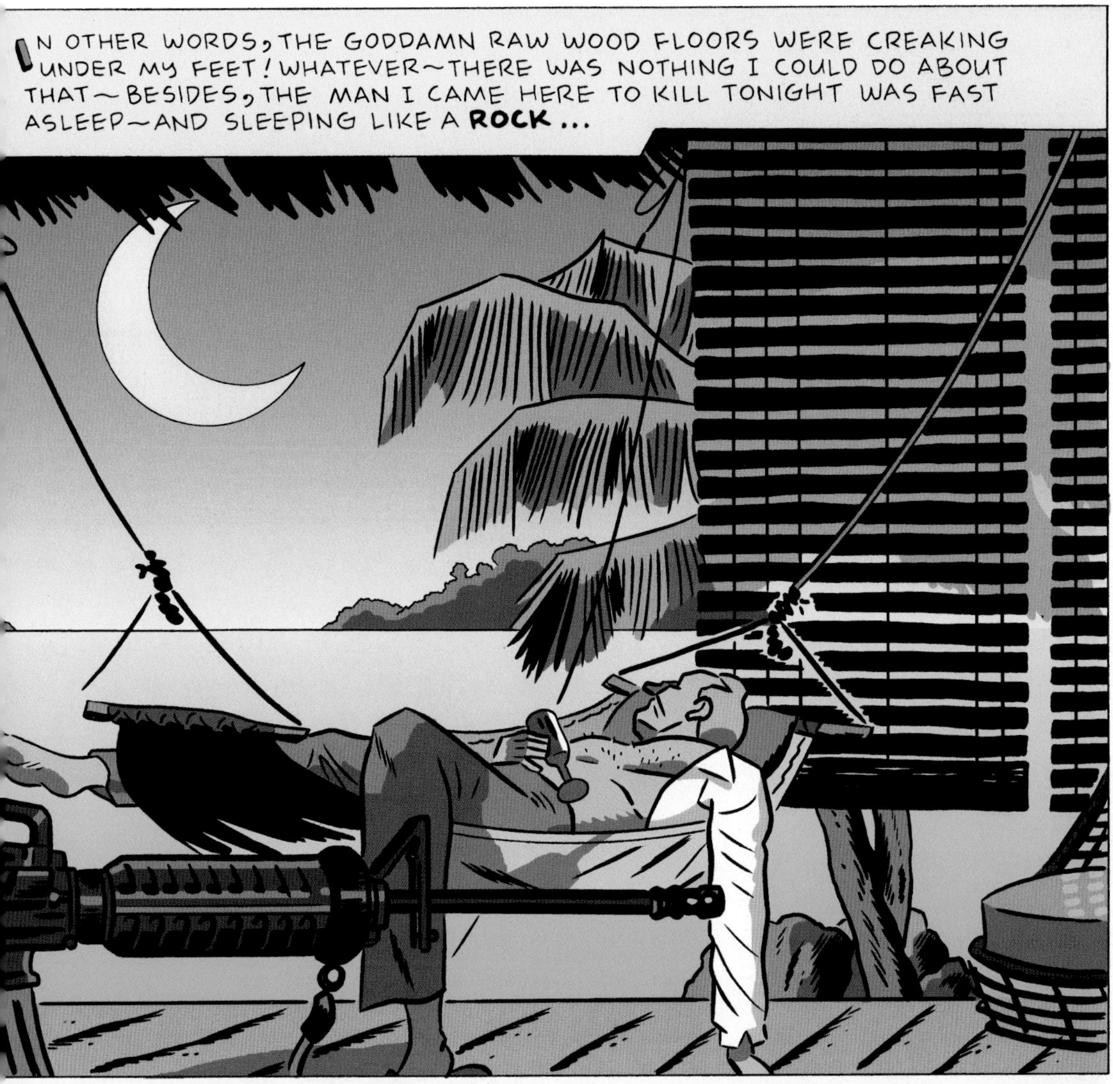
IN OTHER WORDS, THE GODDAMN RAW WOOD FLOORS WERE CREAKING UNDER MY FEET! WHATEVER~THERE WAS NOTHING I COULD DO ABOUT THAT~ BESIDES, THE MAN I CAME HERE TO KILL TONIGHT WAS FAST ASLEEP~AND SLEEPING LIKE A ROCK...

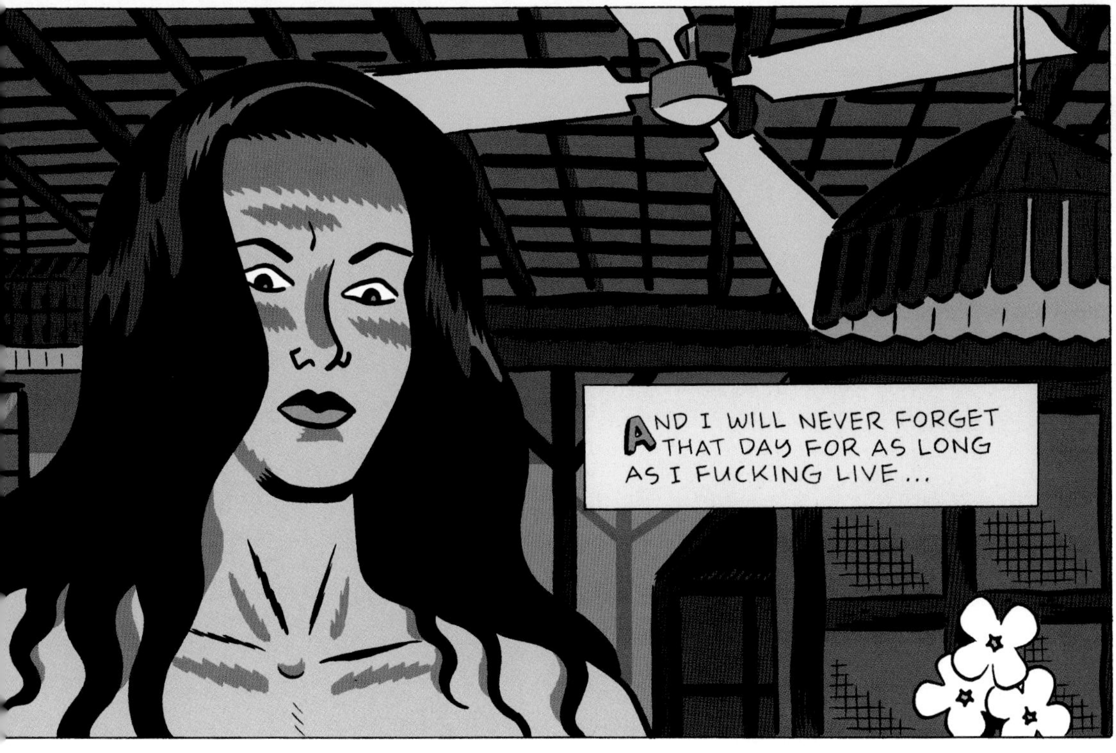
AND I WILL NEVER FORGET THAT DAY FOR AS LONG AS I FUCKING LIVE...

I WAS A CITY KID ~ I GREW UP IN AN **ALL ITALIAN** NEIGHBORHOOD IN THE HEART OF RED CIRCLE -- AS A CHILD I ATTENDED RED CIRCLE PUBLIC SCHOOL #119 ...

ROSEMARY VOLUME SI
GREATEST HITS: ROMERO

WHEN I FIRST SPOTTED THE COP CARS, I THOUGHT MY PARENTS HAD CALLED THEM TO LOOK FOR ME--

BUT THEN I SAW THE SMOULDERIN RUBBLE THAT WAS MY FAMILY BROWNSTON

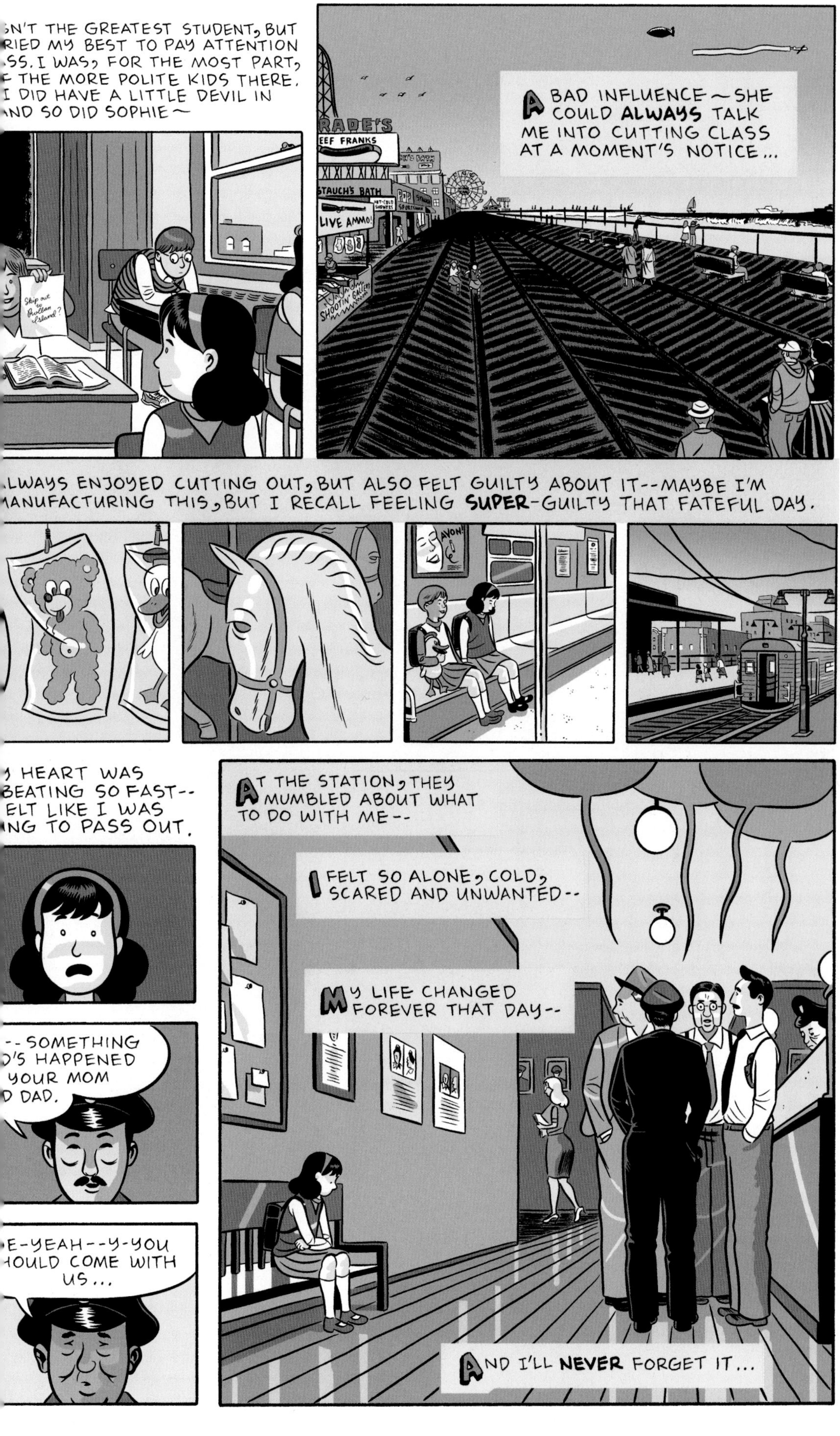

SN'T THE GREATEST STUDENT, BUT
RIED MY BEST TO PAY ATTENTION
SS. I WAS, FOR THE MOST PART,
F THE MORE POLITE KIDS THERE.
I DID HAVE A LITTLE DEVIL IN
ND SO DID SOPHIE~
Skip out to Ptolean Island?
A BAD INFLUENCE ~ SHE COULD ALWAYS TALK ME INTO CUTTING CLASS AT A MOMENT'S NOTICE...
RADE'S
BEEF FRANKS
STAUCH'S BATH
LIVE AMMO!
SHOOTIN' GALLERY
LWAYS ENJOYED CUTTING OUT, BUT ALSO FELT GUILTY ABOUT IT--MAYBE I'M
MANUFACTURING THIS, BUT I RECALL FEELING SUPER-GUILTY THAT FATEFUL DAY.
AVON!
Y HEART WAS
BEATING SO FAST--
ELT LIKE I WAS
NG TO PASS OUT.
AT THE STATION, THEY MUMBLED ABOUT WHAT TO DO WITH ME--
I FELT SO ALONE, COLD, SCARED AND UNWANTED--
MY LIFE CHANGED FOREVER THAT DAY--
--SOMETHING
'S HAPPENED
YOUR MOM
D DAD.
E-YEAH--Y-YOU
HOULD COME WITH
US...
AND I'LL NEVER FORGET IT...

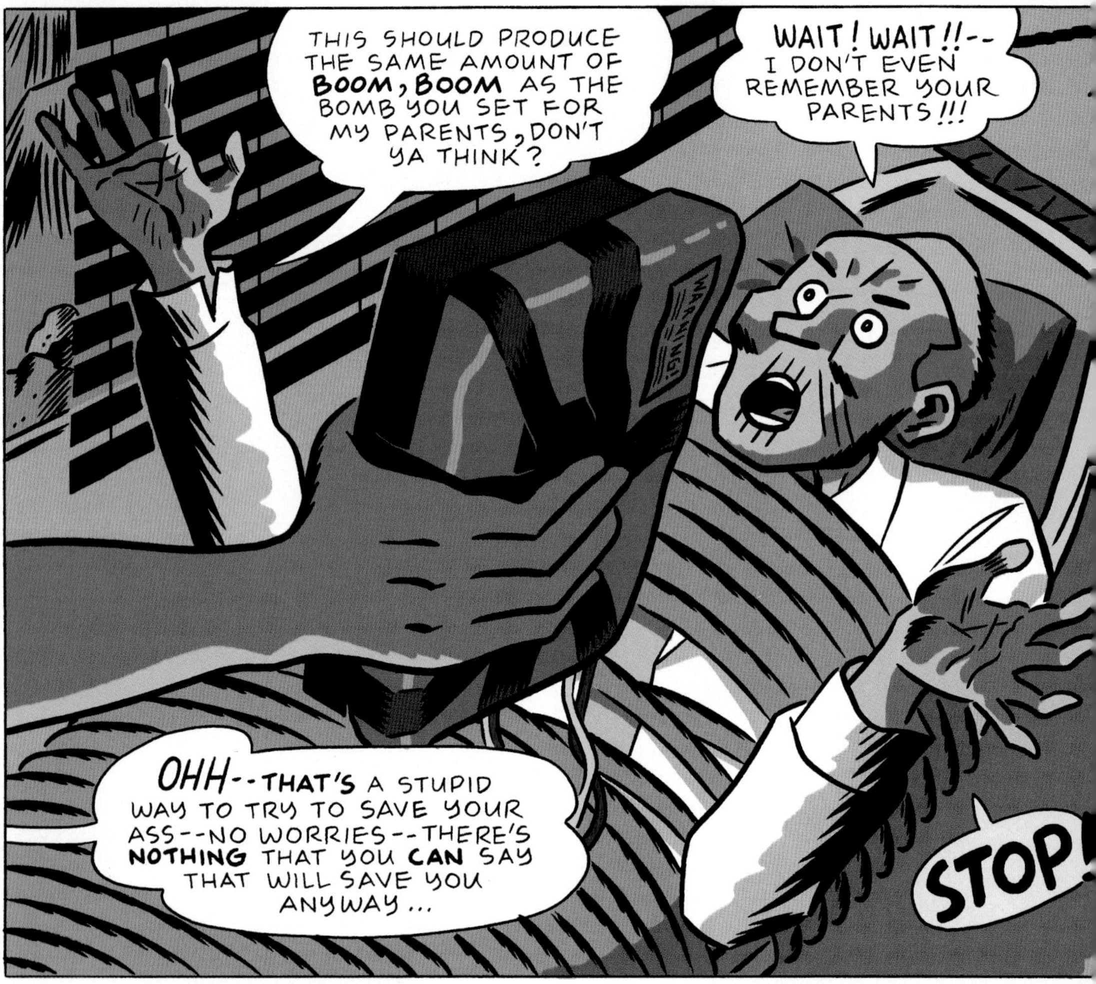
THIS SHOULD PRODUCE THE SAME AMOUNT OF **BOOM, BOOM** AS THE BOMB YOU SET FOR MY PARENTS, DON'T YA THINK?
WAIT! WAIT!!-- I DON'T EVEN REMEMBER YOUR PARENTS!!!
WARNING!
OHH--**THAT'S** A STUPID WAY TO TRY TO SAVE YOUR ASS--NO WORRIES--THERE'S **NOTHING** THAT YOU **CAN** SAY THAT WILL SAVE YOU ANYWAY...
STOP!

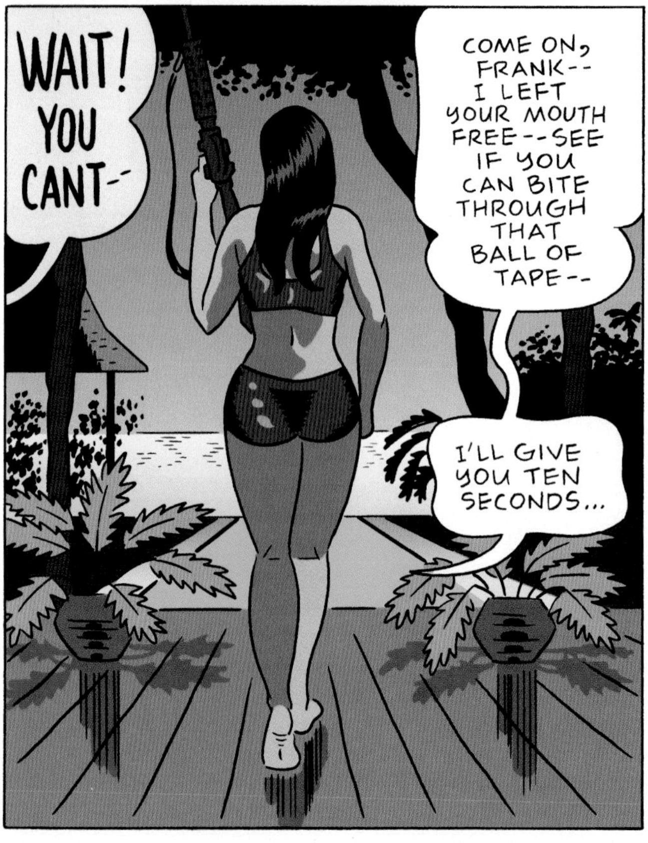
WAIT! YOU CANT-
COME ON, FRANK-- I LEFT YOUR MOUTH FREE--SEE IF YOU CAN BITE THROUGH THAT BALL OF TAPE--
I'LL GIVE YOU TEN SECONDS...

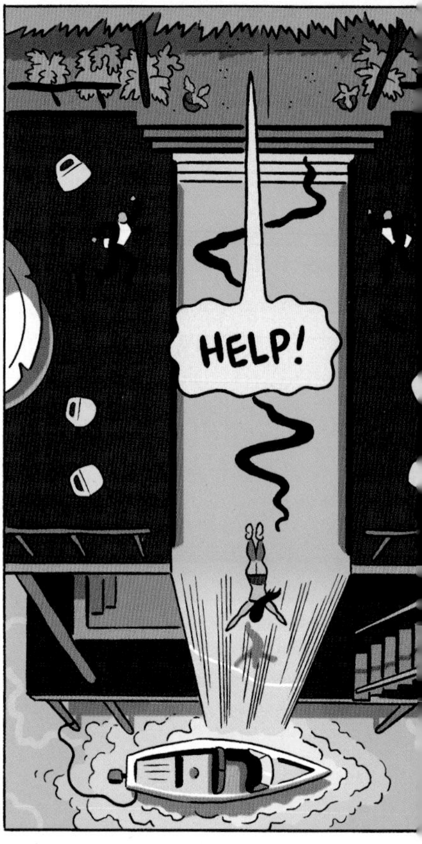
HELP!

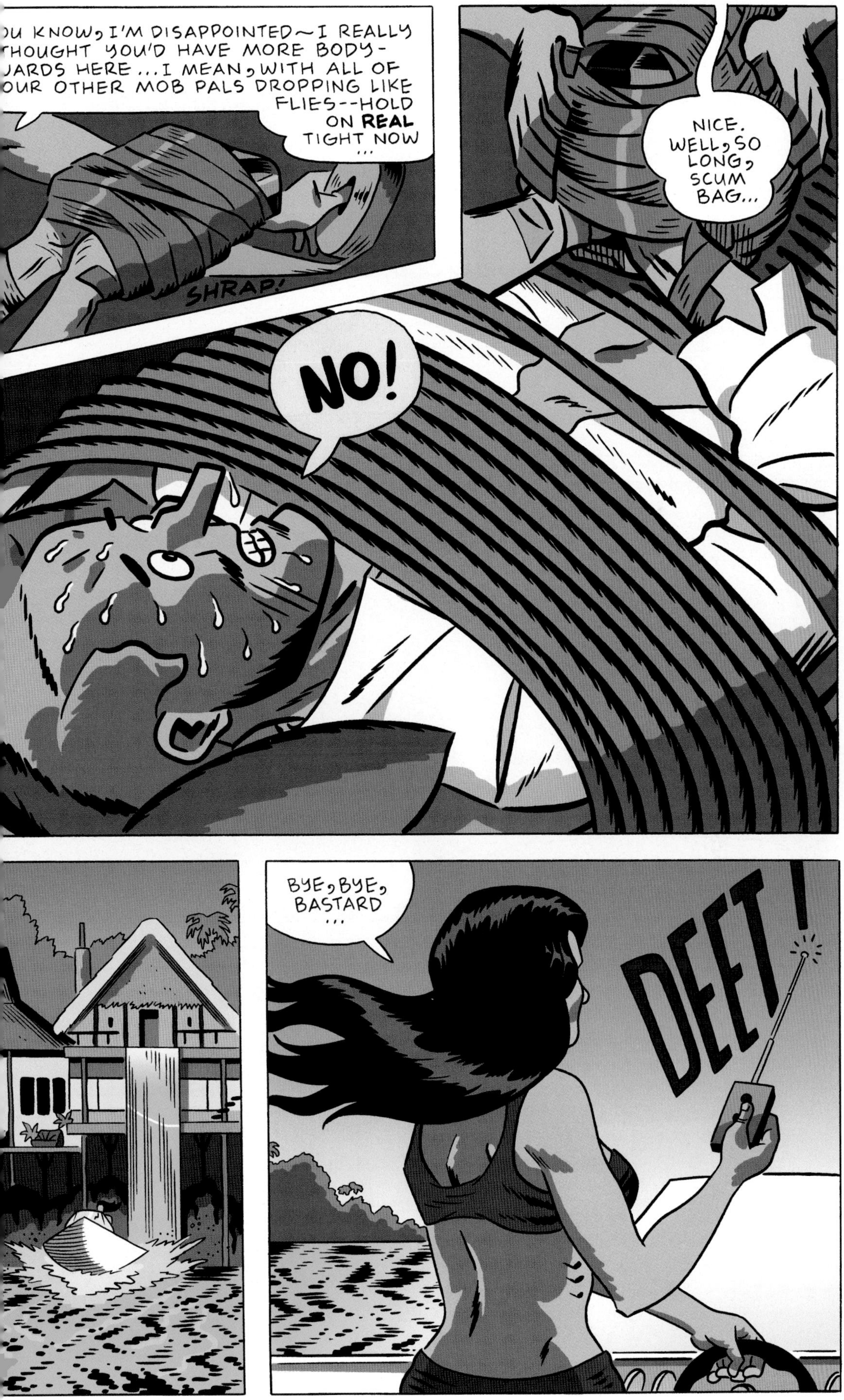

OU KNOW, I'M DISAPPOINTED~I REALLY THOUGHT YOU'D HAVE MORE BODY-GUARDS HERE... I MEAN, WITH ALL OF OUR OTHER MOB PALS DROPPING LIKE FLIES--HOLD ON **REAL** TIGHT NOW...
SHRAP!
NICE. WELL, SO LONG, SCUM BAG...
NO!
BYE, BYE, BASTARD...
DEET!

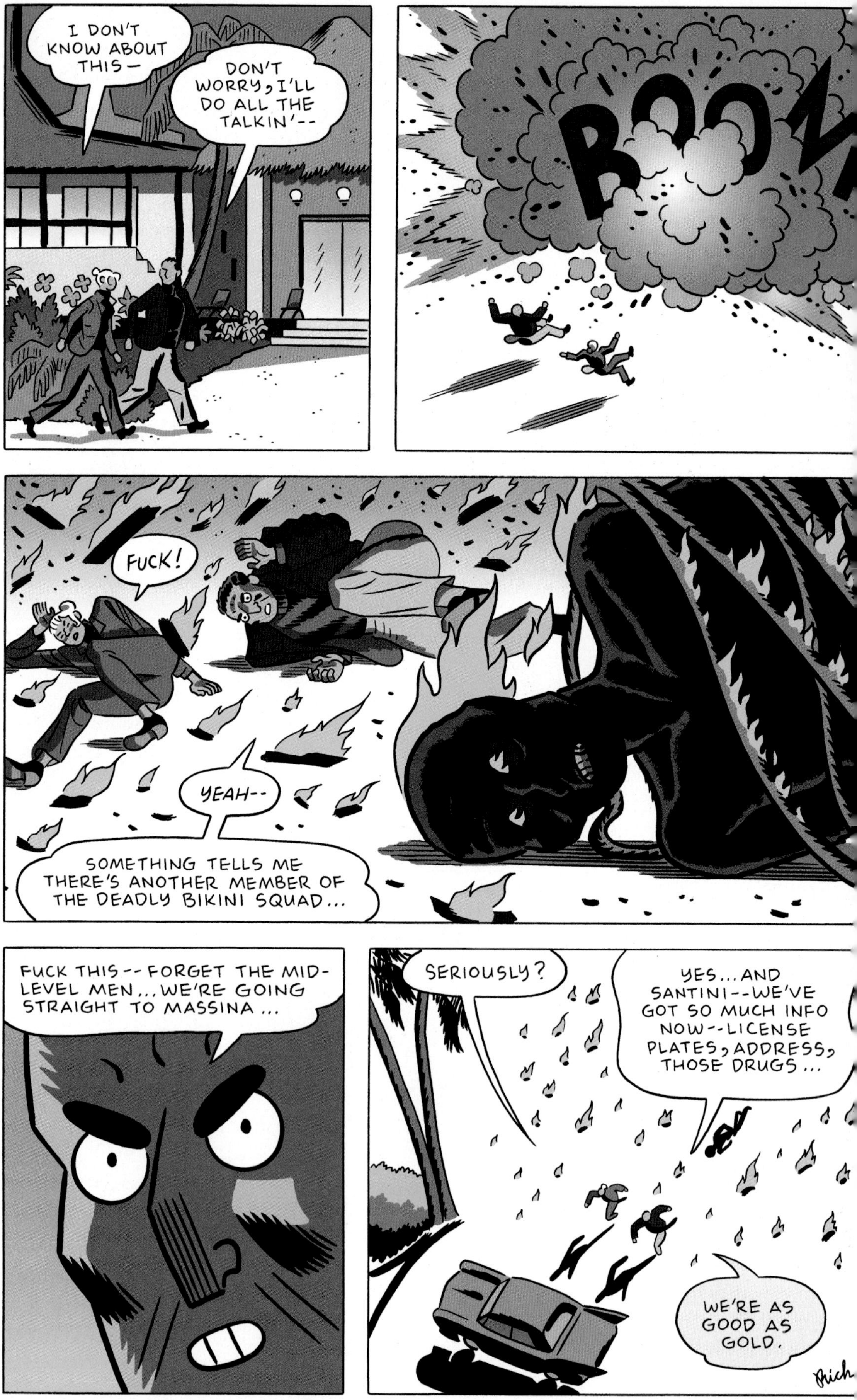
I DON'T KNOW ABOUT THIS—
DON'T WORRY, I'LL DO ALL THE TALKIN'--
BOOM
FUCK!
YEAH--
SOMETHING TELLS ME THERE'S ANOTHER MEMBER OF THE DEADLY BIKINI SQUAD...
FUCK THIS--FORGET THE MID-LEVEL MEN...WE'RE GOING STRAIGHT TO MASSINA...
SERIOUSLY?
YES...AND SANTINI--WE'VE GOT SO MUCH INFO NOW--LICENSE PLATES, ADDRESS, THOSE DRUGS...
WE'RE AS GOOD AS GOLD.

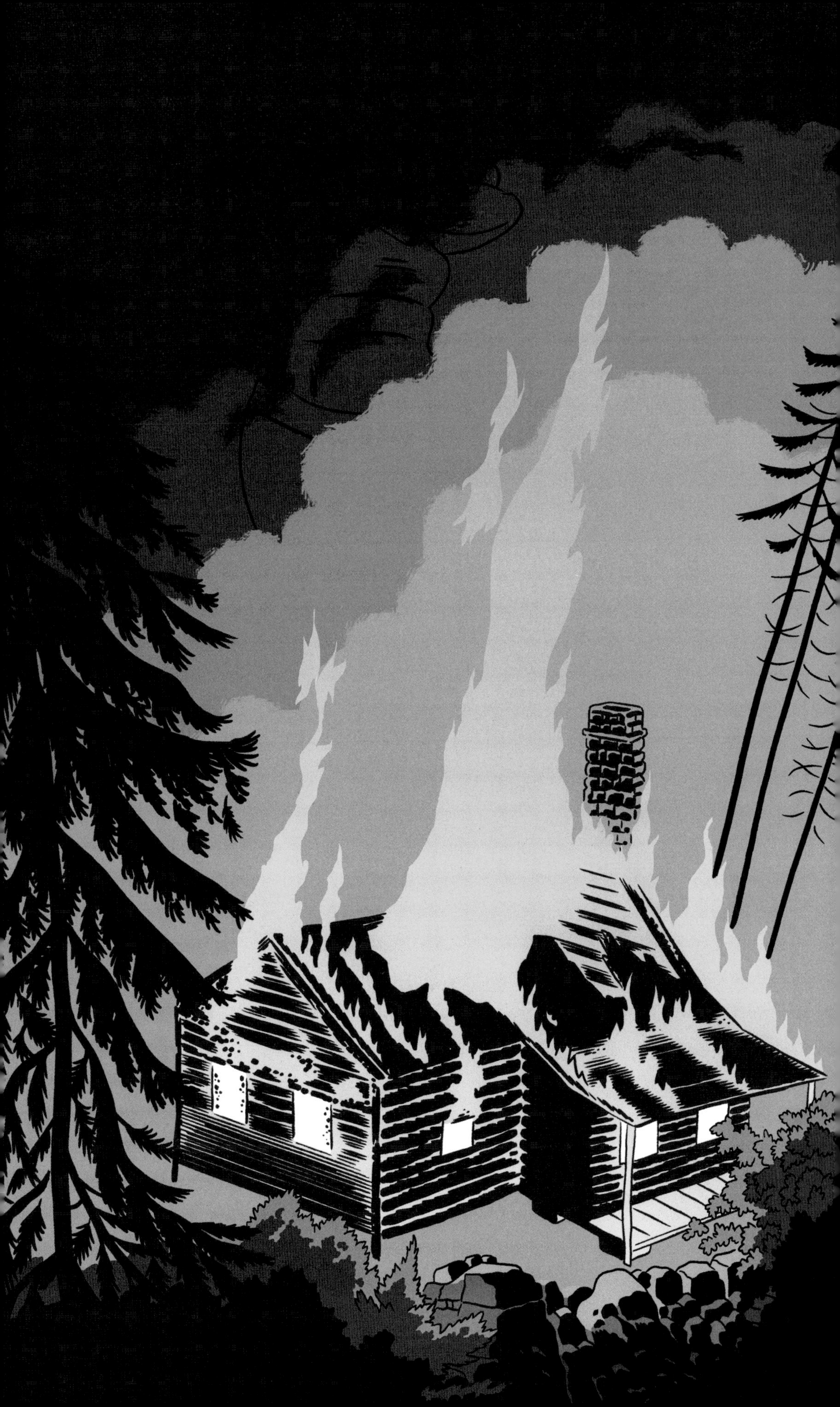

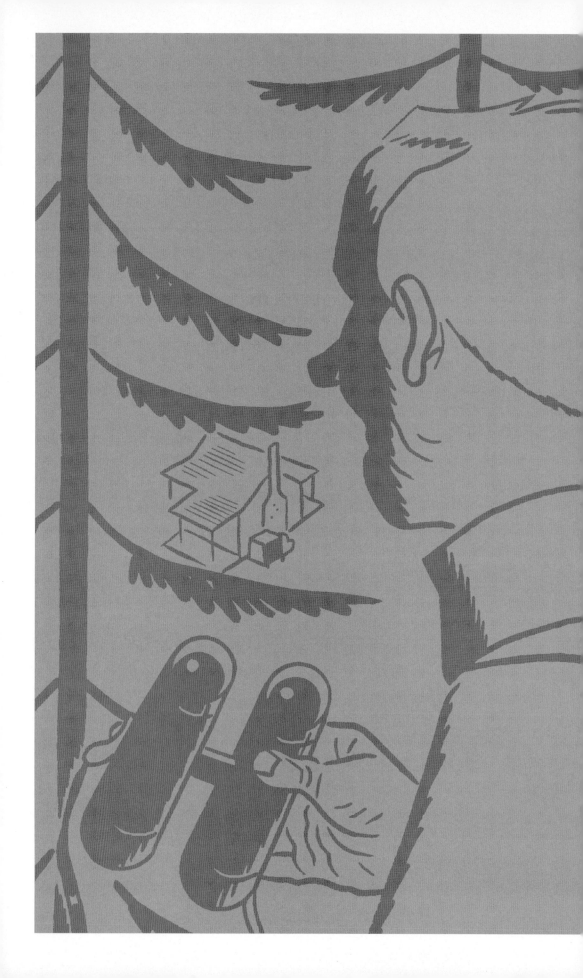

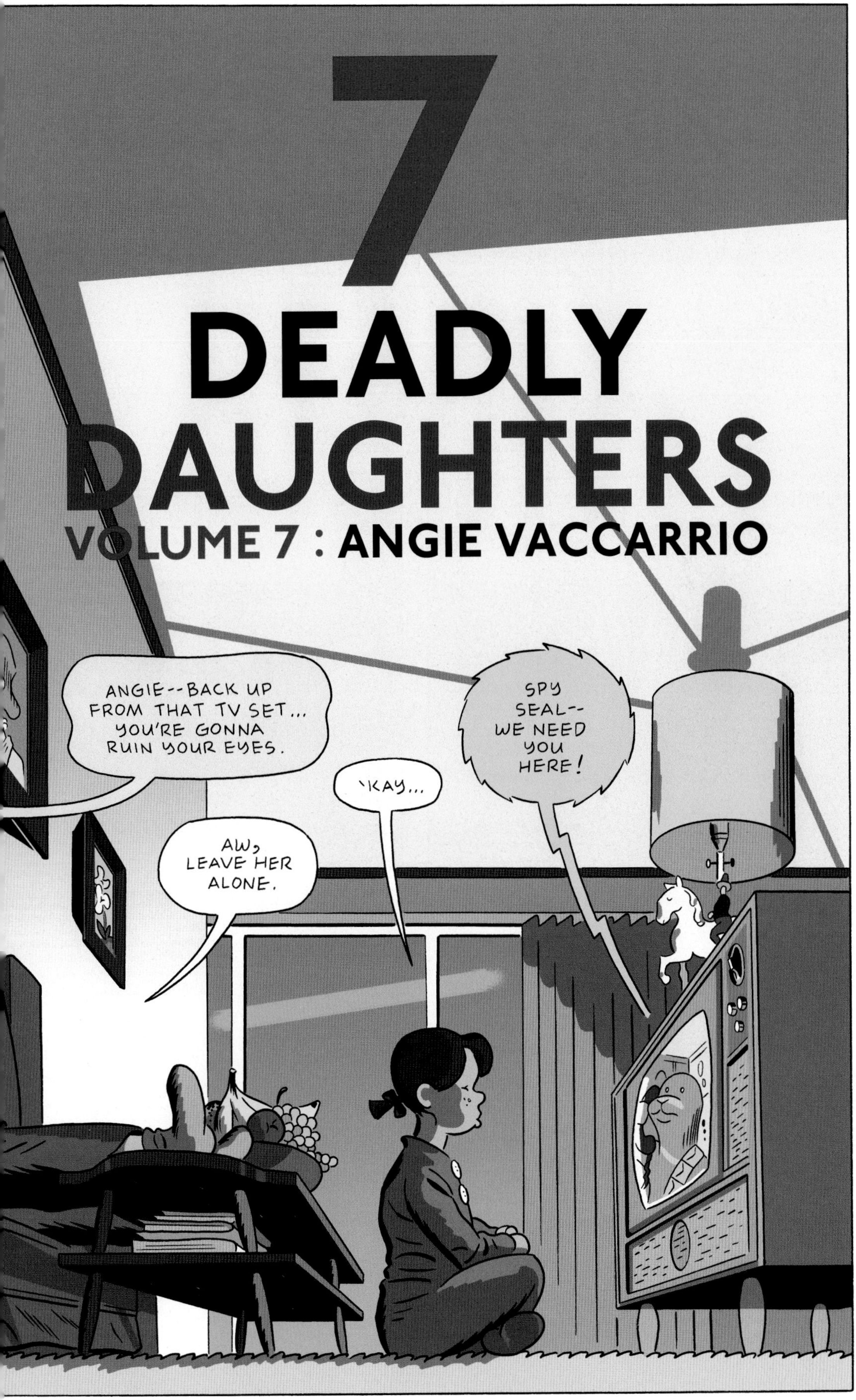
7
DEADLY
DAUGHTERS
VOLUME 7 : ANGIE VACCARRIO
ANGIE--BACK UP FROM THAT TV SET... YOU'RE GONNA RUIN YOUR EYES.
AW, LEAVE HER ALONE.
'KAY...
SPY SEAL-- WE NEED YOU HERE!

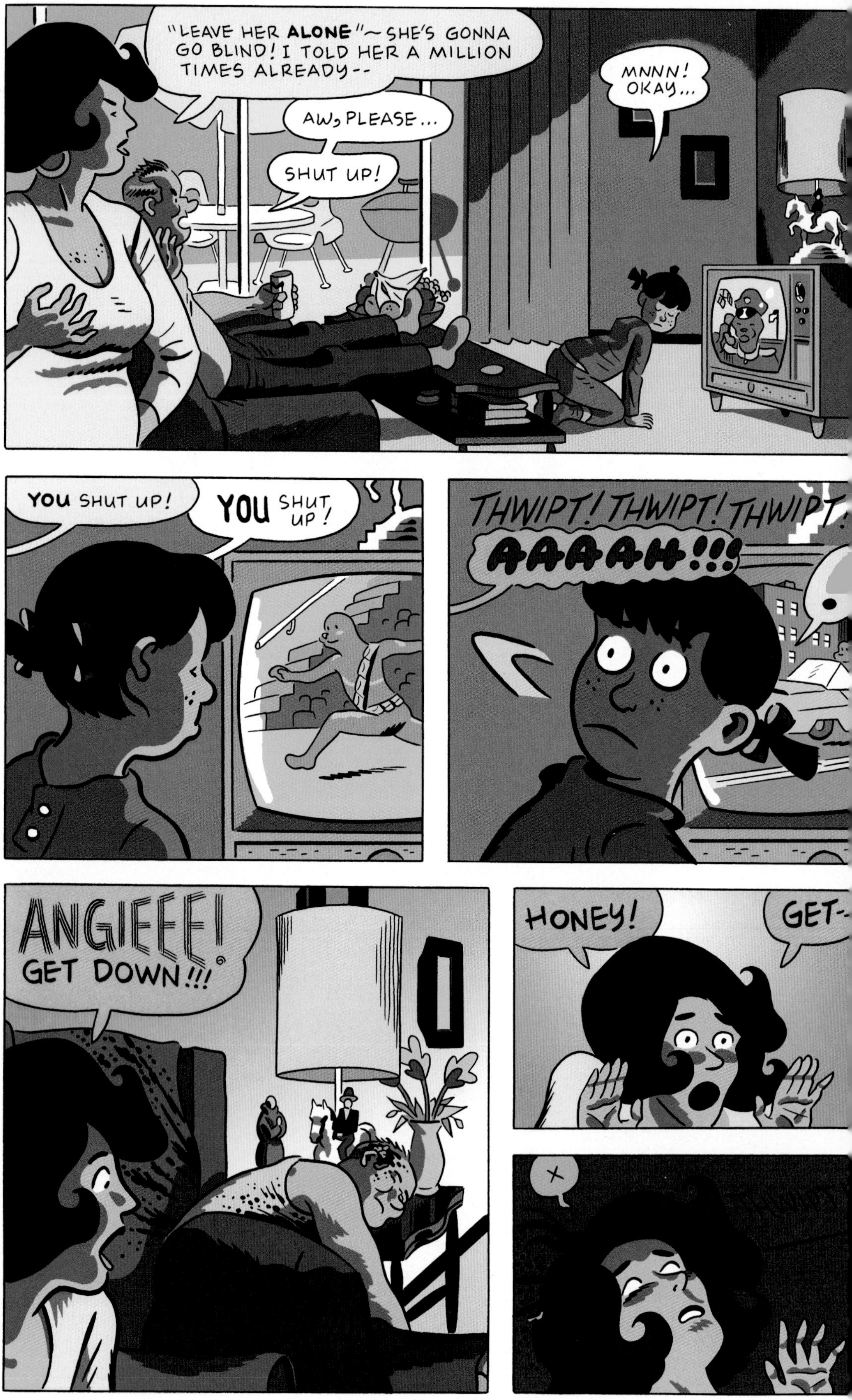
"LEAVE HER ALONE"~ SHE'S GONNA GO BLIND! I TOLD HER A MILLION TIMES ALREADY--
AW, PLEASE...
SHUT UP!
MNNN! OKAY...
YOU SHUT UP!
YOU SHUT UP!
THWIPT! THWIPT! THWIPT!
AAAAH!!!
ANGIEEE! GET DOWN!!!
HONEY!
GET-

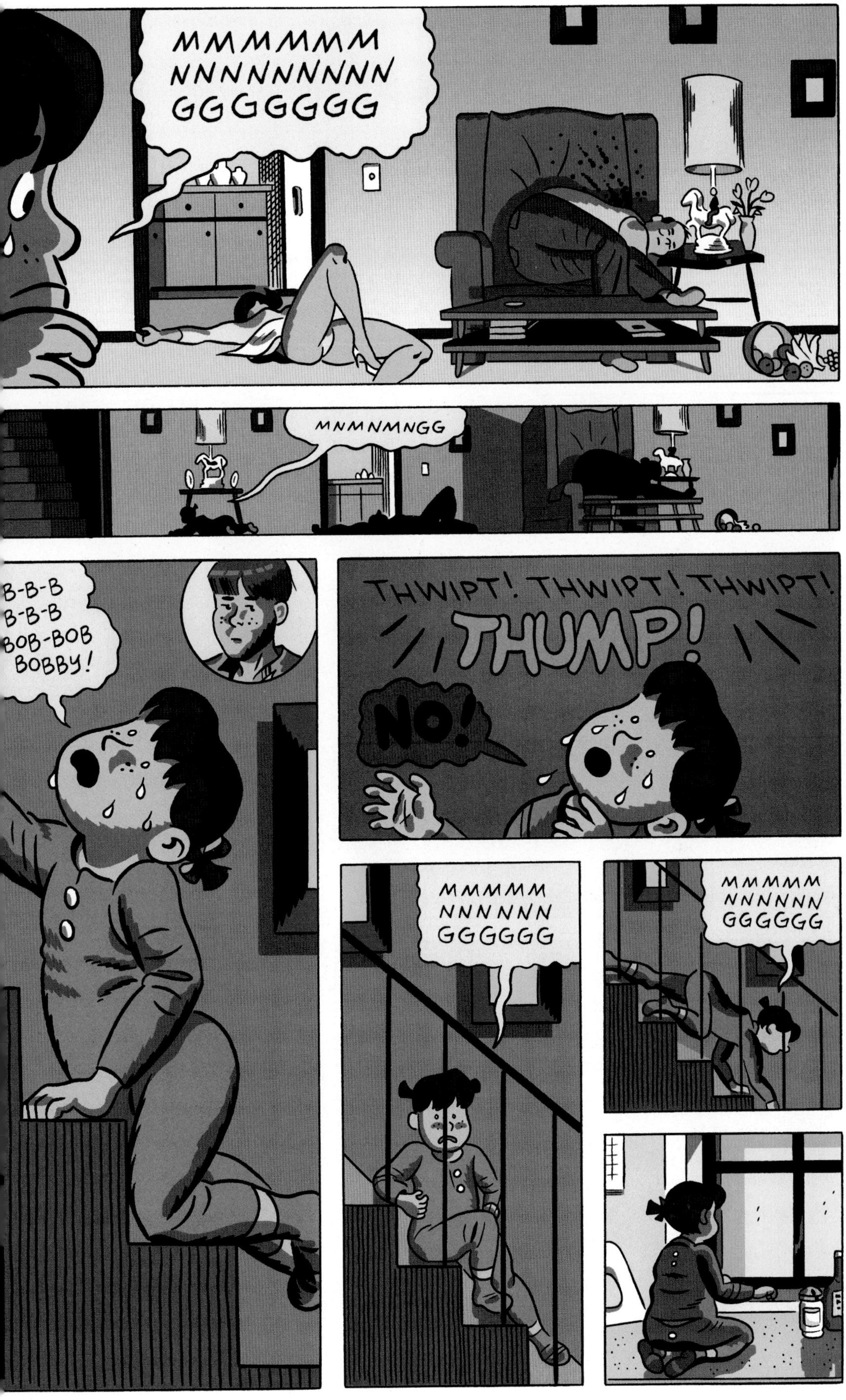
MMMMMM NNNNNNNNN GGGGGGG
MNMNMNGG
B-B-B B-B-B BOB-BOB BOBBY!
THWIPT! THWIPT! THWIPT!
THUMP!
NO!
MMMMM NNNNNN GGGGGG
MMMMM NNNNNN GGGGGG

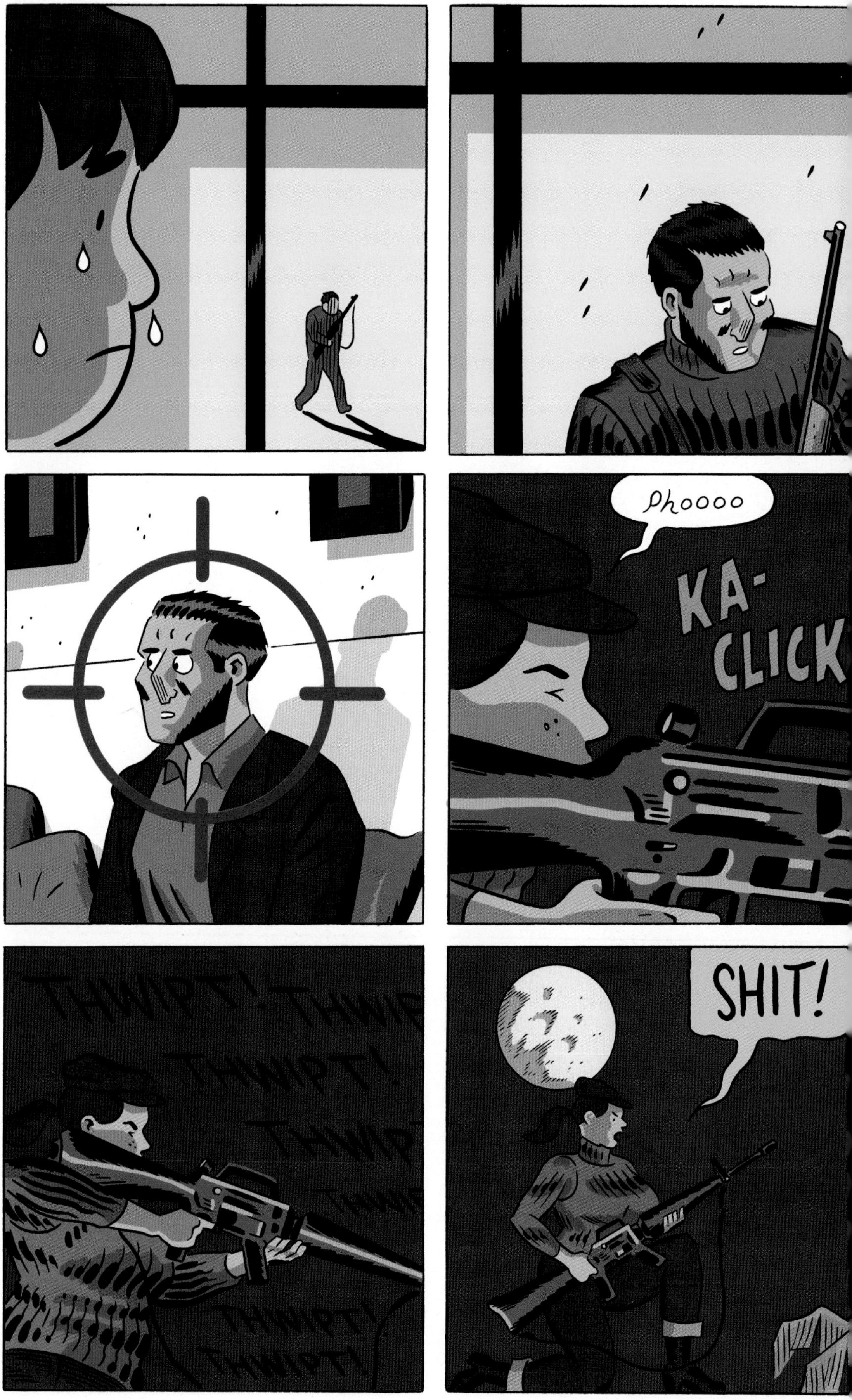
Phoooo
KA-CLICK
THWIPT! THWIPT!
THWIPT!
THWIPT!
SHIT!

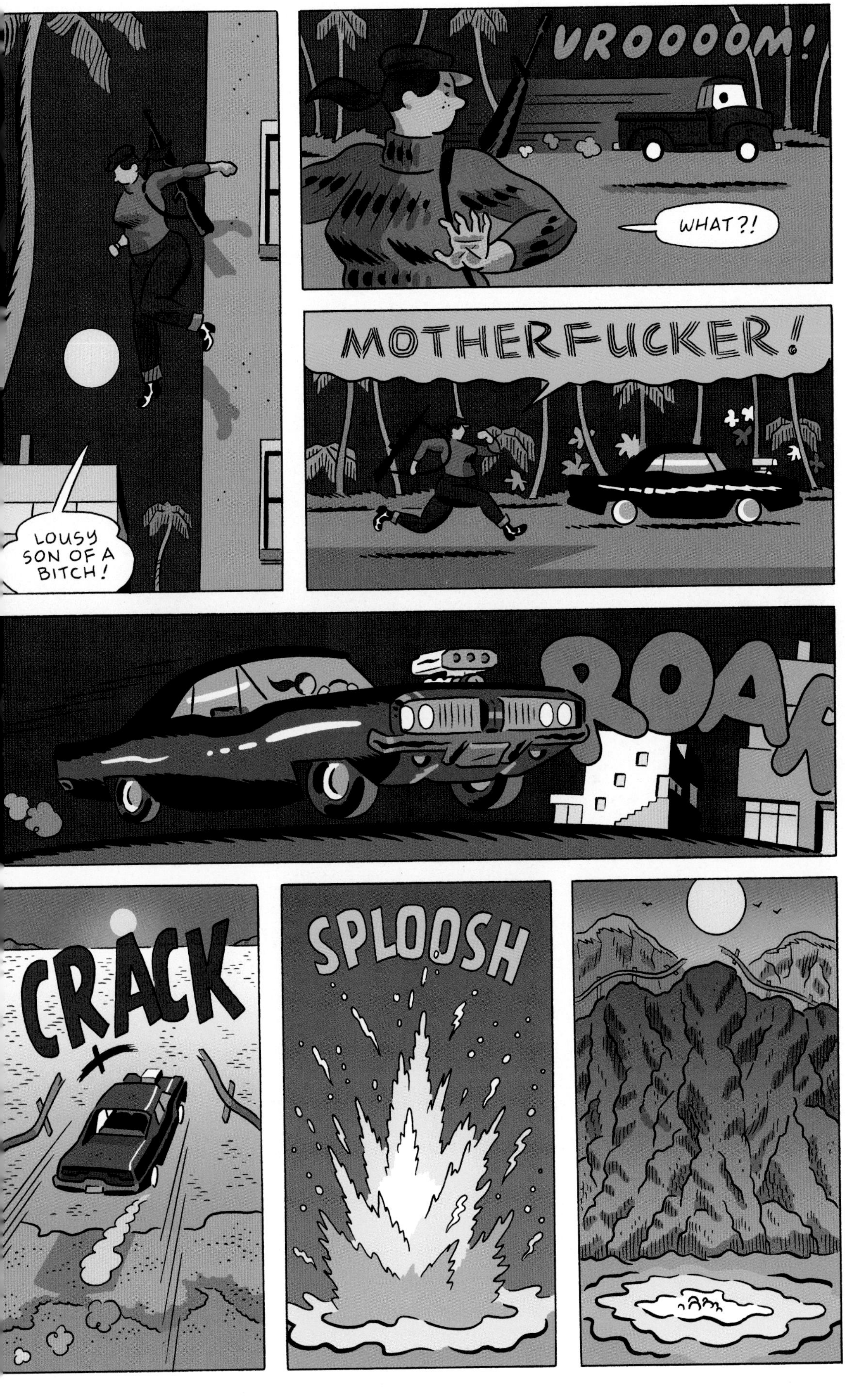
LOUSY SON OF A BITCH!
VROOOOM!
WHAT?!
MOTHERFUCKER!
ROA
CRACK
SPLOOSH

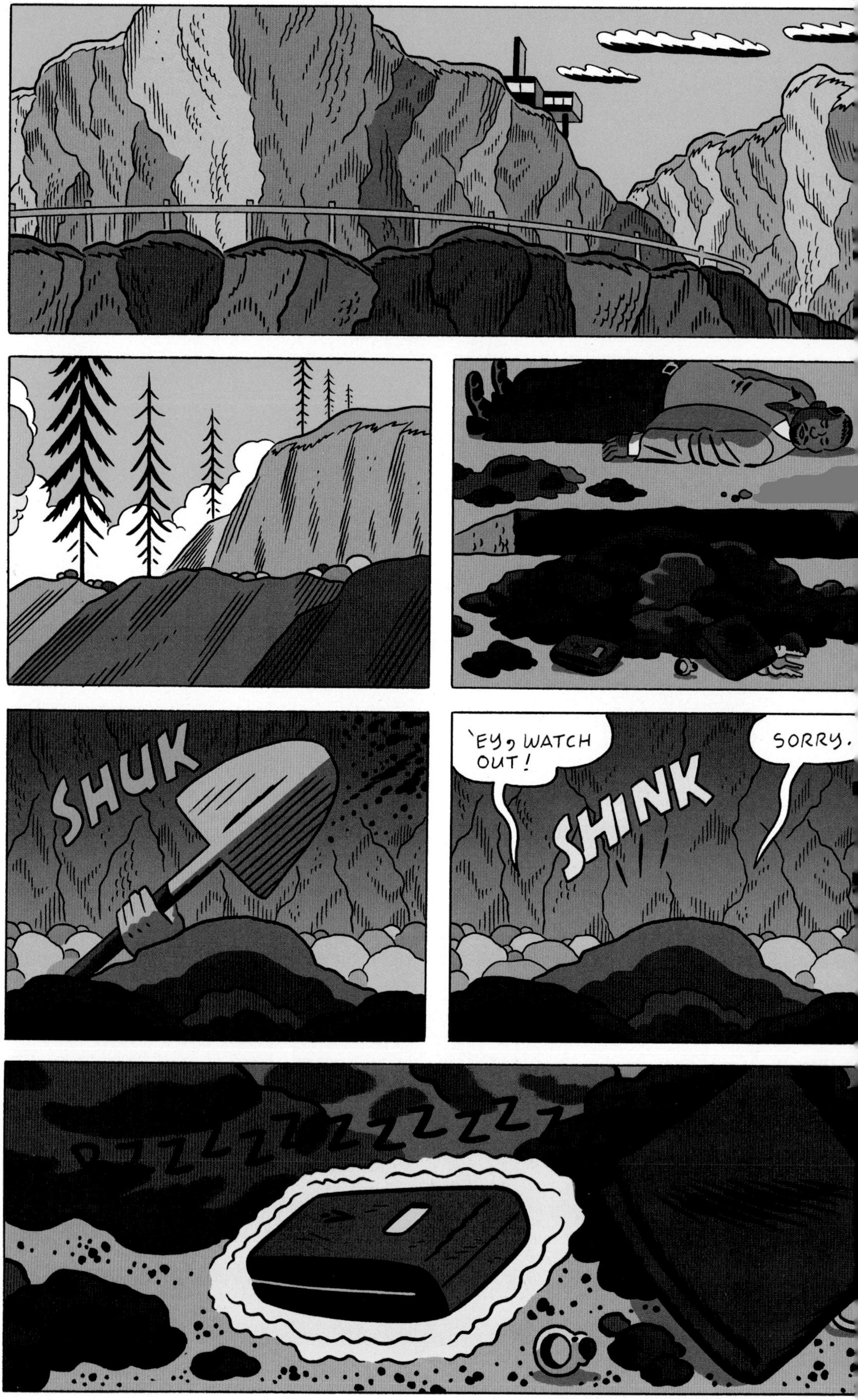

SHUK
`EY, WATCH OUT!
SHINK
SORRY.
ZZZZZZZZZZZZ

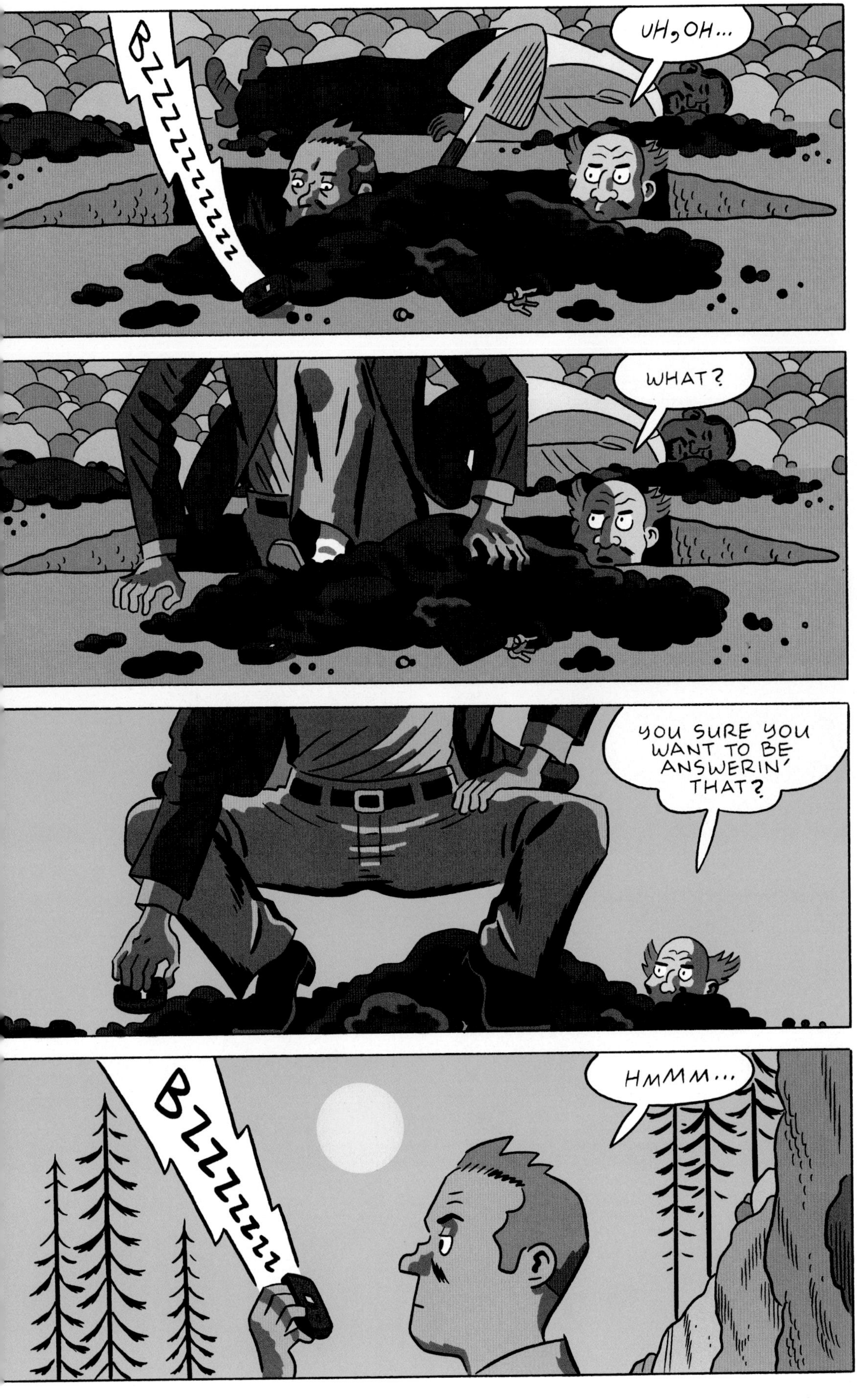
BZZZZZZZZZZZZZ
UH, OH...
WHAT?
YOU SURE YOU WANT TO BE ANSWERIN' THAT?
BZZZZZZZZ
HMMM...

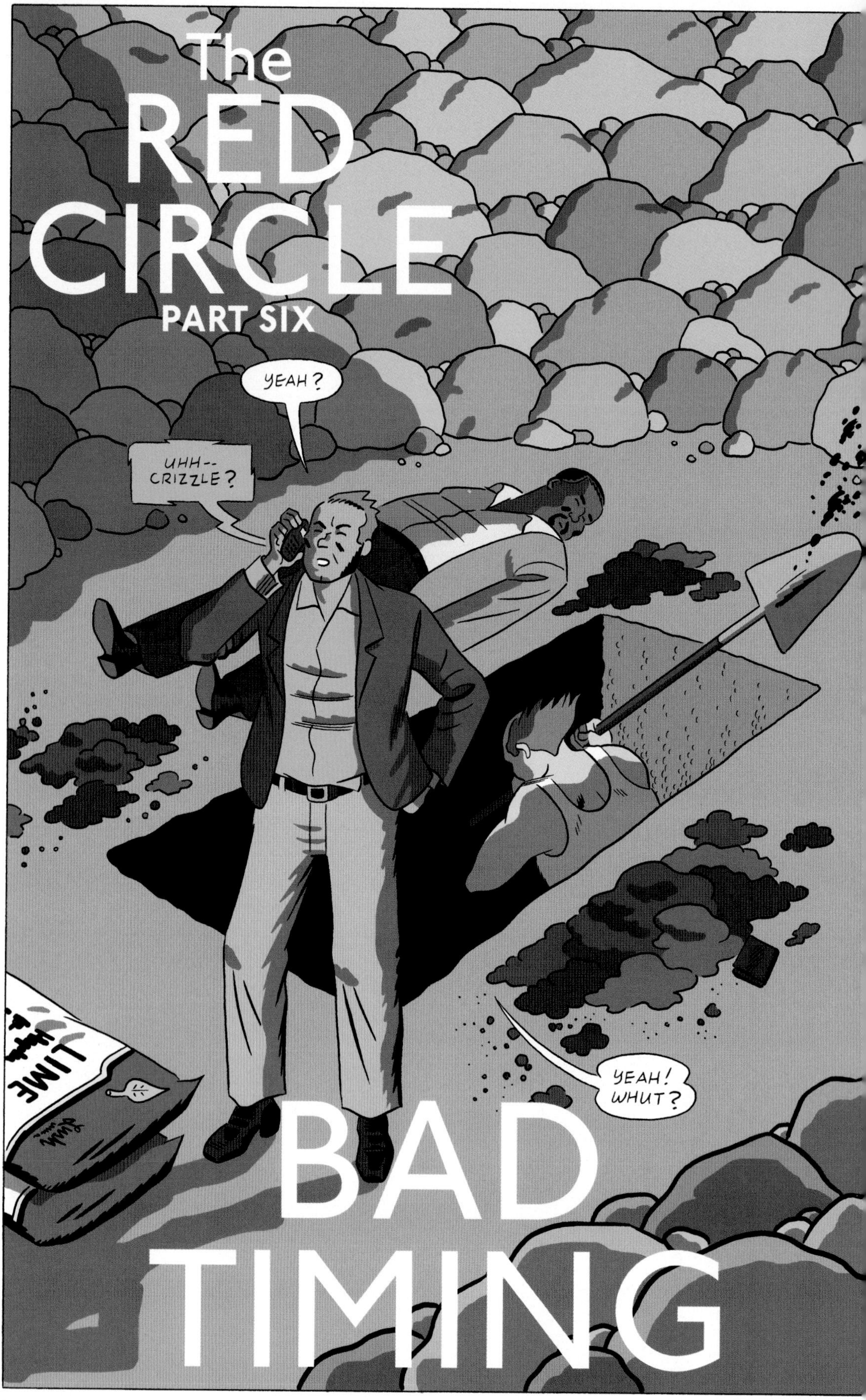
The RED CIRCLE
PART SIX
YEAH?
UHH-- CRIZZLE?
YEAH! WHUT?
LIME
BAD TIMING

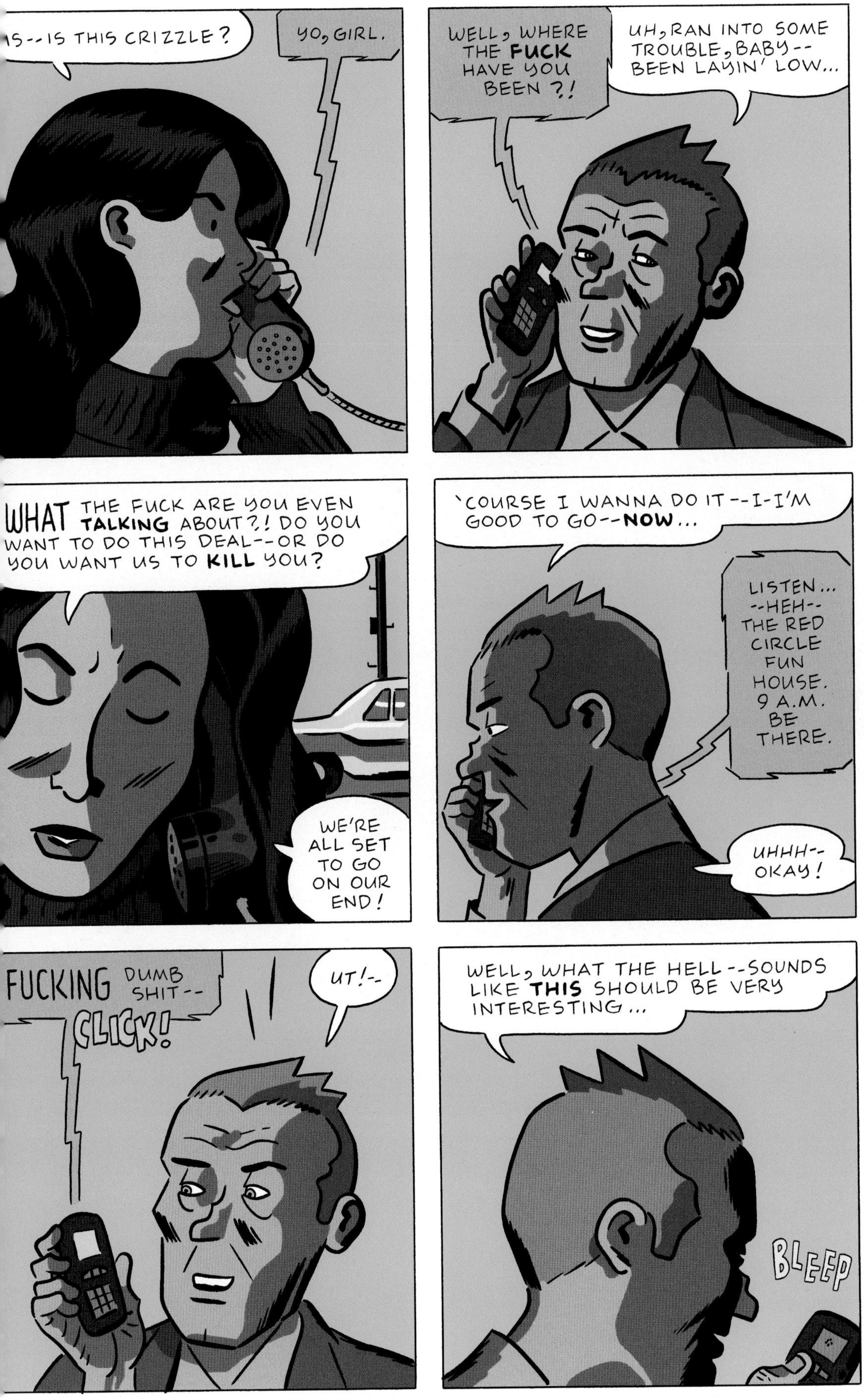
IS--IS THIS CRIZZLE?
YO, GIRL.
WELL, WHERE THE **FUCK** HAVE YOU BEEN?!
UH, RAN INTO SOME TROUBLE, BABY--BEEN LAYIN' LOW...
WHAT THE FUCK ARE YOU EVEN **TALKING** ABOUT?! DO YOU WANT TO DO THIS DEAL--OR DO YOU WANT US TO **KILL** YOU?
WE'RE ALL SET TO GO ON OUR END!
`COURSE I WANNA DO IT--I-I'M GOOD TO GO--**NOW**...
LISTEN... --HEH-- THE RED CIRCLE FUN HOUSE. 9 A.M. BE THERE.
UHHH--OKAY!
FUCKING DUMB SHIT--
CLICK!
UT!-
WELL, WHAT THE HELL--SOUNDS LIKE **THIS** SHOULD BE VERY INTERESTING...
BLEEP

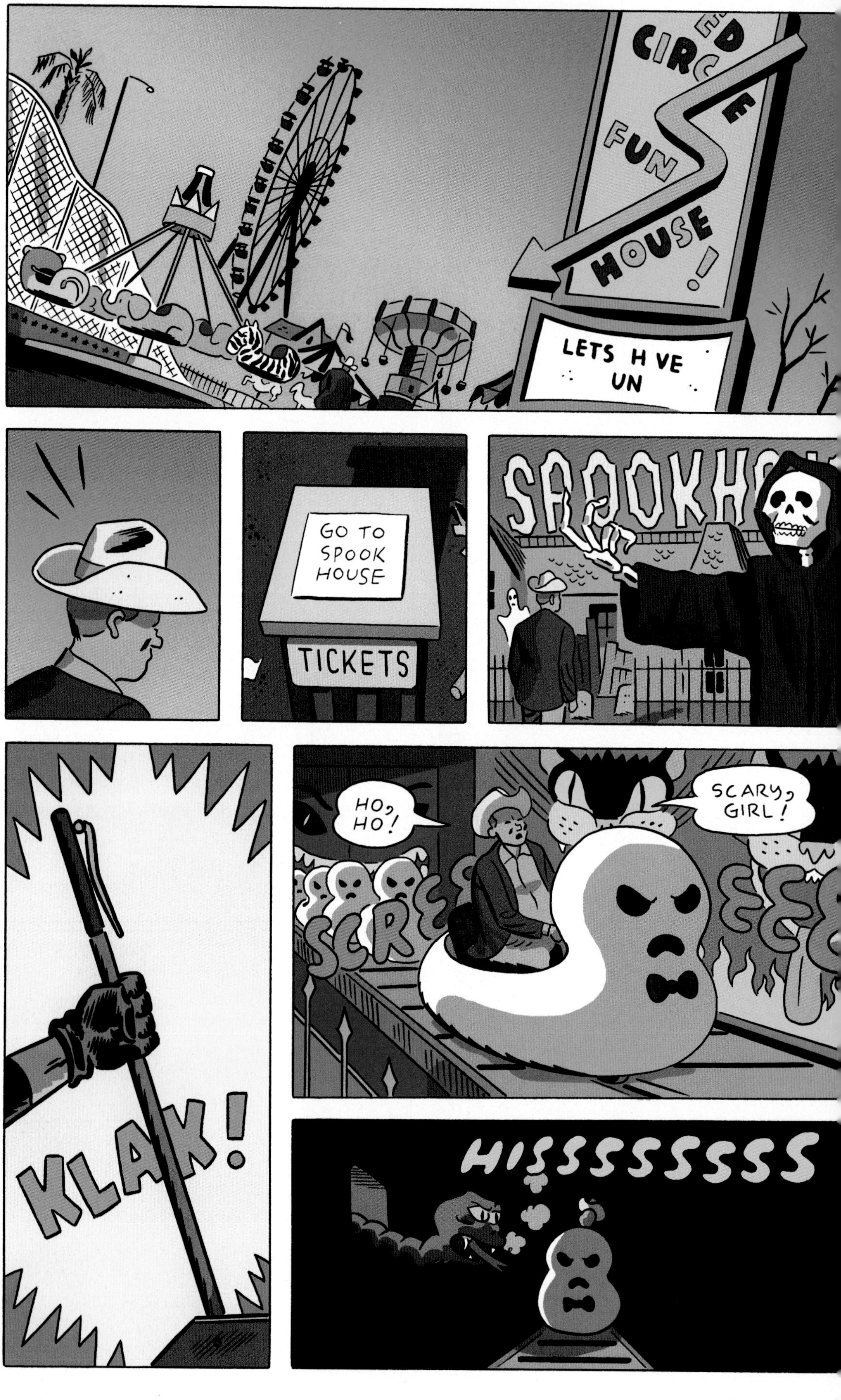
CIRC
FUN
HOUSE
!
LETS H VE
UN
GO TO SPOOK HOUSE
TICKETS
SPOOKH
KLAK!
HO, HO!
SCARY, GIRL!
SCRE
EEE
HISSSSSSSS

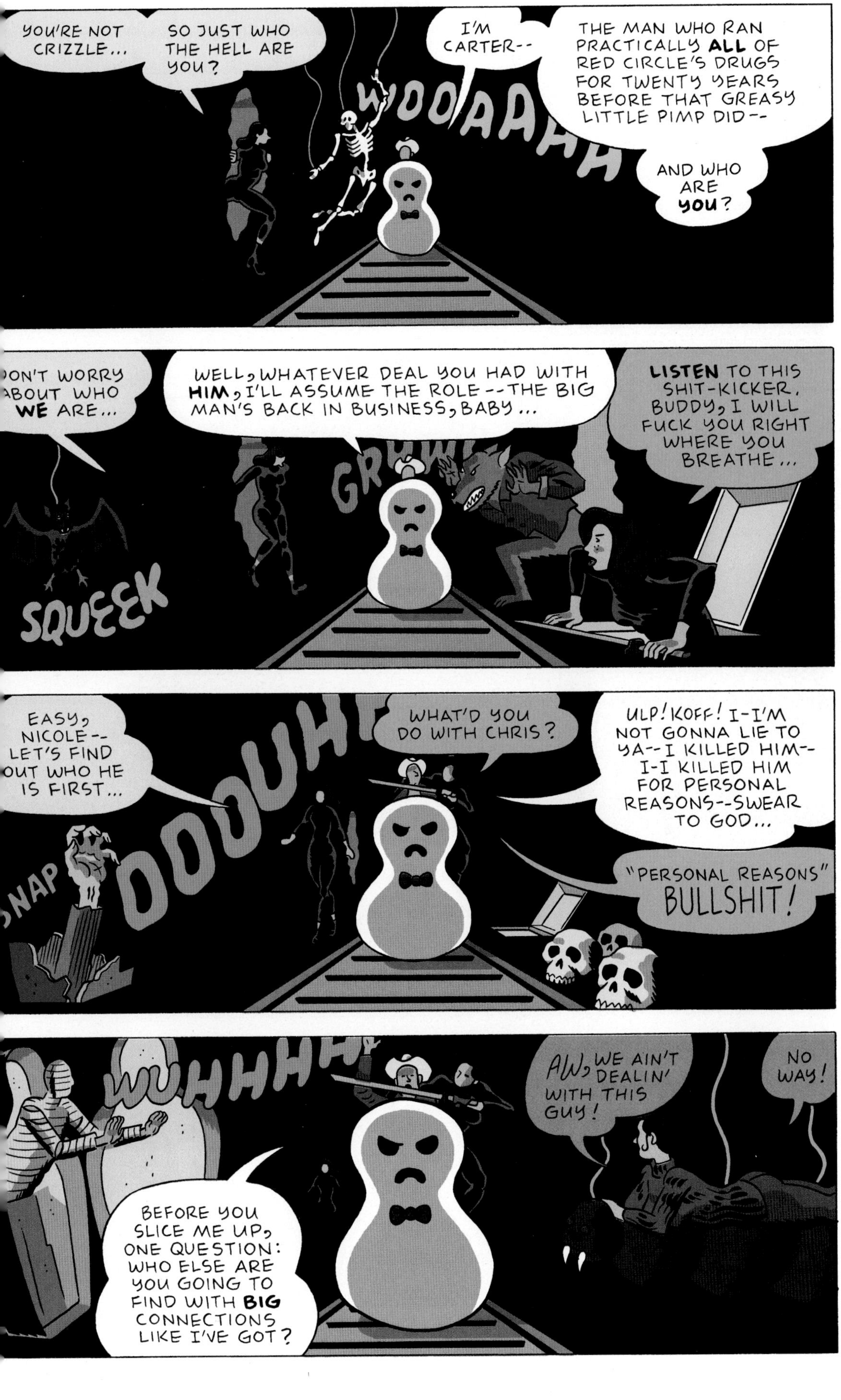

YOU'RE NOT CRIZZLE...
SO JUST WHO THE HELL ARE YOU?
WOOAAAHH
I'M CARTER--
THE MAN WHO RAN PRACTICALLY **ALL** OF RED CIRCLE'S DRUGS FOR TWENTY YEARS BEFORE THAT GREASY LITTLE PIMP DID--
AND WHO ARE **YOU**?
DON'T WORRY ABOUT WHO **WE** ARE...
WELL, WHATEVER DEAL YOU HAD WITH **HIM**, I'LL ASSUME THE ROLE--THE BIG MAN'S BACK IN BUSINESS, BABY...
LISTEN TO THIS SHIT-KICKER, BUDDY, I WILL FUCK YOU RIGHT WHERE YOU BREATHE...
SQUEEK
EASY, NICOLE--LET'S FIND OUT WHO HE IS FIRST...
OOOUH
WHAT'D YOU DO WITH CHRIS?
ULP! KOFF! I-I'M NOT GONNA LIE TO YA--I KILLED HIM--I-I KILLED HIM FOR PERSONAL REASONS--SWEAR TO GOD...
"PERSONAL REASONS" BULLSHIT!
SNAP
WUHHHH
AW, WE AIN'T DEALIN' WITH THIS GUY!
NO WAY!
BEFORE YOU SLICE ME UP, ONE QUESTION: WHO ELSE ARE YOU GOING TO FIND WITH **BIG** CONNECTIONS LIKE I'VE GOT?

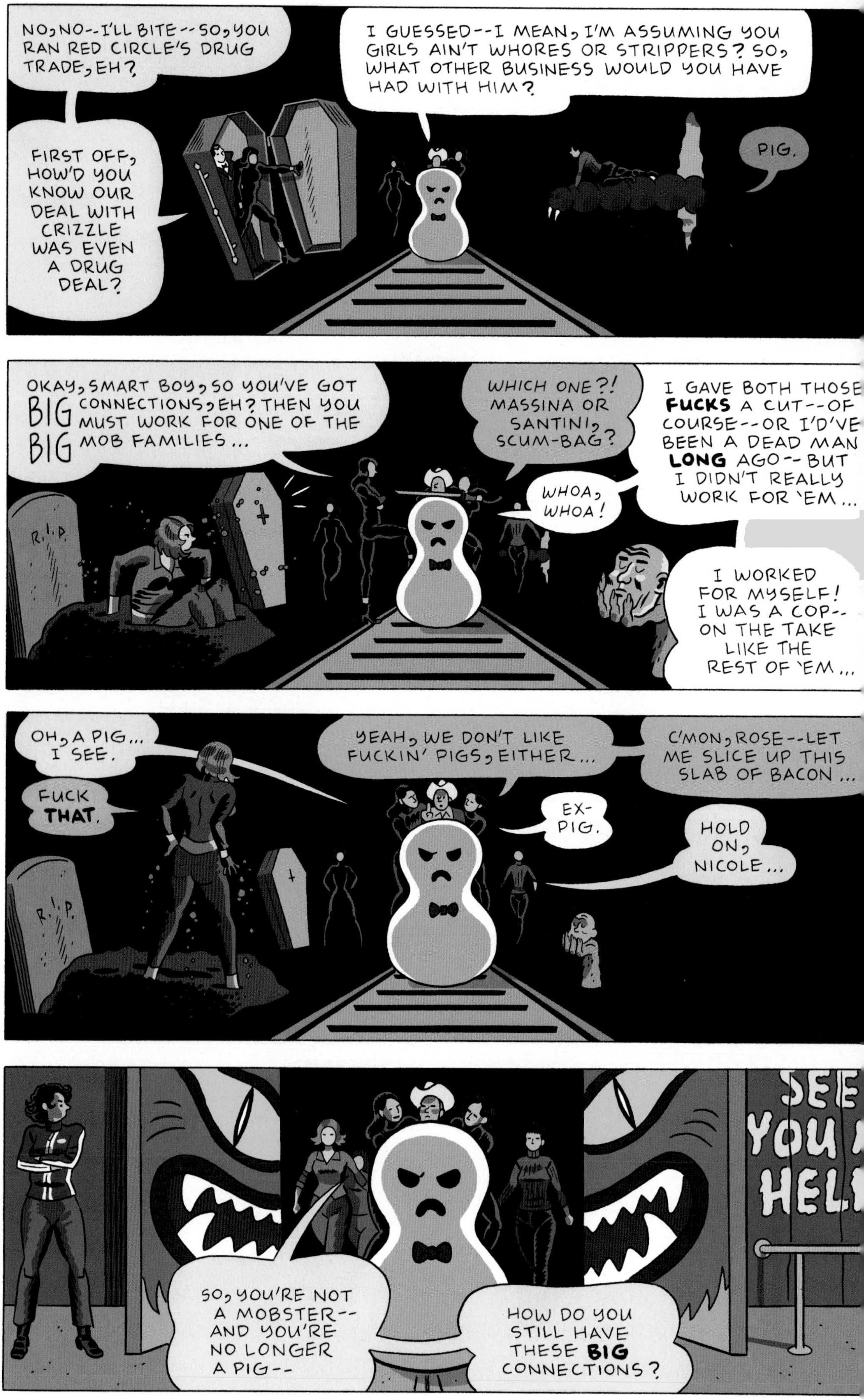
NO, NO--I'LL BITE--SO, YOU RAN RED CIRCLE'S DRUG TRADE, EH?
FIRST OFF, HOW'D YOU KNOW OUR DEAL WITH CRIZZLE WAS EVEN A DRUG DEAL?
I GUESSED--I MEAN, I'M ASSUMING YOU GIRLS AIN'T WHORES OR STRIPPERS? SO, WHAT OTHER BUSINESS WOULD YOU HAVE HAD WITH HIM?
PIG.
OKAY, SMART BOY, SO YOU'VE GOT BIG CONNECTIONS, EH? THEN YOU MUST WORK FOR ONE OF THE BIG MOB FAMILIES...
WHICH ONE?! MASSINA OR SANTINI, SCUM-BAG?
WHOA, WHOA!
I GAVE BOTH THOSE FUCKS A CUT--OF COURSE--OR I'D'VE BEEN A DEAD MAN LONG AGO--BUT I DIDN'T REALLY WORK FOR 'EM...
I WORKED FOR MYSELF! I WAS A COP--ON THE TAKE LIKE THE REST OF 'EM...
OH, A PIG... I SEE.
FUCK THAT.
YEAH, WE DON'T LIKE FUCKIN' PIGS, EITHER...
C'MON, ROSE--LET ME SLICE UP THIS SLAB OF BACON...
EX-PIG.
HOLD ON, NICOLE...
R.I.P.
SEE YOU
HEL
SO, YOU'RE NOT A MOBSTER--AND YOU'RE NO LONGER A PIG--
HOW DO YOU STILL HAVE THESE BIG CONNECTIONS?

I NEVER **LOST** THEM--EVEN WHEN I WAS LOCKED UP AND THAT SHIT-HEEL CRIZZLE HAD TAKEN MY PLACE OUT ON THE STREET--

KLAK KLAK KLAK KLAK KLAK

Y'KNOW, WHEN I FIRST GOT SPRUNG I FELT SO TIRED--SO OVER AND DONE WITH ALL OF THIS DIRTY BUSINESS--

YEAH, YEAH, OKAY...

WUHHH HHH

BUT ONCE I GOT A TASTE OF THE GOOD LIFE--BIG MONEY AND FAST WOMEN AGAIN, I'LL TELL YA--

ALRIGHT, ALRIGHT!

WHEN I WIPED-OUT THAT GREASE-BALL, EVERYONE KNEW WHO WAS IN FUCKIN' **CHARGE** AGAIN--

ENOUGH, ENOUGH! WE DON'T GIVE A SHIT!

YOU'RE BACK ON THE THRONE AGAIN, I GET IT...SO, DO YOU THINK YOUR CONTACT CAN HANDLE MILLIONS OF DOLLARS IN HEROIN?

YEP.

KLAK KLAK KLAK

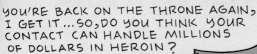

PROVE IT...

BE HERE, WITH YOUR CONTACT AT 5 A.M.

OR ELSE WE SLICE AND DICE YOU.

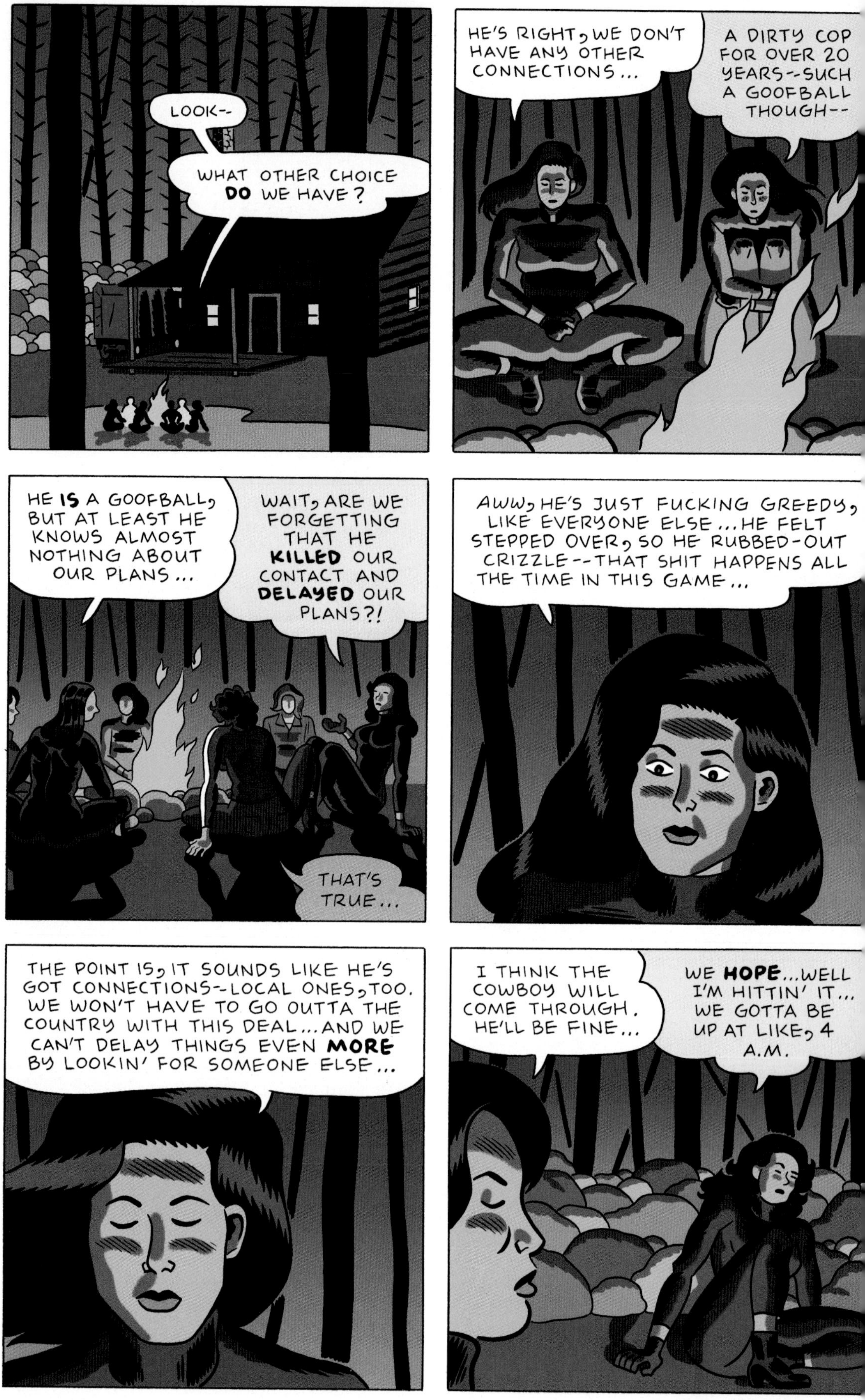
LOOK--
WHAT OTHER CHOICE DO WE HAVE?
HE'S RIGHT, WE DON'T HAVE ANY OTHER CONNECTIONS...
A DIRTY COP FOR OVER 20 YEARS--SUCH A GOOFBALL THOUGH--
HE IS A GOOFBALL, BUT AT LEAST HE KNOWS ALMOST NOTHING ABOUT OUR PLANS...
WAIT, ARE WE FORGETTING THAT HE KILLED OUR CONTACT AND DELAYED OUR PLANS?!
THAT'S TRUE...
AWW, HE'S JUST FUCKING GREEDY, LIKE EVERYONE ELSE...HE FELT STEPPED OVER, SO HE RUBBED-OUT CRIZZLE--THAT SHIT HAPPENS ALL THE TIME IN THIS GAME...
THE POINT IS, IT SOUNDS LIKE HE'S GOT CONNECTIONS--LOCAL ONES, TOO. WE WON'T HAVE TO GO OUTTA THE COUNTRY WITH THIS DEAL...AND WE CAN'T DELAY THINGS EVEN MORE BY LOOKIN' FOR SOMEONE ELSE...
I THINK THE COWBOY WILL COME THROUGH. HE'LL BE FINE...
WE HOPE...WELL I'M HITTIN' IT... WE GOTTA BE UP AT LIKE, 4 A.M.

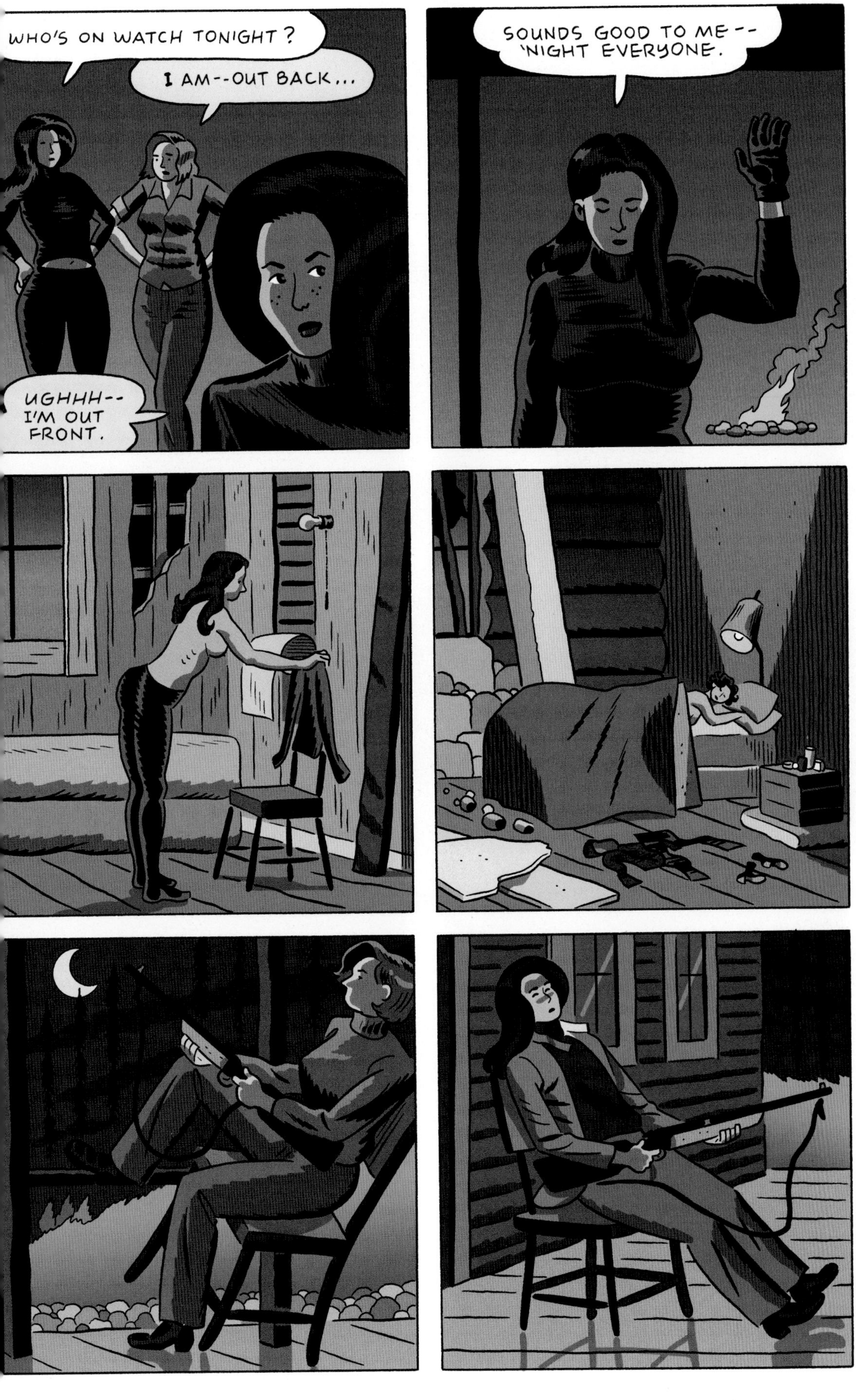

WHO'S ON WATCH TONIGHT?
I AM--OUT BACK...
UGHHH-- I'M OUT FRONT.
SOUNDS GOOD TO ME-- 'NIGHT EVERYONE.

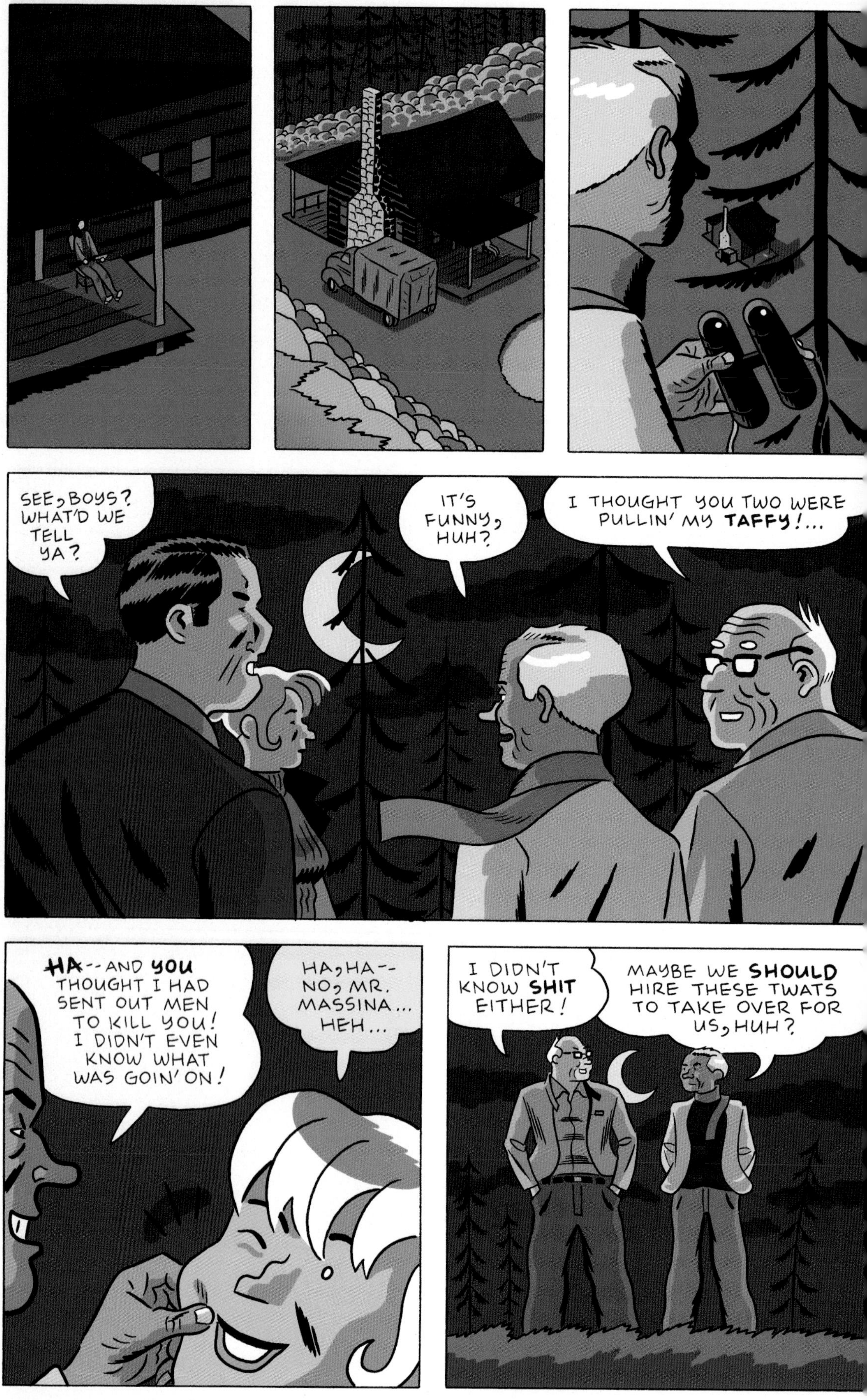

SEE, BOYS? WHAT'D WE TELL YA?
IT'S FUNNY, HUH?
I THOUGHT YOU TWO WERE PULLIN' MY **TAFFY**!...
HA--AND **YOU** THOUGHT I HAD SENT OUT MEN TO KILL YOU! I DIDN'T EVEN KNOW WHAT WAS GOIN' ON!
HA, HA--NO, MR. MASSINA... HEH...
I DIDN'T KNOW **SHIT** EITHER!
MAYBE WE **SHOULD** HIRE THESE TWATS TO TAKE OVER FOR US, HUH?

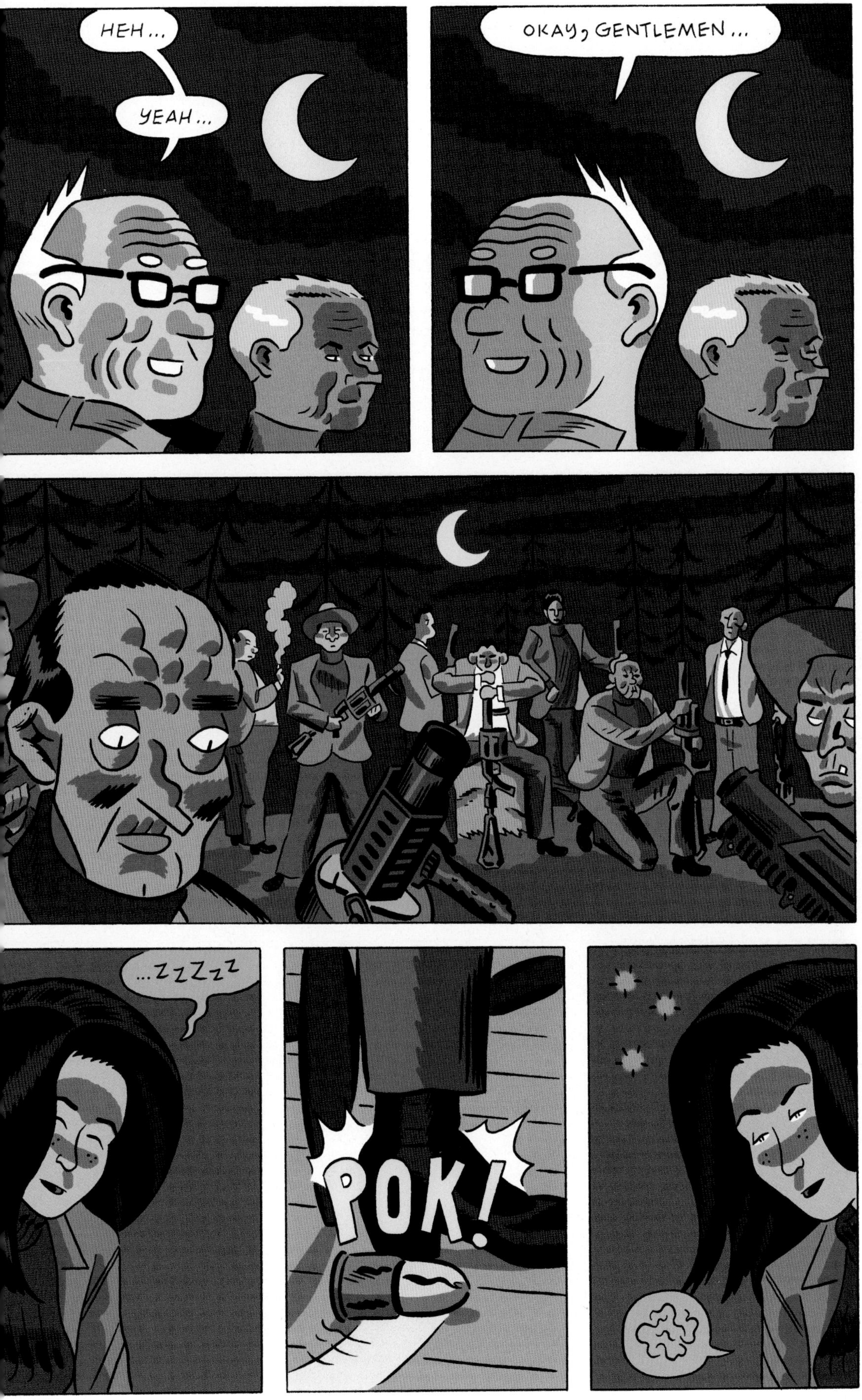
HEH...
YEAH...
OKAY, GENTLEMEN...
...ZZZZZ
POK!

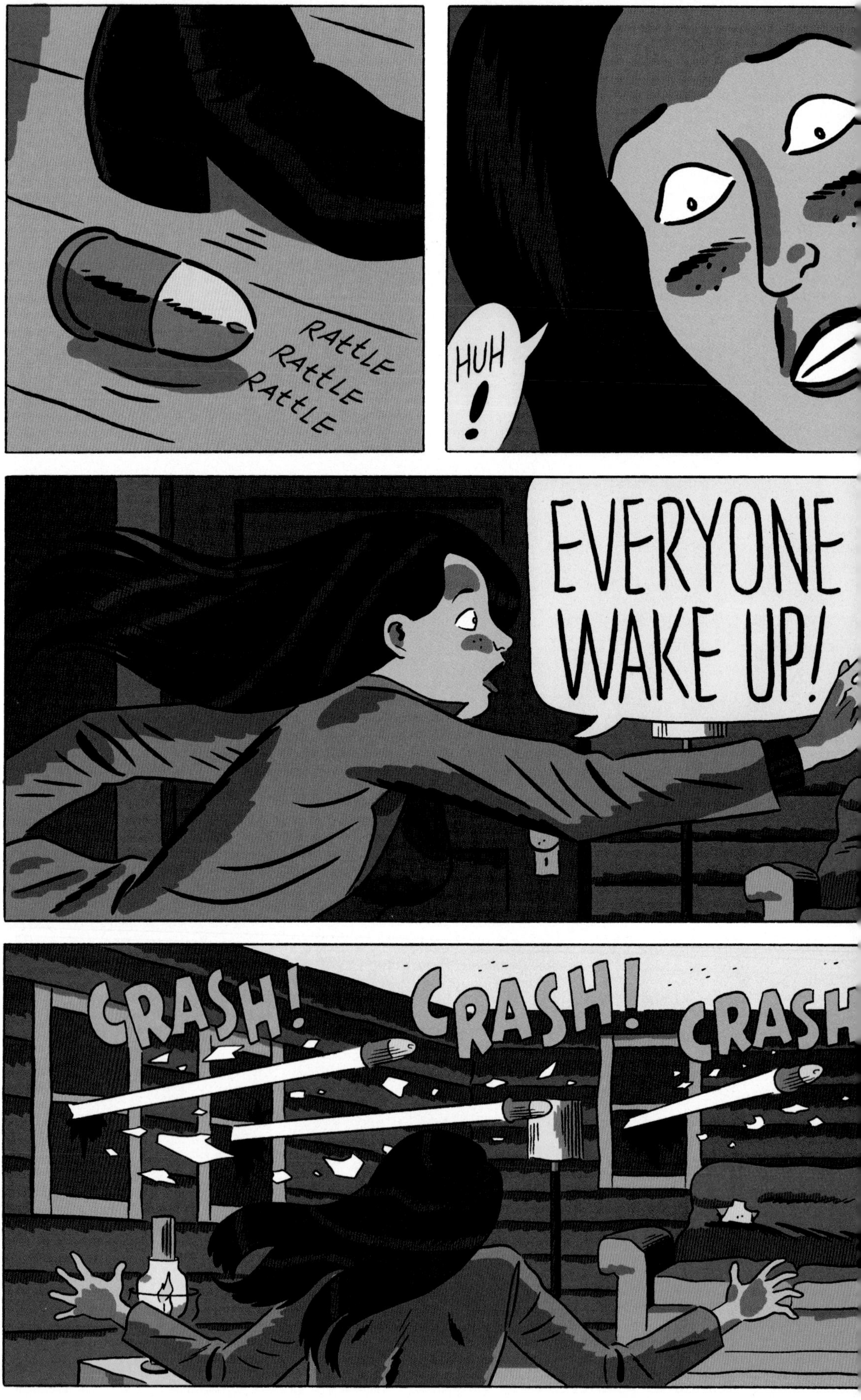
RATTLE
RATTLE
RATTLE
HUH!
EVERYONE WAKE UP!
CRASH!
CRASH!
CRASH

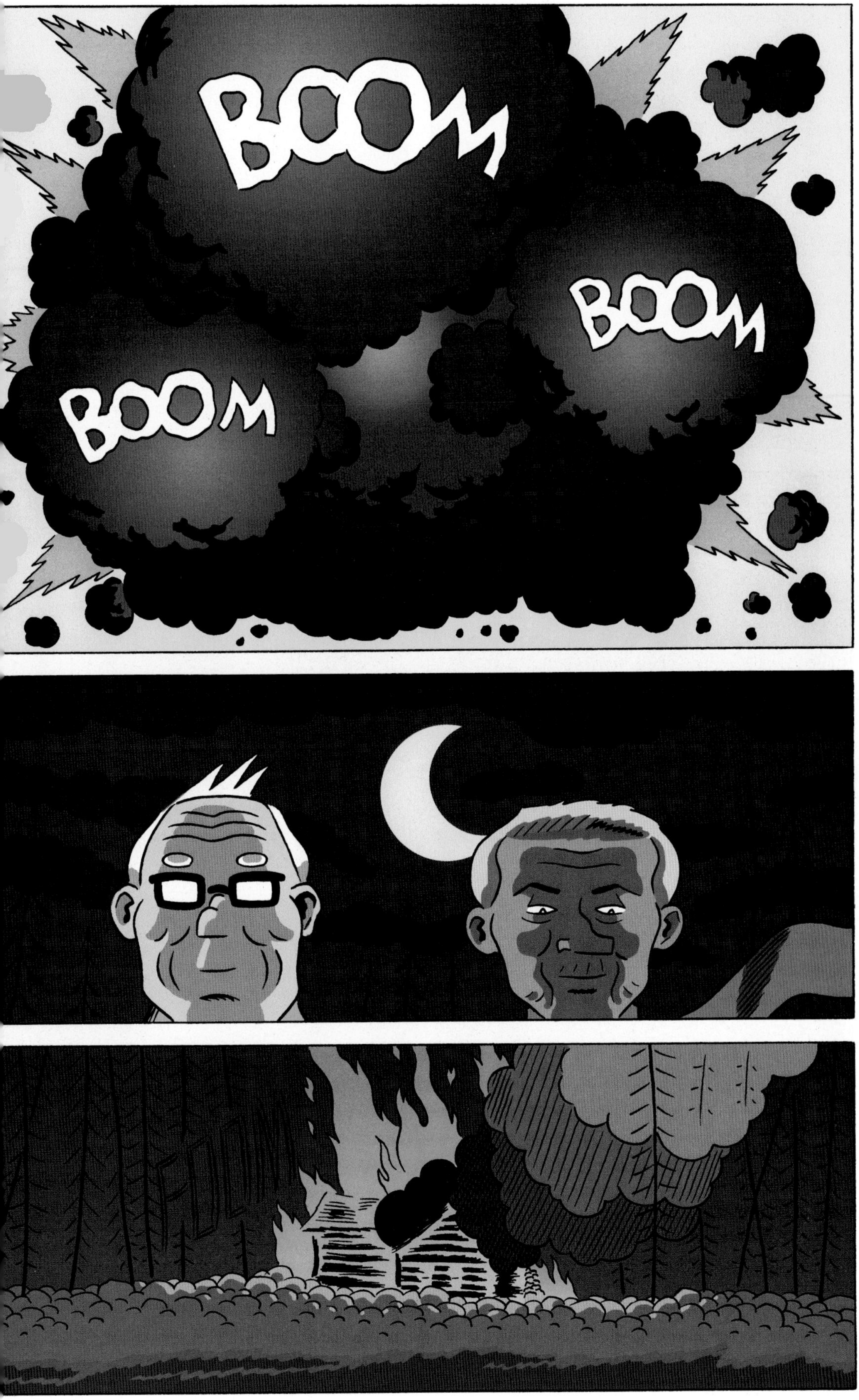
BOOM
BOOM
BOOM

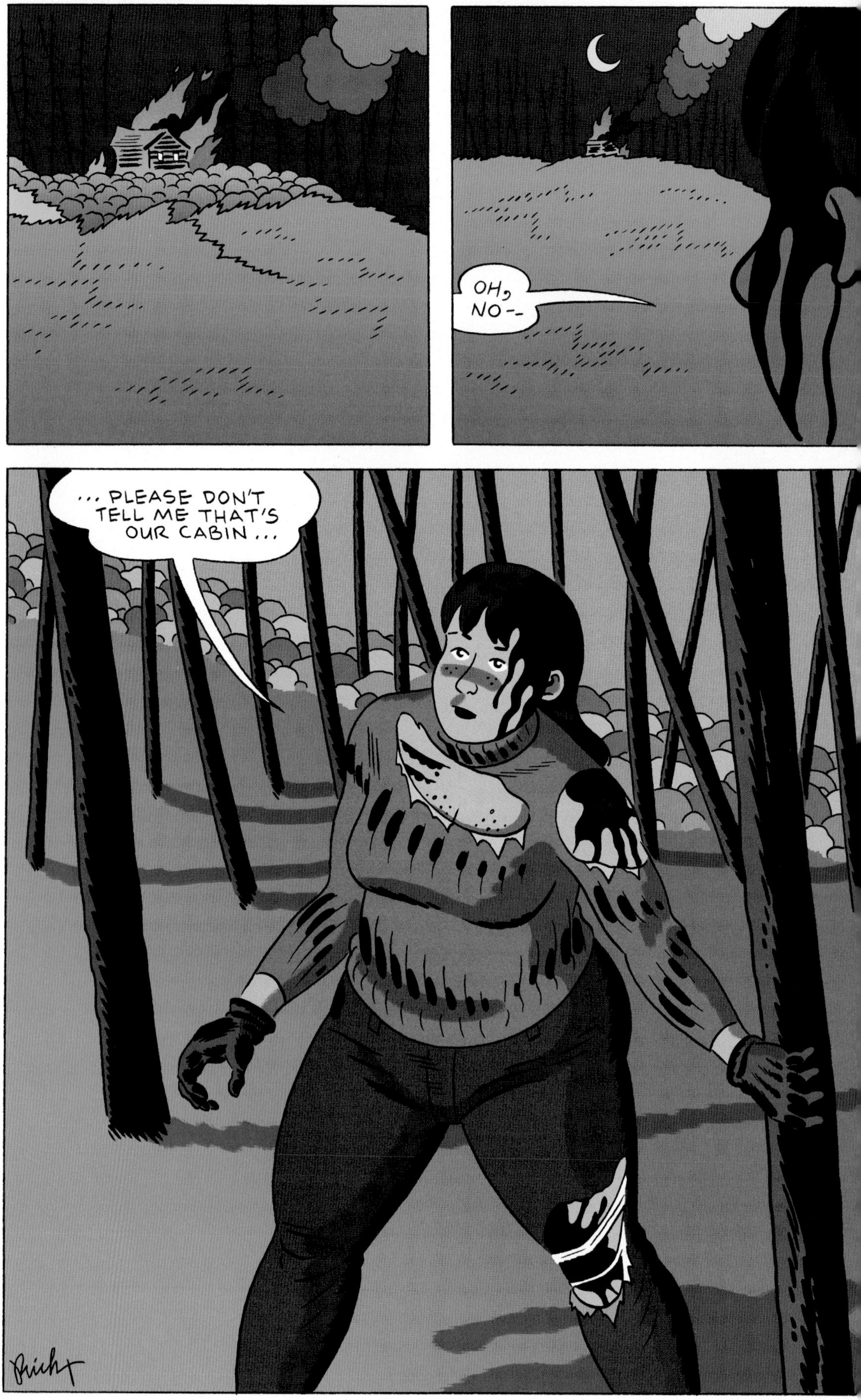
OH, NO--
... PLEASE DON'T TELL ME THAT'S OUR CABIN ...

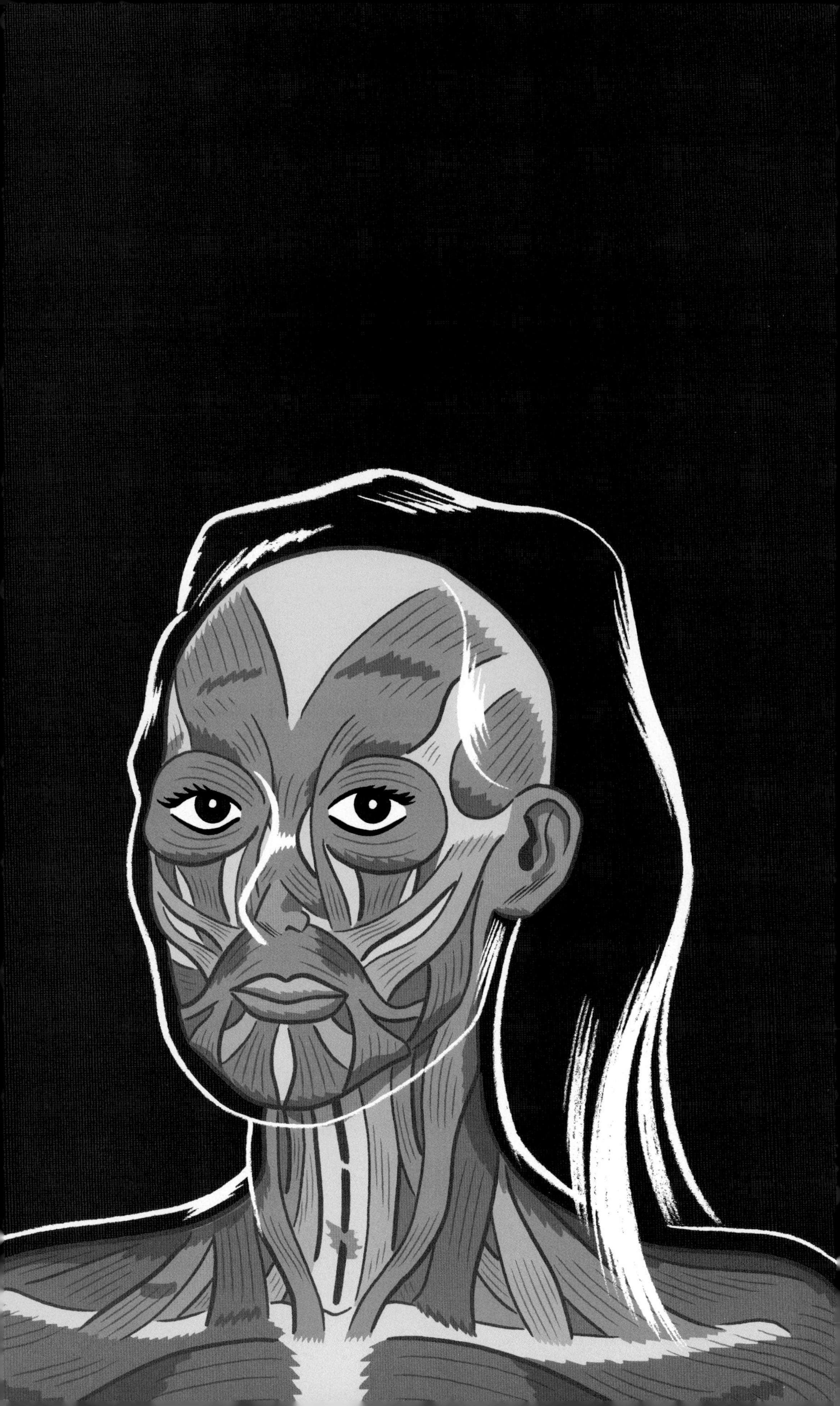

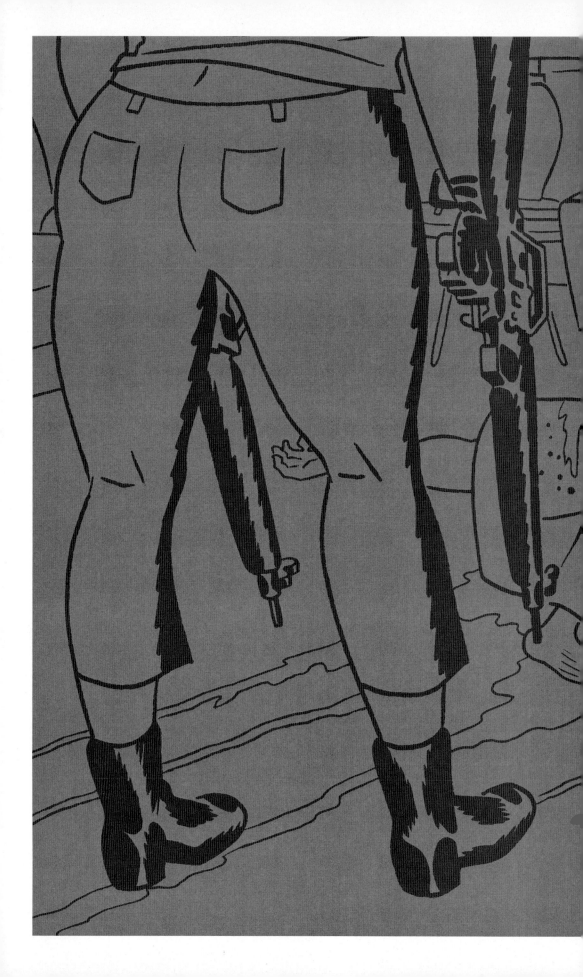

The RED CIRCLE

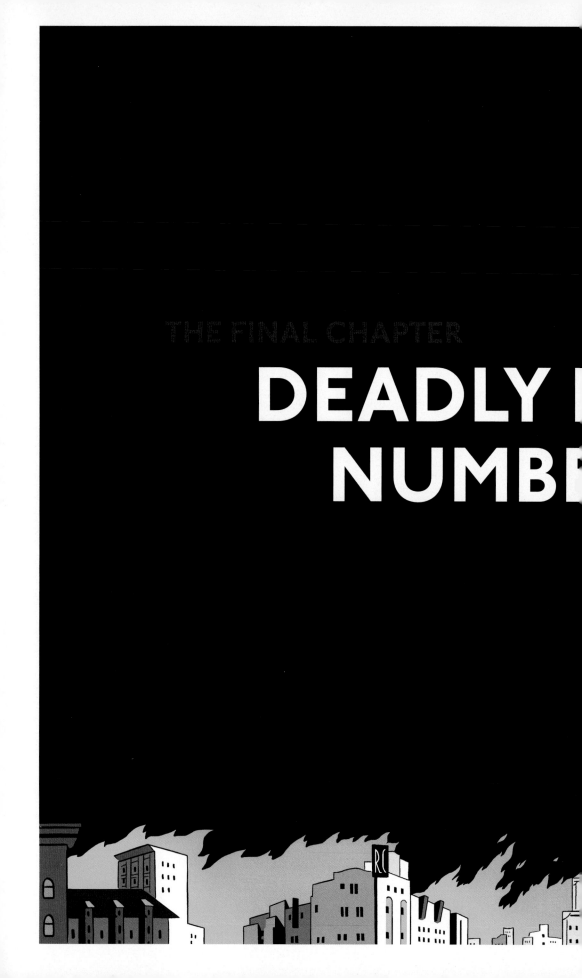

THE FINAL CHAPTER

DEADLY
NUMB

AUGHTER
SEVEN

BY RICH TOMMASO

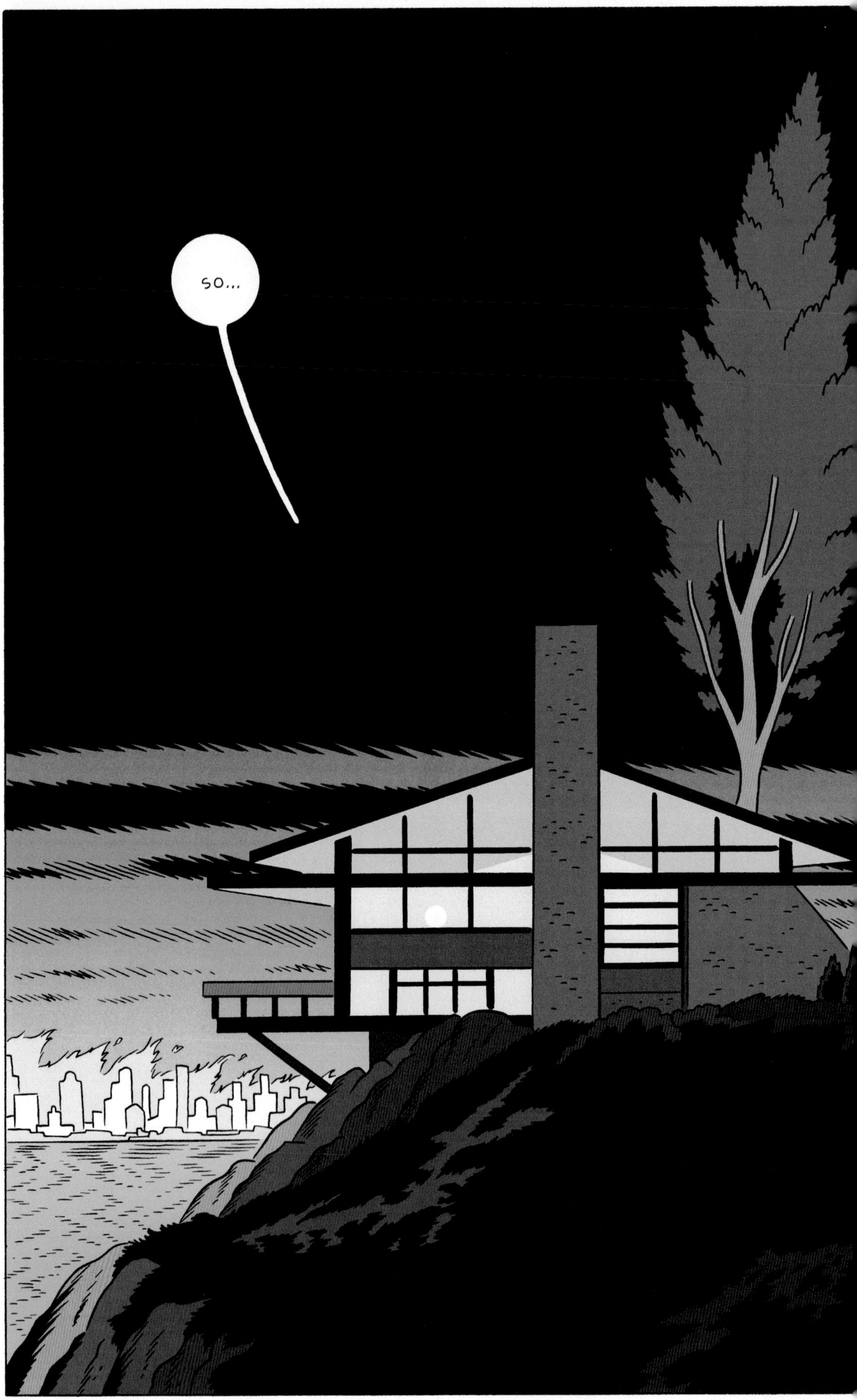
SO...

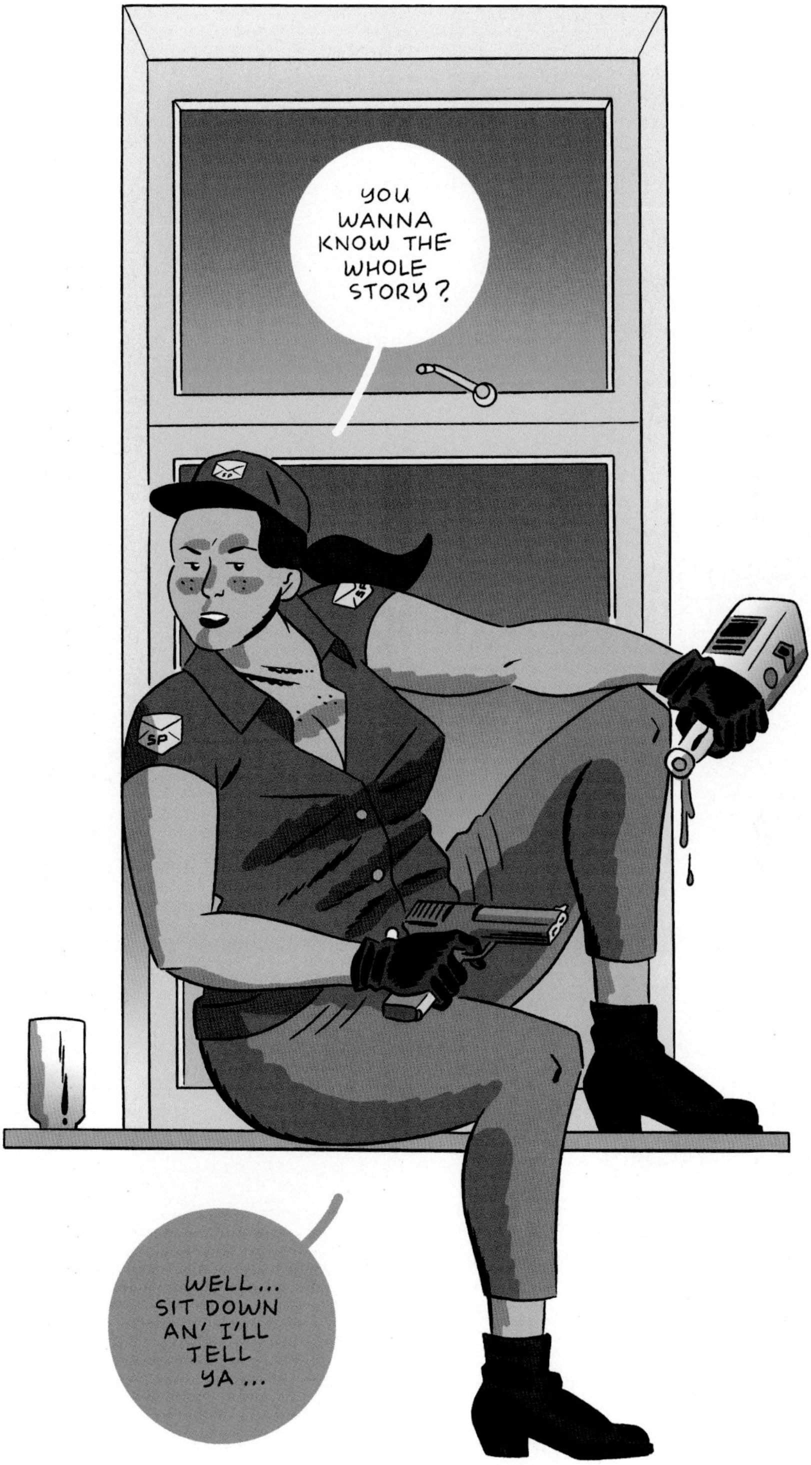
YOU WANNA KNOW THE WHOLE STORY?
WELL... SIT DOWN AN' I'LL TELL YA...

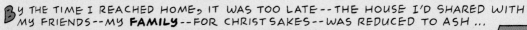

By THE TIME I REACHED HOME, IT WAS TOO LATE--THE HOUSE I'D SHARED WITH MY FRIENDS--MY **FAMILY**--FOR CHRIST SAKES--WAS REDUCED TO ASH ...

Seeing all of thier twisted, charred-black bodies just broke me in half--

I MEAN, WE HAD BARELY EVEN BEGUN OUR MISSION TO CRUSH THE MOB--

And in one fell swoop, they'd wiped-out **ALL** of my sisters...

What was I going to do now, right?...

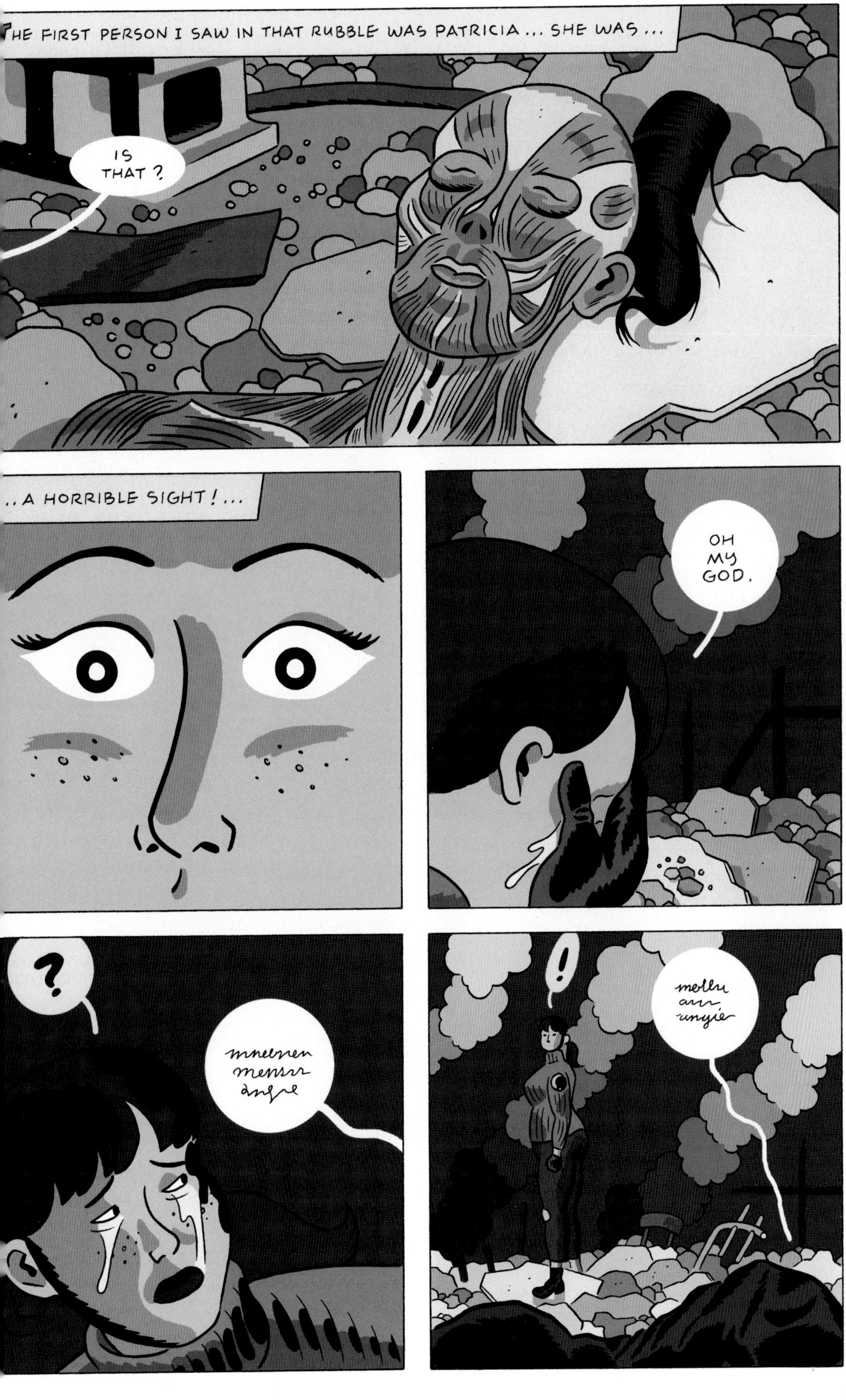
THE FIRST PERSON I SAW IN THAT RUBBLE WAS PATRICIA ... SHE WAS ...
IS THAT ?
.. A HORRIBLE SIGHT ! ...
OH MY GOD.
?
!

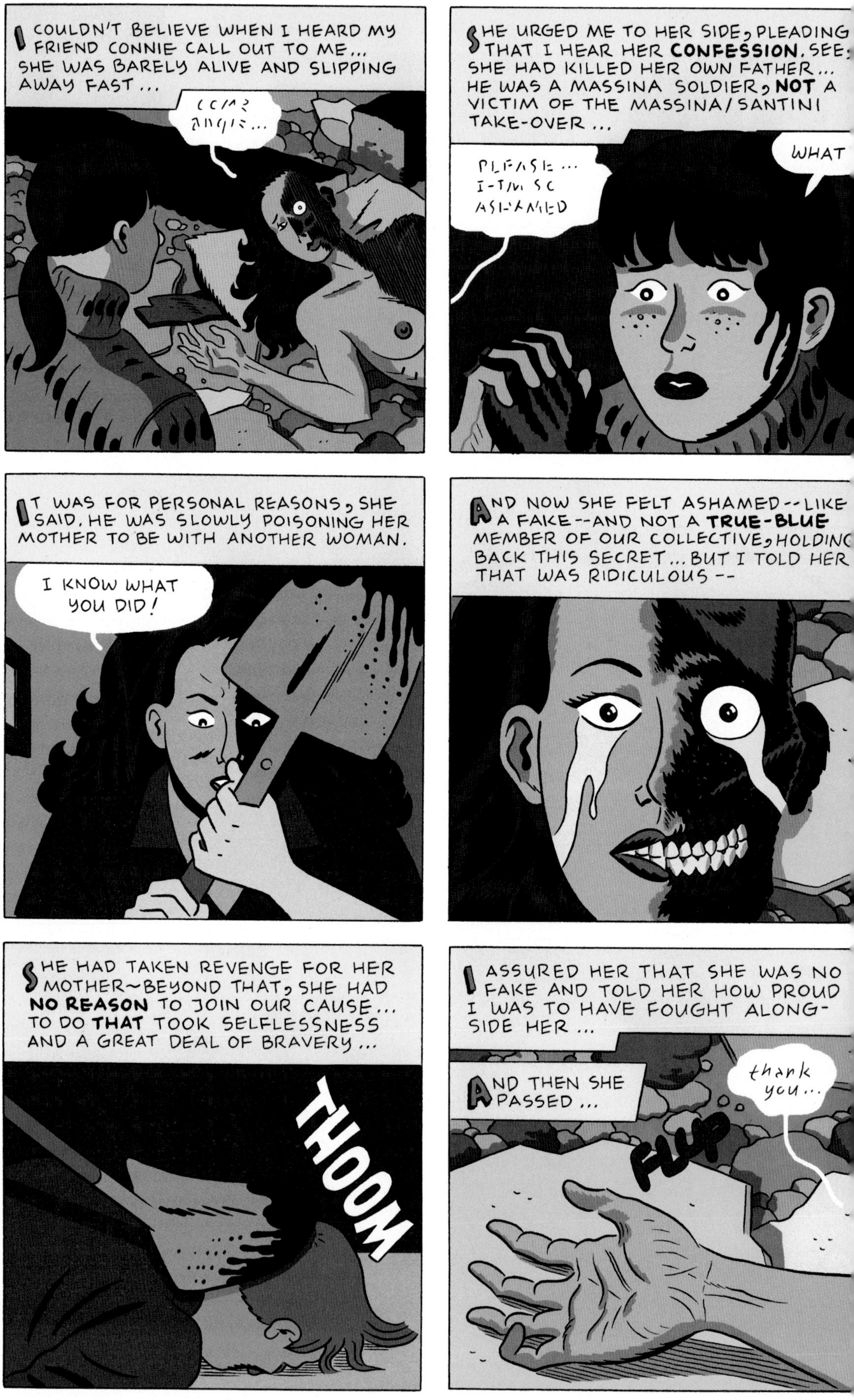
I COULDN'T BELIEVE WHEN I HEARD MY FRIEND CONNIE CALL OUT TO ME... SHE WAS BARELY ALIVE AND SLIPPING AWAY FAST...
come angie...
SHE URGED ME TO HER SIDE, PLEADING THAT I HEAR HER **CONFESSION**. SEE SHE HAD KILLED HER OWN FATHER... HE WAS A MASSINA SOLDIER, **NOT** A VICTIM OF THE MASSINA/SANTINI TAKE-OVER...
PLEASE... I-I'M SO ASHAMED
WHAT
IT WAS FOR PERSONAL REASONS, SHE SAID. HE WAS SLOWLY POISONING HER MOTHER TO BE WITH ANOTHER WOMAN.
I KNOW WHAT YOU DID!
AND NOW SHE FELT ASHAMED--LIKE A FAKE--AND NOT A **TRUE-BLUE** MEMBER OF OUR COLLECTIVE, HOLDIN BACK THIS SECRET... BUT I TOLD HER THAT WAS RIDICULOUS--
SHE HAD TAKEN REVENGE FOR HER MOTHER~BEYOND THAT, SHE HAD **NO REASON** TO JOIN OUR CAUSE... TO DO **THAT** TOOK SELFLESSNESS AND A GREAT DEAL OF BRAVERY...
THOOM
I ASSURED HER THAT SHE WAS NO FAKE AND TOLD HER HOW PROUD I WAS TO HAVE FOUGHT ALONG-SIDE HER...
AND THEN SHE PASSED...
thank you...
FLUP

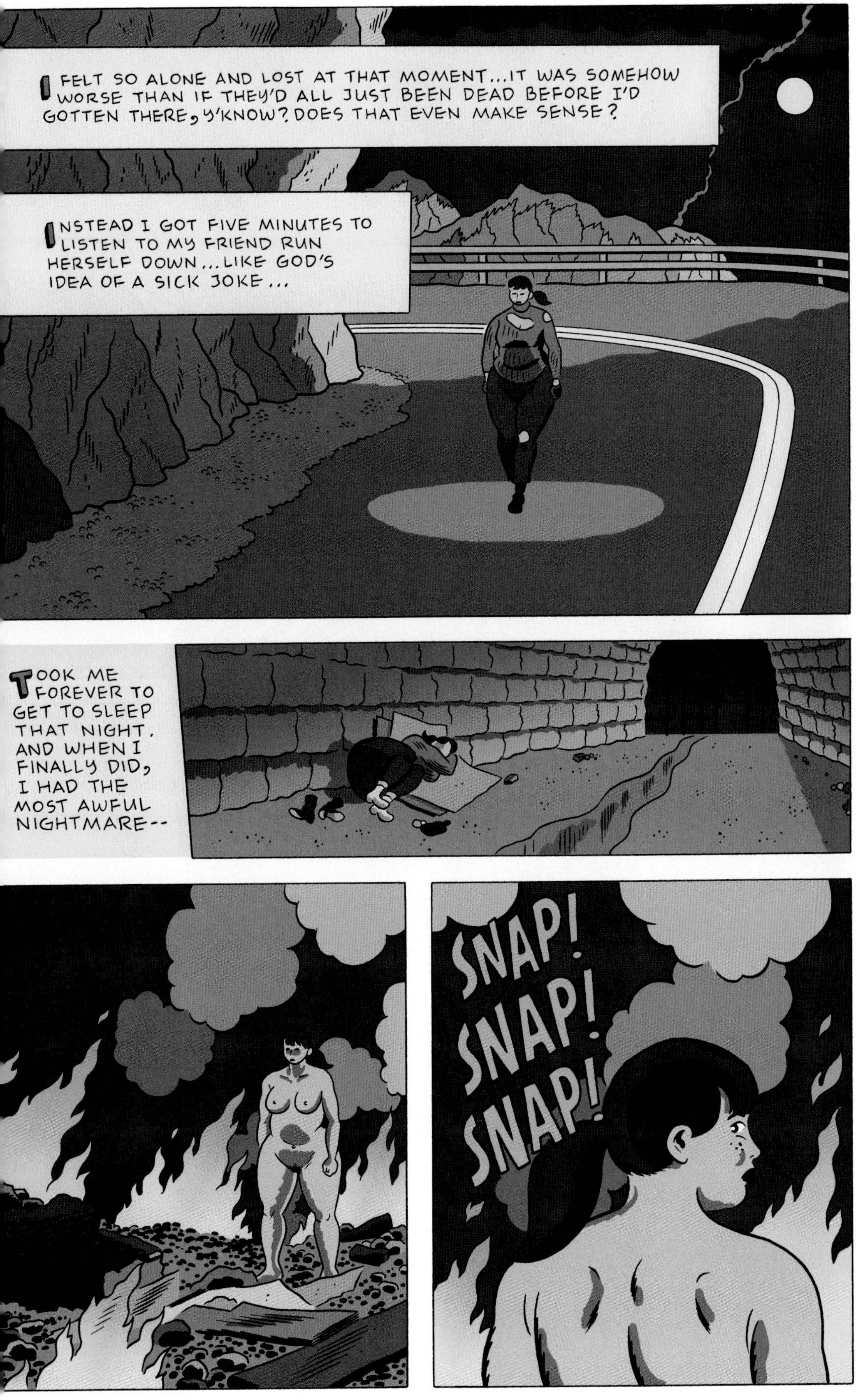
I FELT SO ALONE AND LOST AT THAT MOMENT...IT WAS SOMEHOW WORSE THAN IF THEY'D ALL JUST BEEN DEAD BEFORE I'D GOTTEN THERE, Y'KNOW? DOES THAT EVEN MAKE SENSE?
INSTEAD I GOT FIVE MINUTES TO LISTEN TO MY FRIEND RUN HERSELF DOWN...LIKE GOD'S IDEA OF A SICK JOKE...
TOOK ME FOREVER TO GET TO SLEEP THAT NIGHT. AND WHEN I FINALLY DID, I HAD THE MOST AWFUL NIGHTMARE--
SNAP!
SNAP!
SNAP!

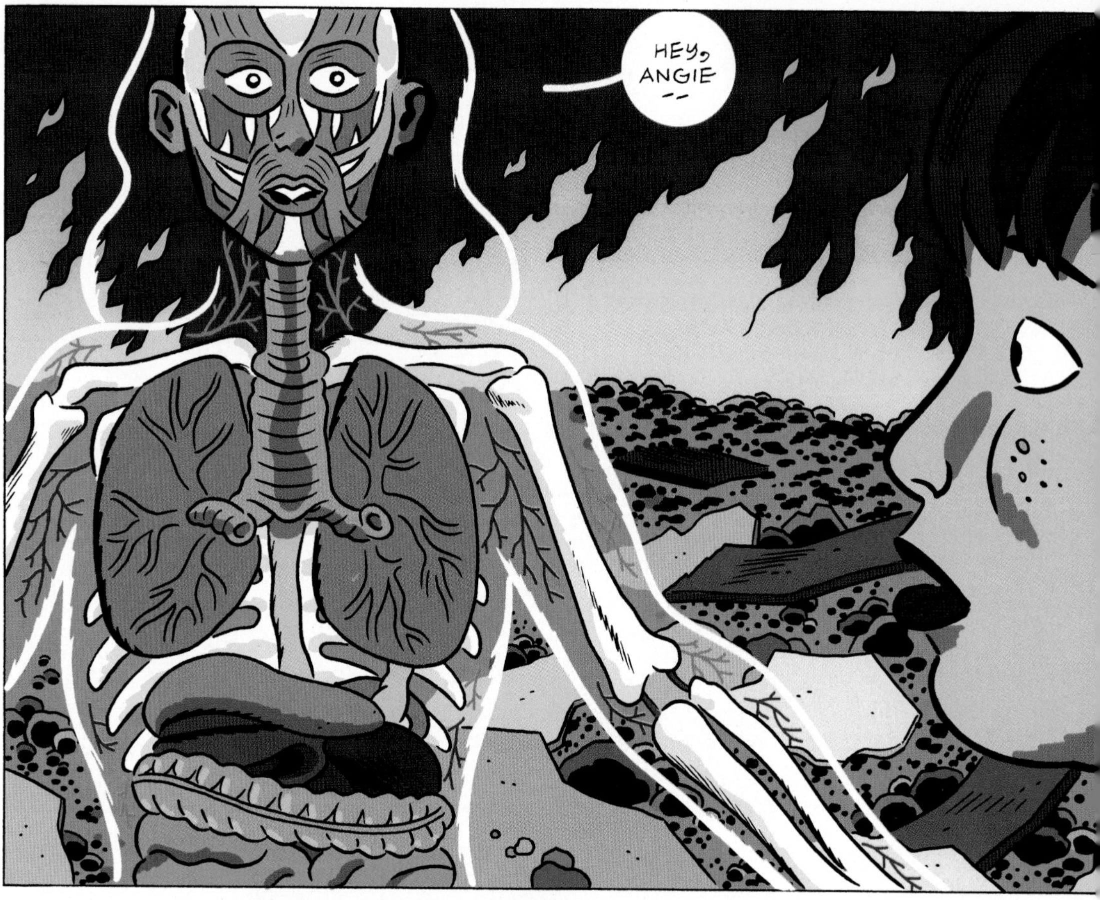
HEY, ANGIE --

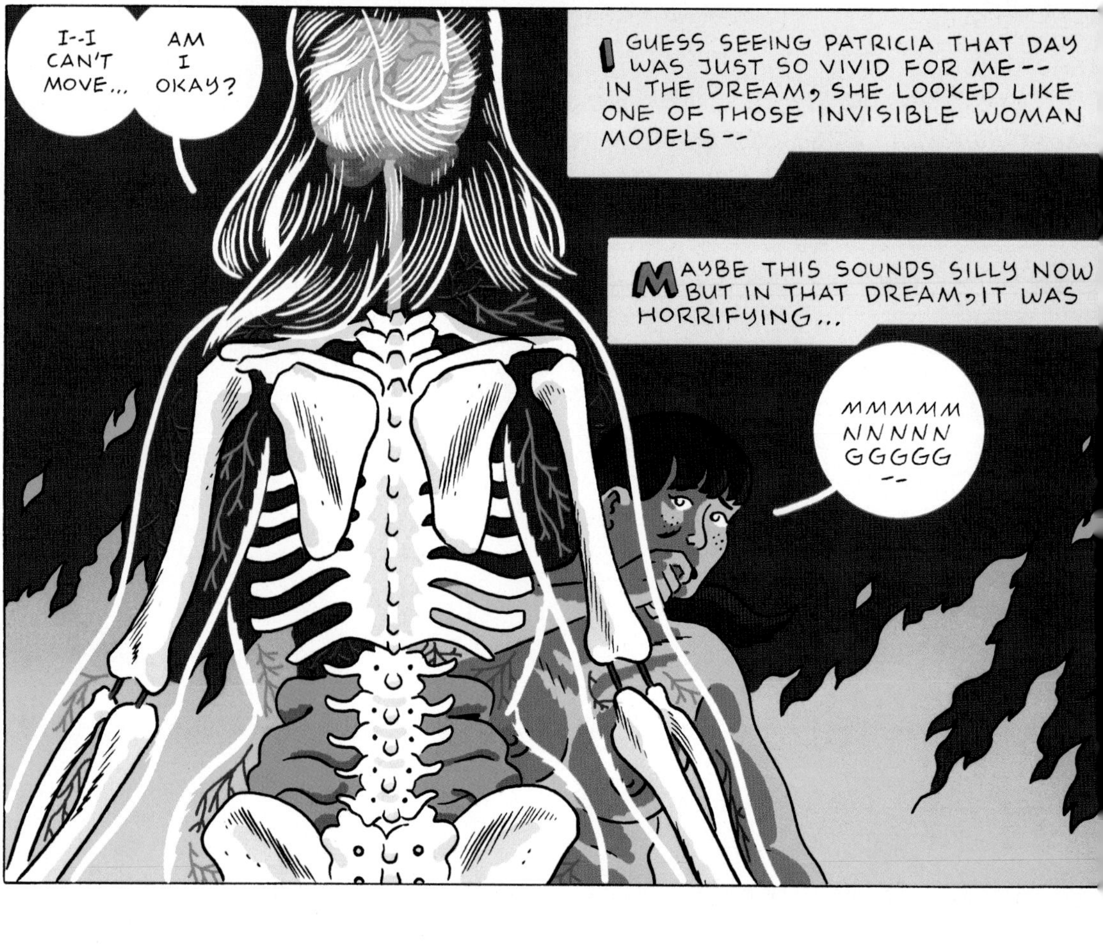
I--I CAN'T MOVE...
AM I OKAY?
I GUESS SEEING PATRICIA THAT DAY WAS JUST SO VIVID FOR ME -- IN THE DREAM, SHE LOOKED LIKE ONE OF THOSE INVISIBLE WOMAN MODELS --
MAYBE THIS SOUNDS SILLY NOW BUT IN THAT DREAM, IT WAS HORRIFYING...
MMMMM NNNNN GGGGG --

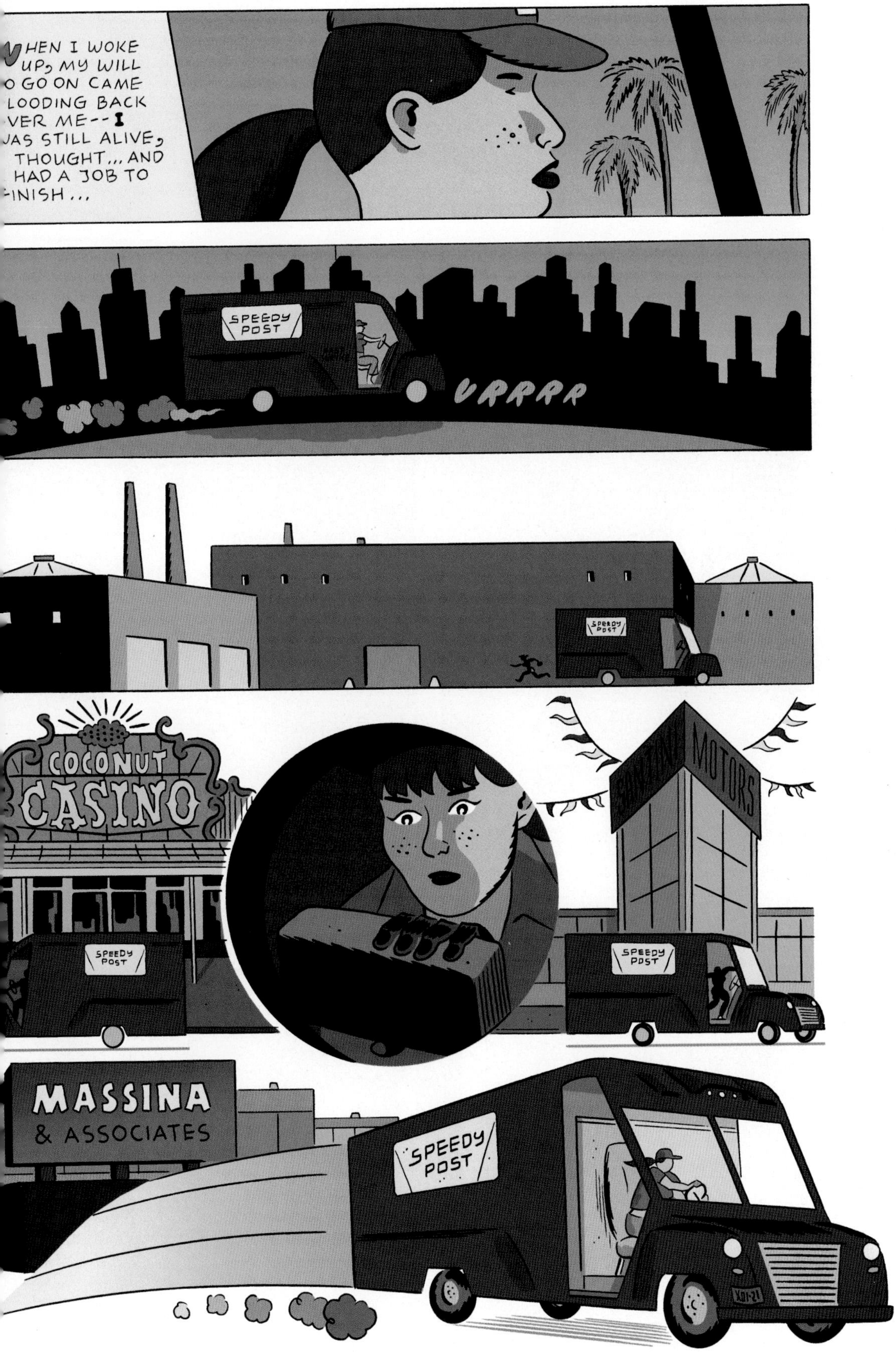
HEN I WOKE UP, MY WILL O GO ON CAME LOODING BACK VER ME-- I JAS STILL ALIVE, THOUGHT... AND HAD A JOB TO INISH...
SPEEDY POST
URRRR
SPEEDY POST
COCONUT CASINO
MOTORS
SPEEDY POST
SPEEDY POST
MASSINA & ASSOCIATES
SPEEDY POST

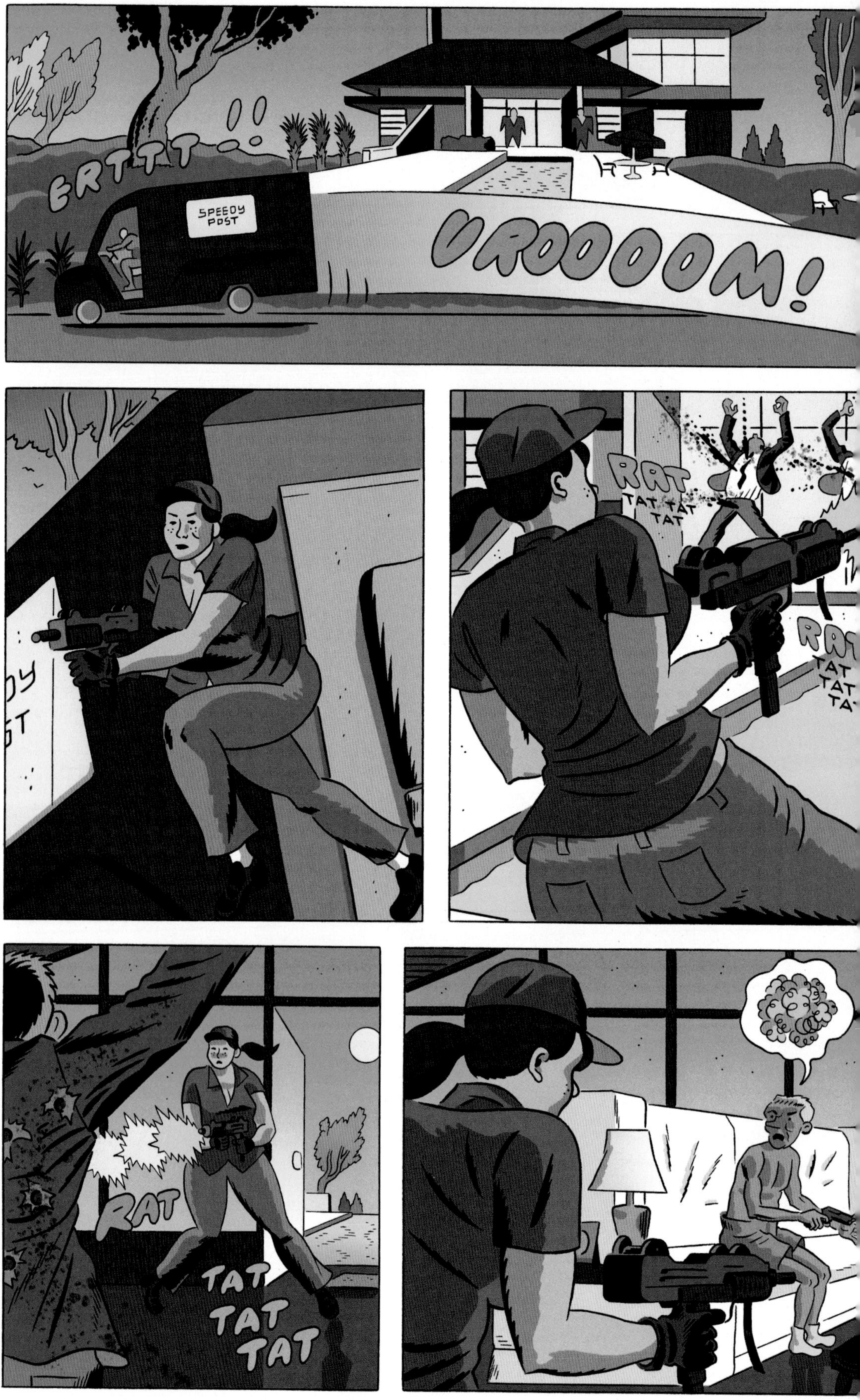
ERTTTT--!!
SPEEDY POST
VROOOOM!
RAT TAT TAT TAT
RAT
TAT
TAT
TAT

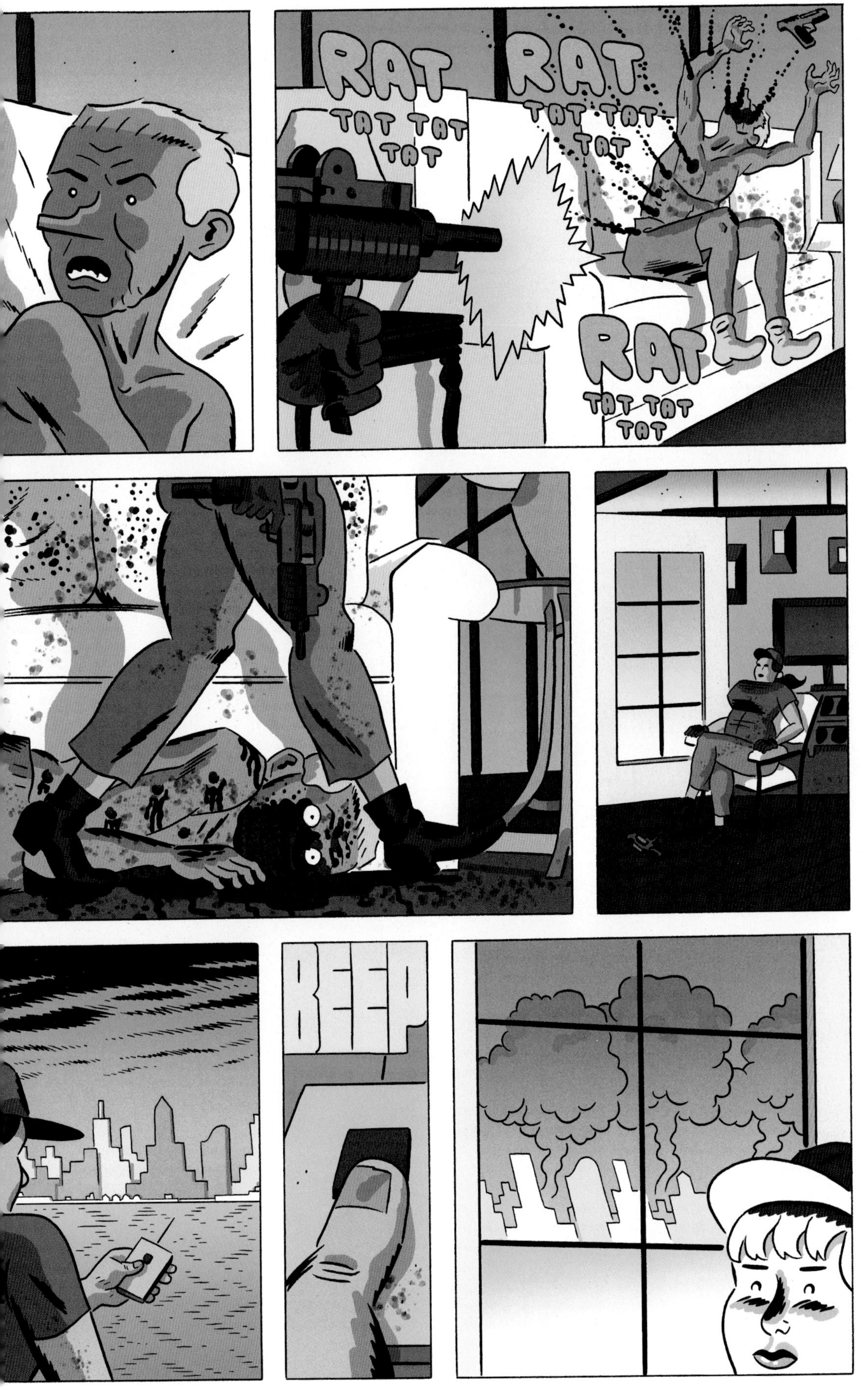
RAT
TAT TAT
TAT
RAT
TAT TAT
TAT
RAT
TAT TAT
TAT
BEEP

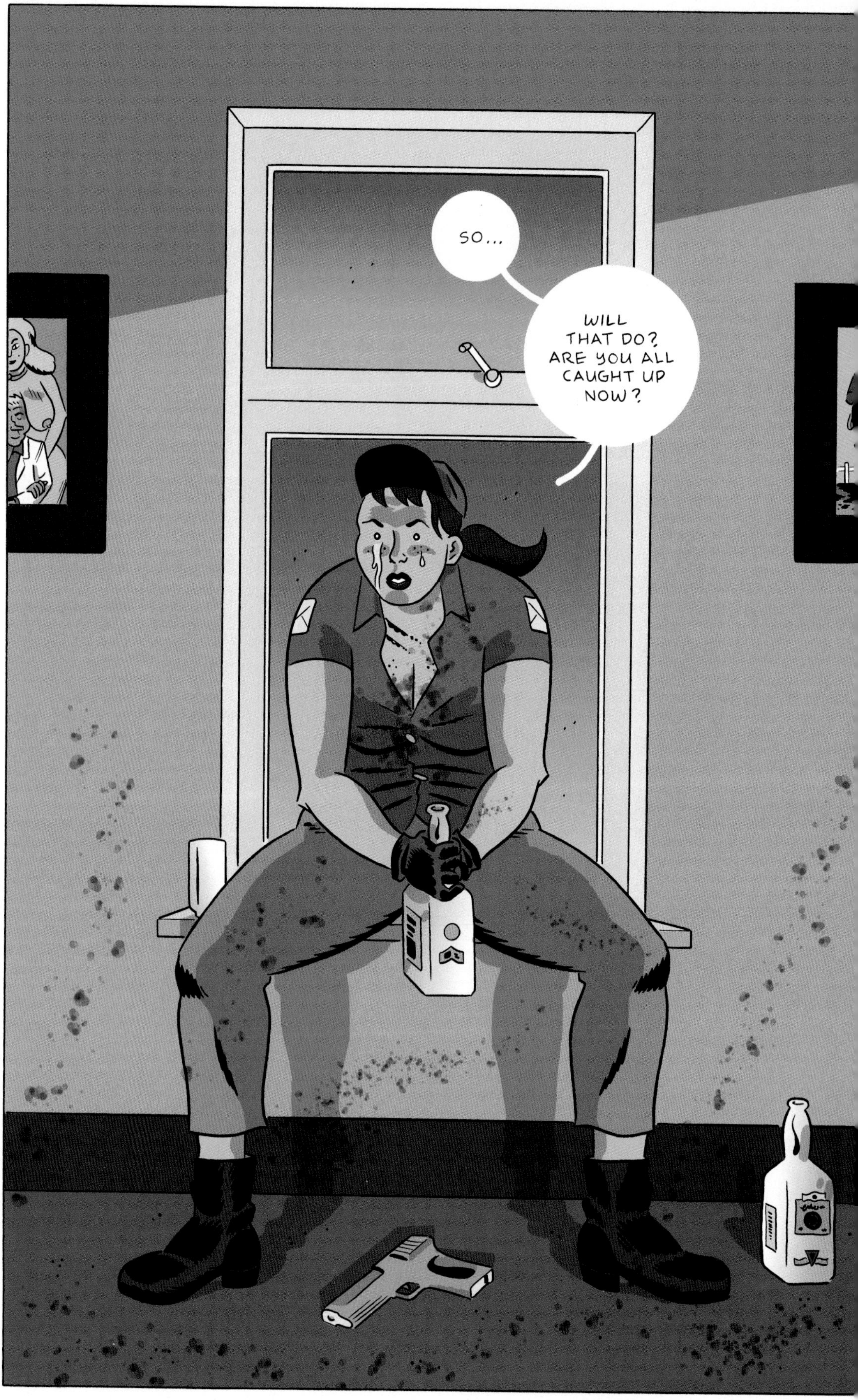
SO...
WILL THAT DO? ARE YOU ALL CAUGHT UP NOW?

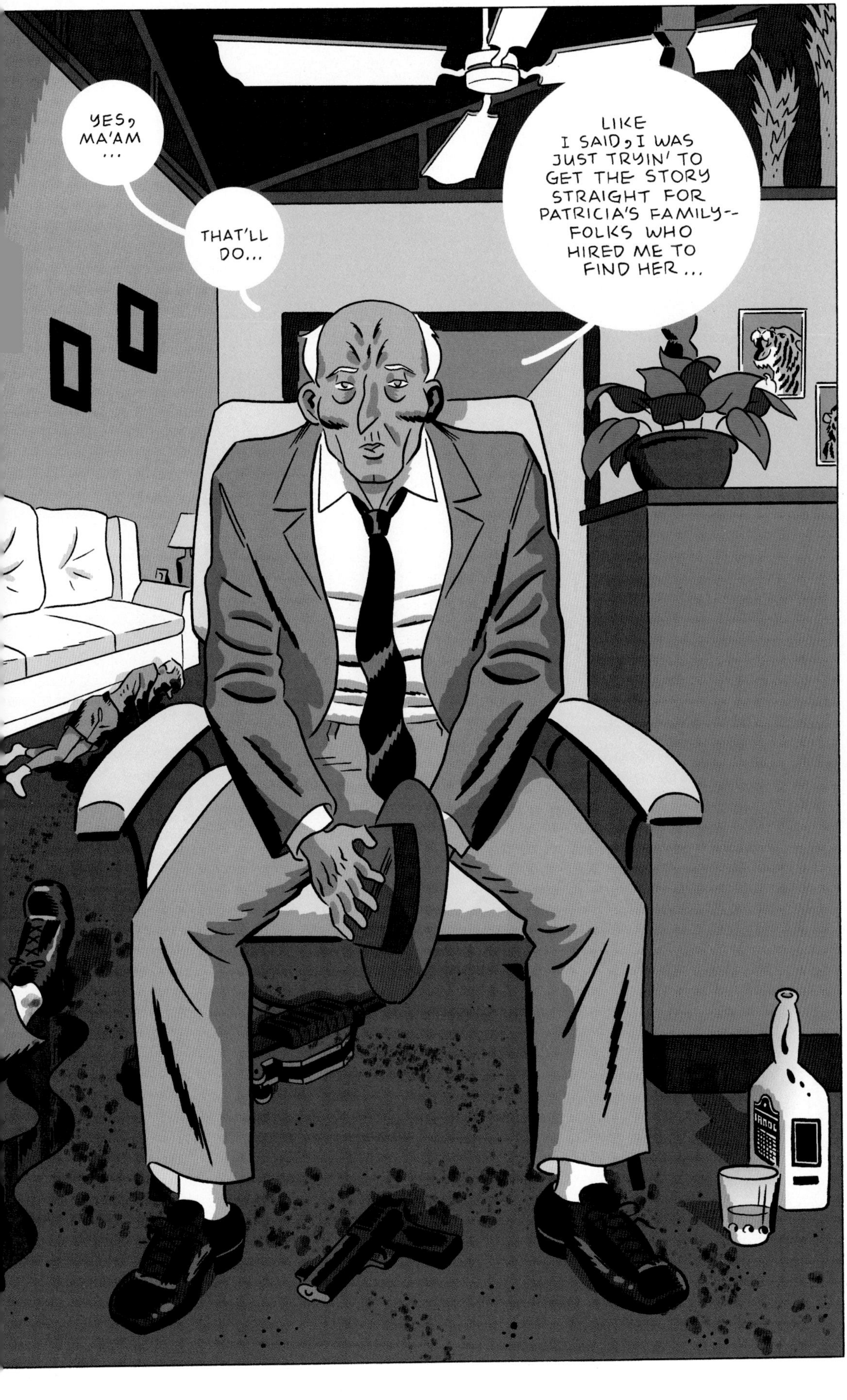
LIKE I SAID, I WAS JUST TRYIN' TO GET THE STORY STRAIGHT FOR PATRICIA'S FAMILY-- FOLKS WHO HIRED ME TO FIND HER...
YES, MA'AM...
THAT'LL DO...

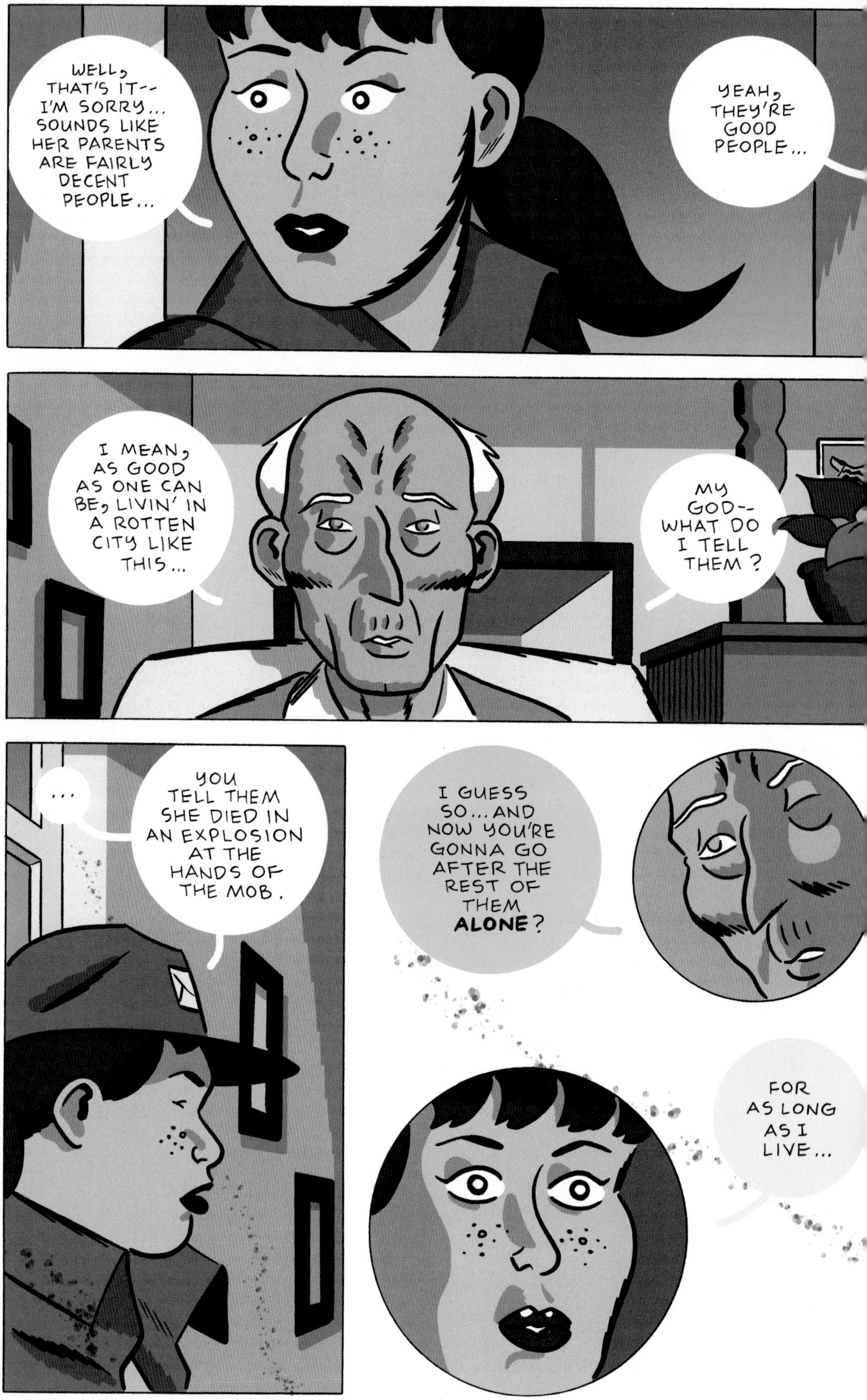
WELL, THAT'S IT-- I'M SORRY... SOUNDS LIKE HER PARENTS ARE FAIRLY DECENT PEOPLE...
YEAH, THEY'RE GOOD PEOPLE...
I MEAN, AS GOOD AS ONE CAN BE, LIVIN' IN A ROTTEN CITY LIKE THIS...
MY GOD-- WHAT DO I TELL THEM?
...
YOU TELL THEM SHE DIED IN AN EXPLOSION AT THE HANDS OF THE MOB.
I GUESS SO... AND NOW YOU'RE GONNA GO AFTER THE REST OF THEM **ALONE**?
FOR AS LONG AS I LIVE...

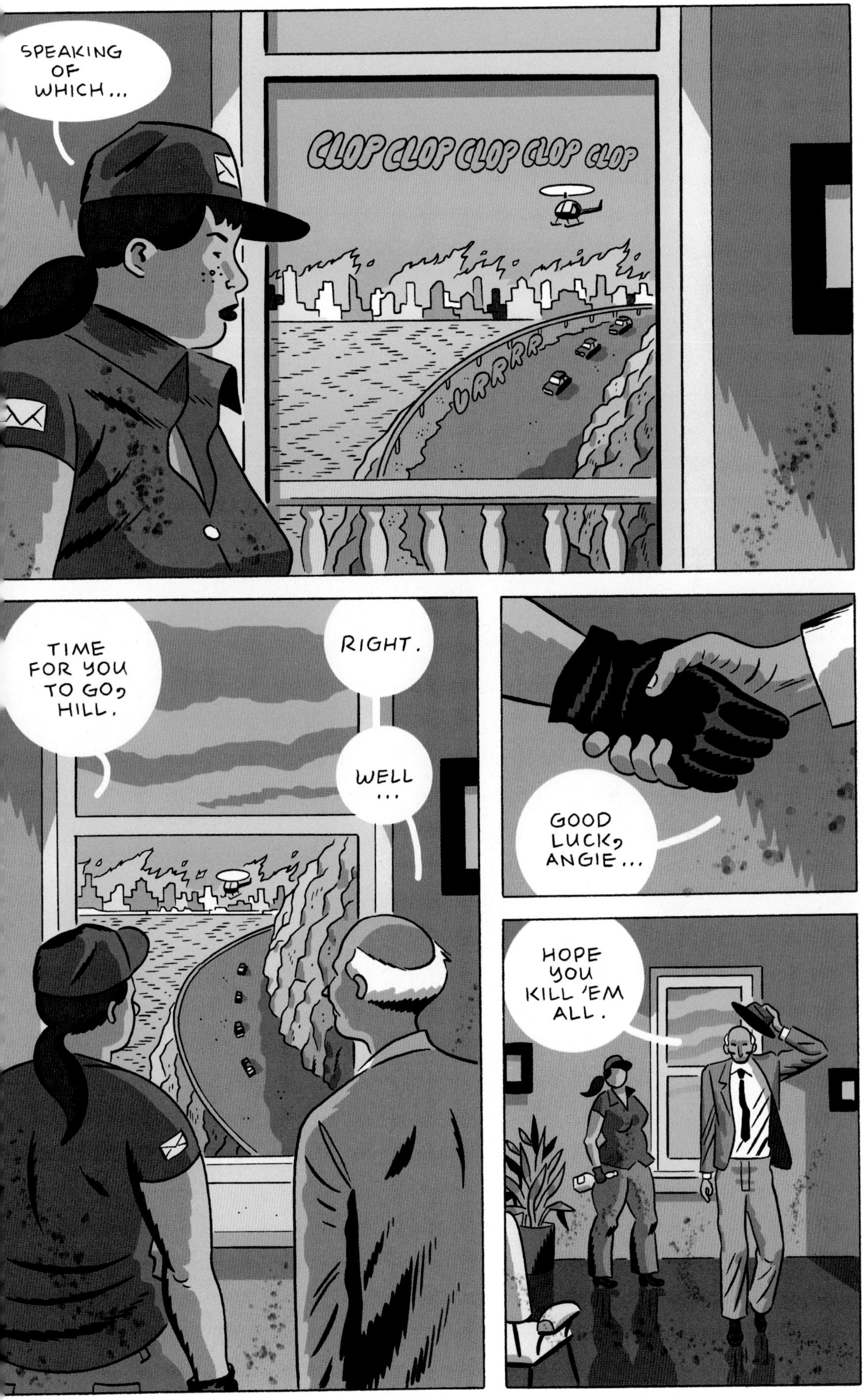
SPEAKING OF WHICH...
CLOP CLOP CLOP CLOP CLOP
URRRR
TIME FOR YOU TO GO, HILL.
RIGHT.
WELL ...
GOOD LUCK, ANGIE...
HOPE YOU KILL 'EM ALL.

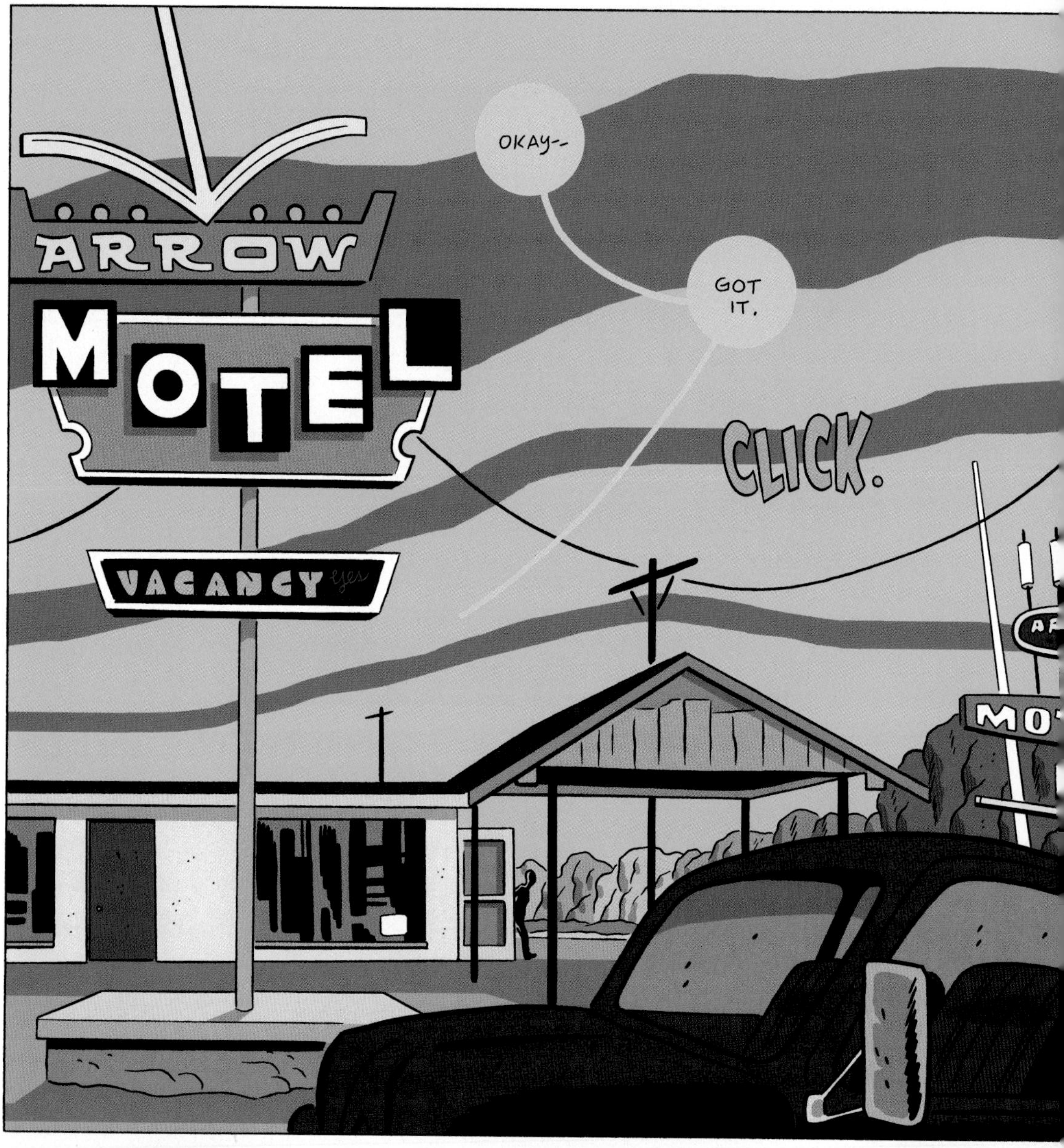
ARROW
MOTEL
VACANCY yes
OKAY--
GOT IT.
CLICK.
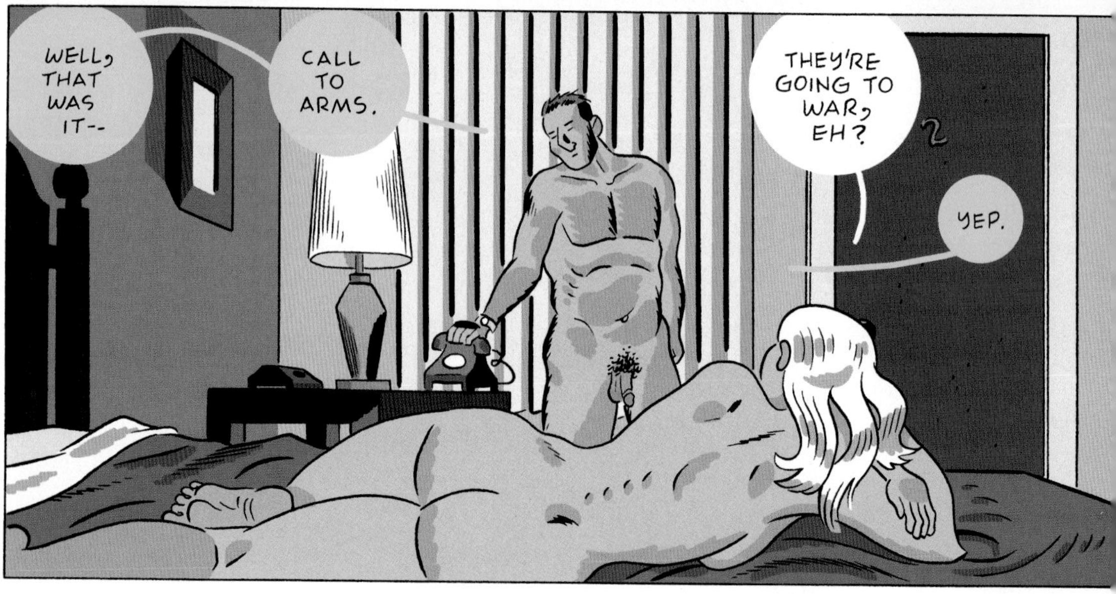
WELL, THAT WAS IT--
CALL TO ARMS.
THEY'RE GOING TO WAR, EH?
YEP.

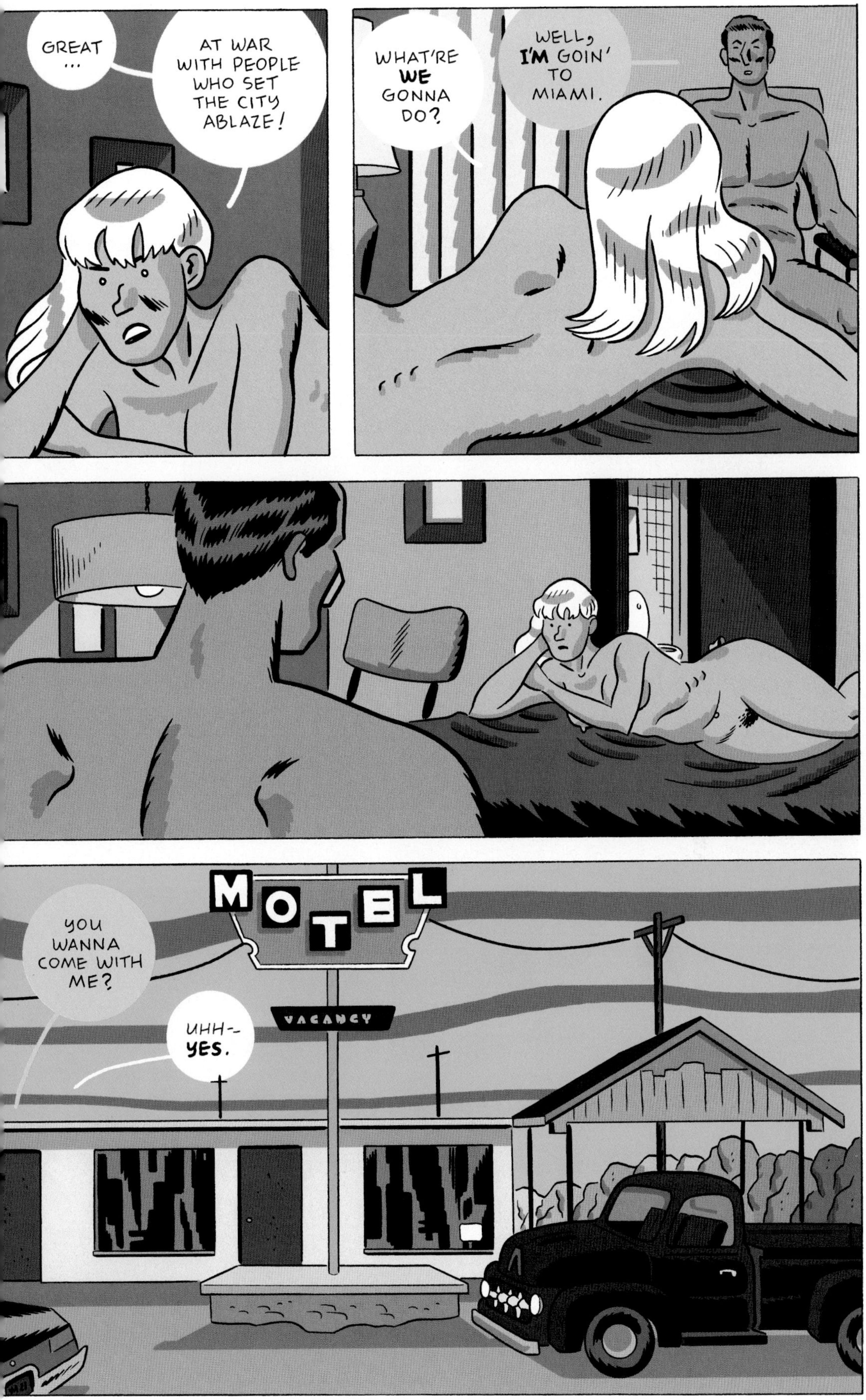
GREAT ...
AT WAR WITH PEOPLE WHO SET THE CITY ABLAZE!
WHAT'RE **WE** GONNA DO?
WELL, **I'M** GOIN' TO MIAMI.
MOTEL
VACANCY
YOU WANNA COME WITH ME?
UHH- **YES.**

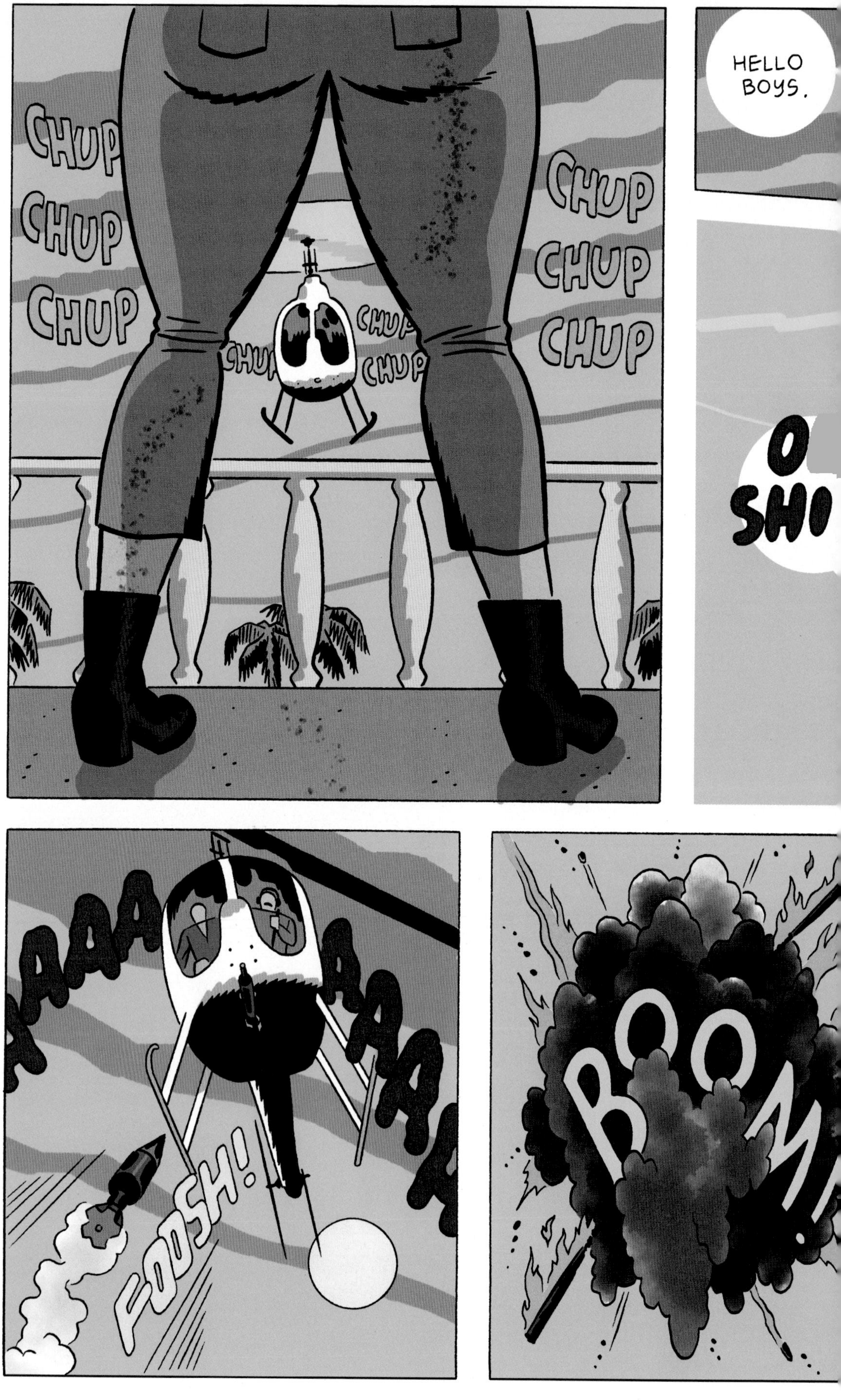
CHUP
CHUP
CHUP
CHUP
CHUP
CHUP
CHUP
CHUP
CHUP CHUP CHUP
HELLO BOYS.
O
SHI
AAAA
AAAA
FOOSH!
BOOM

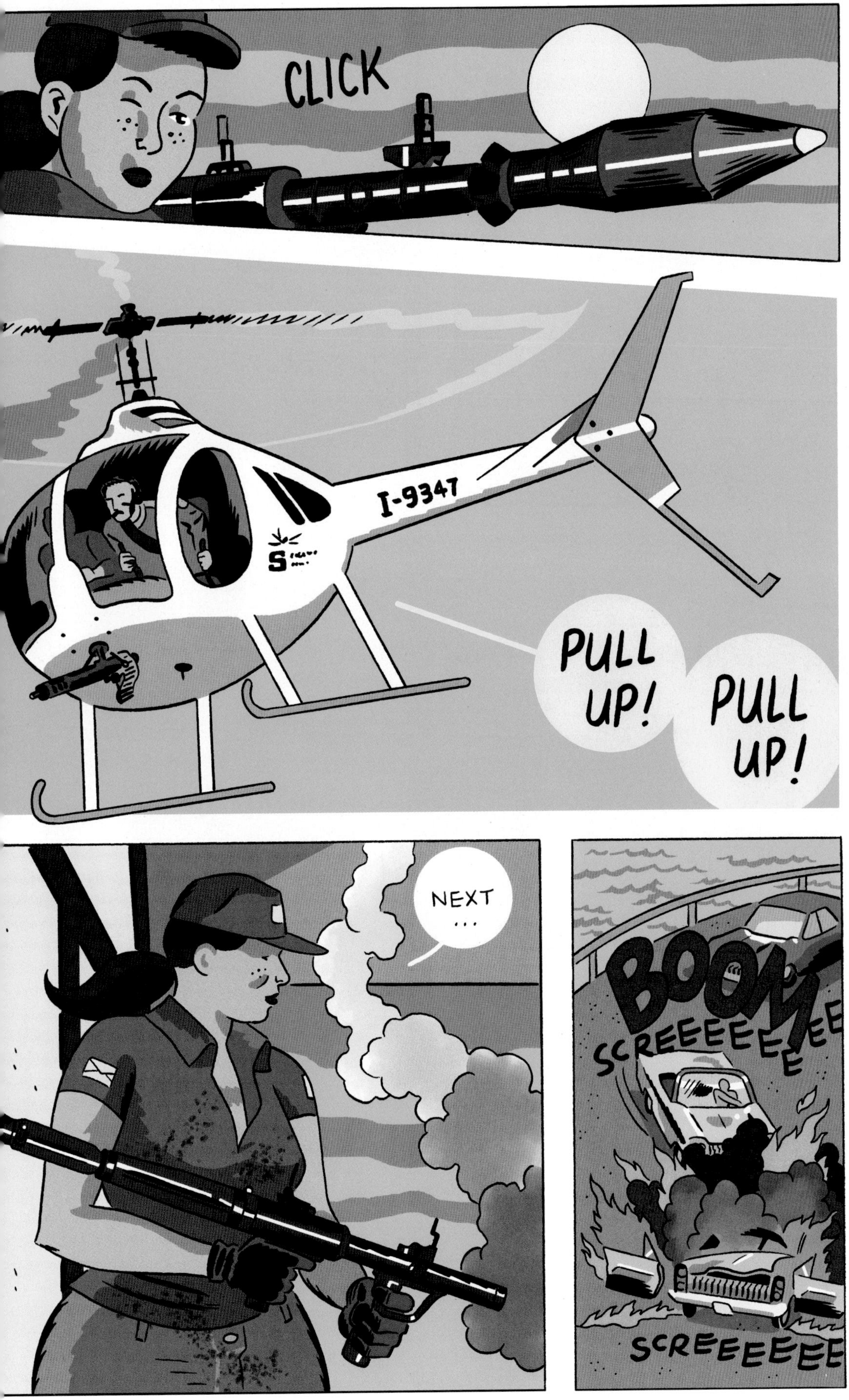
CLICK
I-9347
PULL UP!
PULL UP!
NEXT ...
BOOM
SCREEEEEEEEE
SCREEEEEEEE

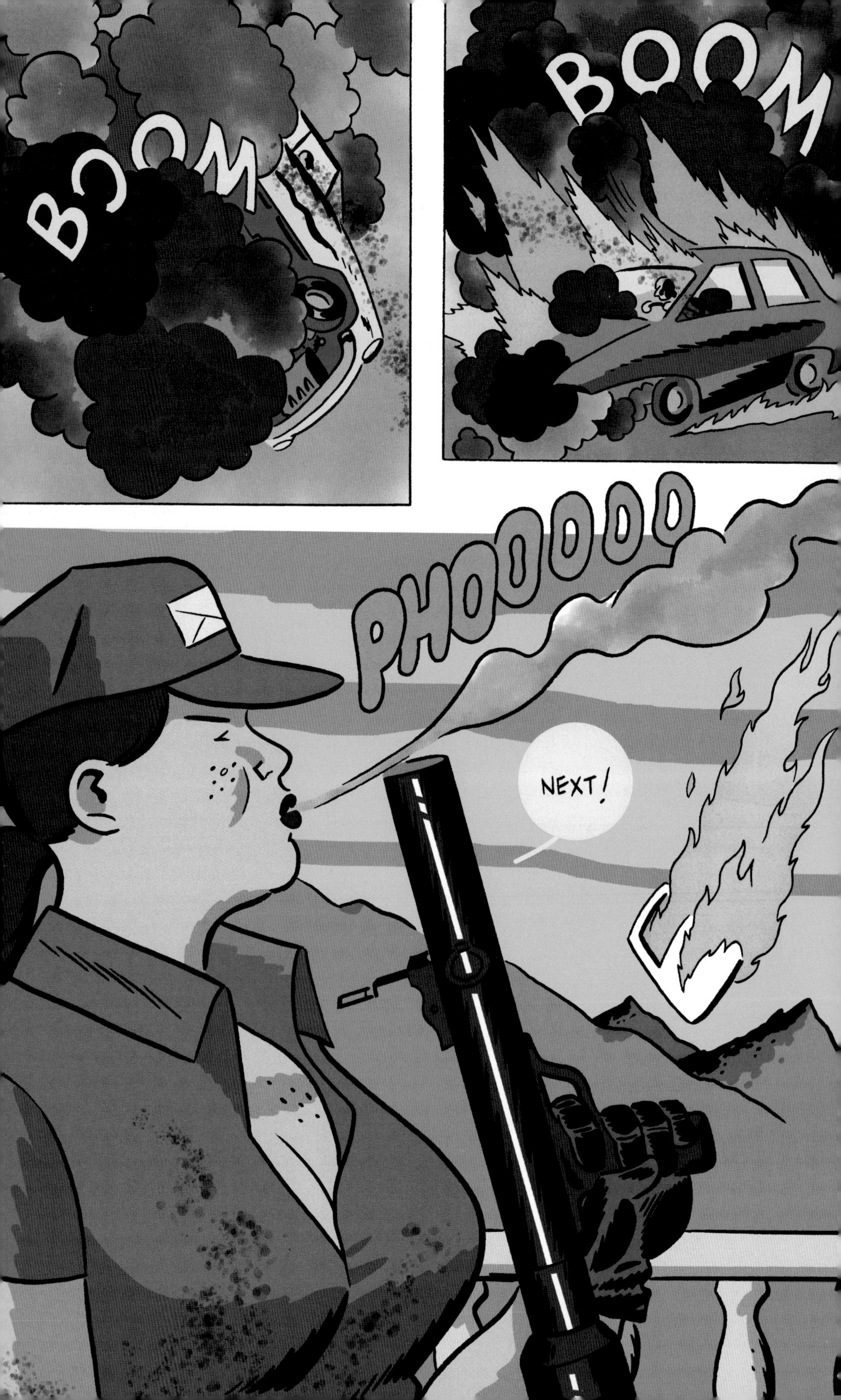
BOOM
BOOM
PHOOOOO
NEXT!

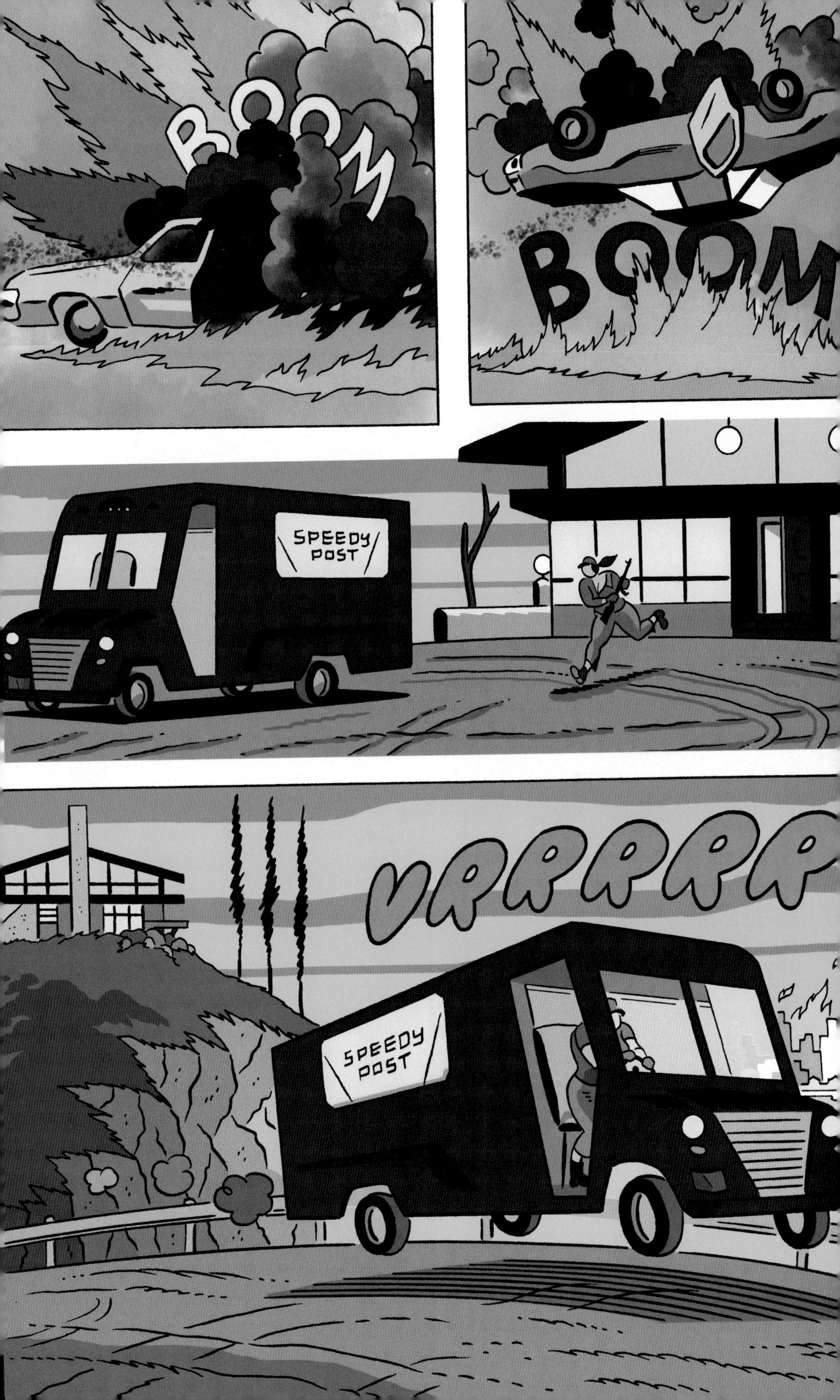
BOOM
BOOM
SPEEDY POST
VRRRRR
SPEEDY POST

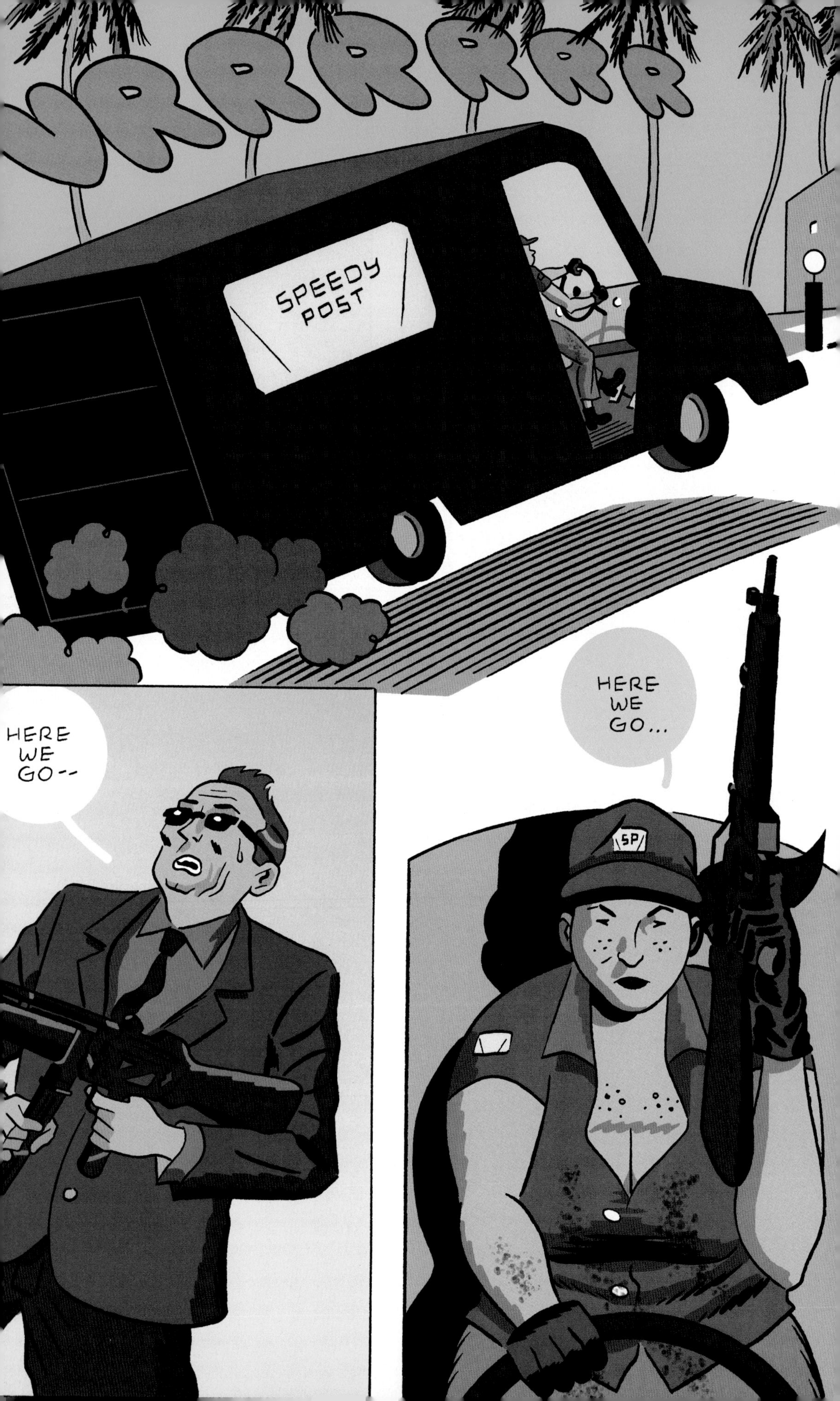
VRRRRRR
SPEEDY POST
HERE WE GO--
HERE WE GO...
SP

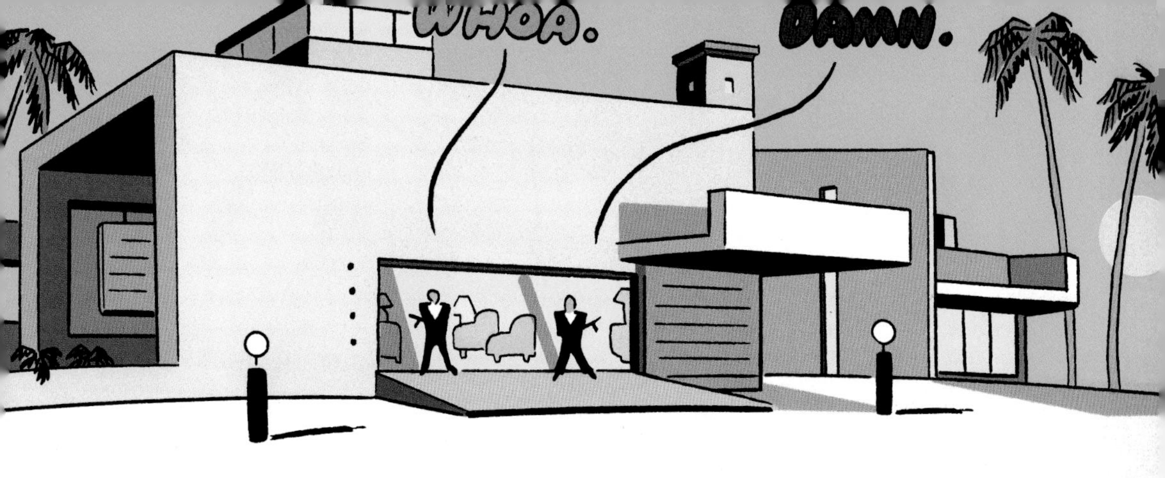
WHOA.
DAMN.

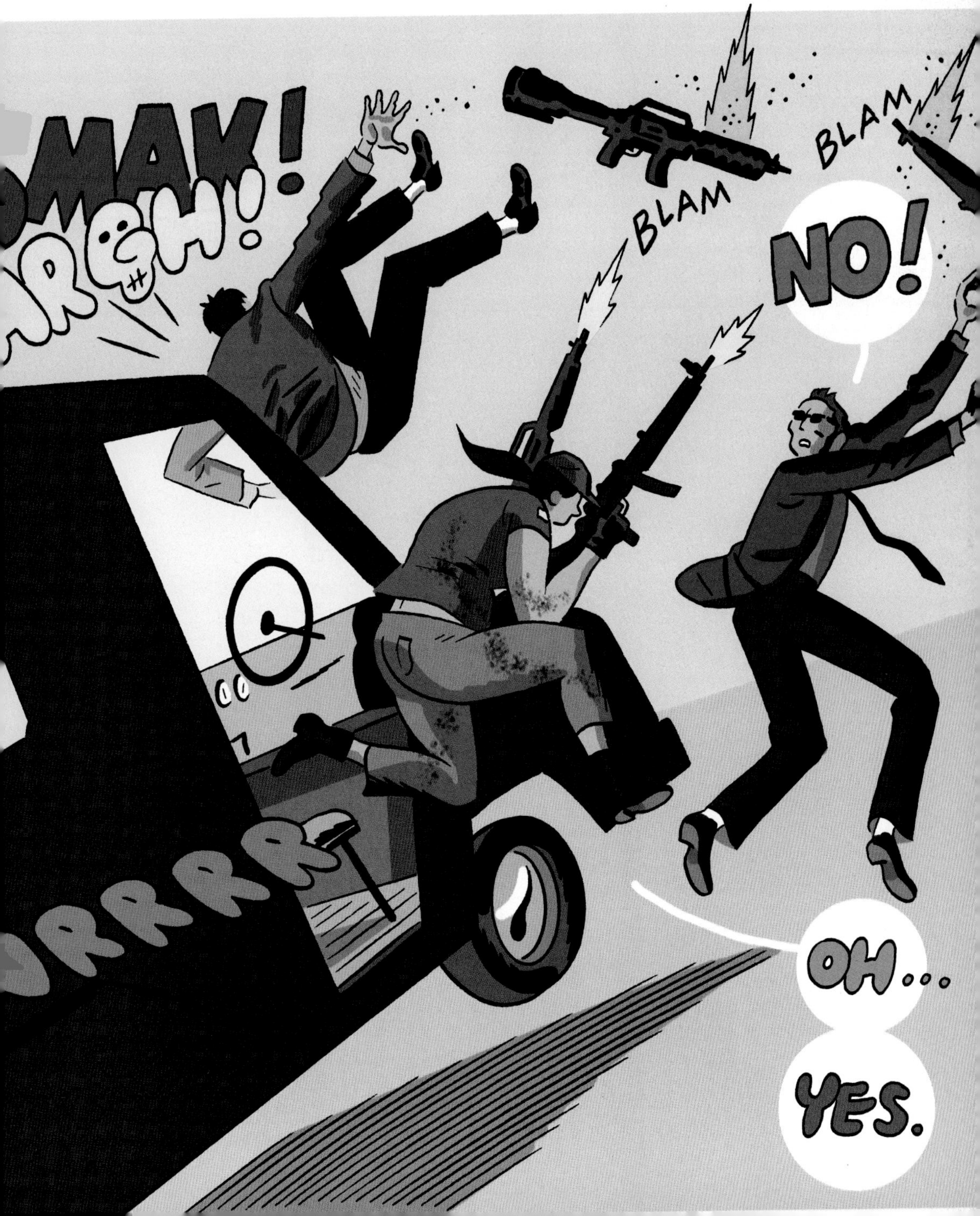
MAK!
RGH!
BLAM
BLAM
NO!
RRRR
OH...
YES.

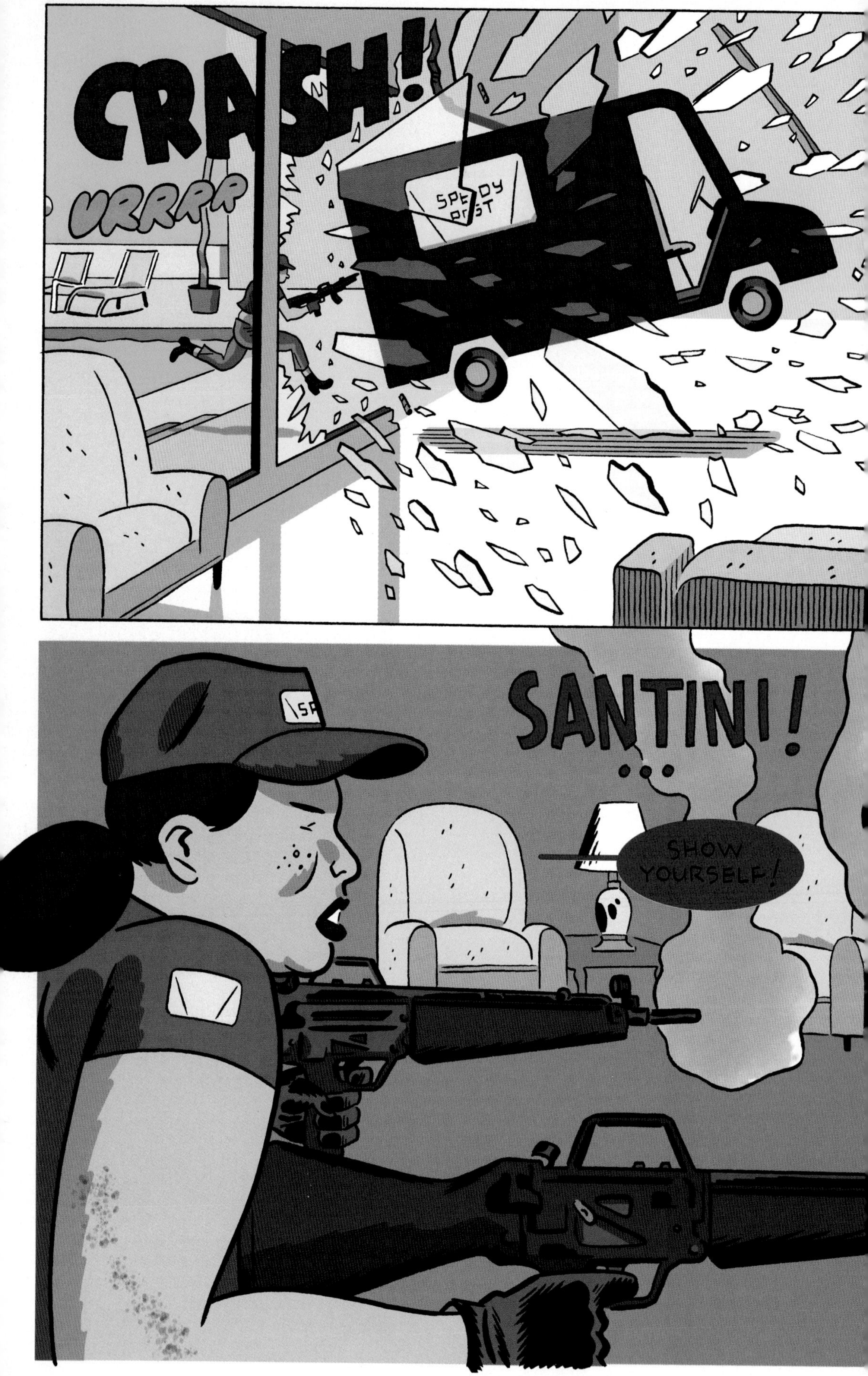
CRASH!
URRRR
SANTINI!
...
SHOW YOURSELF!

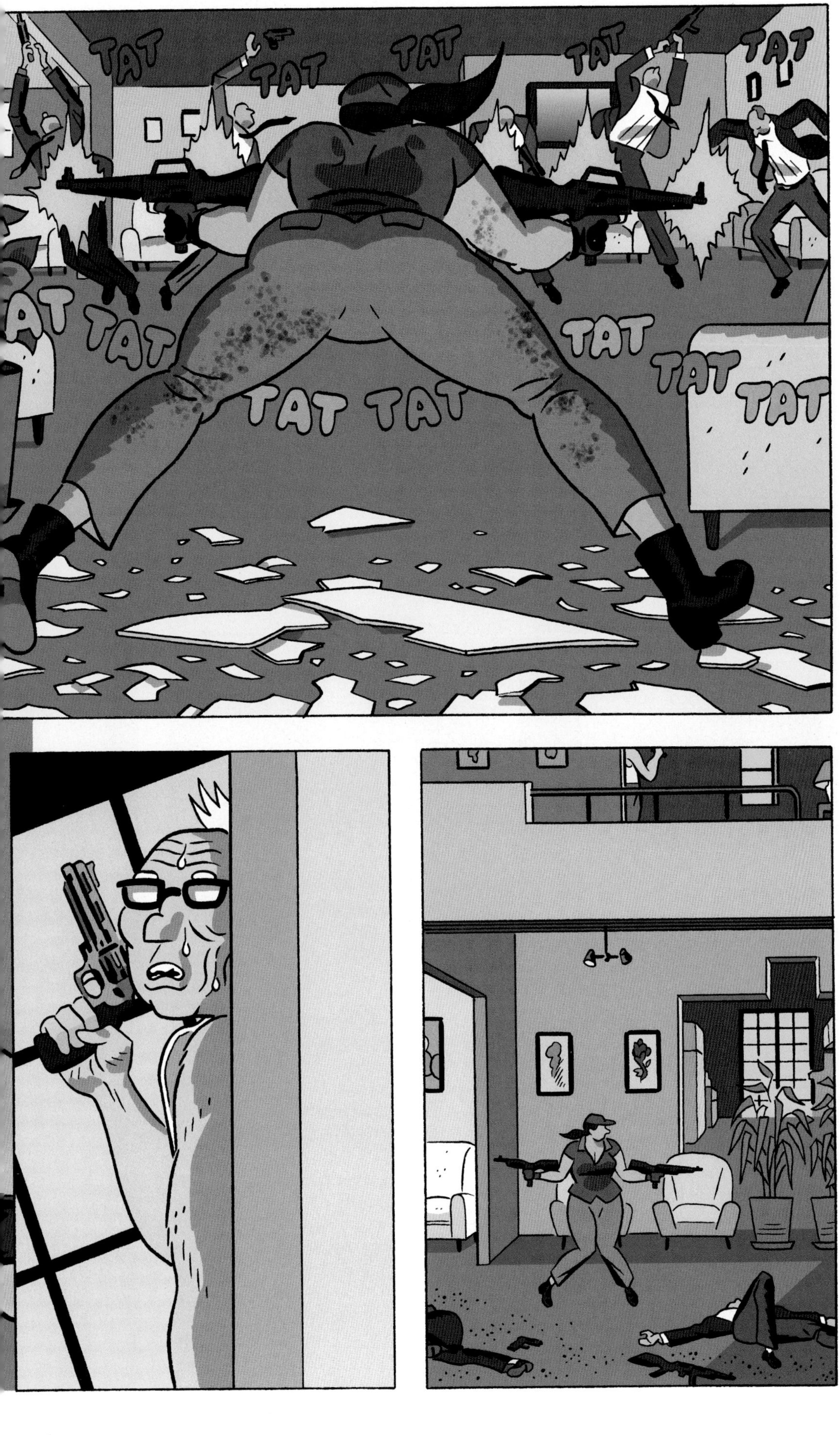

TAT
TAT
TAT
TAT
TAT
TAT
TAT TAT
TAT
TAT
TAT

PHOOO

GAH--

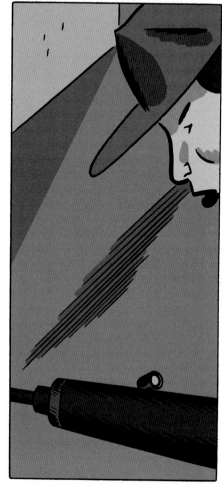

RAT T

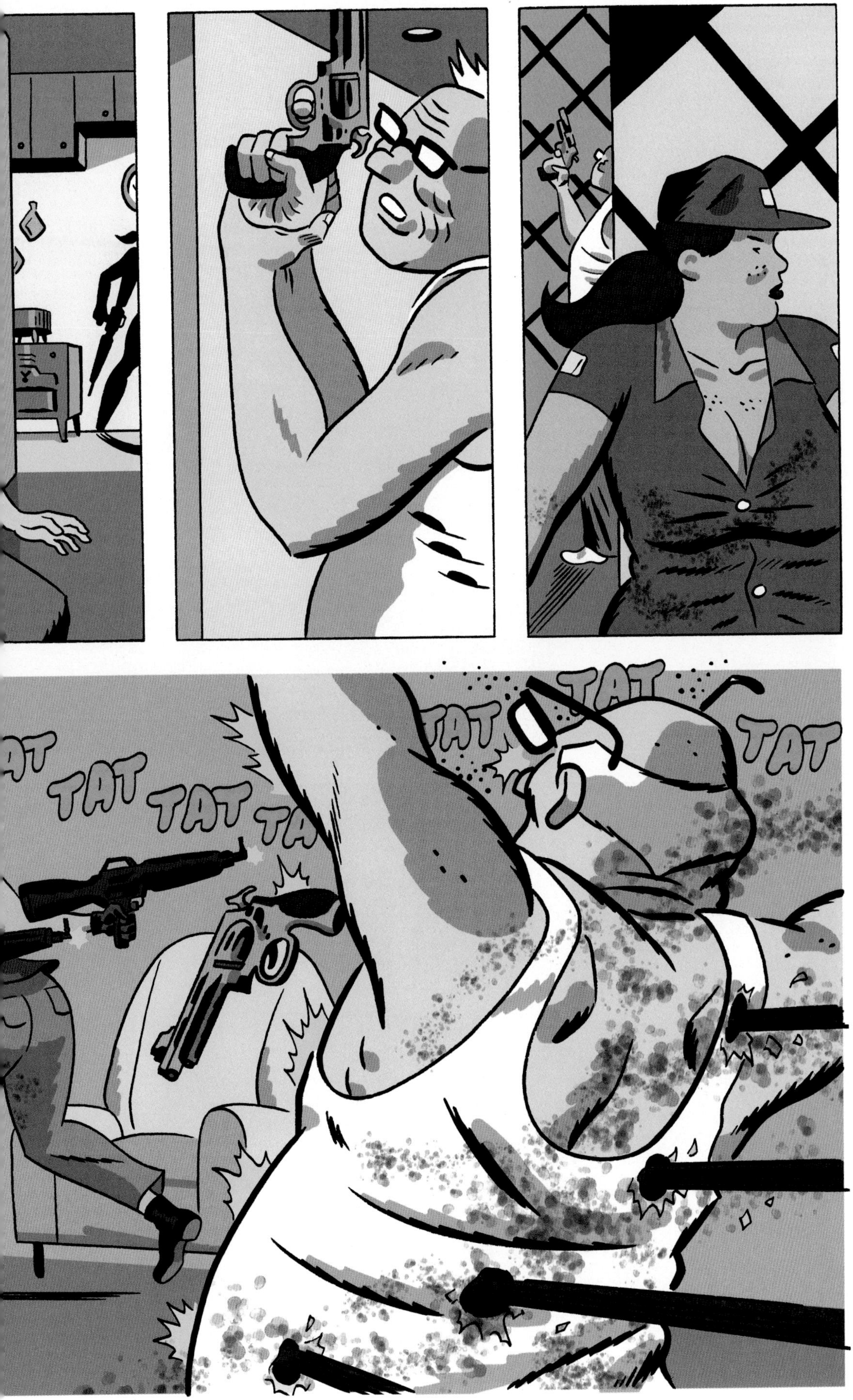

AT
TAT
TAT
TA
TAT
TAT
TAT

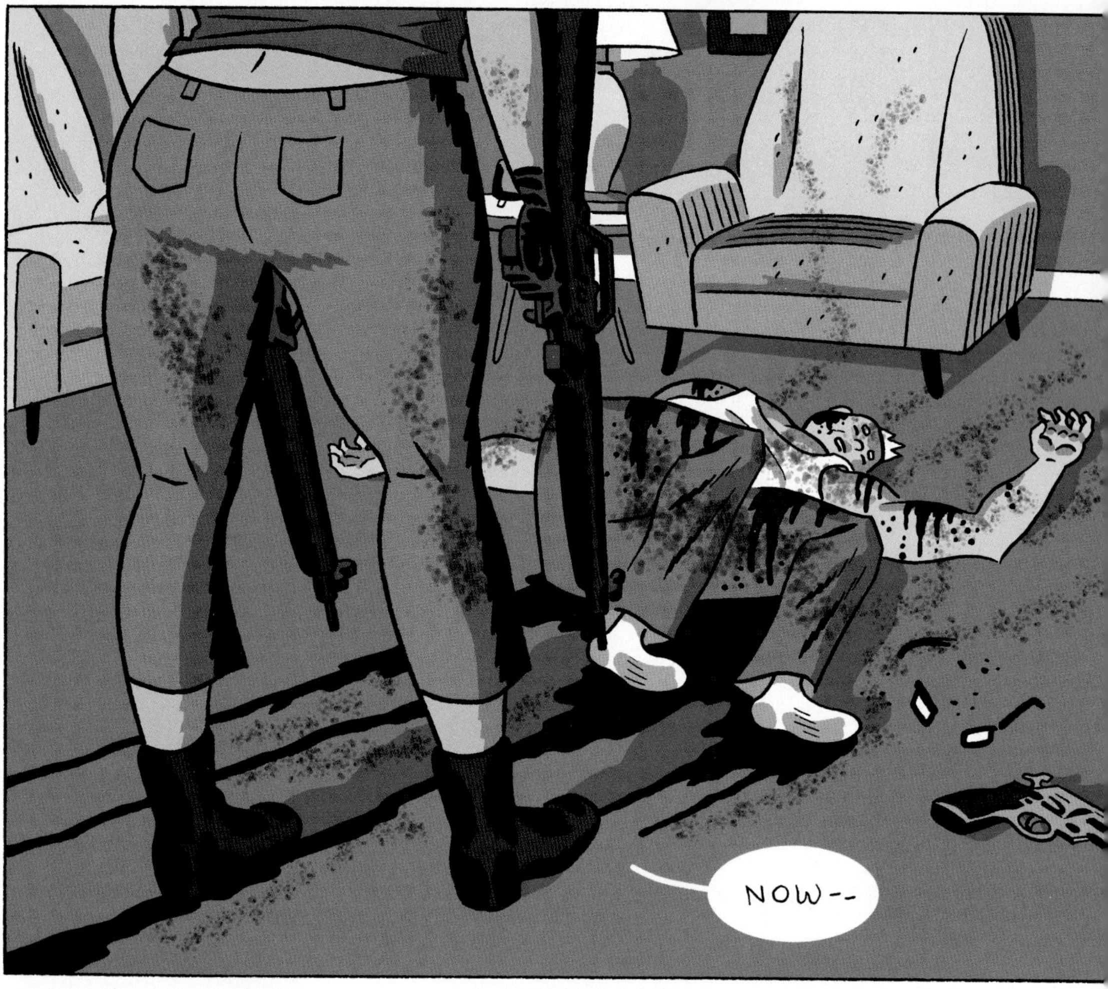
NOW--

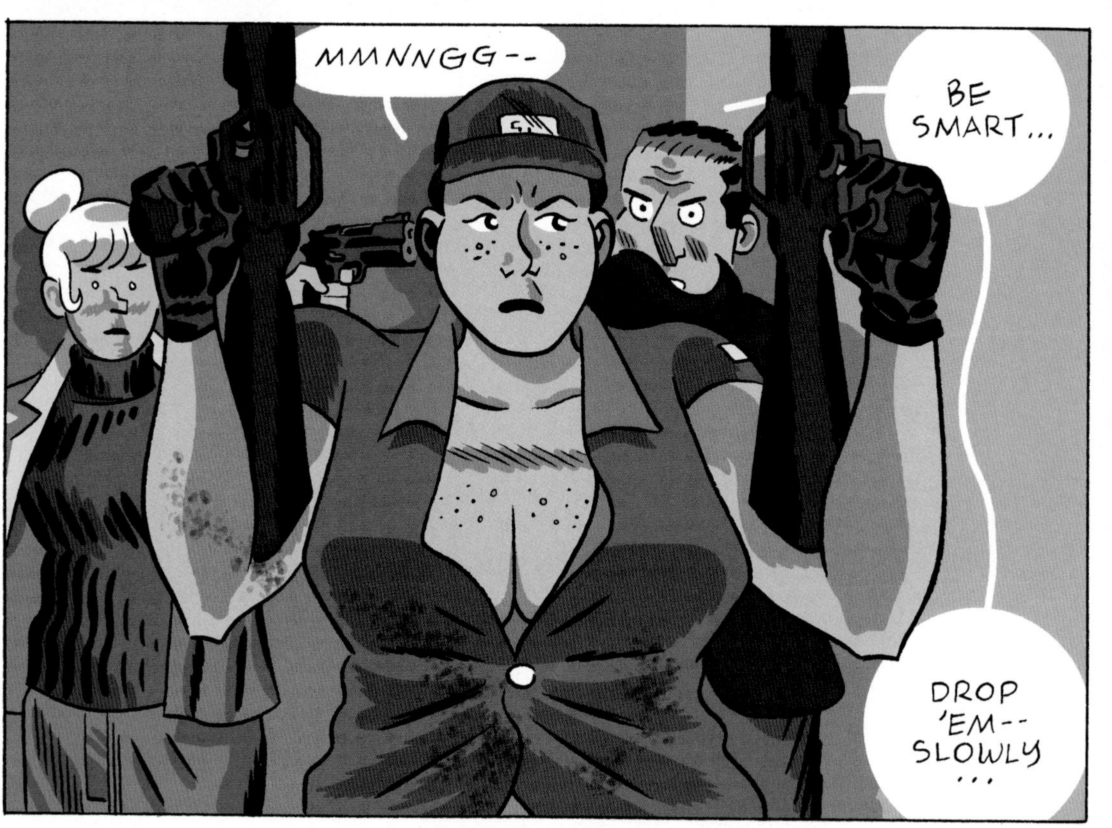
MMNNGG--
BE SMART...
DROP 'EM-- SLOWLY ...

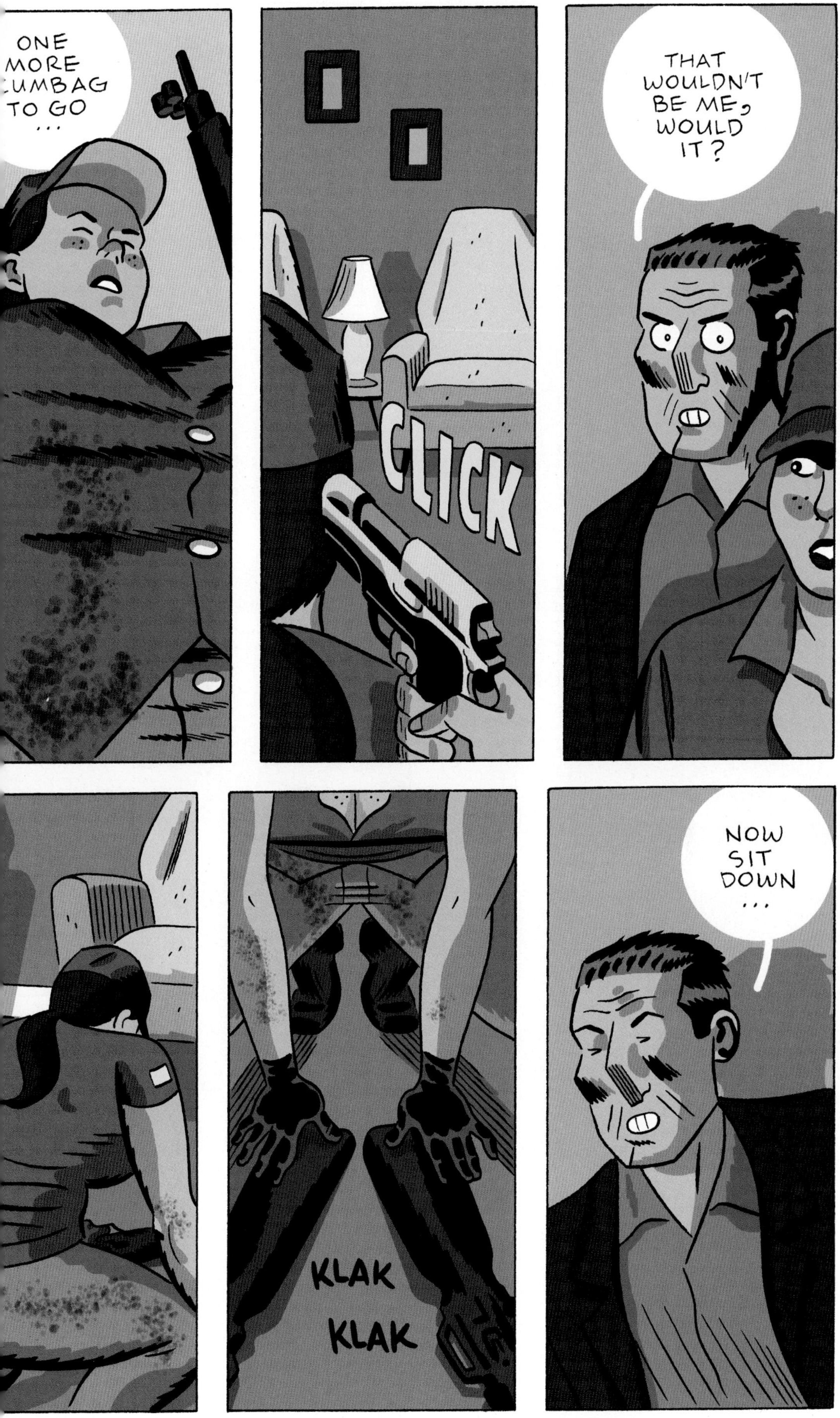

ONE MORE SCUMBAG TO GO ...
CLICK
THAT WOULDN'T BE ME, WOULD IT?
KLAK
KLAK
NOW SIT DOWN ...

YOU KNOW, YOUR FATHER, MOTHER, AND BROTHER WERE **ALL** A BUNCH OF MURDERING THUGS, TOO... ANGIE--
YEAH, I KNOW WHO YOU ARE--WHO YOUR FRIENDS WERE. I KNOW **EVERYTHING** THAT GOES ON IN THIS CITY--
I'VE AVENGED ALL OF MY FRIENDS--THAT'S ALL I CARE ABOUT--SO, WHY DON'T YOU SHUT UP AND JUST FUCKING KILL ME ALREADY--
BLAM
ACK!

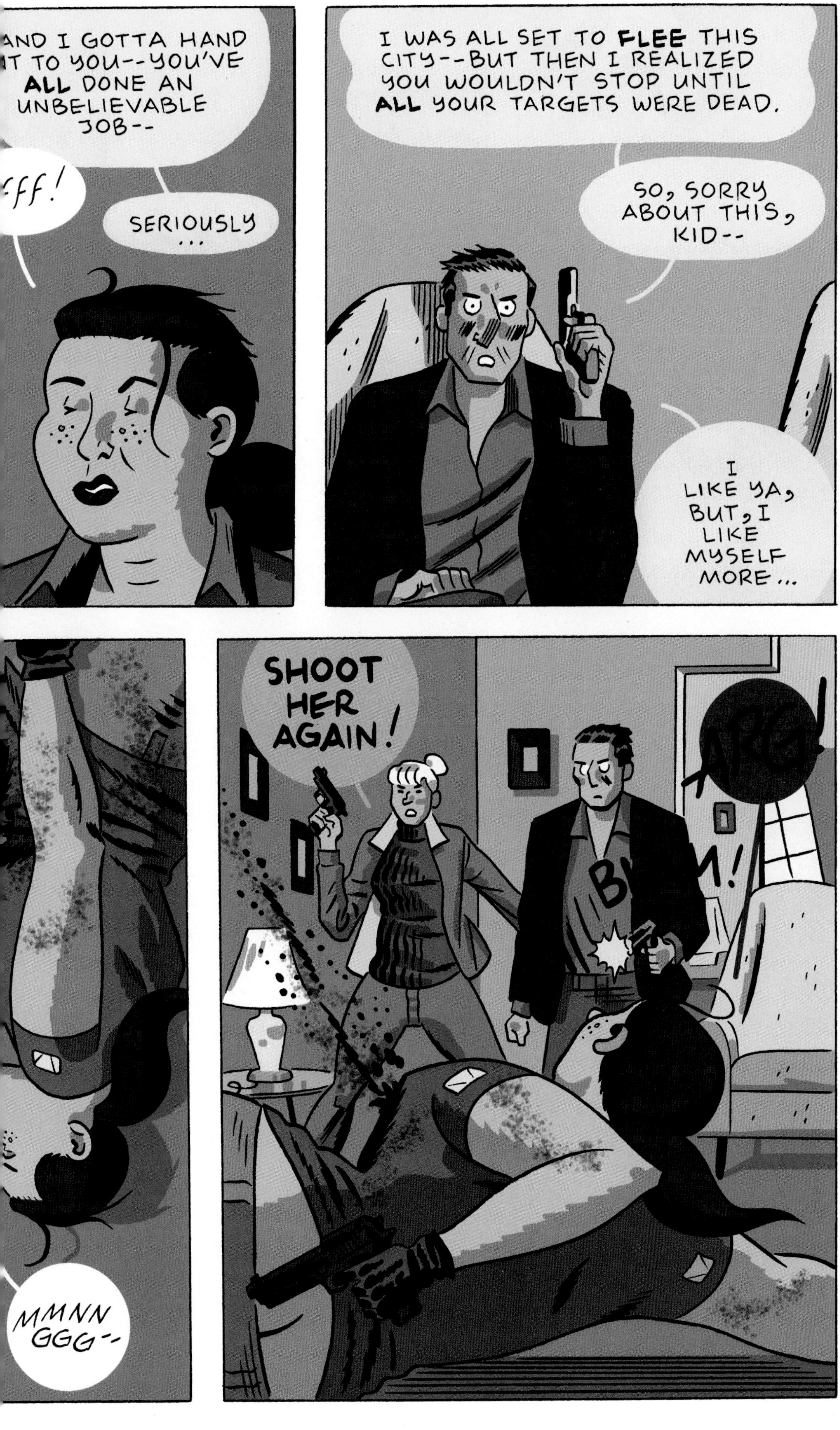
AND I GOTTA HAND IT TO YOU--YOU'VE ALL DONE AN UNBELIEVABLE JOB--
ff!
SERIOUSLY ...
I WAS ALL SET TO FLEE THIS CITY--BUT THEN I REALIZED YOU WOULDN'T STOP UNTIL ALL YOUR TARGETS WERE DEAD.
SO, SORRY ABOUT THIS, KID--
I LIKE YA, BUT, I LIKE MYSELF MORE...
MMNN GGG--
SHOOT HER AGAIN!
ARG!

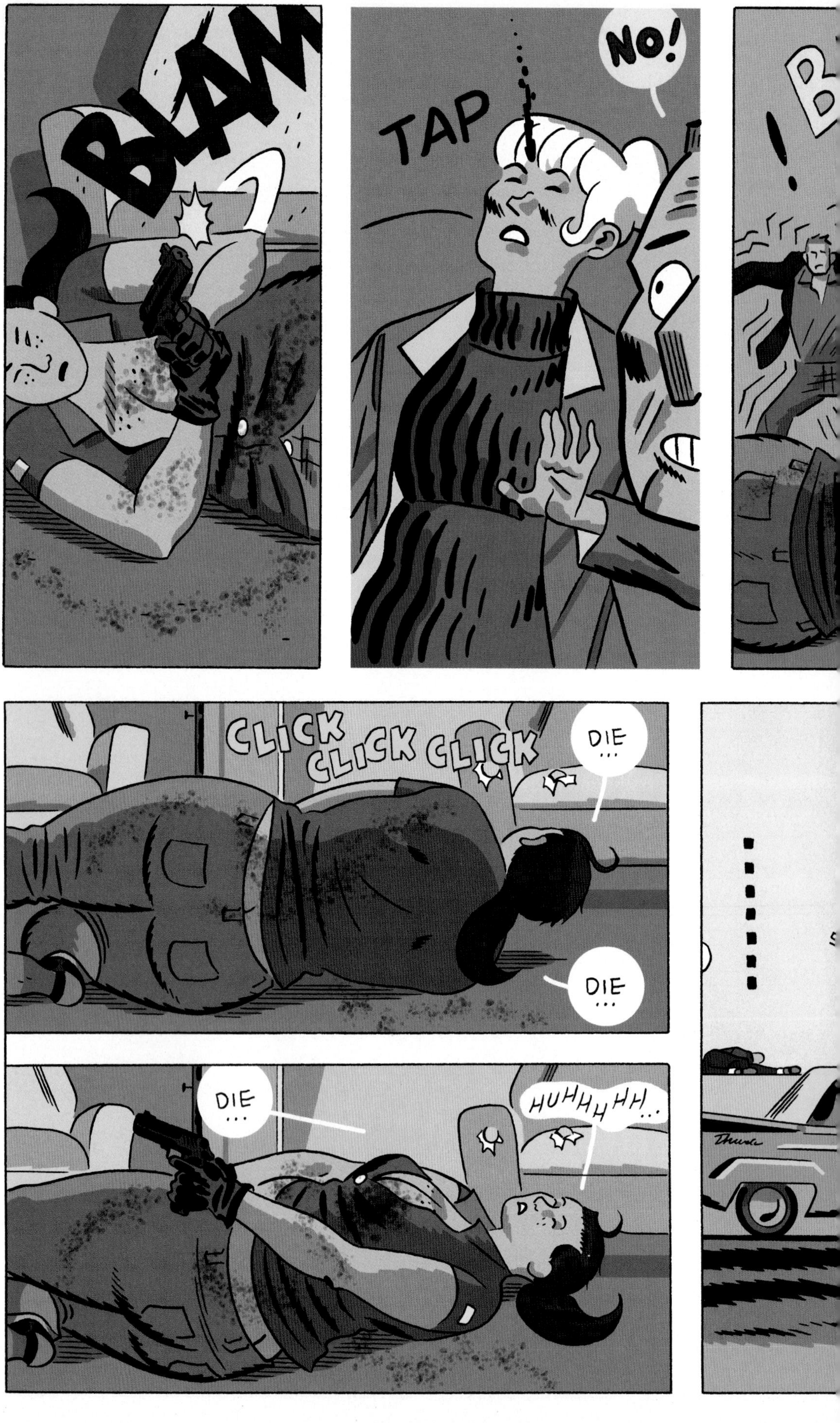
BLAM
TAP
NO!
CLICK CLICK CLICK
DIE ...
DIE ...
DIE ...
HUHHHHHH...

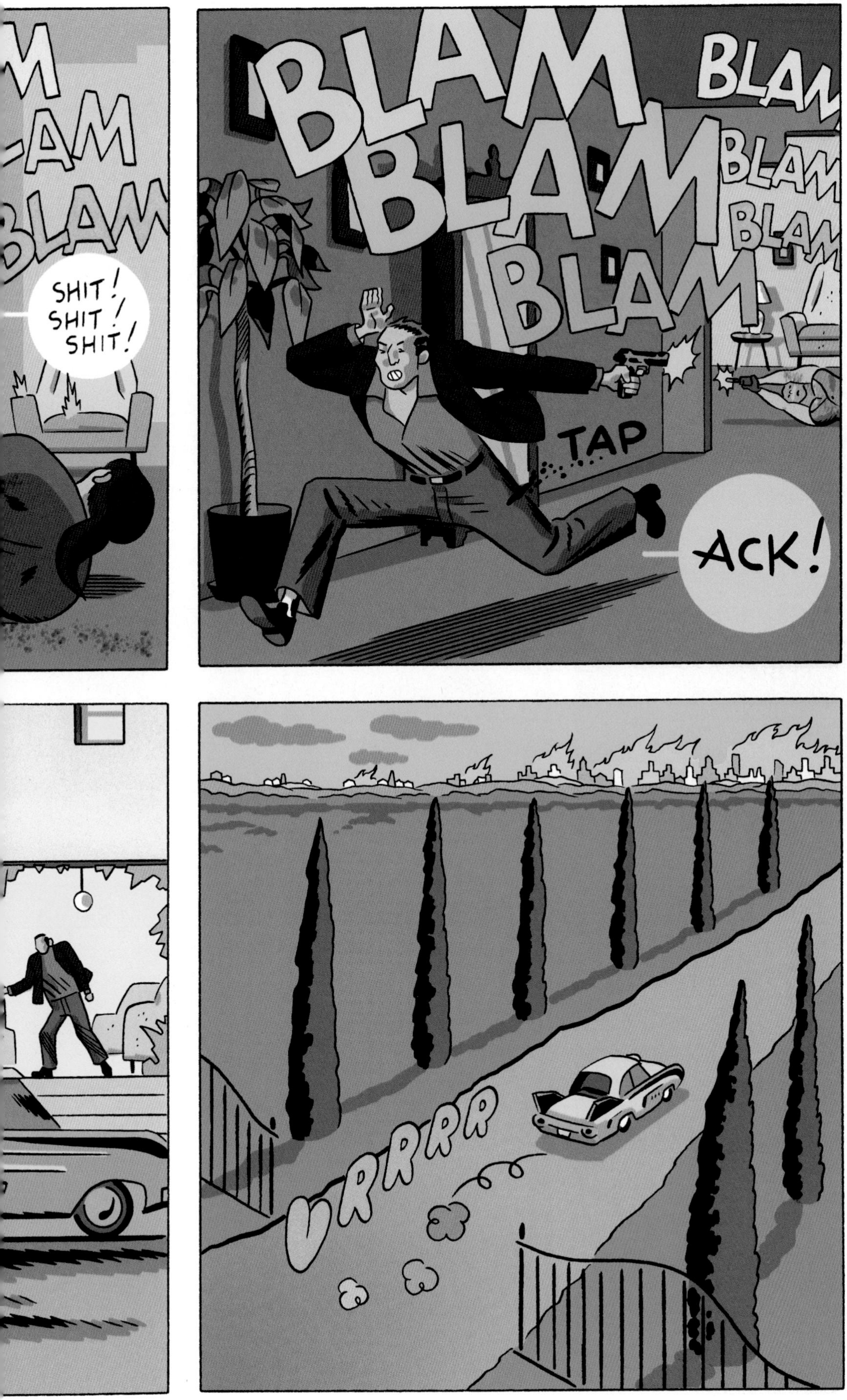

BLAM
BLAM
BLAM
SHIT! SHIT! SHIT!
BLAM
BLAM
BLAM
BLAM
BLAM
BLAM
TAP
ACK!
VRRRR

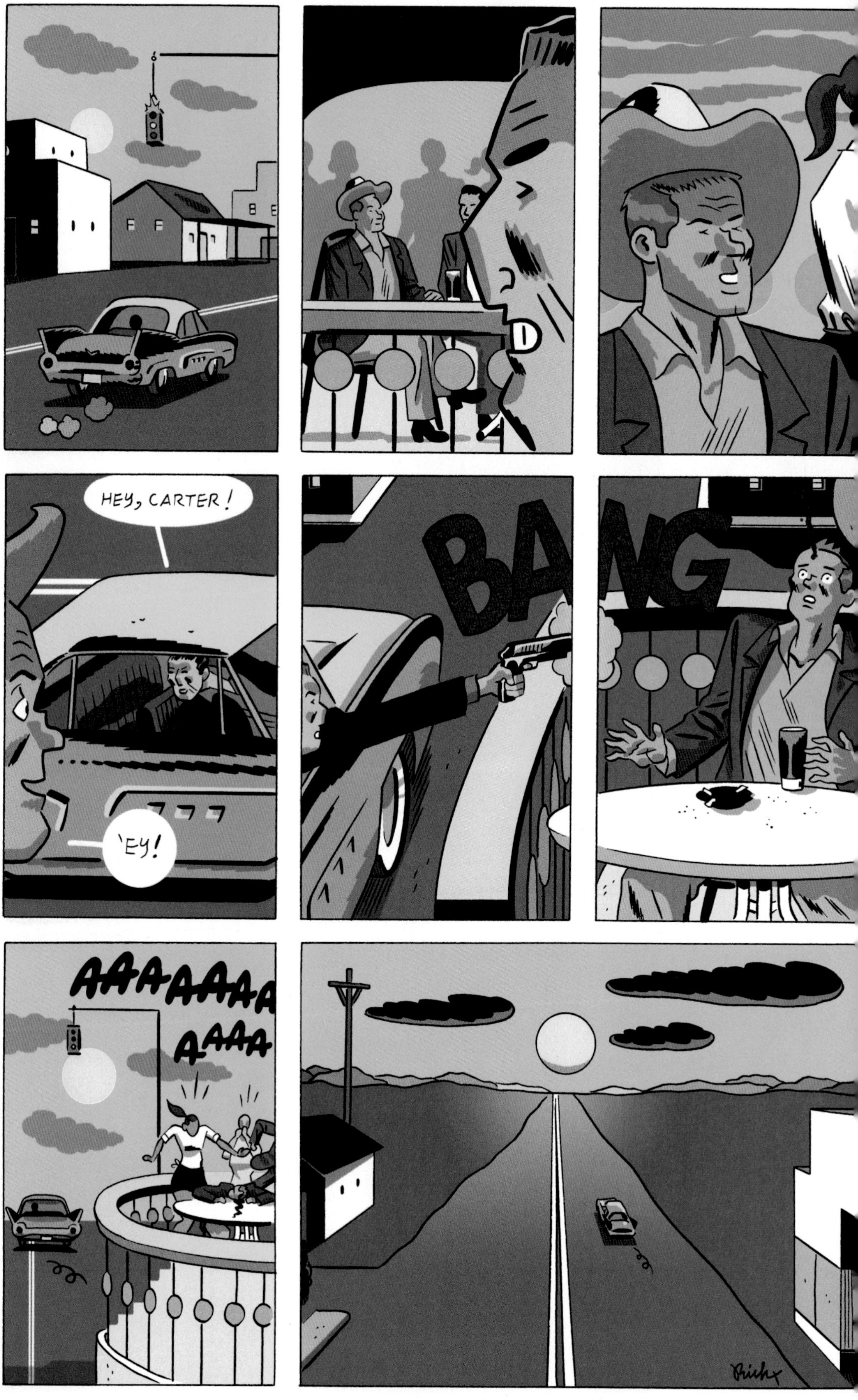
HEY, CARTER!
'EY!
BANG
AAAAAAAA
AAAA
Risch

**THE
END**

She Wolf

RICH TOMMASO

Spell Number One : Shapeshifting

A brand-new
series in stores now!

AVAILABLE NOW

ONLY FROM **image**
IMAGE COMICS

RATED M MATURE